CRITICA

"What grabs me about WATERMAN is the diversity of its utterly believable dangerous men—from hick town power brokers to psycho cracker cops—and its style; the Chesapeake rendered brilliantly in a thousand details; scenes of violence both realistic and hallucinogenic. This broad adventure novel is a triumph."

—James Ellroy, author of
Blood on the Moon
and *The Black Dahlia*

*

"Hornig's best book . . . a good yarn, well told, in a Delmarva locale nicely seen . . . unexpected twists and a strong sense of place."

—*Boston Globe*

*

"A first-rate thriller. The pace builds from leisurely crabbing to a complicated whizbang of an ending. Some of the violence . . . is a bit harrowing but readers will keep turning pages and end up cheering for the protagonist."

—*Publishers Weekly*

*

"Hornig, a very talented guy, has written a redneck thriller with tension oozing off every page and secrets galore."

—*New York Daily News*

*

Also by Doug Hornig

Foul Shot
Hardball
The Dark Side*
Deep Dive*

*Published by
THE MYSTERIOUS PRESS

WATER-MAN

DOUG HORNIG

THE MYSTERIOUS PRESS

New York • London • Tokyo

This is a work of fiction. Grenada is, of course, a real
place and was the site of a real military action. Other than
that, all persons and places depicted herein are fictitious
and any resemblance to real persons or places is entirely
coincidental.

MYSTERIOUS PRESS EDITION

Copyright © 1987 by Doug Hornig

Cover design by Rolf Erickson
Cover illustration by Kathy and Joe Heiner

Mysterious Press books are published in association with
Warner Books, Inc.
666 Fifth Avenue
New York, N.Y. 10103

A Warner Communications Company

Printed in the United States of America

Originally published in hardcover by The Mysterious Press.
First Mysterious Press Paperback Printing: June, 1988

10 9 8 7 6 5 4 3 2 1

One for the boys—
Oscar, Dana and Doug, Sr.

PROLOGUE

WASHINGTON, D.C.
June 1983

The young man closed the heavy oak door behind him. It made a soft thunk, sealing the room off from the outer office. Only the faintest street noise drifted up from the broad avenue eight stories below. The young man smiled.

"Mr. Smith," he said. "You rang?"

"Sit down, Kirk," the other man said.

Kirk crossed the plush-carpeted floor and sat in one of two straight-backed chairs. The other was empty. Smith was on the far side of a substantial executive's desk, enfolded in a soft swivel chair. Above his right shoulder, mounted on the wall, were black-framed photographs of the President and the Director. Other than that, the gleaming white walls were bare. The carpet, too, was snow white, as was the ceiling, with its recessed bank of fluorescent lights behind a fine mesh of white plastic. All the furniture in the room was black leather and chrome.

Smith had a round, smooth-shaven face totally devoid of distinguishing features. His hair was neither long nor short, neither dark nor light. His glasses had unobtrusive plastic frames. He was wearing a gray suit and a dark tie with a muted pattern that would be immediately forgotten. When he smiled, he didn't show any teeth.

3

Kirk shifted in his chair until he found a comfortable position. His movements were casual rather than nervous. He kept a steady gaze on Smith, who sat at a slightly higher level than his guest. Smith's desk was bare except for a white blotter and white modular telephone. The telephone was silent.

Smith had a pencil in his right hand. He tapped it on the desk, slid his fingers down it, then turned it over and repeated the routine. For a moment the tapping was the only sound in the room. Then Smith deliberately laid the pencil on the blotter. He leaned forward, laced his fingers, and rested his forearms on the desktop.

"Kirk," he said, "you're doing a good job."

"Thanks."

"I wanted to say that, even though I know you don't give a damn for compliments. Actually, it's one of the things we like most about you. You're still very young, but you're a professional. The agency recognizes this. It's why we've brought you along so fast. I doubt that you fully appreciate it, but you're a rarity."

"C'mon, Smitty," Kirk said. "Rest the admiration society. What's on your mind?"

"Of course, patience is not yet one of your virtues."

"I haven't yet found the need for it."

Smith leaned back in his chair. "Ah, yes," he said. "Spoken like a true cowboy. The trouble is, you can't be a cowboy your whole life."

"Is there a complaint coming here?"

"Not at all. I told you, the agency is very pleased with your work. You're efficient, you're imaginative, you have courage and brains. It's time to consider your future, that's all. We'd like for you to move up in the organization."

"I don't want a desk job," Kirk said.

"I realize that. I'm not offering one. But there are more highly sensitive field positions than what you've gotten accustomed to. They're more important, in many ways. We'd like to see if you could handle something at that level."

Kirk stroked his close-cropped beard. "Okay, Smitty," he said. "I'll bite."

"Good," Smith said. "How much do you know about Grenada?"

Kirk glanced briefly at the ceiling, then said, "The usual. Small island in the southeastern Caribbean. Former Crown Colony. Population mostly black. Fell to the pro-Communists four years ago. We've got it under embargo." He paused, shrugged. "Anything else?"

"A good bit. The administration is worried about Grenada, Kirk. There are a lot of Cubans there. Some Soviets. They're building a military airport. That's not good news. They're in a very strategic position. Right on the main tanker routes. They threaten Venezuela and Trinidad. We can't afford to have those places compromised.

"In addition, they'd love to export the revolution. As I'm sure you're aware, there are some shaky states down there. Dominica. St. Vincent and the Grenadines. If this thing spreads, we're looking at three or four more Cubas, right in our own backyard."

"The agency's there?"

"Of course," Smith said. "We're doing our best to destabilize. And the administration is turning the usual screws. The pressure is on the EEC not to give any aid until they have elections. The World Bank is keeping its pocketbook closed. And then we ran the 'Amber and the Amberines' maneuvers back in '81. You remember."

"Sure. We invaded Puerto Rico. Wahoo."

"Don't be flip. That was an important operation. The people in power in Grenada know damn well who we meant by 'Amber.' Not that we have any intention of invading, of course. But they've been living with the threat for almost two years now."

Kirk shrugged. "So what's the net?" he asked.

"The net is that the Communists' asses are in a sling. They're feeling the economic pinch, plus they're scared. They understand global politics. They know if push comes to shove, the Soviets aren't going to intervene in this hemis-

phere, any more than we would in Poland. And just between
you and me, the Grenadian army isn't worth diddley shit
without a whole lot of outside help.

"I think they're ready to make some accommodations. The
so-called Prime Minister was just here."

"That's Bishop?"

"Right," Smith said. "Maurice Bishop. He's the head of
the party, and he's got pretty much a one-man show going on
down there. Unfortunately for us, he's generally popular, but
there's a good undercurrent of disaffection. I don't think
they'll go to the wall for him. There're too many people
who're still uncomfortable with Marxists at the wheel.

"Anyway, Bishop's running scared. He knows we can
squash him anytime we want. So he's reaching out a bit.
When he came to the states, the President wouldn't meet with
him, of course. I think that was a good choice. It was a
calculated insult, but it'll increase the fear level, and the
concessions will come more easily later. The President
eventually sent an undersecretary from State to see him. The
guy is dying to deal."

"So deal with him."

Smith began to play with the pencil again. "Not so
simple," he said. "By the time we deal, we want to be sure
we'll get it all. Elections, opposition parties, free press, the
works. Bishop's not ready to go that far yet. I'd say we're at
least six months away. That's six months of heavy pressure
too."

Kirk shrugged again. "And what do you want from me?"
he said.

"We want someone in place down there."

"You've got people in place."

"We want someone who's not involved with destabilizing.
Look at it as a carrot-and-stick number. We've been whack-
ing the stick; now we're ready to start dangling the carrot.
Unofficially, of course. That's why they want to use the
agency."

"That's not my bag, Smitty. I'm a field man."

Smith sighed. "Listen, Kirk," he said. "This is a

tremendous opportunity. By your standards it's not a glamour job. All right. But it's important. It'll require a wide variety of skills. It's a hell of a challenge. If you do well, believe me, a lot of doors are going to open. This administration has a lock on another four years unless they do something incredibly stupid. Keep in their favor and there's no telling how high you can go."

"You're still not telling me why me."

"You've got a good track record with blacks."

"Come on. That was Africa. And they *wanted* our help."

Smith waved his hand. "Listen," he said. "Racism is something that runs wide and deep, even within the agency. I hate to say that, but it's true and you know it. We've got guys who couldn't get close to a black if their lives depended on it."

"So send a black, for Christ's sake."

"Negative. Bishop wouldn't credit him. Besides, he knows that white means serious. You're a rare man, Kirk. You're one of the whitest men I know, and yet you can somehow get a black man to trust you. You've proven that. We want you for this assignment. We *need* you."

Kirk paused, shaking his head. "I don't know," he said. "How long are we talking?"

"Six months min, like I said. A year max."

Kirk was silent for a long moment. He stared hard at the other man. "All right, Smitty," he said. "Off the gloves. Do I have any choice?"

Smith grinned. "Not really. But that doesn't negate anything I've said. It's a plum, I mean that. And for once you won't be risking your neck. Or anyway, the downside is very manageable."

"I do love your euphemisms," Kirk said sweetly. He paused, then sighed. "Okay, fill me in. How's it all go down?"

"Good boy," Smith said. "You're not going to regret this.

"Now, technically, you'll be representing State. You'll get all proper credentials from Caribbean Affairs. The idea is to convince Bishop that you're an unofficial official spokesman for the administration, if you get what I mean. We wouldn't send someone to negotiate out in the open, because of our declared posture. Bishop understands that. He wouldn't trust it any other way."

"How much freedom do I have?"

"Enough. The beard'll have to go, of course."

Kirk stroked it again. "Shoot," he said. "Do you know how hard this came?"

"Small price," Smith said. "We need the right image. You're not just a message bearer, you know, you're liaison. We expect you to maneuver the man to where he's all heart when the *real* bargaining begins. The administration wants to avoid strong-arm tactics, so that puts a lot of responsibility on you."

"It occurs to me that there are probably people down there who are not going to like what I'm doing."

Smith smiled. "It occurred to us too," he said. "Your State cover is for Bishop and anyone who's important enough for need-to-know. As far as the general public is concerned, you'll be from the private sector. You'll be trying to work out some trade agreements that are acceptable to both sides. No one'll be surprised if that keeps you there for months. But it will be a tricky balancing act at times."

Kirk made a brushing gesture. "I can handle it," he said. "Who's going to be running me?"

"Who would you rather have?"

"You."

"Done."

"What about backup?"

Smith shook his head. "You're on your own," he said. "We can't take the chance of your being identified. You won't know any of our other people."

"Who pulls me out if it gets hinky?"

"Your contact is a local named Quartermain. Drives a taxi. He's one of ours. Very good man, very resourceful. Use him when you need to get around. He can get our back-and-forth done safely. I don't want to meet you direct more than once a month, tops. Even then we have to be very careful. The

Bishop people are always suspicious of Americans. They'll be watching.

"If it comes to emergency evac, Quartermain will fetch you. Don't make the decision yourself. We don't want to yank you unless the gun is cocked. But should it happen, don't worry. We've got plenty of naval presence in the area. Quartermain will get you offshore and we'll pick you up. The escape route is clean."

"You don't have to warn me about crying wolf," Kirk said tersely.

"Don't get testy." Smith smiled. "I just want us to be clear with each other. Now, any more questions?"

"What's the time frame?"

"I'm sending you over to State today for general background. There's a lot to digest. Then you'll need to bone up for your trade cover. We'll get one of our civilians for that. You'll get the agency briefing last. We want to put you in in about a week."

Kirk got to his feet. "Okay," he said. "I'm not thrilled about this, Smitty, but I'll take your word it's something I ought to be doing." He pointed his index finger at the other man. "Don't screw me over."

"Of course not," Smith said, looking Kirk in the eye. "Trust me."

DORSET COUNTY, VIRGINIA

August 1985

WEDNESDAY

CHAPTER 1

It was hot. Ninety-some in the shade, with the humidity hovering close to the same mark. The air was still, without even the hint of a cooling breeze from the Chesapeake.

Front Street was midday quiet. Some of the buildings along it had window air conditioners. The machines hummed and wheezed and dripped and rattled against their frames. Between cars, which were infrequent, these were the loudest sounds to be heard. The sidewalks were empty.

A pickup rolled into town from the west. It was the color of an aged brick building and was weathered about the same as the building would be. It was a Ford, over twenty years old. On the bumper it carried a sticker that said, "I'd rather push a Ford than drive a Chevy." From the sound of it the owner might be doing just that before long.

The red pickup pulled to the curb. The driver didn't turn off the motor.

"Don't want to stop her," he said to his passenger. "Times in this weather, she's right contrary."

"No problem," the passenger said. "Thanks for the ride. 'Preciate it."

The driver nodded and his passenger got out. The passenger was a man in his early thirties, a little above

15

average height, with a medium frame. He was wearing a plain white T-shirt, jeans, and blue nylon running shoes. His biceps filled the sleeves of the T-shirt, the cotton stretched taut across his chest, outlining his pectoral muscles, and there was no outward sign of his belly. The jeans fastened at his waist with a drawstring. They were loose, with the boot-cut cuffs well down over his shoe tops.

The man's skin was the reddish brown of someone who never tans without burning a little. His eyes were an unremarkable gray-blue. But his hair was striking. It was pale blond and silky fine. He'd lost a bit from the front, but the rest lay on his head like spun white gold. It bounced and ruffled as he moved.

He shifted his weight from the ball of one foot to the other. With one hand he lifted a large duffel bag and a gray metallic suitcase from the bed of the pickup. He set them on the sidewalk. His arms hung loosely at his sides, and he rocked slightly, forward and back. He looked around as the pickup clattered off in the direction of the Bay.

There wasn't much to see. The pavement shimmered in the heat. On the other side of the narrow street there was a row of wooden buildings that were a good hundred years old. The buildings were shaded by a wood awning that reached out over a cement sidewalk with grass growing up through the cracks.

One of the buildings had an American flag flying above it and a bronze plaque on its front that read:

U.S. POST OFFICE
BRAWLTON, VIRGINIA,

followed by the ZIP code.

Another was identified as Graves' Mercantile. It was identified by a hand-painted sign over the door that was in need of restoration. The words *Graves' Mercantile* were arranged in an arch. Below the arch was the message, "If We Don't Have It, You Don't Need It." On the wall next to the door was a rusted metal frame enclosing a mercury bulb thermometer. The Hire's Root Beer logo could just be discerned through the rust. The thermometer read eighty degrees. It was much hotter than that, but that's what the thermometer read.

In front of Graves' Mercantile was a slatted wooden bench and an old-fashioned barrel encircled by corroding metal strips. Rakes and hoes protruded from the barrel. A gaunt black dog was asleep under the bench.

There was also a tall, thin man. He stood in the shade, leaning against the store's wall rather than using the bench. He was dressed in bib overalls with no shirt. Thick, wiry black hair curled around the edges of the bib. The man's haircut was homemade. His right cheek was distended, and from time to time he spat tobacco juice into the alley that ran alongside the store. He watched the stranger with no decipherable expression on his face.

An old black woman came down the sidewalk. She walked carefully, favoring her left side. She was apparently coming from the small supermarket that was visible farther down the street, because she carried a large, fully packed grocery bag. She moved slowly along in the heat.

The woman passed Graves' Mercantile. A few yards beyond, she turned her head to look at the man in the bib overalls. It was a quick, automatic motion. As she did it her foot caught on something and she stumbled. She fell. The grocery bag was pitched forward, and its contents spilled onto the sidewalk. Small hunks of shrink-wrapped budget meat lay there, the blood glistening against the underside of the plastic. Wilting greens filmed over with the dust of the street. Canned beans and boxes of cereal lay next to soap bars and rolls of toilet paper.

The woman raised herself to a sitting position and rubbed her left hip. She stared mutely at the mess. The thin man in the overalls spat tobacco juice into the alley. He smiled at the blond stranger, showing stained teeth with a couple of dark gaps among them.

For a moment the stranger looked on neutrally. Then he sighed and came across the street. Without speaking, he helped the old woman up. He gathered her spilled purchases and repacked the bag, quickly and efficiently. He handed the bag to her.

She frowned slightly as she looked at the stranger, but she said, "Thank you, mister. God bless."

"You all right?" he asked.

"I be fine," she said, and she started again for wherever she was going. She limped a little.

The stranger glanced at the man in the overalls. The thin man smiled his brown smile and spat again. The stranger had begun to turn when the other man spoke.

"What's that thing?" the thin man asked.

"What thing?" the stranger said.

"That metal thing." He pointed across the street.

"It's a suitcase."

"Damnedest suitcase I ever seen. Looks like a safe. You got in it, guns?" He grinned, showing the gapped teeth and an expanse of yellowish brown upper gum.

"Uh-huh, guns," the stranger said, and he walked away. The thin man in the overalls watched him go. He continued to lean against the storefront.

In one motion the stranger hoisted the duffel bag onto his shoulder and picked up the metallic suitcase. He walked down the street to the east end of town. He stopped in front of a place called Sandi's Café, across from the market. Sandi's was made of wood and had at one time been painted white. Now it needed a couple of fresh coats. There was a small red-white-and-blue neon sign in the window that read: BUDWEISER, KING OF BEERS. Underneath the ad for Bud was a chalkboard. On it someone had written:

TODAY'S SPECIAL
CRAB CAKES W/FRIES AND COLE SLAW
$4.95

Sandi's Café had a screen door held in place by a long spring. The stranger opened it and went in. Behind him, the screen door banged twice against the frame, and the spring vibrated for a few moments.

Inside, there was a long, narrow room. It was a little stuffy. The café did not have air-conditioning. The windows were open and the muggy air was being circulated by a pair of oscillating fans, one at each end of the room.

Along the wall that fronted on the street were four high-backed wooden booths. There were no cushions on the seats. The tables were wood with Formica tops. In the center of the café were six round tables, also with Formica tops. Each table had four spoke-backed chairs around it. At the rear there was a counter with eight or ten stools. The stools were bolted to the floor. They looked like leggy mushrooms. They were chrome-plated and their swivel tops were covered in red plastic. People would stick to the seats.

The countertop was pink Formica speckled with gold. On it were several black-and-chrome metal napkin dispensers, plastic salt and pepper shakers, white china mugs containing packets of sugar and sugar substitute. There was also a pedestal tray that held sticky buns sealed in cellophane. The tray was covered by a cracked plastic dome with a little knob on top.

Behind the counter was a rack with pegs that held broad-brimmed caps for sale. The caps had mesh tops and adjustable plastic straps. They had cloth patches sewn on their fronts. The patches said things like "Peterbilt," "Kiss My Bass," and "Fishermen Do It Deeper."

On the wall was the menu. It was a white slotted board with black plastic letters. Next to it was a sign detailing the rules of the game: "Beer On/Off. No Off Sales After Midnight. No Consumption of Off Alcohol on Premises. We Do Not Serve Minors—Positive ID Required."

There were no customers in Sandi's Café. At the far end of the counter were two girls who would have been required to pass the positive ID test. One was moving a rag in lazy circles. She had dark hair and eyes. The other was blond and leaned on her elbow, looking vacantly toward Front Street. Both of the girls wore white nylon uniforms that made whisking sounds when they moved. They were chatting when the stranger came in. They looked up casually, then looked again. They stopped chatting.

The stranger set his gear by the door, walked to the counter, and sat on one of the stools.

"Beer," he said to the dark-haired girl.

"Sir," she said. "Ah, what kind?"

"Cold."

"Sir."

She opened the cooler below the counter and pulled out a bottle of Busch. The cooler was old and had a built-in bottle opener with a metal box to catch the caps. The girl used the opener rather than twisting off the top. She took a glass from the shelf behind her and poured the beer, being careful not to generate too much head. She set the beer in front of the stranger.

"Thanks," he said, and he drained half the glass in one swallow.

The dark-haired girl moved to the end of the counter. On the way she surreptitiously poked her blond friend, then continued on through the swinging door in the back wall. The door had a diamond-shaped window in it. It swung in and out a couple of times before coming to rest. The blond girl went through the door, and it swung a few more times.

In the back was the kitchen and storage. There was a small frozen food locker, a refrigerator, a couple of deep fryers, a dishwashing machine, two stainless-steel sinks with rubber spray hoses, stacked cases of food in cans and jars and boxes, huge tins of potato chips, gallon bottles of mayonnaise and relish and ketchup, five-gallon plastic tubs of dill pickles. In one corner was a push broom, a sweeping broom, and a swiveling dustpan, but the area was not especially clean.

As soon as the blond girl entered the back room, the dark-haired girl grabbed her hand and pulled her to one side.

"Janine," the dark-haired girl said, a little out of breath, "*who* is *that*?"

"I dunno," Janine said. "Never seen him before."

"God. He's *beau*tiful."

"Come on, Susanna. You just got this older men thing."

"He's not *that* old," Susanna said.

"Spare me, will you? What is it, you turn twenty-one and nobody looks old anymore? This guy's gotta be over thirty."

"That's not old. Well, maybe it is to you."

Janine crossed her arms. "I'll thank you to remember I'm only two years younger than you," she said, "and to keep the smart comments to yourself."

"Okay, okay. Besides, he's got a young face. And what a body, that ain't an old man's body. He looks like that guy, what's-his-name? The one on that old TV show they show the reruns of on Sundays. *Kung Fu.* You ever watch that?"

"David Carradine. Yeah, I've seen it," Janine said.

"Right. David Carradine. What do you think he's doing *here*?"

"Beats me. But he ain't David Carradine, I'll tell you that. David Carradine wouldn't be caught dead in Brawlton. Nobody in their right mind ever comes to Brawlton. This guy's probably just passing through. Shit, I wish I was just passing through."

"You'll get out, Janine. But hell, wouldn't you stick around if there was something like that walking the streets?"

Janine shrugged and said, "Ain't no man worth sticking anywhere for."

She was a slight girl with narrow shoulders and hips and knobby knees. She had lively gray eyes behind her contact lenses. Her face would have been pretty except for her nose, which had been broken at some point in the past. It was still crooked. It made her features seem slightly askew. Her hair, now pinned back in a bun, was golden blond and, when loose, would fall halfway down her back.

Janine looked at her friend Susanna. The other girl had dark, wavy hair framing an oval face that was saved from delicacy by being just a little fleshy. Her large, deep brown eyes were set well back in her head. Her primary problem would be with her weight. She would always walk the line between voluptuous and plump. At the moment she was safely on the near side of the line.

Susanna had a glowing smile on her face. Her mind was obviously elsewhere.

"Earth to Susanna," Janine said.

"Huh?" Susanna said.

"I don't think he's so much. Take a lot better-looking man than that to get *me* interested."

"Looks can be deceiving." Susanna grinned.

"Anyway," Janine added, "you don't even know him."

Susanna patted her friend's cheek. "But I will, honey," she said, and she went back into the front room. When she walked, her body rolled freely from side to side. Janine followed her after a while, her carriage stiff and controlled compared to that of her friend.

The stranger had finished his beer. His elbows were on the counter, his forearms raised and fingers interlaced. He was resting his chin on his knuckles and staring at the display of caps on the wall in front of him.

"Another?" Susanna asked him.

The stranger nodded and Susanna got him another beer. Again she poured it very carefully and again he paid no attention. He drank deeply.

"What's your name?" she asked him.

"Craik," he said, not looking at her.

"Howdy, Mr. Craik. I'm Susanna Holder."

He turned his eyes to her and tipped his beer glass. "Hello, Susanna Holder," he said. "Pleasure." There was just the trace of a smile. He went back to his drink.

Susanna got the rag and started doing the lazy circles on the countertop again. She started near Craik's end of the counter.

"What're you doing in Brawlton?" she asked while carefully watching her working hand.

"Nothing yet."

"Where y'all come from?"

"North."

"You gonna stay?"

"Now why would I want to do that, Susanna Holder?"

"I don't know," she said. "It's an interesting place." At

the other end of the counter Janine rolled her eyes heaven-ward. "There's a lot of good fishing and . . . stuff. History, and like that. Sailing on the Bay. Do you sail? I bet you sail."

"Some," he said. "How about fixing me one of your specials?"

"Right. One special!" she yelled with more volume than necessary. Janine gave her a disgusted look and went into the kitchen to prepare the food.

"I go sailing sometimes," she said. "On my uncle's boat. Well, it's not really sail sailing, it's more of a motor-type boat. I believe it's the biggest one around here. We go out on the Bay and sometimes down to the shore. It's plenty big enough for that. He's the rich side of the family, Uncle Forrest. Judge Holder, they still call him, though he hasn't done any judging, oh, five years now, I believe. But he *was* the District Court for twenty years before that. All the time I was growing up.

"Anyway, he's the success story, like I say. Daddy didn't do all that well, but he's Uncle Forrest's brother, you know, so we ain't ever gonna be hurting. There'll always be a job with the company. That's Uncle Forrest's company. He buys the stuff the fishermen catch and packs it up, ships it to Baltimore and D.C., New York, everywhere. Me, I think I got Uncle Forrest's smarts. Maybe Mama's looks. I don't suppose with that combination there's much can—"

"Susanna," Craik said.

"Huh?"

"Do you always talk so fast?"

"Uh, no, sir."

She began to polish the counter with renewed vigor. She remained silent for a few minutes.

Then she said, "Do you mind? I mean, me talking to you like that."

"No," he said, "I don't mind. But you talk fast like that, people are going to think you're a renegade Yankee hiding out down here." He smiled at her. "How about refilling my glass?"

"Sure," she said. "Sorry." She opened another beer. The

top fell into the little collecting box, making a sound like a coin dropping into a vending machine.

"No problem," Craik said. "What are you doing working in here if you've got a rich uncle?"

"Oh, well, Daddy and Uncle Forrest, they think it'll be good for me. You know, to work for a living and all. I went to the university, but I dropped out after my sophomore year. Actually, they sort of asked me to leave. I was majoring in good times, you might call it. They'd let me back, I suppose. Daddy says that if I work here for a while, I'll learn to see the value of a college education."

"And have you?"

"Seen the value? I guess so. As opposed to *this*." She indicated the rest of the room. "I mean, who wouldn't? But I don't know what I want to do yet."

"Me, neither."

"Really. I thought . . ."

"Thought what?" Craik asked.

"I don't know. It just seems, you seem like someone who knows what he's doing."

Craik smiled and winked at her. "No one knows what they're doing," he said.

Janine came out of the kitchen with the crab-cake platter. She laid it in front of Craik and asked if he wanted anything else with it. He shook his head.

"No ketchup, nothing?" She studied him frankly.

He shook his head again. Janine shrugged and went back to the other end of the counter where she took over the rag-moving job. As she passed Susanna she raised her eyebrows. Susanna just smiled.

Craik ate in silence, his attention concentrated on his food. From time to time the beginnings of a small afternoon breeze would swirl up from the Bay, and the screen door would rattle gently against its frame. A fly landed on one of the strips of sticky paper that was thumbtacked to the ceiling. It buzzed madly in its struggle to free itself.

Susanna leaned against the far wall and watched Craik eat.

Whenever he would look up, she would quickly shift her attention elsewhere.

"Where you staying?" she asked as he was finishing.

"No place," he said.

"You want to stay in Brawlton?"

"Maybe."

"Hey, Janine," Susanna said. "Isn't Miz Vickers' place for rent?"

"Yeah," Janine said. "Since that guy took off."

"It ain't much," Susanna said to Craik. "But she don't want much for it."

"Might be worth a look," Craik said. "How do I find Miz Vickers?"

"Easy. She just lives down a block and over one. I really think you're gonna like it here."

As she was giving him directions two men came into Sandi's Café. One of them was big, and the other one was bigger. Both men wore khaki trousers and short-sleeved khaki shirts. Each was carrying a gun, and each had a small gold star pinned over his breast pocket. The less big man tugged briefly at the seat and crotch of his pants. Otherwise neither looked discomforted by the heat.

When the two men entered the room, Susanna stopped talking. The silence was broken only by the soft whirring of the fans. The fly had ceased struggling and begun dying. Janine stared at the men coldly. Craik picked at the last of his crab cakes. He didn't turn around.

The larger of the two men smiled. "Hello, girls," he said.

"What you want, Brent?" Susanna asked.

"Hot day," he said. "Me and Charles might could use a cold brew."

Brent was about six-three and weighed close to two-thirty, very little of it fat. He was dark-complexioned, with a round face, wide nose, and thick, sensual lips. His chin was square and slightly blue with the kind of stubble that never can be quite fully scraped off. His black hair had been cut by a professional. It had been fluffed and blow-dried and was not quite collar length. He sported a neatly trimmed mustache.

His eyes were invisible behind black sunglasses with gold rims. On his right hand was a heavy gold ring in the shape of the initials *BF.*

Charles was a tad shorter, six foot or so, and about thirty pounds lighter. He also had dark, straight hair. While it was of moderate length on the top, at about the midpoint of his ears it became so closely cropped as to all but disappear. The effect was similar to the old-fashioned mixing-bowl cut. His face was rectangular, with flat features except for a highly prominent brow ridge. He wore mirrored sunglasses.

"Sheriff ain't gonna like you drinking on duty, boys," Susanna said.

"And who is it might tell him, sweetheart?" Brent said.

They stared at each other for a moment, and then Brent said, "C'mon, Charles," and they walked over to one of the booths. Their thick boots pounded heavily on the wooden floor. The silverware on one of the tables clinked.

The two men settled themselves onto their seats with large sighs. Charles removed his shades and dangled them from his index finger. He studied the stranger's back.

Susanna let out a sigh of her own. "See what they want, Janine," she said.

Janine grimaced but picked up an order pad and went to their booth.

"Hi, honey," Brent said to her, pushing the gold sunglasses down his nose. "When you and me gonna get together?"

"Never," Janine said.

"Now that's a shame. It truly is." He grinned and turned to his partner, giving him a wink. "Well," he said, "I know what I'd like to eat. What about you, Charles?"

"I ain't hungry," Charles said. He was still carefully studying Craik's back. His eyes peered from behind thick, half-closed lids.

"Ah, all right," Brent said. "Just bring us a couple of Budweisers, will ya?"

Janine nodded and turned toward the bar. Brent reached out and grabbed a handful of butt. Janine slapped savagely at his hand.

"Don't you ever," she growled back at him.

"Aw, honey, it's only love. Can't you tell?"

She walked away without looking back.

"Hey, buddy!" Charles yelled. "You, at the bar! Look on over here!"

Craik turned his head so that he could see the booth. Charles checked him out for about five seconds, then said. "Never mind. Forget it." Craik returned his attention to his beer.

"What in hell was that about?" Brent asked.

"Nothing," Charles said. "Guy just looked familiar. Thought I recognized him from somewhere."

Brent laughed. "Yeah, you did," he said. "He looks just like the guy used to be on that TV show *Kung Fu,* don't he?"

Charles laughed. "Yeah, that's it," he said. "Damn if he don't. Funny-looking fucker. Wonder what he's doing here. Think we oughtta find out?"

"Charles, I don't have the time to be keeping track of every half-assed tank-town drifter that comes passing through. And neither do you. Maybe he decides to stay awhile, we'll see, okay?"

"Yeah, I guess. I just don't believe I like his looks, though. Hey, Kung Fu! Show us some moves, huh? You got some moves?"

Craik didn't turn around again. Charles laughed. He snorted when he laughed. Brent laughed with him as Janine set the beers in front of them.

"Thanks, beautiful," Brent said.

He slid his hand up her leg, under her uniform. She yelped, tried to slap him, but he caught her by the wrist. He bent her arm back with one hand while with the other he explored the soft folds between her legs. Tears welled in her eyes. Charles was watching the action with a remote grin.

"What's the matter, honey?" Brent said. "I could be real good to you. You ever had a *man* before?"

"Janine!" Susanna called. "What—"

Craik swiveled a quarter of the way around on his stool. He could see the two men, the larger one holding on to the

young blonde's wrist. Susanna looked from the scene back to
Craik. He was watching intently, his eyes slightly hooded.
His face was impassive.

She hurried down to the end of the bar and then over to the
booth. She stood with hands on her hips.

"Let her be, Brent," she said.

"This your concern, little Miz Holder?" he said.

"Uh-huh. And Uncle Forrest's."

With a tremendous wrench Janine pulled herself free of
Brent's grip. She rushed from the room, sobbing. The kitchen
door flapped back and forth three times.

"You're scum, Brent Fyke," Susanna said. "You're trash
and that's all you ever will be. Why don't you just crawl back
under whatever rock you come up out of?"

Brent grinned. "The girl do have a mouth," he said to
Charles. Then to her, coldly, "You know, little miss, you're
damn lucky you got Judge Holder to hide behind. You know
what I mean?"

"I don't need my uncle to protect me from the likes of
you."

"That so?" He clucked, smiling again. "My, you are a
tough one. I like that. It's a shame I do prefer blondes."

"Why don't you'all prefer yourselves right on out of
here?"

Janine emerged from the kitchen. She'd stopped crying.
Except for Susanna, everyone was watching her. She walked
purposefully to the far corner of the room where a jukebox
stood. She dropped a coin in and jabbed at the buttons. Then
she turned, folded her arms beneath her breasts, and glared at
Brent and Charles.

The song came on. It began slowly. The singer's voice was
raw, as if he'd smoked too many cigarettes and drunk too
much cheap whiskey in the dead-end bars of his town.
Steadily, relentlessly, the backbeat rhythm drove the song
along, building its intensity until it exploded into the chorus.
It was a song called "Never Surrender." The singer hurled
the defiant words out into the room.

Susanna turned slowly and went back behind the bar.

Janine leaned against the jukebox, her jaw clenched, her lips bloodless, her eyes never leaving the men in the booth. Craik looked from them to her and back again. Then he smiled.

"What's so funny?" Charles said.

There was no reply.

He raised his voice. "I said, what's so funny, shit eater! You got a joke, share it with us, huh?"

"No joke," Craik muttered, turning his back.

Charles started to get up, but Brent motioned him down. "Finish your beer, Charles," he said, then he shook his head and smiled. "Ballsy. You got to like her spirit, don't you? Yes, I believe I do."

"I don't like that *guy*," Charles said.

"Leave it be. He's just some jerk-off. Nothing to get bent about. C'mon, let's go out and—"

"—catch us some—" Charles said.

"—*criminals!*" the two of them finished together.

They laughed, drained their beers, and got up. The heavy boots beat a path across the floor.

"You watch yourself in this town, buddy," Charles called to Craik's back. He reached out with the toe of his boot and nudged Craik's duffel bag, which was resting against the wall by the door. The bag rolled over a couple of times. Craik never looked around.

Outside, the officers adjusted their sunglasses in the afternoon glare, ran their hands around their waists to make sure their shirts were tucked in. They looked up and down Front Street. There was nothing moving but the gaunt black dog, changing sides of the road. Its tail hung limply between its legs.

They stepped unhurriedly to their cruiser, parked at the curb. It was a tan Ford, current model year and nondescript. On its door was a seal, a circle with a star in the middle. Around the upper half of the circle were the words *Sheriff's Office;* around the lower half, *County of Dorset.*

The two men got in, Charles on the driver's side. He started the engine and twisted the air conditioner fan switch until it was on full. He raced the engine for a moment, then let it fall back to idle. The engine made a small ticking sound. He stared at the instrument panel.

"Fyke," he said, "you know, this sumbitch got twenty thousand miles on her."

"I know," Fyke said. "Hard miles, way you drive."

"Hee haw. You think maybe we get a new one soon?"

"Well, I reckon that might depend on the election."

"Oh, hell, Brace'll win. Judge Holder'll see to that."

"That's what I mean, Deputy Tilghman. Kemp's kind of a chintzy bastard." Fyke winked. "Much money as that man makes."

"Yeah, well," Tilghman said. "But he does right by us other ways." He thought for a moment, then said, "Look, I still think we oughtta pull that boy in for something."

"The one in Sandi's?"

"Yuh. I just don't like the looks on him."

"Let's check it with the sheriff first, huh?" Fyke said.

"Right. Brace'll want to know."

The cruiser pulled away with a jerk, noisily leaving part of its tires behind. The man in the bib overalls, who'd moved to the bench in front of Graves' Mercantile, watched it go. He spat tobacco juice after it. The stream of juice didn't quite reach the street. It dripped down over the edge of the sidewalk and began to turn gummy in the sun.

In the café Janine said, "I wish somebody would kill that bastard."

"How come somebody hasn't?" Craik asked.

"They're afraid of him," Susanna said. "Or they're afraid of Sheriff Kemp. Or they're afraid of my uncle."

"Everyone in this town's scared of something," Janine said. "God, I can't stand it much more."

"But don't get the wrong idea, Mr. . . . Craik," Susanna said. "Ain't all of us like that. There's some great folks . . . here. You can't use creeps like Fyke and Tilghman as an example. They're just animals. You'll meet the good ones."

"Mmmm, I don't know."

"You aren't gonna be leaving right away, are you?" Susanna said, then looked abruptly at the far wall.

Craik half smiled. "Well," he said, "I can't say. I don't like being leaned on, though."

"You don't mind 'em leaning on girls," Janine said. Her face was still flushed. "Not so's anyone'd notice."

Susanna shot her a quick, angry look. Craik turned to her and said softly, "Janine . . . What's your last name, Janine?"

"Devereaux."

"Janine Devereaux. That's a nice name. I believe you're a nice girl, Janine. And I believe you're an intelligent girl too. I believe that you realize the last thing I want my first day in Brawlton is cop trouble." He grinned at her. "But if you want to kill the man, I don't guess I'd interfere."

Susanna laughed, and Janine smiled a little.

"Besides," Craik said, getting up, "it looks to me like this friend of yours is someone to be reckoned with around here." He pointed at the hat rack. "Let me have one of those caps there," he told Susanna.

"This one?" she asked, selecting a black-and-yellow one with a patch on the front that read, "Cat."

"Yeah, that one."

"It's a nice cap," Susanna said, brushing it with her sleeve. "I like the colors. It's my favorite one too." She handed it to him.

Craik took out his wallet. He laid a ten-dollar bill and a five on the counter.

"That about cover it?" he asked.

Susanna nodded her head. "You gonna go see Miz Vickers?" she said anxiously.

"Yeah, I think I might."

"You'll like her. She's a . . . funny old lady. She's got a wooden leg." Susanna laughed. "I mean, it's not funny that she's got a wooden leg, but . . ." She laughed again, unable to control herself.

"I'm sure I will. Like her," Craik said.

He walked over to his gear. He raised the duffel bag and

brushed off the dust it had acquired when Tilghman kicked it. He shouldered it, picked up the metallic suitcase, and left the restaurant. The screen door splatted against its frame.

"Wow," Susanna said. "He is something else. They sure don't make 'em like that around here. Didn't make 'em like that down to the university, either."

"I don't know," Janine said. "He was gonna let that bastard Fyke do whatever he wanted with me."

Susanna looked her friend in the eye. "You know something, Janine," she said. "He wouldn't've. He really wouldn't've. There's a lot of hard cases in this town, but I swear you something. Outside of my uncle and Sheriff Kemp, that's the first man I've ever seen wasn't afraid of Brent Fyke. Wasn't afraid at all. It was like he didn't need to be, like the idea woulda never got into his head."

"What're you thinking of, Susanna Holder?"

Susanna grinned from ear to ear. "I'm thinking that if he don't take Miz Vickers' place, I don't know *what* I'm liable to do."

CHAPTER 2

Craik followed Susanna's directions. He wound up in front of a small two-story house with shiplapped siding painted a fresh, clean white. There was a neat white picket fence around the yard. Attached to the front of the house was a porch supported by columns. On the porch was a bentwood rocker, and in the rocker was a woman in her early sixties.

The woman had a ruddy face, seamed and weathered, and a close-fitting cap of short white hair. Her head was small, her blue eyes set wide apart in her face. The small head sat on a stout, powerful-looking body. The woman was wearing a thin cotton floral-print dress. She was smoking a pipe. Next to her on the porch lay a sleeping dog. It was medium-sized, brown and white, of no easily discernible breed.

"Miz Vickers?" Craik called.

The woman pulled the pipe from her mouth. It had a short, straight stem and a pebbly corncob bowl. The dog raised its head, eyed the stranger for no more than two seconds, and went back to sleep.

"Who's looking?" she asked.

"My name's Craik," he said. "I understand you have a place to rent."

"Could be." She nodded. "Come up and let's have the sight of you."

Craik opened the small gate in the fence and let himself into the yard. When he did, the dog looked up again and emitted a soft growl.

"Lucky," the woman said, and the dog shut up. But it continued to keep an eye on the visitor.

Craik set his baggage down and climbed the steps to the porch. The woman held out her hand.

"I'm Marla Vickers," she said.

"Scott Craik. Pleasure."

"All mine, Craik. You're a fine-looking youngster, if you don't mind my saying so."

Craik smiled. "You live alone here, Miz Vickers?"

"Marla. Yeah, since Edward died. Ten years now. He was a waterman. Most of them are, and lot of them die young. It's a hard life. I know."

She rapped on her left leg with the bottom of the corncob bowl. "Fake," she said. "Lost the original back in sixty-three. Out tonging for oysters in December and a swell hit the skiff, and before I knew it, I was in the Bay. Never was that good of a swimmer, but I hung on till somebody picked me up. Time they got me to the hospital and all, they had to work like hell just the save the other one. Lost a fine pair of tongs too."

"Let me guess," Craik said. "Six months later you were back on the Bay again."

"Mmmm-hmmm. Don't believe it was that long, though,"

Vickers said. "Edward needed me, you know. It's tough enough in the business without you try to make it alone."

"And now?"

She shrugged. "I rent the cottage. I still go tonging now and again in season. I take what the government gives me. Wouldn't do it when I was younger, mind you. Whole trouble with this damn country. But it don't seem wrong at my age."

"You want to rent me your cottage?"

"I don't know, Craik. What do you do?"

She sucked at her pipe. It made a gurgling sound. When she exhaled, she broadcast a bluish white cloud of smoke. It hung without moving, slow to mix and dissipate in the hot, damp air.

"I'm looking for work," he said.

She laughed heartily. "Work," she said when she'd recovered. "Now that's a good one. You come out here to the end of God's earth looking for work. I believe you're short of brains, young man."

"There's some would agree with you."

"Including your mamma and daddy, I'll bet."

"Including them. Unfortunately, it seems like I favor places like this."

"You running from the law?"

"No, ma'am," he said.

She eyed him intently. "You're running from something," she said. "You got the look to you."

"I suppose you could say that. I've tried the city. Didn't take to it. If you want to say I'm running from too many people in too little space, you can."

"Any skills?"

"I can pound nails," he said. "But I'd rather work outside. I was hoping to catch on with one of the watermen."

"Boy comes down from the city, wants to work on the Bay." She shook her head and chuckled. "Now I *know* you're crazy."

"Why? It seems like honest work to me."

"Oh, it's honest, all right. The water don't lie, not never. You fall into it in winter, it'll freeze you stiff. That's honest as you ever find it. You need that kind of truth in your life when you got other choices, I'd sure have to wonder about you."

Craik started to get up.

"Look, Marla," he said, "maybe I'm not—"

"Sit down, son," she said. "Come on, sit." He sat. "It's nothing personal against you. Actually, you seem likable enough. But I been working the Bay for fifty year now. It's hard. It ain't what you'd call a . . . romantic way of life."

"I'm not looking for romance."

"Uh-huh. You're just looking for a job. You're out here looking where everyone has God's own time just making ends meet. Where you come from, Craik?"

"Up north."

"No jobs up there?"

"There's jobs," he said. "Like I told you, they don't appeal to me."

Vickers puffed at her pipe and looked thoughtfully out at the dirt road that ran in front of her house.

"I suppose, by my age," she said finally, "that I know when a man's trying to leave something behind. And I know when it's better not to ask what that something is. So what does that leave me? I'll tell you. It leaves me depending on my own judgment, which in my experience is right about half the time. I don't know about you, Craik. I don't dislike what I see, mind. But then you got your looks going for you. Probably you'll end up giving me more trouble than I've got stomach for." She smiled. "But what the hell, don't nobody else want to rent the damn place."

Craik smiled back. "Marla," he said, "I think we're going to get along just fine."

"We don't, it won't be the first time. Nor the last." She heaved herself up from the rocker. "C'mon and take a look at it."

She stepped down off the porch. Craik followed. She walked with a limp but only a slight one. From the rear, what was most noticeable was the breadth of her shoulders and the heft to her back and arms. Except for the white hair, she looked more like forty than sixty.

Craik picked up his gear and they started down the dirt road. They were heading south. As they walked, the neighborhood deteriorated steadily.

"How long you planning on staying?" she asked him.

"Don't know. I'll front you a month's rent if you want."

She made a brushing gesture. "I ain't worried about that. If I'd've been, you never would've got offered the place."

"Marla, I believe you must be right a bit more often than half the time."

Her faded blue eyes twinkled. "Yeah," she said, "I might be at that. But we've got a saying around here. Never trust a man until you see what he does when you hit the water. You might want to keep that one in mind yourself."

"Okay."

They'd turned down another dirt road, and the houses were a little farther apart. There was more junk in the yards. Work-related things like skiffs and nets, traps and oyster tongs. But also the rusting shells of cars, discarded refrigerators, old wringer washers, hubcap collections, forgotten middens of glass and plastic failing to decay even in the sun and the salt air.

Marla Vickers stopped in front of one of the houses and extended her hand, palm upward.

"Ta da," she said.

The house was clapboard and had once been white. It rested on stacks of brick. There was a front porch that sagged a little. The roof was tin, its silver paint streaked and spotted with the red of rust. It, too, sagged a little. A door and two windows faced the road. None of them was plumb. The yard was unfenced and it needed mowing, but there was no junk in it. The house was flanked on either side by a large live oak.

"I know," Vickers said, "it needs sprucing up, don't it? I find I can't keep up both places. You might say the other house is my pretty side and this one is my ugly side. But the roof don't leak and the frame's in good shape, best as I know. I'd knock some off the rent, you wanted to fix it up."

"Let's go in," Craik said.

They went up the front steps. Both the steps and the porch

creaked under their feet, but that was all. Vickers opened the screen door, which hung loosely on its hinges. Beyond it was a substantial, solid wood door with a spring-bolt lock. It was unlocked and opened smoothly.

"No key?" Craik asked.

"There's a key," she said. "Back at the house, if you feel like you need one. We don't get much breaking-in around here. Sheriff Kemp is tough, and the kids all know it."

"He's got a couple of deputies go a little beyond tough."

"Yeah, he does. Which ones in particular?"

"One named Brent and another called Charles."

Vickers nodded. "Fyke and Tilghman," she said. "They're two bad apples. Think the badge gives them the right to do any damn thing. I wouldn't mind seeing either one of them go missing. Don't nobody step out of line around here, though. You've got to say that along with the other."

"Why, because they're afraid?"

"Yeah, I reckon."

"Well, it works, all right. But if the people who might step out of line are afraid, then it's a good bet the ones who wouldn't are afraid too."

She cocked her head at him. "Perhaps I'd best advise you, Craik," she said. "Could be a lot of folks in this county prefer you didn't have any opinions about them before they get to know you." She raised an eyebrow and he nodded. "Now, how about we have a look round the cottage?"

"Okay," Craik said, and they went inside.

The air within the cottage was thick with the mustiness of not having been lived in for a while. The place needed to be swept, but basically it was pretty tidy. Almost three-fourths of it had been opened out into one big room. Living area to the left, dining to the right, kitchen behind that. There was a brick chimney in the center of the room but no fireplace, only a flue that was closed off with a tin pie plate. Next to the kitchen was an open door that revealed a small bathroom. There was a closed door at the left rear.

"Let a little fresh air in, what do you say?" Vickers said, and without waiting for an answer she pushed open the front

windows. Because of the humidity, it took some effort, but
she grunted and cursed and finally managed it. The windows
weren't counterhung and had to be propped with sticks that
were lying on the sills. Neither of them had a fitted screen,
although someone had nailed rectangles of screening over the
outside of both.

Craik walked around.

In the living area was a threadbare but serviceable sofa,
one nonmatching overstuffed chair, and a low table with
several magazines lying on it. *Popular Mechanics, National
Fisherman,* a small yellow pamphlet containing phases of the
moon and tide tables. There was a single standing floor lamp
with a shade that had once been off-white but was now
yellow. Tassels dangled from it. They swayed slightly in the
first breeze from outside. On the floor was an oval braided
rug that had been colorful when new.

The centerpiece of the dining area was a circular table that
had been painted, had the paint stripped off, and never been
either finished or repainted. There were two varnished wood
chairs snugged under it. On the tabletop was a set of glass salt
and pepper shakers with metal tops. There was a covered
bowl with a spoon handle protruding from it. And there was a
cheap white porcelain vase, slender at the base and wide at
the mouth, with some sort of sculpted porcelain vines
climbing up its sides. In the vase were some unidentifiable
flowers, wilted and brown. A handful of brittle dry petals lay
nearby, almost covering the initials J. H., which someone had
carved into the tabletop long ago.

The kitchen contained a gas stove with four blackened iron
burners, stainless-steel double sinks, some counter space
with storage underneath, and an old refrigerator, of the sort
that closes with a latch instead of magnets and has a tiny
freezer box inside that melts ice cream. Over the sink was a
cupboard with two doors. In the far corner, between the sinks
and the refrigerator, was a door to the outside. It had four
small windowpanes set in it. One had been broken and
patched with a piece of cardboard. The others gave a view of
the backyard. About thirty feet from the cottage was a

weathered gray board-and-batten shed. The kitchen's floor was bare wood, as was the dining area's.

All of the walls that could be seen—kitchen, living room, and dining area—were Sheetrocked. The Sheetrock had been hung with minimal professionalism. It had originally been painted off-white. Much of it was now stained, spotted, or discolored, and there were tears here and there in the outer layer.

Craik peered into the bathroom. There was a toilet, a sink, a medicine chest with a mirror, and a clawfoot bathtub. A tubular steel frame had been erected around the bathtub, and plastic shower curtains hung from it. The curtain was patterned with drawings of four-masted sailing ships. The tub's faucets had been fitted with a contraption that allowed the use of a plastic shower attachment on the end of a long, flexible metal hose. Cracking linoleum with a black-and-white checkerboard pattern covered the bathroom floor.

Craik gestured at the closed door.

"Bedroom," Vickers said. "Go on in."

He went into the bedroom. It was small and particularly musty. There was a four-poster double bed with a ribbed white spread on it. An oak bureau with two full and two half drawers, and an oval mirror on dowels, so that it pivoted freely. There was a tiny walk-in closet and a well-scuffed rose print rug on the floor. In one corner was a short stack of cardboard boxes.

Marla Vickers was standing in the doorway. "That's Henry's stuff," she said.

"Who's Henry?" Craik asked.

"Henry Beadle," she said. "C'mon out and set down."

They went back into the living room. Vickers settled herself into the overstuffed chair while Craik sat on the sofa. She fidgeted with her smoking materials until she had the pipe fired up again.

"Now, I don't want to spook you, Craik," she said, "but you don't really look the type. Henry's the fella used to live here. It's why the cottage is for rent."

"He took off and left his stuff?"

"Kinda. Actually, I don't know where he is."

"Disappeared."

She nodded. "About six weeks now. I let the place sit a month for him, but I get a taker, I'm not gonna let it sit longer. I'll move his stuff over to my place."

"He leave anything of value?"

"Some money, not a lot. His clothes. All the furniture's mine, such as it is."

"And no one knows where he went?"

"Nope. Like I said before, there's a lot of men out there on the run from this and that. They run and they get tired and they stumble into my life. I seem to have met up with more than my share. Why I asked about you, you see."

"Uh-huh." He looked around the room again. There wasn't anything personal, possibly excepting the magazines. "What did Henry do?" he asked.

"Worked the Bay, like most. Pretty good at it, I suppose, but I don't believe his heart was in it."

"He work alone?"

"We all do, one time or another. Mostly he crewed with Brendan Shields, though. He could have been doing some night fishing alone. Thought had occurred to me. A lot of things happen at night." She shrugged. "Right damn lot of things. Some of them don't leave a body around."

"You think he's dead," Craik said.

"Could be. Or some woman led him off by the nose. He's gone, anyway, and I don't find as I care that much. I got a place to rent. You want it?"

They looked at each other for a long moment, then Craik smiled. "Yeah," he said. "Yeah, I do. What happens if Henry Beadle comes back from the dead?"

"I guess I'd have to start going to church again."

Craik laughed. "Tell me something, Marla," he said, "what about Beadle's partner, he looking for somebody?"

"Shields? Maybe. He ain't taken on no one yet."

"You know him?" he asked. She nodded. "Good man?"

"Yup. Good man."

"Local guy?"

"Off and on," she said, puffing at the pipe. "Born here. He's left a time or two, and he come back a time or two. You'll find every waterman to curse the Bay, but you won't find many as will turn away from it for keeps."

"Okay, I'll give him a try. You know where he lives?"

"Well, most of the time you'll find him on *Murphy's Law*. . . ."

"His boat?" Craik asked.

Vickers nodded. "Most name 'em for a woman. Daughter, maybe a wife when they can stand her. Leave it to Brendan to be different. Lord knows he'd have a time picking a woman out of the crowd. Anyway, you find him there, or either down at the harbor. That is, if he ain't at Jimmie and Sook's." She winked.

"Who're Jimmy and Suke?"

"Jesus, Craik," she said. "You want to be a waterman, you better learn how to talk. Jimmies and sooks are crabs. You don't know that this time of year, ain't nobody gonna hire you."

"So what're you saying," he asked, "that he's probably out crabbing?"

"This late in the day, I doubt it. It's where the watermen drink. Cute, eh? Call it Sook's for short and make like you always knew. It's on the main road, just west of town. You had to passed it coming in."

"Cinder-block place? Green roof?"

"Uh-huh."

"Okay. Suppose I don't find him. Where's he live?"

"About a mile out, then north toward the Pawchunk. He's right on the river." She gave him directions, then hoisted herself from the chair. "Hundred bucks a month, Craik. You paint the place, the first month's a ride. After that we'll see what else needs doing."

"Fine."

"I'll have someone to fetch Henry's stuff."

"Whenever."

They shook hands and Vickers left. At the edge of the yard she paused and turned around, shifting her weight onto her good leg. She stared at the front of the house, her head slightly cocked, her brow a little furrowed, her lips pursed. She held the position for perhaps ten seconds. Then she turned again and started down the dirt road.

Inside, Craik stood in the center of the room. The mustiness was beginning to fade, though the tobacco scent lingered. A few random insects plinked against the screens. Other than that, the only sound was from the occasional traffic over on Front Street.

Craik picked up his bags and set about moving in.

CHAPTER 3

By six o'clock, some of the heat had gone out of the day, but not much. Fyke and Tilghman were cruising the road from Dorset, the county seat, to the bayside town of Brawlton. The scenery was somewhat monotonous. The land was flat, nowhere much above sea level. There were patches of pine woods and patches of pine mixed with hardwoods. This late in summer, the only color other than green was provided by the flowering crape myrtle, its blossoms ranging from a pale pink to a deep wine red.

Nearly all of the open land was under cultivation, but there were only two crops being grown, corn and soybeans. The corn was tall and still green. Soon it would begin to brown. When it had fully dried in place, it would be cut and ground into meal, stalks and cobs and all. The soybeans were about knee-high. They, too, were being grown for animal fodder. No farms grew food for people any longer. The only human food produced locally was what was taken from the Bay.

The two deputies were protected from the evening heat by the cruiser's air-conditioning, still wide open. Fyke was driving. He was hatless, whereas his partner chose to continue wearing his wide-brimmed trooper's hat with the strap that went around the back of his head. The police radio was turned down and the FM radio turned up. The latest from George Strait thumped the interior of the cruiser. Fyke beat on the steering wheel in time with the record. Tilghman hummed along disinterestedly. He was far off-key.

They passed a concrete-block house set near the road, painted pink. A woman was working in the garden in front of the house. She wore running shorts and an abbreviated halter top. Tilghman swiveled his head as they drove by. He gawked.

"C'mon, darlin'," he said, "bend on over now. That's it. Oh, my Lord, I believe I could crawl in there and never see the light of day again. I could die a happy man."

The pink concrete house and its garden slipped out of sight. Tilghman faced forward again. He shook his head, sighed, and made a clucking sound with his tongue.

"Only way you find yourself someplace like that is you trip and fall and they can't get clear in time," Fyke said.

Tilghman looked at his partner coldly. "That ain't so," he said.

"Oh, yeah? You gettin' a lot lately, Charles? Tell me about it?"

Tilghman opened his mouth to speak. Then he closed it again. He folded his arms across his chest and faced forward. "I don't have to do that," he said.

They drove in silence for a while, then Fyke said, "Sheriff seemed a bit bent."

"I think the Judge leaning on Brace," Tilghman said.

"Beadle."

"Yeah, maybe. Been six weeks now. That's a long time. Man *was* Shields' partner, but it don't seem like the Judge cares that much for the Shields. They ain't but half kin."

Fyke ran his hand through his thick hair, arranging it. "Yeah," he said. "And anyway, he don't have to take it out on us."

"He don't. Damn if I don't feel like taking it out on somebody back."

"I mean," Fyke went on, "sometimes it don't seem like they *want* us to find the man. You know? I don't give a shit, you want the truth. Be nice if they'd tell us what was going on, though. We do a good job, and nobody tells us dick."

Tilghman removed his hat, smoothed what hair he had, and fitted the hat carefully back on.

"I believe it'll blow over, Brent," he said. "Take it easy. Get yourself laid or something."

Fyke smiled. "Yeah, maybe I'll hit on Janine Devereaux. I do love that busted nose."

"The bitch don't like you, old man."

"I don't give a shit. I don't need her fucking *permission*."

"Tough guy," Tilghman said. "Big talk."

Fyke jammed on the brakes and spun the cruiser to a stop on the shoulder. Tilghman banged the dash and then was thrown sideways into his partner. Fyke flicked him off with an elbow, then grabbed a handful of shirtfront and mashed him against the passenger-side door. He pulled him forward and slammed him backward again. Tilghman made no effort to resist.

"Charles," Fyke said precisely, "I want to listen to an asshole, I'll fart, you know what I'm saying? You don't never talk that way to me. Not until the day you come three sizes bigger to what you are now. If I tell you I can have the bitch on her knees with her mouth open and love in her eyes, then all I want to hear from you is, 'Yeah, Brent, you sure could do that.' We got us an understanding about this?"

Tilghman stared at him, his own eyes as dull as the surface of the Bay on a cloudy day.

"Whatever you say, Brent," he said finally, mechanically. "Whatever you say."

Fyke released Tilghman's shirtfront and brushed at it. He patted his partner twice on the chest. Then he punched the cruiser into gear and jerked off the shoulder, throwing up a plume of gravel. The Toyota he cut off in the process fishtailed as the driver fought for control, gaining it only after narrowly missing a pickup that was headed in the opposite direction at well over fifty-five. Horns shrieked, but Fyke didn't look in the rearview mirror.

"What it is, Charles," he said as if lecturing, "I'm bigger than you and I'm smarter than you and I got more years in this job than you. But all that ain't worth walking two feet to piss on. The only thing you got to always remember is that I'm *meaner* than you. That's what's important." He nodded as if confirming the fact to himself.

"You got a bigger prick too?" Tilghman said.

"Well, I don't know about that." He laughed. "But I sure as hell ain't gonna let *you* find out. Only ones get to see my cock are the ones *glad* to see it coming."

The two men laughed together, Fyke loudly and Tilghman carefully, as the cruiser rolled into Brawlton. They made a circuit of the town, giving it a visual inspection. They drove down Front Street, past the small cluster of businesses, through a tree-shaded residential area and down to the Bay.

There wasn't much activity at the docks. The warehouses were padlocked, and the only people at the processing plant were cleaning up. There was a single blue-and-white panel truck in the lot, with HOLDER SEAFOOD CO. painted boldly across its side. Underneath the company name was the slogan, "Fruits of the Deep." A station-wagonful of tourists was out on the main loading pier, the adults snapping photos, the children fighting over some unidentifiable scrap of junk that each wanted for a Chesapeake vacation souvenir.

The cruiser didn't stop. The deputies checked the fleet of workboats tied up in the small harbor. There was nothing there to see. They continued on around and back out Front Street. As they approached Sandi's Café the stranger came out onto the sidewalk. He was dressed the same as he had been earlier in the day, except that now he was wearing the yellow "Cat" cap.

"Well, well," Tilghman said, "what do you think?"

"I think we ought to give the boy a lift," Fyke said.

Tilghman smiled and wet his upper lip. "Uh-huh," he said.

The cruiser slowed until it was keeping pace with Craik,

who was walking west, away from the harbor. He glanced at it, then away. Tilghman rolled down his window.

"Hey," he said.

Craik stopped. The cruiser stopped too. Craik turned and faced Deputy Tilghman. His expression was neutral.

"Evening," Craik said.

"Yeah," Tilghman said, smiling. "That's what it is, all right."

"Can I do for you?"

"Like to offer you a lift." Tilghman gestured at the rear door of the cruiser. The car's engine raced briefly, then settled down again. It ticked softly.

"Thanks," Craik said. "Rather walk." He turned away. The cruiser followed him.

"Buddy," Tilghman said. He wasn't smiling anymore. "Get in the goddamn car, will you?"

Craik stopped and looked at Tilghman's face. It was the face of someone who had put on a dime-store tough mask. It didn't blink, the set of it didn't waver at all. Craik sighed, went over to the cruiser, and got in the backseat. Fyke jackrabbited off down Front Street, leaving behind some tire tread and one irate pedestrian.

After a couple of minutes of silence Tilghman said, "Don't you want to know where you're going?"

Craik shook his head. He leaned back in the set, his hands resting lightly on his thighs.

"My partner asks you a question," Fyke said, "we want to hear what you got to say."

"No, I don't want to know where I'm going," Craik said.

"Dorset," Tilghman said. "Ever been to Dorset?"

Craik shook his head.

"Say what?" Fyke said.

Craik sighed. "I've never been to Dorset," he said.

"You'll like it," Tilghman said. "Nice place. Sheriff Kemp wants to meet you."

"Fine."

"You ain't got much to say, do you?"

Craik shrugged. "Not to you," he said.

"Boy's got a mouth on him," Tilghman said to Fyke. "Think we oughtta check for cavities?" They both laughed.

"I used to been right good at home dentistry," Fyke said, and they laughed some more.

Craik looked out the window. It was seven miles from Brawlton to Dorset. The three men covered the rest of the distance in silence. Halfway there, they passed the pink concrete-block house. The woman wasn't working in her garden anymore. Tilghman was audibly disappointed.

The town of Dorset wasn't much bigger than Brawlton. What there was of it lay strung out along the state road, on either side of the County Courthouse. This was an imposing building of nineteenth-century brick, weathered and pitted, with four massive white columns in front. At the peak of its roof was a domed bell tower, also painted white, with no bell inside.

The cruiser turned down a hard-surface driveway that ran between the County Courthouse and a small frame building with a hanging wooden sign announcing that it belonged to a branch office of the Virginia Marine Resources Commission.

Behind the County Courthouse was a miniature replica of it. The details were all there, the columns, the bell tower, but on about a one-third scale. It was also obviously newer. The bricks had not yet begun to flake and crumble. A discreet white sign proclaimed that this was the Office of the Sheriff of Dorset County. The cruiser stopped in front of it.

"Home sweet home," Tilghman said.

He got out and opened the door for Craik, since there were no handles on the inside of the cruiser's rear doors. Craik stepped onto black tarmac, still soft from absorbing the heat of the day. Tilghman tried to take his arm, but Craik pulled away. They looked at each other for a moment, neither betraying emotion, then Tilghman inclined his head toward the brick building. The three of them went inside.

They were in a large waiting room. It was cool and very clean, with bright fluorescent lights overhead. The lights provided a steady background hum.

"Sit there," Fyke directed, and Craik sat on a plain wooden bench that ran along one wall.

The two deputies walked to a chest-high counter that separated the waiting area from the remaining two-thirds of the room. On the other side of the counter was a reception desk and two other desks, some filing cabinets, an inverted-bottle watercooler, a copying machine, a cubicle with a dispatcher's radio in it, some tables with books and papers stacked on them. Fyke talked to the overweight officer at the reception desk, and the man made a short phone call. After he had hung up, a buzzer sounded and the deputies went through a door in the partition. They each pulled a rolling chair out from under one of the empty desks, sat, and propped their feet up. Fyke smoked a cigarette. Craik sat motionless, his arms loosely folded and his eyes half closed.

Fifteen minutes passed. During that time no one entered or left the building. There was one phone call, concerning something evidently routine, which the dispatcher handled quickly. Fyke and Tilghman occasionally exchanged words, their voices pitched so that they couldn't be heard across the room.

Then the phone buzzed again. The dispatcher answered it, said "Right," and hung up.

"Sheriff'll see you now," he said to Craik. "Go through that door, down the hall, second door on your left."

Craik followed the directions. The door was closed. It was wood and frosted glass. SHERIFF KEMP was painted in black on the frosted glass. Craik knocked and was told to come in.

Craik went in and closed the door behind him. He looked around. The sheriff's office was clean and tidy but otherwise was unlike anyone's image of a sheriff's office. The walls were blond wood paneling. The chairs were real leather. There was a deep, plush carpeting on the floor. A number of paintings hung on the walls, primarily seascapes and fishing scenes. They were well-executed originals, professionally framed. The sheriff had an oak executive's desk, perched on a carpeted platform at the far end of the room. Behind him were three large windows that looked out on a rectangle of manicured green lawn with two large sycamores lending shade. On the desk was a modern phone console and an antique brass lamp.

The sheriff stood when Craik entered the room. He was in his late forties and of medium height. At first glance he might be taken for thin, but his body was lean and hard. His gray hair was cut close to his head, no more than bristles. His eyes were pale blue smudges in his narrow face. They looked out at the world from behind silver-rimmed glasses. He had clean-shaven leathery skin, the kind that requires patience to raise a respectable beard.

Craik walked over to the oak desk. The sheriff held out his hand in a friendly manner. Craik shook it without hesitation.

"I'm Bracewell Kemp," the sheriff said.

"Scott Craik."

The sheriff released his hand. "Sit down, Mr. Craik," he said, indicating a leather chair that was considerably lower than his own. Craik sat in it.

"Am I being charged with something?" Craik asked.

Kemp smiled. He walked around to the front of his desk and perched on the edge of it, one foot on the floor, the other dangling. He rested a forearm on one knee. He was looking down at Craik.

"Dorset County is the smallest in all of Virginia," the sheriff said. "Did you know that?" Craik shook his head. "It is. We have less than ten thousand people here. Now, I've been on this job for fifteen years, and I like to think I know just about every one of those people. When someone new comes to our county, I prefer to know who he might be."

Craik's face was expressionless. "Am I being charged with something?" he asked again.

"There's no need to be hostile, Mr. Craik. You're not charged with anything. I wanted to make your acquaintance, that's all."

"Pleased to meet you. May I go now?"

"You're free to go at any time," Kemp said, gesturing briefly at the door. "However, I would like to remind you that your stay in Dorset County will be a great deal more

pleasant if we are on . . . speaking terms. Don't you think
so?" He smiled.

Craik shrugged. "What do you want from me?" he asked.

"Just a little chat."

"I don't like to talk much."

"I can see that. Why is that, Mr. Craik?"

"Look, Sheriff, if you've got something you want to ask
me, go ahead and do it."

Kemp dropped off his desk and walked over to one of the
windows. He clasped his hands behind him and looked out at
the lawn. He tapped one foot to a music that wasn't playing in
the room. After about fifteen seconds he turned back to his
guest. His face was still genial, except around the eyes.

"Where are you staying, Mr. Craik?" he asked.

"Marla Vickers's cottage. In Brawlton. I've rented it."

"For how long?"

"By the month."

"How long did you intend to stay here?"

"I don't know."

Kemp returned to the desk and resumed his earlier posture.

"What brings you to Dorset County?" he asked.

"It's nice. I like the water. I like peace and quiet. I *like*
being left alone."

Kemp smiled. "I appreciate your sense of humor," he
said. "Man's got a good sense of humor, I often take to him.
And where do you come from, Mr. Craik?"

"Up north."

"That covers a lot of ground."

"I move around some. Last place I lived was New York.
What's the difference?"

"You wouldn't have been in trouble with the law, would
you?"

"No."

"I'll check, you know."

"Feel free," Craik said.

"All right. And what do you do for a living?"

"I'm looking for work."

Kemp laughed. "This is not exactly Boomtown," he said,

"as you might have noticed. *Especially* for someone without any skills. You do have some kind of skills, don't you?"

"I've fished before. I'll find something."

"You realize that the watermen are a pretty close-knit bunch. They don't tend to warm up to outsiders."

Craik shrugged. "Maybe I'll take Henry Beadle's place," he said.

Kemp's head jerked slightly backward. "What do you know about Beadle?" he asked.

"Nothing."

The sheriff leaned toward Craik. His face was serious. "I asked you a question," he said.

Craik looked up at him, then said slowly, "He used to rent the place I've got now. Miz Vickers said he's been missing for a while and his partner might be looking for help. I thought I'd check it out."

"You don't know Henry Beadle?"

"No. Why would I?"

"You wouldn't know what happened to him, would you?"

"Of *course* not," Craik said. "What the hell is this, Kemp?"

"*Sheriff* Kemp."

"Sheriff Kemp. What are you getting at?"

The sheriff peered at Craik's face as if searching for something. Then he said, casually, "Nothing. A man disappears in my county, I like to know the reason. I like to know what things mean, Craik. I don't like mysteries. Why I'm a cop. You come in here, a stranger, start talking about Henry Beadle, it seems odd."

"Well, it isn't. I needed a place to stay, that's the one I found. I don't care where Henry Beadle went, or why, or anything else about him."

Kemp got up. "All right," he said, "I believe you. See you stay out of trouble in Dorset County." And he turned away.

"Can I go now?" Craik asked his back.

"Of course," Kemp said to the windows. "Have a nice day, Mr. Craik."

Craik sighed and got up. He went back down the hall and into the waiting room. Tilghman and Fyke were still there. They were laughing about something when he arrived. Tilghman was snorting heavily.

"He's finished with me," Craik said.

Fyke glanced over at him. "Oh," he said. "Well, 'bye now."

Craik looked at him, then at Tilghman. Tilghman had a smug smile on his face.

"Jesus," Craik muttered, and he walked out of the building. Behind him, the deputies were laughing once again.

Outside, Craik moved at a relaxed pace. He paused in front of the courthouse building and examined a glass case near the massive doors. In the case was a listing of the various offices to be found within.

Besides housing the circuit and district courts, the building also contained offices for the Registrar of Voters, the Commonwealth's Attorney, Division of Social Services, Health Department, and Board of Supervisors. According to the listing, the Board of Supervisors' functions included the overseeing of county administration, building inspection, zoning, parks and recreation, and wetlands protection.

Craik turned his back to the courthouse. As he stepped to the road a man came out of the building next door. He had on a rumpled blue suit and a tie that was hanging unknotted against his shirt. The man locked up and went out behind the County Courthouse to the parking lot. He got into a dark, late-model sedan with "Commonwealth of Virginia Official Use" license plates and drove out to the road. Craik was hitchhiking. The man picked him up and they headed east.

"Not much traffic on this road," the man said. "Where you going?"

"Brawlton," Craik said.

"I can take you part of the way there," the man said.

"Thanks." He paused. "Working late?"

The man chuckled. "You guessed it," he said. "I don't always stay as late as this, but it isn't as rare as it might be. The Marine Resources Commission is a bit understaffed."

"That who you work for?"

"Yeah. Me and the select few. They've got less than a hundred and fifty of us covering the whole Bay. Virginia's part, anyway."

"You a cop?" Craik asked.

"Uh-uh. More than half of the payroll is, but not me. The rest of us have to run the offices. We maintain at least one in each of the counties that borders on the Bay. It stretches us pretty thin. Sometimes I wish I *was* in the Enforcement Division. They get to work outside, at least. But then, I don't know. It's getting dangerous. Our officers are unarmed. Now that there's so much drug smuggling and whatnot going on, I'm not sure I'd want to be out there. Those people are dangerous."

Craik nodded. "It's serious business. Lot of big money, lot of desperate people."

The man looked over at him. He cleared his throat. "Well," he asked, "what are you doing here? You don't live here, do you?"

"Just passing through," Craik said, and he turned and looked out the side window at the darkening day.

"Oh."

The man wet his lips, and they drove in silence for another mile. From time to time the man glanced at Craik out of the corner of his eye. Craik didn't look back. Eventually, the man pulled off the tar and the sedan came to a stop.

"This is it," the man said quickly. "I'm headed down that road there." He pointed twice to the left. "I, uh, hope you make it to Brawlton okay."

The man looked down at the steering wheel as Craik turned to him.

"Thanks for the lift," Craik said. He got out. The sedan threw up a spray of gravel as it reentered the road. The pellets flew at Craik, who made no effort to get out of the way. A number of them bounced off his legs and rattled to the ground, making a sound like a fistful of thrown dice. Craik stood on the shoulder and waited.

CHAPTER 4

After Craik had gone, the sheriff stood gazing at the sycamores for a while, his hands locked behind him. Then he turned and strode purposefully to his desk. He placed a phone call.

"Yeah," he said, "this is Sheriff Kemp. Let me speak to the Judge. . . . Yeah, I'll hold."

It was five minutes before he spoke again.

"Judge," he said, "sorry to bother you. Something I thought you oughtta know. There's a new kid in town my boys just brought by for a visit. . . . I don't know, he don't talk much. He says he's from up north someplace. Anyway, he's in Henry Beadle's old place. . . . Don't think so. Looks like a coincidence. But when he said Beadle's name, I grilled him. . . . I know, I don't much believe in coincidences myself, but they happen. Still, I think this guy's clean as far as Beadle goes. But there's something about him. He don't seem an ordinary sort of drifter. He's got his lip awful tight zipped. . . . The other thing is, he was in Sandi's this afternoon. Fyke and Tilghman saw him talking to Susanna. Probably just ordering food, but what with the rest of it, I think it's best I have the boys keep an eye on him."

"Okay," Judge Holder said, "and look, I want to see you. . . . No, not tonight. Tomorrow. . . . Yes, here. Come by in the afternoon, around five. . . . All right, Brace. . . . No, it's all right, I *want* you to interrupt me. Anything suspicious, you get on the phone right away, y'hear? . . . Tomorrow afternoon."

Holder fitted the tan plastic receiver into its slot amid the array of buttons and gizmos that constituted a modern phone console. He opened the bottom drawer of his desk, punched the appropriate buttons on the recorder, and played back a tape of the conversation he'd just had. He sat, listening, his chin rested on his knuckles, his face impassive.

Forrest Holder was just over sixty and looked younger. He stood five-eight and weighed one-eighty. The weight was well distributed. His body tapered very little between his shoulders and his hips. When he stood with his legs slightly spread, his shape was almost perfectly rectangular.

The Judge still had most of his hair, and its chestnut brown was only slightly streaked with gray. He wore it long and combed back in carefully controlled waves. His head was large. It seemed well suited to his body. His face was round and symmetrical, his ears prominent. His eyes were a very dark brown.

When the tape finished, Judge Holder reset the recorder and closed the desk drawer. He got up and walked over to one of the wall cabinets. The cabinet was constructed of oiled black walnut, as were the bookcases that encircled his library. The bookcases were crammed with law books and other volumes with embossed bindings that looked as if they had never been opened. There was a deep red and gold Oriental carpet on the floor. The chairs were buttery dark leather. In one corner of the room was a walnut table with a twenty-five-inch Sony monitor and a VCR on it.

The Judge opened the cabinet. It housed an assortment of bottled whiskies and liqueurs, and a collection of Waterford lead-crystal glasses and goblets. He poured himself two fingers of Glen Calder single-malt Scotch whisky and drank it down. Then he went back out to the dining room.

"I'm sorry, Jess," he said to his guest.

"I understand," Jesse Mills said, smiling. "Business."

"Yes, business."

"Your affairs continue to run wide and deep, don't they, Forrest?"

Holder didn't answer. Instead, he poured the Courvoisier.

The dining room table was capable of accommodating twelve without crowding. That night it had been set only for two, but it had been set well. Irish linen, crystal, sterling silver. In front of each of the men was the remains of dessert, a peach Melba with fresh, lightly whipped cream. As Holder was filling the brandy snifters a man in formal attire appeared with a gold cigar box. He offered a cigar to Mills, but Mills declined. The Judge took one, ran it briefly under his nose, bit off the end, and fired it up.

He exhaled and said, "Thank you, Stayne. Please see that we're not disturbed now."

The formally dressed man said, "Yes, sir," removed the dessert dishes, and left the room.

Mills gestured at the cigar. "Cuban?" he asked.

The Judge nodded. "Of course. You ought to take them up. They become a politician."

"I'll pass," Mills said. "But your contacts never cease to amaze me. Autographed by Fidel, I suppose." He laughed. "Anyway . . . the meal was outstanding, as usual. It's been so long between visits, I'd forgotten what a chef your boy is."

Holder shrugged. "Why not the best?" They both laughed. "Speaking of which, how *are* things in Washington?"

"Ah. I thought you might be getting around to that."

"Don't want to spoil dinner."

"Of course," Mills said. "Well, you know how it is. The game never changes. The President wants to cut our favorite programs, we don't want to let him. Most of the Congress is running scared at what we've already done with elections coming up. It's nerve-wracking having to face the voters every two years. To tell you the truth, that's one of the main reasons I wanted to move up in the first place."

"That and the fact that Dillon's more vulnerable than he's ever been."

"The timing is . . . right, isn't it?"

"He's still a tough opponent."

"Of course," Mills said. "You don't get to be a three-term senator by being a pussy. But he can be beaten. I can beat him. I *will* beat him."

Judge Holder regarded Jesse Mills from behind the barrier of cigar smoke. The congressman was still only in his mid-thirties. And he was handsome, with rugged good looks and the healthy appearance of someone who spent a lot of time out-of-doors. He dressed so conservatively as to satisfy even the most reactionary Virginian, yet he wore his hair just long enough that he'd be able to use his sex appeal with the women and his youth appeal with the young. He had a boyish, innocent smile. Though he had only a hint of regional accent, when he spoke, it was with the measured, dramatic pace that Southerners prefer in their politicians.

"I like your style, Jesse," Holder said. "Always have. You've got that sense of timing and you've got just the right amount of confidence. You've got a good shot at senator." He paused to smoke.

"Yeah," he went on, "I remember when I first saw you, when you made county supervisor. You didn't know from shit about politics. Just a bright young kid who'd hustled it on his own. But I said to myself, 'This boy's got it. I can get this boy into the Congress of the United States.' And it's all worked out, ain't it?"

Mills chuckled. "Well, I do happen to believe that I would've beaten Goodwin, anyway."

"Oh, you do, do you?"

"Not that I haven't been grateful for your help, Judge," he added quickly. "You know I've always done right by you. But I think you realize just how far I've come since those days."

Holder twirled the cigar between his fingers as he puffed. "Uh-huh. You reckon you can take Dillon all by yourself?"

Mills flapped his hand to clear the air in front of him of smoke. He studied the Judge's face.

"Come to that," he said finally. "What're we talking about here?"

"What we're talking about is I'm beginning to feel old and only in the way."

"Come on, Forrest. You know I don't think that."

"Do I? Like I said, Jess, I like that self-confidence of yours, but I wouldn't want to see you get cocky as a slum kid with his first knife. No, that wouldn't do at all. It's good we all remember where our roots are."

"I know where my roots are. But my constituency is expanding, Judge. You gotta understand that. If I'm going to be any kind of a senator, I have to represent all of Virginia."

"Spare me the soapbox, son. I've forgot more about politics than you'll ever know. There's only one thing worth understanding, and that's who got you where you are. The rest is just seeing you don't lose your grip. You keep that in mind, you'll do well in this world. You get to thinking you're beyond what put you up there, and you'll hit the ground harder than a blue hits bait when he ain't eaten in the past hour."

"Why'd you have me here, Judge?" Mills asked coolly.

Holder smiled. "You're my friend, Jess. You're my *protégé*."

"Forrest, no offense, but you haven't done anything out of friendship since I met you."

"And your sense of humor," the Judge said, "I like that too. All right, let's talk about your future."

"What about my future?"

"You think you got one?"

"I don't like that kind of question," Mills said.

"You ain't asked for my help yet in this campaign, Congressman. Why is that? I been wondering."

"Do I have to ask?"

"Don't fence with me, Jess. I think you been figuring you might've . . . outgrowed our relationship. I think you figure all you got to do is toady up to the fat party cats in Richmond and they'll throw you everything you need."

"I suppose you'll think any damn thing you want to, Forrest."

Judge Holder leaned forward and rested his arms on the table. He looked hard at Jesse Mills. Mills eventually looked down.

"Now, you listen to me, son," the Judge said. "I believe what I said about you. I believe you got what it takes. You can be senator. I wouldn't be surprised but what you could be the goddamn President. But let's not have any doubt who your biggest backer's been all along. Who your *partner's* been. We're in this thing together. We always have been and we always will be. I don't want that changing 'cause you're putting on the emperor's new clothes here."

"Now *you* listen to *me*, Forrest Holder. I'm a United States congressman. I don't care how much you've done for me, I will not be threatened. Not by you. Not by *any*one! Are you threatening me?"

Holder sat back and shook his head slowly. "Boy," he said more to himself than to Mills, "you really don't understand yet. I wonder how long it's gonna take before you understand."

"I think maybe it's time for me to be going," Mills said.

"Political reality," the Judge said, "political reality. I give the boy every opportunity . . . I don't know." He sighed. "All right," he said, getting up, "come on, I've got something to show you."

Mills got up too. "I don't think I want to see it," he said.

"Yeah, you do. Stick around for a few more minutes, Jess. If you don't, I guarantee you're going to regret it."

Mills hesitated, then said, "What is it?"

"Come on into the library," the Judge said.

Holder led him into the library and closed the door behind them. "Set," he said, and Mills cautiously lowered himself into one of the pliant leather armchairs.

"Drink?" Holder asked.

Mills shook his head. The Judge shrugged. He went over to the TV monitor and turned it on. Then he extracted a tape from its case, slotted it into the VCR, and punched the appropriate buttons. There was a whirring, and some black-and-white snow appeared on the TV screen.

"What the hell is this?" Mills asked.

"Enjoy the show," Holder said. He parked himself behind his desk. His cigar had gone out. He relit it. The only sounds in the room were the sucking noises he was making and the garbled hiss from the monitor.

Then some lines flickered across the screen, and the snow was replaced by the head of a young man. Mills drew in his breath sharply.

"What *is* this, Forrest?" he said. It was the voice of a man who intends to convey menace but can't quite control the undercurrent of anxiety.

The Judge said nothing.

"Hi," the young man on the TV screen said, "my name is Daniel. I live in Washington, D.C. You may not know me back there in Virginia, but I know your congressman *very* well, if you know what I mean."

"Turn that damn thing off," Mills said.

"Oh, it gets better," Holder said.

"I met Jesse Mills two years ago," the young man said, "and I knew right away that there was something between us."

"I said *turn it off*, for Christ's sake!" Mills yelled.

Holder shrugged, got up, and went over to the TV.

"—the first night we met," the young man was saying. "It was in a bar—"

The VCR clicked to a stop as Holder pressed the "pause" button. The young man's face was frozen momentarily in an expression of wonderment. The Judge looked at the screen, slowly shaking his head, then shut off both the VCR and the monitor. He returned to his desk.

"You bastard," Mills said.

"Nature of the game," Holder said nonchalantly.

"I'm a married man," Mills said defiantly, but his voice lacked the force of true conviction. "Everyone knows that. They're not going to believe this."

"Jess, hey. Me, I couldn't care less. I know you're a happily married man. But homosexual, bisexual, it ain't a difference in people's minds. Not around here. Maybe other places in the country you can get away with it these days, but the people of *this* state know what they want and what they don't want. And what they don't want is worrying whether their senator's got AIDS or something."

Mills slumped in his chair. The soft leather enclosed him. He looked smaller.

"How'd you find out?" he said wearily.

"Boy, it's years I been trying to teach you the facts of life. You think I wouldn't have a man on your staff? You think you can fart without I know whether it was in the key of *G*?"

Mills was silent for a long moment. Then he said, "What do you want?"

The Judge spread his hands in a gesture of benevolence. "I want to contribute to your campaign. I want you to still think of me as your friend."

"Never."

Holder stubbed out his cigar. "Jesse," he said, drawing out the word, "there's nothing changing between us. Well, maybe we won't be drinking buddies like we used to. But you're gonna be senator and—who knows—maybe more. I'm still your biggest booster and I always will be. All I'm doing is protecting my interests, you can see that. Like I said, I just don't want you to go forgetting your roots."

"My roots. You mean the ones that are stuck down here in the muck of the Bay."

"No need to be bitter about it. That muck is the most fertile place on the face of the earth, you know."

"Cut the crap, Forrest. What you're trying to do is control my life, like you always have. I wish to Christ I'd never met you."

"I'm sorry you feel that way, Jess. I see it as a partnership, and a hell of a one at that."

Mills massaged his temples. "Let me have that drink," he said.

"Scotch?" Holder asked. Mills nodded, and the Judge poured two glasses of the special Glen Calder.

After Mills had drunk half of his he said, "All right, let's get to it. What exactly do you want?"

"I told you."

"Don't screw around with me. You want to cut a deal or what?"

"No deal," Holder said. "I intend to contribute to your campaign fund. I'll do everything in my power, which is considerable, to get you elected. You're going to be elected. Sometime later on, maybe I'll need your help. Little favors, you know, like you've done me in the past. And you'll get your fair share, of course."

"I told you six months ago I didn't want to help you with your goddamn *business* anymore!"

"Please, I don't do anything that isn't in the best interest of the country, you know that."

"Yeah, while you get rich off it."

"Don't you get sarcastic with me," the Judge said with barely suppressed anger. "If you bastards up there were doing your job, our allies wouldn't *have* to come to me for what they need to defend themselves. You'all could do with a few more balls and a lot less of whatever you're using instead."

"Blame the Congress," Mills muttered.

"Look, Jesse, I don't really know *who's* to blame, the President, the Congress, or the entire American people. But *some*body has to set things right. Otherwise we might as well give our enemies the keys to the city. I know you agree with me."

"I don't care! It's too . . . it's too risky, that's all."

"Easy," Holder said soothingly, "easy. We're not talking about a major change in the scale of things. I'm not a greedy man, Jesse. I've got most of what I need as it is."

"Yeah, everything but a stooge in the Senate."

"I won't jeopardize your career, Jess. I promise you that."

"Sure."

"Of course, there's always the chance you'll be tempted, once you're in there, to . . . Well, I do have another tape. It's not as, ah, genteel as this one, but if you'd like to see—"

"For Chrissake," Mills said, "I get the point!"

"Good. I *know* you're going to learn how this thing works, my old friend. There are some great years ahead for us. Trust me."

Mills sighed. "Jesus," he said, "that's about the last thing in the world I'm ever going to do." He finished the rest of his Scotch in one large swallow.

Holder beamed. "That's my boy," he said. He pressed a button on his phone console.

"Is that it now?" Mills asked.

"I think so. I'll send a man to meet with your campaign manager. They can decide how much money you need. When they figure it out, I'll see that you get it."

"You're all heart, Forrest."

There was a knock at the door. In response to Holder's invitation, the man in formal attire entered the room.

"Stayne," the Judge said, "see Congressman Mills safely to his car, will you?"

Stayne bowed slightly and looked at the congressman. Mills sighed and pulled himself from the clutches of the chair. He left without another word.

When his guest had gone, Holder went over to the liquor

cabinet. He poured himself another glass of Glen Calder and took it to his desk. He leaned back in his tilting executive's chair, his feet propped on the desktop. For the next fifteen minutes he drank slowly, staring with unfocused eyes at something in the middle distance.

CHAPTER 5

"Been a right smart year for crabs, ain't it?" the man in the corduroy cap said.

He was at least seventy. His face was deeply seamed, his hands gnarled. He had thick white eyebrows.

"Don't know," Craik said. "Just got here."

"City boy, ain't you?"

"Sometimes."

"Well, it *has* been a right smart year. Them boys been filling their baskets regular, I believe."

The man in the corduroy cap had picked Craik up next, after the man from the Marine Resources Commission. Craik had been waiting for twenty minutes. Traffic had been light. There were a few tourists, but they didn't pick up hitchhikers. Then the old man had pulled the rackety Plymouth over. He was going to Brawlton.

" 'Course, you never know with the crabs," the old man said. "You on vacation, are you?"

"Sorta," Craik said.

"We don't get near so many as other places on the Bay. But we get us a few. Folks come down here to unwind. They got some dead-end job to the city, they got to have a place to unwind. Now, me, I just go out on the water. Used to been, I went to *work* to unwind!" He laughed. "Don't do it as much now. These things ain't as good as they once was." He held out a hand like a claw. "But I'll tell you, ain't nothing in the world as peaceful as getting out on the water by yourself, and that's the truth. I like to seen the sun come up. I'll bet I seen the sun come up more times in a month than most do their whole lives. It lets you know where you are on God's earth."

The Plymouth was traveling at under forty-five. They passed a church on the right. The sign out front was illuminated by floodlights. METHODISM FOR TWO CENTURIES, it read, PROCLAIMING GRACE AND FREEDOM. The church was the landmark Marla Vickers had spoken of earlier.

"Stop," Craik said.

"Huh?" the old man said.

"Stop the car. I believe I'll walk from here."

"Suit yourself."

The Plymouth pulled onto the shoulder. Craik got out and thanked the man in the corduroy cap. He pointed to the small county road across from where they were stopped.

"That's the way to Brendan Shields's, ain't it?" he said.

"Yuh, sure."

"Okay, thanks again."

The man looked at Craik, standing there with the illuminated Methodist church in the background. "Go with God," he said, and he ground the Plymouth's worn gears and was gone.

Craik crossed the main road to the small county road that headed north, toward the Pawchunk. He walked down it.

The house was a neat, single-level brick rancher. It was on a cul-de-sac in a residential area south of Brawlton, with close access to the Bay. Each resident of the cul-de-sac had a full acre of land. Most of the houses had window air conditioners. They pulsed in the warm, sticky night.

Inside the rancher, three people were seated at a rectangu-

lar table covered with a green tablecloth. It stood in the center
of the room, under a four-armed brass light fixture. Beneath
the table was plush gold wall-to-wall carpeting. The only
other furniture in the room was a tall glass-fronted cabinet
displaying a collection of crystal, porcelain, and pewter. The
remains of a roast chicken dinner lay on white china plates
with blue rims.

One of the people, a dark, stocky, middle-aged man, was
saying, "Susanna, we've got to talk about this."

He had curly hair that was graying at the temples and
thick, heavy eyebrows. His hands, large and uncallused,
were folded on the table in front of him. Next to them was a
half-empty pilsner glass of beer.

"Daddy, we *have* talked about it," Susanna said.

"We have, Stuart," the third member of the group put in.

She was a petite, slender woman of forty, with straight
chestnut brown hair that as yet showed no signs of the aging
process. She opened her mouth only very slightly when she
spoke, and kept her clean, finely proportioned teeth close
together.

She continued, "I don't think there's much point—"

"Felicity," Stuart Holder said, "we *got* to talk about this.
Would you kindly?"

"Would I what?"

"Mama," Susanna said, "Daddy. Let's don't fight about it,
okay?" She looked rapidly from one to the other.

"Susanna," Stuart said evenly, "you are living in my
house, you are eating my food, and until such time as that
changes, I am entitled to know just what it is you intend
doing with your life."

"I don't know, Daddy."

"Fall semester is only a few weeks off, young lady."

"She knows that, Stuart," Felicity said. "We're all aware
of that."

"The university would like to know if you plan to favor
them with your presence again," Stuart said.

"I don't know, Daddy."

"Well, perhaps you could tell us what you *do* know."

Susanna visibly clenched her jaw. She stared back at her father.

"It's all right, dear," Felicity said.

"It is *not* all right!"

"Damn it, she's *my* daughter too! I won't have her treated like some piece of trash that came in with the tide."

"Woman's telling me what she'll have in my own house," Stuart muttered.

"Will you two *stop* it!?" Susanna yelled. "You know, if there's one thing I can't stand, it's people talking about me like I wasn't there. I don't have to put up with that."

She pushed her chair back.

Felicity reached out a hand. "Susanna, wait," she said.

"Yeah, hang on—" Stuart said, but Felicity silenced him with a gesture.

"Perhaps," she went on, "if you'd just share your feelings with us. We're your parents and we're concerned. I think you can understand that. There's no need for anyone to go getting upset." She glared quickly at her husband. "Your father wants the best for you. As I do. Please don't leave."

Susanna hesitated. Then she sighed and slumped in her chair.

"I don't know what I want," she said softly. "I know that I don't want this."

"Don't want what, dear?" Felicity asked.

Susanna gestured in a circle. "All of this. I don't want to live like this."

"What's wrong with this?" Stuart said.

"There's nothing *wrong* with it," Susanna said. "But it's not what I want. It's not . . . I don't know, not enough of something."

"If you go to the university," Felicity said, "you can become anything you want to be."

"The university's boring."

"You're an expert on the university now," Stuart said. "You've tried every field, you've taken every course they've got, you're qualified to say it's all boring."

"Of course I haven't tried everything, Daddy. It's their approach. No matter what you're in, it's the same. Everyone's competing against everyone else. You all study like hell and then you take tests, and some people get good grades and some get bad grades and it's the most unexciting way I can think of to spend my time. I felt like I was suffocating there. Life is an adventure, or it's nothing. Helen Keller said that."

"You want adventure," Stuart said, "become a fisherman. Become a fisher*woman*. That's an adventurous life. Go see Brendan. He'd probably take you on."

"I might just do that."

Stuart shook his head disgustedly and drained his beer.

"Susanna," Felicity said, "you have to think about how you're going to support yourself while you're adventuring. You can always count on us, of course—"

"Don't speak for me, Felicity."

"Well, you can always count on me, dear. But eventually you're going to be on your own. I don't think you'll be happy working at Sandi's Café."

"Of course not, Mama. But I have saved some money this summer. I think I might like to travel."

"Travel, Jesus," Stuart said. "That stuff went out twenty years ago. What do you think, there's still a bunch of flower people out there riding around in Volkswagen vans?"

"I don't think we have the same idea of travel, Daddy."

"Travel, whatever. You take my advice, you get your degree, *then* you can travel all you want. You got that degree, you got something to fall back on. Come the day you want to settle down, you'll be able to get yourself a decent job. That's what's important in this life. God damn it, you're gonna learn that the hard way!"

"Susanna," Felicity said, "think of the comforts you've grown up with, that you've gotten used to."

"Without a decent job," Stuart said, "you can blow all that to hell."

"A decent job like yours?" Susanna said.

"Yeah, like mine."

"And where did that come from?"

Stuart squinted. "Just what do you mean by that, young lady?" he said.

"What I mean is that you didn't come by that job because you had some college degree. You come by that job because of Uncle Forrest."

"I work for my brother. That ain't nothing to be ashamed of!"

"I didn't say it was—"

"And I don't think I like the tone of your voice!"

"Forget it, Daddy. I was just trying to make the point that it isn't always your education—"

"There's nothing wrong with my goddamn edu*cation*!"

Susanna got up.

"Wait, dear," Felicity said.

"Holier than thou, Susanna Holder!"

"Mama, we're not getting anywhere. I'm gonna go out for a while."

"Sure," Stuart said, "go on out and bang your boyfriend, whoever he might be, for all you tell us—"

"Stuart," Felicity said through her teeth, "stop it!"

"Daddy, I'm sorry. I can't be whatever it is you want me to be. Good night, Mama."

She turned and walked quickly out of the house. She pulled the front door carefully behind her.

Stuart yelled after her, "You better get serious about your life, Lady Di the goddamn queen! You—"

Susanna ran to her car, an old red Toyota. She threw herself into the front seat and pounded on the steering wheel. "No," she said. "No no no no *no*!" Then she started the car and jammed it into gear. She backed out into the road. The cul-de-sac was quiet. She accelerated past the quiet houses.

The insects of the night began to splatter against her windshield.

Janine paused at the head of the path and looked at the house. It was small, gray-shingled, with a single crumbling chimney poking from the center of its roof. It sat no more than thirty feet from the dirt road. The porch needed shoring up, and the trim needed paint. At either end of the porch was a trellis, thick with untended roses. A rectangular garden plot lay along the right side of the house. It was growing an excellent crop of weeds. There were no trees in the yard, only grass and weeds and the fine sandy soil.

The girl shook her head slowly, then walked up the path. It cut through the knee-high weeds. Someone had laid a few stones in it so that the way remained fairly clear. There was the screech of insects and the creak of the front steps beneath Janine's weight. She went into the house.

Inside there was a short hall, with a kitchen visible at its end. Janine poked her head through the doorless frame on her left. It led to a small living room. The room's furnishings consisted of a matching blue velour couch and easy chair, both badly frayed, an unfinished end table, and a wheeled metal cart with an old black-and-white television set atop it.

A man was seated in the chair. A glass and a bottle stood on the end table next to him. Each was half full of a clear liquid. The bottle had no label. The man was staring at the television set, although it was not on.

"Hi, Dad," Janine said.

The man turned and looked up at her. He was about fifty. His face was seamed and pitted. His pale blue eyes were sunk deep in his head. Their whites were crisscrossed with a delicate network of red. His hair was a little brown but mostly gray, and he sported about a two-weeks growth of stubbly gray beard. He had the fine, narrow nose his daughter would have had if hers had never been broken. His was showing the blood vessels at its surface.

"Oh, hello, girl," Will Devereaux said. "I didn't hear you come in."

"I just got off."

"Uh-huh." He picked up the glass and, after taking a drink, gestured with it. "I been watching TV. But I . . . sorta lost interest."

" 'Scuse me, Dad, okay?"

He nodded, and Janine went across the hall to her room. It was a tidy room. There was a narrow wood-frame bed and a three-drawer dresser with a mirror. Next to the bed was a low bookcase filled with paperback books. There was a clock-radio on top of it.

There was no carpet on the board floor. Above the bed was a poster of Huey Lewis and the News. On the wall beside the dresser was a long calendar with a photograph of a young girl in white holding out a piece of lemon meringue pie. Under the photo it read "Sandi's Café—Home-Cooked Food" and gave the address, phone number, and hours of business. On one of the other walls was a big poster depicting an Arctic scene of ice and mountains. "The Sound of Silence," the poster read.

Janine shed her work clothes and hung them in a small walk-in closet. She unpinned her hair and stood in front of the mirror. She examined her face, her small breasts, her narrow waist, turned briefly to the side, faced front again. She pushed her hair back behind her ears. Resting one hand on the dresser, she leaned closer, until her face was next to the mirror. With the other hand she reached up and took hold of her nose. She manipulated it this way and that, pulling and flattening it, pinching the nostrils and flaring them, finally letting it go. She stared into her eyes and sighed, nodding her head slightly.

"Shit," she said.

She opened one of the dresser drawers, took out jeans and a blue T-shirt, and put them on. The logo on the T-shirt read, "Save the Bay." She smoothed the shirt down over her, tucking it into her jeans, and went to the kitchen.

The refrigerator was only a little taller than she was. She got out a cold bottle of Dr Pepper. She twisted off the cap and threw it into a plastic waste can. It clinked off another bottle. She took a long swallow and returned to the living room.

She sat on the couch, across from her father. The level of liquid in the glass next to him was higher than it had been; that of the bottle lower.

"How you doing, sweetheart?" he said.

She shrugged. "Okay, I guess. It was hot in the restaurant today. I thought it wasn't ever gonna end."

"Well, you're kinda lucky to have a job at all. There's a lot don't."

"Umm-hmmm. I just wish it'd be somewhere I didn't have to deal with scum like Brent Fyke."

"He been bothering you again?"

She nodded. "He thinks 'cause he's big and he's wearing that stupid uniform that all the girls are just dying to go out with him. Which they may be, for all I know. But I'm not."

"You got to ignore him, honey. Him and his boss can make big trouble for all of us. Best thing to do is just stay out of his way."

"That's a little hard."

"Still, you best try. You know how it goes around here. Fyke is Kemp's boy, and Brace is tighter to the Judge than a sook underside her jimmie. Folks like us don't got a chance dealing with that sort."

Janine nodded. "I know, Dad. That's why I want to leave."

Will took an inch off the contents of the glass.

"I wish I could help you." He sighed. "I wish I could."

"Couldn't you work, Dad, just for a little while?"

"And what'd I do? There's no work for a waterman without a boat. You think I could go down to the company and crate up crabs at my age? You think the Judge would hire me? It's fortunate I get the jobs he finds for me as it is."

"You *could've* still had the boat. You might—"

"Shut up!" Will said harshly. "Don't talk about no 'could've been' around here."

"I just meant—"

"Let it be, girl. I done what I thought was right."

Janine leaned her head back and blew a breath stream toward the ceiling.

"I know you did," she said. "I'm sorry, Dad. I don't mean to be critical. But at least you got to work the water once. Look at me. I ain't built to do that. So what else is there? If I don't go to school, I got nothing."

"That ain't so. You're pretty. You find the right man, you can have yourself a nice home, a family . . ."

"I'm not pretty, either, not with this stupid nose. Besides, I'm only nineteen years old. I'm not ready to get *married*. Didn't *you* want to do anything when you was my age?"

"Sure," Will said. "I wanted to sign on the first freighter that'd have me and ship out for Bali." He chuckled. "I heard the women there went around without any clothes on and you could pick your dinner up off the beach . . ." He paused, drank from the glass. "Sure, you got to have your dreams. But dreams you keep inside of your head. That's where they belong. If I hadn't've gone to work on the Bay, I wouldn't've been able to get your mother to marry me, and then where would you be?"

"That's just it, though. College isn't a dream for me. It's right there. I'm smart enough—"

"I know you are."

"—I can do the work, we got plenty of good schools in this state I could get into. It shouldn't have to come down to whether we got such and such amount of money or some other."

"But it does, honey, it always does."

"Damn it, you take Susanna. She's got it all laid out for her and she don't even *want* it."

"She's a Holder."

"So what? Dad, she's my best friend. I know her real well and I love her like my sister. But it ain't right that she's got a choice and I got . . . what? Sandi's?"

"I'm sorry, Janine. I can't help you. Maybe if you find the right fellow, he'd be able to . . ." He shrugged.

"It's all right," she said softly. "I know you'd help if you could. If Mom was still alive . . . Ah, hell. Couldn't we get a loan or something?"

"And who's gonna pay it back?"

"Me."

Will laughed.

"I don't think that's a joke," she said.

"They don't give loans to girls your age," he said. "You tell 'em your father's a retired waterman and they'll show you to the door, quick as you please. That's what the banks do. They give the money to people like the Holders, who already have money. They don't give it to the Devereauxs. As far as they're concerned, they look at us and we might as well be the air."

"Dad, I'm gonna find a way to do this," she said seriously. "If it kills me, I'm gonna find a way."

"Hey," he said, raising his glass, "more power to you. You get a education and a fancy job, maybe you can afford to send me to Bali, huh?"

"And go a little easy on the corn, will you?"

Will looked at the glass he was holding in front of him.

"Oh," he said. "Sure. Sure I will."

Janine got up and went to her room. She lay on the bed. A tear slid down her cheek and into her hair. She clenched a fist and pushed it hard into her diaphragm.

"No," she whispered. "No way."

CHAPTER 6

The tar road turned to gravel and branched in two directions. Craik stayed to the left, making his way by the soft glow of the waning moon. He followed the gravel road all the way to the end.

The house wasn't visible from the road. Craik walked down the curving dirt drive. A quarter of a mile in, the woods opened out into a clearing. In the near distance was a deep, narrow creek, actually an arm of the Pawchunk two hundred yards to the east. The pallid moonlight outlined a shack down at the creek's edge, with a pier running out into the water. Tied up at the pier was a fishing boat of thirty-five feet or so. There was a bow line, and one at the stern.

At the front of the clearing was the house itself. It was very small. The exterior was weathered, unpainted board and batten. Cinder blocks held the house up off the ground. There was a brick chimney at one end.

Craik knocked at the door. There was no reply.

"Mr. Shields?" he called.

"Yeah," came from the inside of the house. Then there was silence.

"Mr. Shields?" Craik said again.

"You know my name," came the voice from inside, this time more loudly. "So?"

"Mr. Shields, I'd like to talk to you," Craik said.

"Then come in, for Chrissake!"

Craik opened the door and stepped into the room that was a combination kitchen, living, and eating area. It was brightly lit. Shields sat at a scarred circular table. There was a net spread out in front of him. He was repairing a hole in it. He tied little knots, over and over again. It was a very slow process. It might have been made slower by the small stump that served Shields for a left index finger, but it might not have.

Shields pulled a particularly tricky knot tight with his teeth and looked up at his visitor, marking his spot with a broad middle finger that was cracked and yellowed.

"Who the hell are you?" he said.

"Scott Craik," Craik said.

Shields shrugged. "So what?"

"Marla Vickers suggested I look you up."

"I know her." Shields nodded. "What's she to you?"

"My landlady."

Shields nodded again and looked Craik up and down. Craik returned the favor.

Shields was a large man in his mid-forties. He had the look of someone once stocky and muscular, now inexorably aging. His chest was broad, his stomach prominent, his arms and legs meaty. He was going to fat, but it was a hard fat, especially around the belly.

He was wearing paint-splotched khaki pants held up by suspenders. A gray T-shirt with several tears in it covered his upper body except for a strip of pale flesh at the waist that it didn't reach. The flesh was covered with a mat of curly, reddish-gold hairs.

Shields's feet were bare. They were large and needed washing. His hands, too, were large, the approximate size and shape of pointed-end shovel blades. They were stained and deeply seamed. The nails on his wide fingers had dirt under them. One of them was completely black, as if it had been hit with a hammer.

His face was wider than it was high. The eyes were green, the nose red and somewhat bulbous, the hair a wild tangle of sandy curls which, if pulled straight out, would have reached nearly to his shoulders. Bits of gray were just barely discernible against the light background. He sported a three-

or four-day growth of beard. Some of the stubble might also
have been gray. There was a deep furrow down the center of
either cheek, and a network of fine lines radiated from the
corner of each eye.

Shields removed his hand from the spot on the net, reached
for a shirt pocket that wasn't there, swore when he didn't
find it. He twisted on his stool and grabbed a pack of
unfiltered Camels off the countertop behind him. He fired up
a cigarette, offered the pack to Craik. Craik shook his head.

"Sons of bitches," Shields said. Smoke drifted out of his
mouth as he gestured at the table. "Never known it to fail—
twice, three times a year they run their useless frigging yachts
through my nets. And I ain't never had not a one of 'em come
by and say they done it and could they pay for the damages.
Had one of 'em call me up once, though. Told me my net had
fouled his propeller and he burned out a bearing or some
damned thing. Wanted to know what I intended to do about
it. I told him exactly. I said just bring the thing over here and I
would personally shove it where it wouldn't ever get fouled
again. Well, he never did show up, a-course. What brings
you out here, Craik?"

"I'm looking for work."

Shields laughed. His teeth were tobacco-darkened and
chipped here and there.

"Work? Jesus," he said. "Even so, I supposed you got a
right to sit down."

Craik took a ladder-back cane chair and turned it around.
He sat on it, resting his forearms on the back.

"Marla said you lost your partner," Craik said. "I thought
maybe you could use a replacement. If the work's there."

"Work's always there," Shields said. "It's the crabs you
can't never be sure about. But I'm not sure my partner's lost.
He's a funny feller, Henry is."

"Six weeks is a long time."

"I suppose. Especially since we been on to a mess of crabs
this year. Henry did favor the ladies. Wouldn't surprise me if

he chased one clear out of the county, just following along. He wasn't the type to stop in and say good-bye."

Shields cocked his head. From outside came the sound of a distant motor. Shields smoked and listened.

"Bud Blanchard's boat," he said. "She's a lunger. You know, like she got the TB. The bastard'll probably put him in his grave someday, but right now she's keeping him out. You ever worked the water before?"

"I did a little fishing."

"Whereabouts?"

"Up north."

"You know crabs?"

Craik shook his head.

"What kind you done?"

"Surf fishing. Trolling for blues. I've dug clams."

"Trolling for blues," Shields said. "Jesus. I don't know, Craik. The Bay is different."

"I can learn."

"Maybe so. But I get out on the water, I need someone I can depend on. I don't know can you find your way to Jimmie and Sook's, much less what'll happen the first time you piss your boots in a heavy sea. So like I said before, who the hell are you?"

"I'm looking for work," Craik said. "I'm pretty strong. I got good sea legs. I don't mind the hours, whatever they are. If I don't know it, I pick it up fast." He shrugged. "Is that enough?"

Shields lit another cigarette. He looked at the muscles that showed through Craik's T-shirt.

"Depends," he said. "You on the run from something?"

"No."

"Well, what *are* you doing here, then?"

"I don't like the city anymore. I don't like the noise and I don't like the lies."

"What city in particular?"

"This and that. They're all mostly the same."

"Jesus, Craik, you sure don't take the long way round, do you?"

"If something's worth talking about. Otherwise I'd rather not bother."

"There's some," Shields said, "they don't trust a man who won't talk. But I don't care. Everyone's got a right to live their own life, and we all done stuff that we'd prefer to just let it rest. There's some couldn't stand to be on the water with a man shut tight all the time. Drive 'em crazy. And some don't say a word their own selves, so they could care less. Me, I don't give a damn one way or the other. People say I talk too much, anyways. I don't guess it matters if I'm mouthing off at you or the frigging wall. Comes to the same in the end.

"Thing is, though, I like the measure of a man before I go on the water with him."

"You want three references?"

Shields laughed. "Yeah. No relatives. No family doctor. Them as know your work."

"I'll see what I can do," Craik said. "In the meantime, I need a job."

"There is that part of it."

"I'd be obliged if you'd let me help you out. I don't believe you'd be disappointed."

Shields scratched at the stubble on his face. He caught Craik's eye, as if he were looking up at him, and held it. Craik didn't flinch.

Shields wet his lower lip. "Tell you what," he said. "I was about to knock off, anyway. I feel the need to cut the dust a little. Suppose you come along with me and we'll talk on it some more."

"Okay."

Shields carefully arranged the net on the tabletop. He pulled a pair of worn black-and-white sneakers over his bare feet. The laces were knotted in a couple of spots where they'd broken. His big toe protruded slightly from a hole in the front of each shoe. He took a brown cloth cap from the counter and set it lightly on his head.

"Ready?" he asked.

Craik got to his feet and pushed his chair back up to the table. He put on his own yellow "Cat" cap.

"Sure," he said. "Where we going?"

"Sook's. You been there yet?"

"Nope."

"Let's go, then. You'll be okay you're with me. But don't let on anything about fishing you don't really know. Them boys'll fetch up your ass for tomorrow's bait if you do."

Craik laughed. "Thanks," he said. "I'll keep it in mind."

The two men left the house and got into Shields's car. It was an old Dodge Dart station wagon, pitted with rust. At one time it had been all forest green, but the paint had faded haphazardly until in places it was now the color of a lima bean.

The engine, however, started immediately. It belched out one puff of blue smoke, then settled into a smooth idle.

"Best car Detroit ever made," Shields said, nodding to himself. "American iron."

"Uh-huh," Craik said.

"If they'd've stuck to it, you wouldn't see so many of them out of work up there. You damn sure wouldn't."

The drive to Jimmie and Sook's took less than ten minutes. Shields drove slowly and looked around frequently. The two men didn't talk.

When they arrived at the roadhouse, the parking area was already close to full. Most of the cars were American, and most of them were at least three years old. There was a number of aging pickups and one shiny new one, complete with roll bar and oversize tires. It carried a bumper sticker that read: "My wife, yes. My dog, maybe. My gun, NEVER."

Shields and Craik went inside. The front room was large and featured a long bar with stools and a scattering of tables and chairs. People were standing or sitting, talking, drinking draft beer from quart mason jars. The noise level was high, the air heavy with tobacco smoke.

There was a second area at the rear where a coin-operated pool table was set up. Two men were shooting eight ball, while others stood around and kibitzed or silently studied the game. A row of quarters lay on the table's rail, marking spots for those waiting their turn. On one wall was a sign that read: GAMBLING IS ILLEGAL. Under it was scrawled in pencil, "So's everything that helps ease the pain."

One of the players tapped the pocket directly in front of him with the tip of his cue stick. He stretched halfway down the table, steadied his stick, and stroked the cue ball hard. It clacked crisply into the solid-yellow one ball and propelled it into the side rail. From there the one ricocheted off the far end rail, then off the other side rail. Just before its momentum died, it dropped smoothly into the corner pocket called by the player before the shot. His opponent nodded in silent admiration.

"What're you drinking?" Shields asked.

"I'll have a beer," Craik said.

Shields went to the bar and ordered two pints of beer and a shot of whiskey.

A weathered man of about sixty said to him, "Brendan, I heard you pulled a thousand bucks' worth of the blue bastards last week."

"That'll be the day, Samuel," Shields said. "That'll be the day we all retire to the Grand Bahama. How about you? The *Sophie Jane* still out of the water?"

"Damn if it isn't! That worthless, piece-of-junk motor ain't give me a good day since I had her. I swear I'm about to have the son of a bitch melted down. Just melt her on down!"

"For what?"

"I don't *know* for what! She ain't good for one thing, she ain't likely be good for another. I tell you what, I might melt her down, tie her to my leg, and drop her overboard. Let her drag me under, seeing that's what she's doing, anyway."

"Samuel," Shields said, "you're gonna outlast us all and that's a fact, I don't care about your damn motor or what." He grinned. "Besides, there ain't no point your going under the water till there's a few less ladies to be crying the blues when you're gone."

Shields took the drinks and went over to a table by the back wall where Craik had sat down.

At the end of the bar a middle-aged man with dusty black skin and sunken eyes was saying, "Damn me if it ain't true. The prices them Holders pay don't have nothing to do with what they're getting at the other end. You check it out. They got us beholden, and they're about squeezing every cent they can. You can't tell me it ain't so."

His neighbor at the bar said to him, "So quit, Virg."

"I wish I could, Miz Vickers," he said. "I truly do."

"There're easier ways to make a living," Marla Vickers said.

"I can't quit, you know that. It's just I hate to see Judge Holder get richer while we all get poorer."

"That's the way it's always been. Always will be. Unless you fellas figure out something to set up for yourselves."

"Sure, like my daddy."

"Your old man was a good one, Virg," Marla said. "He was just a bit ahead of his time. In them days selling fish on your own was dangerous. What come of him, you won't find that sort of thing to happen anymore."

"Aw, hell. I ain't no businessman."

"Most people ain't. That's how the Holders got to be where they're at. And they're gonna hold on until somebody comes along who's better." She paused for a drink, then looked around the room. She smiled. "Well, have a look there," she said to herself. " 'Scuse me, Virg."

"Yes, ma'am."

Marla Vickers picked up her glass and walked over to the table by the back wall.

"I see you two've met," she said.

"Yeah," Shields said. "Sit down, old woman."

Vickers pulled a chair over and settled her bulk gently onto it. She went through her pipe ritual, filling it, tamping it, and firing it up. She exhaled a thick cloud of aromatic smoke.

"I understand you know this guy," Shields said.

"Sure," Vickers said. "My tenant. You don't reckon Beadle's coming back, do you?"

"Nah. So what do you think of our Mr. Craik here?"

"Good-looking feller, I'd say."

"Marla, Jesus Christ," Shields said. "I don't care you want to get in his pants. Though at your age you oughtta be ready to turn it down a little. I want to know what you think of him. Tell me like he wasn't here."

Craik had his arms folded across his chest. He was smiling.

"I only met the man today, Brendan," she said. "What's to know? He needed a place to stay and I rented him Henry's. I didn't ask was he related to the queen of England."

"He's got a close mouth on him," Shields said.

Vickers sighed. "I know. There's those I can only wish it. Let the man be, if that's what he wants."

"You think I oughtta take him out with me?"

"Lord, how would I know that? I'd never've said Henry Beadle was your kind of man, neither. But you made out okay. The kid's green, it don't take much to see that. Put him on the water is the only way I know to find who he is. If he can't cut it, it won't take long to discover, even for you."

"Thanks for the plug, ma'am," Craik said.

Vickers grinned. "You know," she said, "if I was just a little younger woman, you might die of too much . . . Ah, forget it." She raised her glass, then tipped it back and emptied it. "Constance!" she cried, swiveling her head. "Now where *is* that girl? Ain't never to hand when you need her, that's for damn sure."

A woman in jeans and a blue Jimmie and Sook's T-shirt

appeared at the table. She took Vickers's order for another pint of beer and Shields's for a pint and a shot. Craik's glass was still three-quarters full, and he shook his head slightly.

Connie carried her serving tray back to the bar. Vickers's place there had been taken by a grizzled old man in overalls. He was talking to the younger man next to him.

"Old Bob," he was saying. "We're gonna miss him, Virg. We sure are."

"He was a good one, L.B.," Virgil said.

The old man nodded his head. "No one like him," he said. "Best navigator on the Bay, and that's the truth. Always knew where he was at. I ever tell you about the time the boys tried to trick him?"

Virgil shook his head slowly. "I don't think so."

"Damnedest thing you ever heard," L.B. said. "But you had to knowed Old Bob. Back in them days we didn't know nothing about your fancy navigating techniques. Hell, I don't believe Old Bob even owned a compass. But he never got lost, not that I heard of.

"Now, most of us could get around pretty good. We could use landmarks, sight with our own two eyes and whatnot. But when the fog come in, well, we pretty much had to stay to home. Or either drop anchor, if we was on the water. Except Old Bob, of course."

A couple of other watermen had heard the story developing and had drifted over. One of them grinned and nodded knowingly.

"How'd he navigate in the fog?" Virgil asked.

"Just like everywhere else," the old man said. "He had this little bucket, and he just tossed it over the side and brung up whatever was on the bottom. He'd take a look at what come up. Stick his finger in there and taste the mud. Then he'd adjust his course, simple as that. It was a fine thing if you could get within shouting distance of Old Bob's boat, 'cause then you could just follow him on home."

L.B. drained off some of his beer.

"Now, I tell you," he went on, "it ain't that his crew didn't appreciate his talent. We all did. But them boys got to talking among theirselves one day, and they decided to see if they could trick Old Bob. So one of them snuck into his backyard one night and dug up a bagful of dirt. Then the boy went next door to Miss Effie's and dipped up a little stuff from her outhouse and mixed it in. Next foggy day, he took it all with him on the boat.

"They went out, of course. They was drudging for oysters, and Old Bob took advantage of them foggy days when nobody else would be on the water. Well, when it come time to get on home, Old Bob called for a bucket from the bottom. The boys was out of his sight at the time, so they just dipped up some seawater and mixed it with the stuff that had come off the land. Then they called Old Bob to come and tell 'em where they was.

"Old Bob come out on deck and took a look at what they had in the little bucket. He looked at it a good while. He stuck his finger in there and tasted the mud. Then what do you think he done?"

Virgil grinned. "Puked," he said.

"Not Old Bob," L.B. said. "Had a stomach of iron on top of everything. What he done was he turned to the boys and said, 'I guess we better drop anchor, men, 'cause we're about halfway between my house and Effie's shithole.' Then he went back in the cabin and laid down to sleep. He kept them boys out there all that night and most of the next day before he let them pull the anchor up. They never did try to trick him again after that."

Some of the men were laughing, but L.B. just stared down into his beer. "Old Bob," he said. "Gonna miss him around here."

"Old Bob," Virgil said, shaking his head.

The front screen door opened, and Susanna Holder came in. A couple of the men in the bar glanced at her, then turned back to their conversations. No one greeted her except one husky young man with long, straight blond hair and a single earring. He sidled up to her.

"Susanna," he said, "long time."

She continued looking around the room. "Could have been longer, David," she said, "and it wouldn't've hurt none."

The man touched her shoulder with his forefinger and went, "Sssss. Ouch."

"You got it," she said, and she walked to the rear of the room. "Mind if I join you?" she asked Marla Vickers's back.

Vickers turned and smiled up at her. "Hello, girl," she said.

"Hello, yourself," Susanna said, and gave her a quick hug. She got herself a chair. "Hi, Uncle Brendan," she said. "Mr. Craik."

"Lord, child," Shields said, "I told you not to call me uncle. I ain't your damn uncle, and your daddy's plenty happy about it. And if I was, hell, they could lock me up, some of the thoughts I have about you."

Susanna grinned and punched Shields lightly on the arm.

"You know this girl, Craik?" Shields asked.

"We met," Craik said.

The waitress returned with the drink tray. Susanna immediately grabbed the shot of whiskey and gulped it down. She sipped from one of the pints of beer. Connie set the other in front of Marla Vickers. Shields looked dejected.

"Well, knock me back, look at that," he said. "Girl's gonna come up kin, after all. Get me another round, will you, Connie? Better make it two rounds of each. I don't know *what* kind of thirst this child's got on her."

The waitress moved away from the table. Susanna took a long swallow of beer and said, "Aaaaah."

"Ain't seen you in here in a while, Susanna," Shields said.

"Only when I need it," Susanna said.

"Let me guess," Shields said. He looked up at the ceiling, then back at her. "Stuart and 'licity are on your back again."

"Yeah."

"What's the matter?" Craik asked.

Susanna shrugged. "My folks want me to go back to the university. I just don't think that's where it is. All the kids there are so . . . slick. Like they knew what they wanted to do when they were three years old. You ever go to college, Craik?"

"Uh-huh. Some."

"Watch out, Brendan," Vickers said. "That's a *educated* fool wants on your boat now."

"You drop out or what?" Susanna said.

"Or what," Craik said.

"I tell you, Craik," Shields said, "you got a college education on you, it sure don't show."

Craik shrugged. "There're more important things," he said.

"That's what I know," Susanna said over the top of her glass. She smiled. "I wouldn't mind finding out what they are, either."

Connie set Shields's order in front of him.

"You been to college," Vickers said, "you mind telling me what you want to be a waterman for?"

"I told you this afternoon, Marla. I don't like the city. I like it here. That's all there is."

"Have you traveled a lot?" Susanna asked.

"I don't know," Craik said. "What's a lot?"

"Have you been to Europe? Have you been to . . . South America? I'd like to go to South America. Peru. Someplace like that."

"I've traveled some," Craik said. "I've never been to South America."

"I believe I agree with you, Susanna," Shields said. "I never saw much sense in going to college. You get a college degree and then you got to go live in the city to get a good job. But once you've lived here, you don't want to live in the city, anyway. At least I never did. I guess that's something me and Craik here are gonna agree on. You'll see lots of men leave the water to try their luck in Richmond or someplace, and you'll see most of them back before the year is out.

"I tried that Richmond for a while, you remember. People in the city hardly know each other and don't care shit if they do. On the water, at least, we all know each other and we take care. Now, I ain't saying we don't fight, Craik. Marla'd be the first one to agree to that. When we fight, we do it up right. But get us on the water and we're all the same couple of inches from going to the bottom. Which we realize. We're looking out for the next boat and he's looking out for us."

"I don't know, Brendan," Vickers said. "I wouldn't want to live anywheres else, but what is there here for a girl like this? She gonna get married? You want to get married, dear?"

"Hell, no."

"So there you have it. You don't know what kind of choices we got, Shields. Little and none. It's hard enough of a life on a man, but women got nothing. You ain't never heard such a word as 'water*woman*,' did you?"

"You did it," Craik said.

Vickers snorted and drank some beer. She wiped the foam from her upper lip with her sleeve.

"Yeah, sure," she said. "But I got born with them damn waders on. They could skin me up for some glove leather. This little girl, I don't believe she's been cut for the water."

"It's not what I want, anyway," Susanna said.

"Going back to school might be the best thing for you," Vickers said. "Give you some idea what other choices you got in the world. Woman's got a few more than she used to."

"May be," Susanna said. "But I don't think school's where you find out. I think if you want to know about the world, you have to go out in it. Like Mr. Craik, here, done."

Craik laughed. "I'm not sure you have the right idea about me, Susanna," he said.

She studied him for a long moment over the top of her beer glass. She took a swallow.

"Yeah, I do," she said.

They were silent for a while, then Shields ordered another round of drinks.

"Here's *to* you, Susanna," he said. "You do what you feel like. Anything else ain't but treading water. What do you say, Craik?"

"I wouldn't be here if I didn't agree with you," Craik said.

"Where *would* you be if you weren't here?" Susanna asked.

"Probably home asleep."

"Come on," she said. "You know what I mean. Where would you be if you weren't here in Brawlton?"

Craik shrugged. "A lot of things might have been," he said. "I try not to worry about them. I found they just eat you up on the inside."

Behind them, in the vicinity of the pool table, someone had begun yelling.

"You son of a bitch! You moved the goddamn cue ball!"

"No, I didn't," a quieter voice said.

"Yes, you did! I turn my back, you move the goddamn cue ball! You can't beat me, so you *cheat*!"

"I don't need to cheat to beat you."

"You son of a *bitch*!"

There was the sound of scuffling, a punch thrown, and other voices saying, "Hey, hold on" and "C'mon, you two, cool down." Craik and Shields turned so they could see into the back room.

The angry man was in his early thirties, of medium height, and wiry. His face was sharply angular, like that of a carnivorous bird. He had black hair, liberally oiled, combed up in the front and then straight back. He had a drooping mustache. His T-shirt was cut off at the shoulders, revealing on the outside of his upper right arm a tattoo of a heart with a lightning bolt through the center of it. At the moment there were two men standing between him and the object of his anger, a slight, balding man in his mid-twenties who continued to proclaim his innocence. The two men running interference were saying calming words.

Shields shook his head. "Rodney Crowe," he said to Craik. "He's a bad one. They oughtn't let him in a place like this, but God knows what he'd do if they didn't."

"I've seen the type," Craik said.

"Okay," Crowe was saying in a low voice. "It's okay. Just stand back, will you? Give me a little room to breathe."

The two men looked at each other, shrugged, and stepped back. When they did, a knife materialized in Crowe's hand. He swept it in a wide arc, and the two men jumped back even farther.

"Lester," he said, staring at the slight, balding man, wiping a trace of blood from the corner of his mouth, spacing the words, "you don't *never* go and lay a hand on me. But it seems like you just don't understand that, don't it? I believe I'm gonna have to teach you why not. You about to get cut three different ways, boy. Up, down, and across the side."

Lester retreated, but there was nowhere for him to go. He glanced wildly around him. A couple of his friends started to move. They stopped when Crowe flashed the blade their way. Behind the bar, the bartender was dialing a phone.

"C'mon, Rodney," Lester said. "I didn't mean it. Here." He stuck his chin out and pointed to it. "Hit me back. Go ahead."

"Lester," Crowe said, "I ain't gonna *hit* you, I'm gonna *cut* you."

Shields looked at Craik. Craik sighed, then briefly inclined his head in the direction of the pool table. The two men got up and walked toward the altercation.

"Crowe," Shields called. "Put it away, Crowe. We don't need no knifing in here tonight."

Crowe moved so that he could see the two men advancing toward him while still watching Lester on the other side of him. He was balanced on the balls of his feet and swayed slightly from side to side. He held the knife loosely, his palm up, and flicked it once at the intruders.

"Stay out of this, Shields," Crowe said. "It ain't nothing to do with you."

Shields stopped. "We know how good you are with that thing, Rodney," he said. "You got nothing to prove here."

"I ain't *trying* to prove nothing. The man cheated on me and then he hit me. Everybody seen it. I got a right."

Shields shook his head.

"Put it away," Craik said.

Crowe shifted his eyes to Craik. "The fuck are you?" he said.

"Someone not to mess with, Rodney," Shields said.

Crowe shifted his attention back to Shields. He smiled. "Oh, yeah?" he said.

As he did, Craik moved, very fast. He stepped past Crowe's side, bringing his arm down in a blur of motion, clamping Crowe's knife hand in his grip. He twisted the wrist three-quarters of a turn, raised Crowe's arm, and took a step backward, as if beginning a formal dance.

"Let it go," he said.

Crowe sneered and threw a punch with his free hand. Craik did nothing but give the wrist a further turn. Crowe yelped. His punch froze in mid-swing and the knife dropped to the floor. One of the other men immediately rushed in and scooped it up. Crowe glared at Craik, his anger obviously tempered with pain.

"Time to leave," Craik said, turning the wrist a little more.

Crowe gasped. "All right, all right," he said, and the two of them moved off, Craik steering the other man by his immobilized arm. They stopped as they passed the bar, and Craik look questioningly at the bartender.

"Crowe," the bartender said, "you can get out of my place and not come back, or you can wait for the sheriff's boys to get here. Your choice."

"Fuck you," Crowe said, but he started for the door. Craik followed, still holding on to him. Behind them, the conversational noise level began to rise.

Outside, Craik released his prisoner. They faced each other across a distance of about three feet.

"Sorry," Craik said. "But I did you a favor."

Crowe spat at the ground. "Don't tell me what you done," he said in a low growl. "I don't know who you are, buddy, but you ain't seen the last of me, not by a *long* ways." He turned abruptly and strode off across the parking lot. He got into a black Camaro and jerked it out of the lot in a flurry of flying gravel.

Craik watched the taillights recede through a cloud of dust. He continued to watch until the car was long out of sight. Then he went back into Jimmie and Sook's. As he did, the spinning blue light of the sheriff's cruiser appeared in the distance.

The place fell silent as he walked back to the table. Everyone was staring at him.

"Hey! Show's over, folks!" Shields yelled.

Craik sat down, and slowly people returned to whatever they had been talking about. Susanna had followed his progress across the room, smiling to herself.

The front screen door banged open, and Deputies Fyke and Tilghman entered. Again there was quiet. The deputies looked around, then walked heavily to the bar. They had a brief dialogue with the bartender, at the end of which he gestured toward the table along the back wall. Fyke and Tilghman looked at the table, glanced at each other, and made their way to where the two men and two women were seated, Fyke leading, Tilghman a step behind him.

Fyke stood over the table, meeting the eyes of each of the people before settling on Craik.

"Craik," he said, "looks like you got yourself a little trouble in our town already."

"C'mon, Fyke," Vickers said. "All the man did was save Lester from getting hisself cut."

Fyke looked toward the pool table. "That right, Lester?" he called.

"Ah, I don't know," Lester said cockily, "I reckon I could've—" He stopped when his friends began to chuckle, and glared at them.

"Uh-huh," Fyke said. "So you're the big hero," he said to Craik.

Craik shrugged. "We asked him to put the knife down," he said. "He didn't seem inclined to do it."

"He didn't seem in*clined*," Tilghman said.

Fyke leaned down and rested his hands on the tabletop. He held Craik's eye.

"You realize," he said, "that around here you best leave law enforcement to the law. Otherwise there ain't no telling what might happen."

"Let him alone, Fyke," Shields said.

"I'll keep that in mind," Craik said. "Officer, sir."

Fyke pushed himself back upright. "Good," he said.

"The boy done fine," Shields said. "You ought to be thanking him."

"I'll thank *you* not tell me my job, Shields," Fyke said. "C'mon, Charles, there ain't much else we oughtta do here."

The deputies clomped out of the bar. Connie came over to the table with a tray loaded down with glasses of beer, shots of whiskey, packages of nuts and beef jerky, pickled eggs. She spread it all out in front of them.

"On the house," she said, and returned to her rounds. In a short time the place was raucous once again.

At the table the other three all looked at Craik.

"Wow," Susanna said. She was still smiling.

"All right, cut it out, will you?" he said. "The lot of you. It's over and done with now."

"Boy's right," Vickers said. "I'll drink to that," and she hoisted her glass.

Shields put his elbows on the table and rested his chin on his hands. He kept his eyes on Craik.

"Okay," he said finally. "I suppose I could use somebody out on the water with me. Might as well be you. You do got a style to you, son."

Craik grinned. "Good," he said.

"You'll need to get your crabbing license tomorrow, over to Dorset, so that's out. We got to be on the water early. Start Friday morning. Meet me at the dock down the end of Front Street. Five o'clock."

"Fine."

Shields downed half a glass of beer. He belched.

"I tell you one thing, though," he said. "I'd sure as hell like to know where you learned to move like *that*."

THURSDAY

THURSDAY

CHAPTER 7

Susanna stood on the porch of the clapboard house. There was a small paper bag in one of her hands. She stared at the door, finally raised her other hand and knocked.

A few seconds later Craik opened the door. He had on his jeans but no shirt or shoes. Susanna glanced at his bare torso, then looked self-consciously at his face.

"Hi," she said.

"Good morning."

"Didn't get you up, did I?" He shook his head. "I thought you might be hungry." She held out the paper bag. "I brought you some doughnuts."

Craik chuckled as he took the bag from her. "Thanks," he said. "You make them?"

"Yeah," she said. "Well, sort of, anyway. Me and Janine made them. They're out of a mix we get down at the café. Can I come in, Mr. Craik?"

"Scott. Sure, come on in and have a doughnut."

They went inside. Susanna peered around. The room was still gloomy. It hadn't yet caught the morning sun.

"Kind of a grungy place, isn't it?" Susanna said.

Craik shrugged. "It'll do for now. I'm gonna start fixing it up this weekend, beginning with some badly needed paint. You won't recognize the place. Coffee?"

"Nah. Already had plenty."

"Good, because there's none here. Henry Beadle didn't care for it, or he cared for it so much, he took it with him. That and a lot of other things. Today is shopping day. Sit down."

She sat at the scarred circular table and broke out the doughnuts. Craik fetched two glasses of water and joined her.

"Who do you think J. H. was?" Susanna asked, pointing at the initials carved into the tabletop.

"Don't know. Old as this house is, it might've been John Henry."

"That's a coal-mining song."

"Maybe he really retired to the Bay and ended up a waterman."

"Like you?"

Craik smiled. "I never dug coal," he said. "And I ain't retired and I'm sure not a waterman yet."

"Then who are you?"

"Susanna, you know, you got an awfully large nose on you."

She rubbed her nose. "Actually, I'm quite fond of it. And you haven't answered my question."

"Do you pull this crap on everyone?"

She grinned. "Uh-uh."

Craik scratched his head. "I wish I knew why I don't just toss you the hell out of here."

"Because you like my doughnuts. And you *still* haven't answered my question."

"Susanna, look, I'm just a drifter. My mama thinks I'm a bum. Always has, probably always will. Come to that, she may be right. I don't know how to do much of practical value, and I never gave a lot of thought to learning. The only reason I'm here is because I'm not someplace else. How's that?"

"It sucks."

Craik laughed. "You got me all figured out, eh?"

"Well, not completely. But I've lived here all my life. We get our share of drifters. Not many but some. They slide on in here and they slide on out again, if the sheriff don't get to them first. I've seen them. I never did see one like you before, though. Plus I was in Sook's last night, don't forget. You took out Rodney Crowe in about two seconds, and Rodney Crowe is *bad*. Wasn't a man in that room would've gone up against Rodney once he had his knife out."

"So I'm dumb," Craik said.

"You ain't dumb. You knew exactly what you were doing in there."

"I went after someone I shouldn't have gone after, and I got lucky, that's all."

"No way, Cap'n. Rodney Crowe ain't even in your *league*."

Craik sighed. "Okay," he said. "Crowe is a punk. The street I grew up on, we had a dozen guys tougher than he'll ever be. I learned how to fight. Had to. There's nothing particularly wonderful about that."

"And you've traveled."

"Some. It's what you do when you're young."

"*And* you been to college," she said with a broad grin.

"So? A lot of people have."

"Sure, including me if you can believe it, so I know a little bit about the subject. College is where you learn how to live somebody else's idea of your life. You ain't like the guys I knew there, either."

"Meaning what?"

"Meaning that Brawlton is a very boring place and you're an interesting man, and I got a lot worse things to do in the morning than bringing you doughnuts." She smiled. "Just don't let it go to your head."

He held up his hands. "I promise not to expect them," he said.

"Okay. But you enjoy them and maybe someday you'll let me in on just what you're doing here. I'll tell you one thing, though, good buddy. If you're a dope dealer, you best watch your step. This county is about dry as it could be. My uncle

hates drugs, and he keeps real tight control on what goes on.
Most of the time there ain't even any reefer around. If the
Judge gets suspicious, you're in for a hard ride."

"Thanks for the advice, but I'm afraid I have to admit that
I am definitely not a dope dealer."

"Well," she said, getting up, "it was either that or a spy. I
guess it's a spy."

He raised his right hand. "Susanna, on my honor, I am
neither a dope dealer nor a spy."

"Uh-huh. You're just some flake from up north, who
always wanted to be a fisherman."

"There you go," Craik said. "You got it."

Susanna shook her head. "You think I'm a twit?"

"Not at all."

"Then don't treat me like one. Look, I've gotta get back to
Sandi's or Janine'll be on my case for the rest of the day.
When'd you say you were gonna paint this hole?"

Craik laughed. "This weekend. Sunday, probably."

"I'll come help," she said, and turned to go.

"You don't have to—"

"Quit it, Scott," she said over her shoulder. "Try thinking
on your good fortune, why don't you?"

She continued out of the house without breaking stride and
let the screen door flap behind her. She stopped at the edge of
the porch, stretched her arms straight out to the side, and
rolled her head back. She stood that way for a moment, then
hopped down off the porch. As she made her way down the
path she kicked occasionally at tufts of grass growing along
its edge.

Craik watched out the window until Susanna reached
the road and turned toward Front Street. He went back to the
table, ate another doughnut, and resumed sweeping out the
cottage. When he'd finished, he walked into town.

It was another hot, windless day. There were few people on
the street. The ones Craik did pass nodded to him and went
on their way, taking it slow.

Craik went into the small IGA at the east end of town. He
bought a loaf of whole-wheat bread, butter, eggs, milk,

cheddar cheese, bacon, fresh and canned vegetables, some local fish, coffee, sugar, two six-packs of beer, matches, a Thermos, cleaning powders and liquids, scrubbing pads, paper towels, toilet paper, a small pad of paper, and a ballpoint pen. He paid in cash. It made for two heavy paper bags full, which he carried back to the house without setting them down.

He worked into the afternoon, cleaning and defrosting and straightening up. Then he had a sandwich and a beer and hitchhiked to Dorset. There, he went to the Marine Resources office. He purchased a nonresident harvester's permit. It cost eight dollars and allowed the taking of blue crabs by trotline and/or dip net. Craik pocketed the permit and went back outside.

As he did, one of the Sheriff's Department cruisers came down the adjacent drive. Bracewell Kemp was inside, alone. The sheriff glanced briefly in Craik's direction but didn't stop. He continued down to the state road and turned left.

Kemp drove three miles toward Brawlton before turning north on a county road, in the direction of the Pawchunk. A mile later he turned left again, onto a narrow strip of asphalt. A sign read: PRIVATE ROAD. NO OUTLET. NO TRESPASSING.

The private road wound up the side of a hill, with dense woods on either side. Halfway to the top there was a wrought-iron fence with a double-wide gate barring further progress. Kemp stopped and rolled down his window. Next to the car was a post with a metal box atop it. On the face of the box was a button and a speaker grille. Kemp punched the button.

"Yes?" came a voice from the box.

"Sheriff Kemp," Kemp said.

"Yes."

The two halves of the iron gate creaked slowly apart. Kemp drove through it, and it closed behind him, more quickly. Two hundred yards farther on, the woods opened out, revealing a grassy knoll of five acres or so. At the summit of the knoll was a nineteenth-century mansion, gleaming white, with an imitation Monticello front. A long stable lay below and to the left of the mansion. The top of a guest house showed above the far side of the hill.

Kemp stopped in a gravel area in front of the mansion. He got out and took a quick look around. There was a panoramic view of the countryside. The Pawchunk River to the north. Brawlton and the Bay to the east. Small farms and woodlands to the south. Dorset, to the west, would be visible from the other side of the house. The knoll was the highest point for miles around.

The sheriff went up the broad brick steps and past thick white columns. As he approached the front door it opened.

"Stayne," Kemp said.

"Afternoon, sir," Stayne said. "Judge Holder is expecting you in the library."

An amber light glowed on the telephone console in front of the Judge. He pushed a plastic button and the light went out. Then he opened the bottom desk drawer. He punched a button on the tape recorder. A tiny red light came on. Nothing else happened. The Judge cleared his throat and the tape advanced slightly. He closed the drawer.

Stayne knocked, then entered, Kemp close behind him. Holder got up.

"Brace," he said, indicating the chair on the other side of his desk. "Drink?"

Kemp nodded. "Judge. Bourbon and water." He sat down.

"I'll have Glen Calder," the Judge said, seating himself.

Stayne went to the bar along the side wall and prepared the two drinks. He set the Scotch on the desk in front of Holder and put the other into Kemp's hand.

"Thank you, Stayne," the Judge said. "I'll ring you if we need anything."

"Very good, sir," Stayne said, and he left the room.

The Judge cleared his throat. "Well," he said, "anything to report?"

"Nothing new," Kemp said. "Just this fella the boys brought in yesterday."

"What's his name?"

"Craik."

The Judge jotted on a pad in front of him. "How's that go? C-r-a-i-k?" Kemp nodded. "First name?"

"Scott."

"Where's he from?"

Kemp shrugged. "North somewhere," he said. "Craik ain't exactly loose up with information about hisself. I figured it weren't quite time to lean on him yet."

"Describe him," Holder said.

Kemp gave a detailed description of Craik. The Judge jotted more notes on the pad, then put his pencil down and leaned back in his chair.

"You run a check on him?" Holder asked.

"Uh-huh. He's clean, least as far as the Commonwealth of Virginia is concerned. Outside of that, who knows? I wanted to check with you before I went on the national wire."

"Let's hold off on that. With our . . . position here, I don't want to go outside the state unless I absolutely have to. Not officially, anyway. I'll see what I can get through my own channels, if you think I should. What's *your* take on the man?" Holder asked.

The sheriff took a sip of bourbon before answering. "I don't know," he said. "He don't seem a drifter to me. Drifters are scared people, which is how come they drift so much. Running from this and that, afraid it's gonna catch up with them. This guy didn't bat an eye when we hauled him in. He was cool, like all we did was *bore* him or something. It ain't the way they act, in my experience. Then . . . well, there was this thing down to Sook's last night."

The Judge raised an eyebrow.

"Yeah," Kemp went on, "and Craik was in the middle of it. I ain't talked to no one was there yet, but my deputies got called in and they heard the story right out. Seems Rodney Crowe got out of hand and pulled his knife on Lester Dent. Craik was there, drinking with Shields and Marla Vickers and . . . your niece."

"Oh?"

"Well, I don't know what all that means. Craik is renting

from Marla and seems to be crewing up with Shields. Susanna got there late on, from what I understand, and sat down with them. It mightn't be anything. She's probably just pissed at Stuart and 'licity again and gone out and set down with the first friendly faces she seen."

"Perhaps," Holder said. He jotted some more notes. "But I don't like this, Brace."

"He went home alone."

"Fine. But now you've also got him in Henry Beadle's old job."

"I know, I know. The whole thing is weird. But there's also the possibility that we got us a snake's nest of coincidences here."

"Uh-huh. I'm a little old for coincidences. But let it ride for now. What happened with Crowe?"

"Well," Kemp said, "apparently this Craik went in there and disarmed him."

"With his bare hands?"

"Yeah."

The Judge whistled softly. "Jesus," he said, "I ain't even sure *Fyke* would try something like that. Crowe's the best man with a knife in the damn county. What in hell did the boy do?"

"Beats me," Kemp said. "Weren't too many people seen it. All the deputies could find is that one minute Crowe had Shields and Craik under his knife, and the next Craik had Crowe's arm all bent around and the knife was on the floor. I tell you something, though. Craik had to been fast as a three-dollar whore to do that."

"Which brings us back to the number-one question. If he isn't a slab-ass drifter, who is he? You think the Fib's decided to have a look at us?"

Kemp sipped some bourbon and shook his head. "Don't think so. If he was an FBI man, I doubt he'd have tipped his hand so early on. He'd be afraid we'd make him and he's still young enough, it'd probably be an important assignment for him. He'd've let Rodney carve Lester three ways before he stepped in. Still, there's always the chance. I think we're gonna have to let him be for a while, 'cause if he is fed and we make the wrong move, the store'll have to be closed down until it all blows over."

"Shit," Holder said.

He drained the rest of his Scotch, and the two men sat in silence for a while.

"All right, let him be," the Judge said finally. "What the hell else have we got? Anything new on Beadle?"

Kemp shook his head. "Nothing," he said. "I don't think we're gonna find anything, Judge. If he skipped, he skipped. If the D.C. boys are in on it, they might not want us to find him. Might think it's better to keep us in a sweat. You heard from them?"

"No. Not since last week."

"Maybe they've given up."

Holder laughed mirthlessly. "Fat chance," he said. "They'll keep at it until they win or we show them they can't. It's in their blood."

"Never did like the types, myself," Kemp said.

"Yeah. Here we are supporting their brothers all over the damn hemisphere and what do we get for it? A bunch of clowns wanting to screw up the whole works."

"Ain't fair."

"Fair or not," Holder said, "you've gotta keep them off my back, Brace. That's the bottom line here, and I don't much care how you do it. Use the deputies. Use Crowe and his friends if you have to. But keep the greasers out of my county. Figure that's what I'm paying you for now. You don't mistake my meaning, do you?"

"We'll do the job," Kemp said tersely.

"Good." The Judge pushed a button on the phone console. "Okay, keep an easy eye on this Craik character. He does anything at all suspicious, I want to know about it yesterday. And anything else you see, anything that looks like the D.C. boys, the same."

"Right."

The Judge got up as the door opened and Stayne entered. Sheriff Kemp got up too. Stayne led him from the room.

When they'd gone, Holder went over to the bar. He poured himself another two fingers of Glen Calder and returned to his chair. He sat, replaying the tape of the conversation with Kemp, sipping at the whiskey until it was gone.

Then he ejected the tape from the recorder. He printed something on it, placed it in a protective case, and laid it on the desktop. He opened a new tape and slotted it into the recorder. The tiny red light continued to glow. Next to the recorder was a small black box with three toggle switches. The Judge flipped one of them up and another down. He closed the drawer, tapped a two-button combination on the phone console, and leaned back in his chair. In a few seconds a female voice came from the phone speaker.

"Congressman Mills's office," the voice said.

"Let me speak to Jesse," Holder said.

"I'm sorry, the congressman is in conference at the moment. May I—"

"C'mon, Allie, it's Forrest Holder."

"Excuse me, sir, I'll see when Mr. Mills might be available."

There was a click, and the woman's voice was replaced by music. It was a bland version of "If I Was a Rich Man." The Judge whistled softly along with the tune.

"What is it, Forrest?" Jesse Mills's voice said.

"Jess," Holder said. "You don't seem pleased to hear from me."

"I'm a busy man. I *am* trying to serve my constituents, you know."

"Good. And I'm one of them. I just need a small favor . . . Jess, are you there?"

Mills sighed. "Yeah, I'm here," he said. "What do you want?"

"Small, I said. I need you to run a check on someone. You got a pencil handy?"

"Yeah. Go ahead."

The Judge picked up the pad from his desk and held it in front of him.

"Guy's name is Scott Craik, C-r-a-i-k," he said. "Don't

know where he's from. Here's what he looks like." He read the detailed description. "And that's all I got, Jesse."

"What're you looking for?"

"Whatever you've got. I'd like to know who the son of a bitch is."

"How bad?"

"Go as deep as you can without getting anybody riled up. Source of request confidential, of course."

"Yeah, sure," Mills said. "What do you want to know for?"

"Business reasons."

"I should know better. All right, when do you need it by?"

"Soon."

"I'll try for the first of next week, if I can. Some of these people are slow. Is that it?"

"That's it."

Mills hung up. He massaged his temples.

"Son of a bitch," he muttered to himself. "Goddamn bastard."

He pushed a button on his phone and a voice said, "Yes, sir?"

"Come in here please, Richards," Mills said.

A moment later one of the side doors in Mills's office opened, and a young man in a blue suit and striped tie came in. He stood in front of Mills's desk. Mills held out a sheet of paper to him.

"I want a background on this man," he said.

"Yes, sir. How deep?"

"Just moderate. And confidential. But don't call in any important favors."

"Very well. FBI, IRS, SSA?"

"Yeah. Do the Pentagon, too, army records. And the DMV network. Don't bother with the media. I don't think that's worth anything."

"Intelligence?"

Mills drummed his fingers on his desktop. "No," he said. "Not yet, anyway."

Richards nodded. "Under your name, sir?" he asked.

"Sure. Routine background. See what you can get me by Tuesday."

"No problem. Will that be all?"

"That's all. The report's for my eyes only. Okay?"

"Certainly, sir."

Richards left, and Mills rested his head in his hands, massaging his temples. He stared down at his desk.

"Bastard," he muttered. "What is it this time, you bastard?"

FRIDAY

CHAPTER 8

The early-morning air was still hot, though it was a little cooler down by the water. Craik sat at the end of the pier, propped up against a piling. One leg dangled over the side. He hummed a song to himself.

Men, and a few women, were arriving around him, firing up diesels old and new, cursing the ones that wouldn't start, drinking coffee and gossiping, casting off. The water was calm, and a boat left the harbor every few minutes. Most of the watermen agreed that it was going to be a fine day for crabbing.

At ten minutes after five o'clock a boat came around the end of the breakwater and motored up to the dock. Shields nudged the boat skillfully up to the pilings. Craik picked up a brown paper bag, and Shields handed him aboard. The waterman returned to the wheel. Craik steadied himself on the balls of his feet and shifted his weight from one leg to another as he adjusted to the rhythm of the water. *Murphy's Law* chugged slowly out of the Brawlton harbor.

Shields's boat was a thirty-five-footer, long and narrow, of the Bay style known as deadrise. It had a *V* bottom with a shallow draft. There was a small wheelhouse forward and a long, open deck aft. The wheelhouse contained a few basic instruments; the deck was strewn with gear, boxes, bushel baskets. At about the boat's midpoint was a small boom and a set of controls that allowed its speed and direction to be governed from there.

Craik sat on a bench in the wheelhouse while Shields guided the boat out into the Bay. Shields rubbed his chin.

"Good day for crabs," he said. "I can feel it."

"That's what they were saying on the dock," Craik said.

The boat cleared the breakwater, and the sea became a bit more choppy. There was a very slight breeze.

"Wind's in our favor too," Shields said.

"How so?" Craik asked.

"Out of the southwest she's most of the time dry. She shifts around to the southeast, then you watch out. That's when you get your bad squalls." He looked over at Craik. "So," he said, "you made it."

"I can get up at four-thirty if I have to."

"You get so you *want* to, then you're a waterman. Some of these boys, they get so they can't even sleep right on land anymore. Get up in the middle of the night, put their clothes on, and come down and sleep on board. There's a few wives don't understand what that's all about."

"I don't wonder," Craik said.

"Think their men are off screwing some little twist, and that ain't it at all. Some of 'em like to eat on the water too. Their wives'd get up, even early as this, and cook breakfast if they wanted it, but no, they make up some excuse about coming down beforetimes and tinkering with their motor or something. Then they end up eating and shooting the shit with their friends. Swear that food just don't taste as good when you're eating it inside of a house. I know some like that. And it's the same damn stuff they'd be getting at home."

"Uh-huh," Craik said.

Shields had turned the boat north and was following the coast. He gestured back toward Brawlton, whose lights were quickly being lost.

"So what do you think of our fine city?" he asked.

"I'm learning to like it," Craik said.

"You ain't much of a swamp rat, are you?"

"I suppose not."

"Well, you got your . . . *talents,* though you might be a little out of time. Yeah, I'd say you belong about, oh, two hundred year ago." He chuckled. "You know how Brawlton got its name?"

Craik shook his head.

"Brawltown," Shields said, "that's what it used to been called. They just shortened it up after a while. Back when they first settled into this area, it was all woods, you know. But them English bastards, they come in and cut all the trees down. Planted tobacco everywhere. Hogged all the land to theirselves.

"Then there was the watermen. They didn't have no land, so they kind of stuck together down by the Bay. Might have a little one-room log shack and a little boat and that was it. Lived on oysters and bread and not much else. They was a bad bunch back then. Hated the tobacco men, not that it did them any good. The boys with the money controlled the cops, just like they do now. So they fought amongst themselves, mostly. Drank a lot. Didn't a week go by but what there was somebody cutting up somebody else.

"Brawltown they came for miles around to drink and fight. It was the roughest place this part of the coast. If you'd've gone into whatever they called Jimmie and Sook's in those days, you'd've had three or four guys trying you before the night was over." Shields glanced over at Craik and grinned. "And I ain't prepared to say *how* you would've done, either."

"Probably not too well," Craik said. "I don't like to fight all that much."

"Nowadays I'd say that's a good thing. For the other guys."

Craik shrugged. "I've done some," he said. "I can hold my own. But all fighting is, is marking time between when the innocent people start getting hurt. I've seen too much of that. Anyway, you seem to know your local history."

"Ought to. It's where I'm from."

"I'll bet not everyone knows as much."

"You'd be surprised," Shields said. "You know what's happened before, and it helps you out now."

"Yeah. A little history can help you see something coming at you. Then again, sometimes it doesn't help at all."

Craik took a Thermos out of his brown paper bag and poured himself some coffee. He offered it to Shields. The waterman produced a mug and a bottle of Irish whiskey from one of the compartments in the cabin and fixed himself a low-rent version of Irish coffee. The two men drank.

"I hope I ain't making a mistake with you," Shields said after a while.

"You're not," Craik said.

"Like, for example, what do you know about a boat like this?"

"I'm a good listener."

"Nothing, huh? About what I thought. Well, *Murphy's Law*'s good as some and better than others. Motor's good. I'd say ain't a finer motor been set into a boat than this one. We talk to each other, tell us what's wrong. We done a few miles and'll do a few more. You do some, you'll get to know her too."

Shields swept his arm around the wheelhouse. "Now, this here," he went on, "it ain't as *modern* as some. I don't give a damn about that. I want to be able to get out, and I want to get back, and I want to catch something while I'm there. Some of these boys've got radar and Loran and that kind of shit, and I say, who needs it? This is the Bay, not George's Bank or some damn thing. You don't *need* but three things, and I ain't dead certain about them, either. But I got them. A CB." He gestured at the radio resting in a bracket slung from the ceiling. "A compass." A large marine compass with bold white numerals, floating in its housing atop a metal tripod. "And this son of a bitch." A video display tube with dials and switches.

"This here's a depth sounder," Shields said. "When it works, you use it all the time." He kicked the metal cylinder that supported it. "When it don't, which is a lot of the time, you throw a line and sinker overboard and see how far down it goes. In the old days that was all they had. They used to stick some tallow wax on the end of the sinker too. Then when they pulled it back, they could tell what the bottom was like by what the wax brung up. Supposed to been there were guys who could navigate the entire Bay by what come up on the tallow line."

"How's it working now?" Craik asked.

"The sounder? Beats me. We'll find out when we get there."

"Where's 'there'?"

"You'll see. Ain't no point in filling your head with that kind of stuff yet. Besides, it's time to be baiting the trotline."

Shields took a piece of rope that was tied to the cabin wall and attached it to one side of the wheel. He did the same on the other side. The wheel's rotation was reduced to a narrow arc.

"That ought to hold her good enough," Shields said. "It ain't that rough today."

He crooked his finger, and Craik followed him back onto the open deck. Near the wheelhouse were two wooden boxes, two barrels, and a steel drum. Shields reached into one of the boxes.

"This is the trotline," he said. "Three-sixteenths manila, about three thousand foot of her. We catch us some crabs with her or we don't. A good number of the boys gone to pots, and I say to hell with them. You're never through with a pot, what with hauling them and cleaning them and moving them around, putting them in and taking them out. Cost you a pretty penny and then you lose the half of them before the season's out. That's why I'm a trotline man.

"Okay." He held up a red-and-white float. "This marks the end of the trotline." He pulled out thirty feet or so of line and came to a length of iron chain. "Chain holds the float in place, of course. And after the chain you got the trotline proper." He pulled out ten feet of it. "Every five feet you got one of these." He indicated a short length of thin filament line, attached to the manila rope. "This is your snood. You tie it around the bait. We get lucky, we get a crab on the bait every five feet, we got us six hundred crabs. A-course, we ain't gonna do that well.

"And here's the bait." He opened the drum. "Salt eel. Crab's basically a garbage-eater. They'll get into most anything, long as it's rotten. This is one of their favorites, though." He took out an eel and pulled a knife from his belt. "Cut it up about this much. A lot of the boys call me a heavy baiter, and maybe I am. But I'll tell you this. If I get on some crabs, I want to catch them, and the big ones ain't gonna come to your table if you cheat them on the food.

"That's about it. If you ain't a moron, you can do it. Bait up the trotline and you best get started. I done the one, so you got about five hundred and ninety-nine to go. The only other thing is, you feed the baited line into this barrel here. And coil it nice now. When it come out, we don't want it all tangled up. Think you can handle it?" He passed the knife to Craik.

"Sure," Craik said. He took the eel and began to slice it into bait-sized chunks. Shields returned to the wheelhouse. The sky was beginning to lighten.

When the sun made its first appearance, Craik was only half finished. Shields had *Murphy's Law* laying off the mouth of a creek about a quarter of a mile across.

"How you doing, son?" Shields called. "We're onto the best time of day here."

"I got a ways to go," Craik said.

"How're your fingers?"

"Fine."

Shields chuckled. "I'll bet," he said. "Okay."

He killed the engine and went back to where Craik was working. Together the job went more than twice as fast, with the two men alternating snoods. Shields worked as if the index finger weren't missing at all. The barrel was soon full of baited line. Shields returned to the wheelhouse and restarted the engine. He jockeyed the boat around, moving it here and there in a seemingly random way. Craik observed.

"I'm sighting on that big oak," Shields said, pointing.
"What're we looking for?" Craik asked.

"Sandbar," Shields said. "That's where you find the best crabs. This one's my personal spot. Been working it a good many years now and it's rarely disappointed me. I think we'll be on a deal of crabs today."

He fiddled with the dials on the depth sounder, cursed, pounded it with his fist.

"Ah," he said, "there we go. Now, look here. This is your profile of the bottom. See where that line dips down there? That's the sandbar dropping off. It's fifteen feet, then it drops right quick to twenty-five. We want to lay the trotline right close to the edge. Crabs'll come out to investigate, but they won't go over. Let's shade it a hair, make sure we don't miss it."

He maneuvered the boat again.

"Okay," he said, "pitch the anchor line. Back towards shore, six feet or so."

Craik followed instructions. In a moment the float bobbed steady in the water.

"Play the line out," Shields called, and he eased the boat forward, perpendicular to the flow of the creek. Craik guided the coiled line from the barrel into the water. Within a few minutes all three thousand feet of trotline had gone overboard. A second buoy marked the far end of it.

"Nothing to it," Shields said. "Now let's get us some crabs."

The big waterman turned the boat and guided it to the beginning of the trotline. Then he slipped the engine into neutral. He walked back amidships, bringing with him a long-handled dip net and the empty box.

"Set up like this," he said to Craik. He arranged the wooden catch box with several bushel baskets around it. "I'll dip, you sort." He handed Craik a set of steel tongs. "Better use these until your hands toughen up. Number-one jimmies into that basket there. Sooks there. Can you tell the difference?"

"Males are blue."

"All over. Sooks got the red tips to their claws. Peelers in this basket. You flip them over, look at the underside. If you see a pink line down the middle here, or the shell beginning to come apart, that's a peeler. Whities can go in with the peelers.

"And then, this time of year, we're apt to run into some doublers. That's a couple of crabs screwing. The jimmie gets a good lock on his old lady and they stay stuck together for a while. We get any of those, put them in a separate basket. And watch yourself with the sooks. Them that've already mated, they're wild, I tell you. They'll go for you. Getting toward the fall, they're about the meanest thing you'll find in the Bay, and I include a damn bluefish in there.

"Oh, yeah, we got a size limit too. I'll try not to dip up anything too small, but you check them out. If it looks less than five inches, put it in a separate basket. We'll go over them later. The little ones we can take home and eat ourselves. Now, you get it all?"

"Sure," Craik said. "I got it."

"Let's do her, then."

The boat drifted toward the marker buoy. When it got close enough, Shields reached down with a boat hook and fished up the line. He raised it up and laid it across the small boom that extended a couple of feet out over the water. At the end of the boom was a roller sandwiched between two chocks. Shields threaded the line into the groove of the roller. Then, with the lever controls, he started *Murphy's Law* moving, very slowly and parallel to the trotline. As the boat moved, the line was drawn to the surface. Shields leaned out over the gunwale, his left hand resting on the controls, his right wielding the dip net.

The first snood neared the surface. There was a blue crab feeding at it. Shields dipped quickly and the crab was in the net. The next snood had two crabs. Shields dipped once, twisting his wrist and snared both of them. He turned, dumping the three crabs in the catch box, and immediately shifted his attention back to the trotline. Craik sorted.

The line unrolled. Shields plunged his net, sometimes

feverishly, five or six thrusts in a row, sometimes only after a lengthy pause. Once he leaned so far out that he almost went overboard. Craik grabbed at his shirt and pulled him back. Shields turned and glared briefly at him, showing an empty dip net. Craik didn't interfere with him again.

Before long the chain clanked against the roller. Shields dropped it back over the side. He wiped his forehead.

"End of run number one," he said. "Let's see what we got."

Craik shook his head. "And you do all that by yourself?" he said. "Plus what I was doing?"

"If I have to," Shields said. "You get used to it."

He slipped the engine into neutral and carefully inspected the bushel baskets.

When he'd finished, he said, "Not bad, Craik. You are a pretty good learner, after all. Only problem is you got some whities mixed in with the hard shells." He started resorting some of the crabs. "Crab's got to shed his shell," he went on, not looking up, "or he dies. When they're young, it's every few days, but when they get old, only every couple months. Just before it happens, you got a peeler, which you recognized. Hard shell on top, new one underneath. Just afterward you got a whitie." He held one up and poked it. "See? Shell's still soft. They're easy to catch, 'cause they used up all their energy getting rid of the old shell—this one seems about half dead—but they ain't much of a market for them.

"Otherwise you done good. Let's just rearrange things here a little." He got another basket and shifted some of the crabs into it. "You mix the jimmies up a bit, bigger ones and smaller ones together, try to make the baskets about even. I believe we might get a few bushels of number-one jimmies today.

"What'd we get, one doubler?" Craik nodded. Shields searched it out. "Break it up. Get them from behind like this and pull them apart. Watch your fingers, 'cause they ain't gonna like it any more than you'd like being pried off *your* favorite lady." He demonstrated. "Sook with the womenfolk, jimmie with his buddies." He tossed the separated crabs into different baskets and brushed his hands together.

"We got about fifty," Craik said. "How's that?"

"Decent. But it won't keep us in beer money. Now we do it again. I warn you, it's a boring life, Craik. You do the same thing, over and over."

"I imagine it takes a while to get it right, though," Craik said.

Shields was moving the boat back to the start of the trotline.

"Yeah," he said. "Like how you bring the line up. Too fast and they'll just skitter right off. Too slow and you drag them along the bottom. They don't like that any better. Plus, on a calm day like this, sometimes they won't stay with the bait until you can get them. It's almost like they can see what's gonna happen. Hell, maybe they can, I don't know."

They ran the trotline again. And again and again. Some times there were a lot of crabs, sometimes few. The baskets began to fill. Other boats nosed into the area as the morning passed. Each time the captain would hail Shields and ask how he was doing, and each time he'd tell them he thought the place was about fished out. One of the boats stayed, laying line on the other side of the creek mouth. It didn't land nearly as many crabs as *Murphy's Law*.

Shields chuckled. "That's a nice feller over there," he told Craik. "Hell of an oysterman. But he ain't much at crabs. I could follow right after him and take out twice what he done. He just don't have the instincts. 'Course, in winter, it's me that'll be following him around. All works out in the end. That's why we don't grudge the next guy what he's getting."

After about five hours of steady work Shields said, "I think this spot's about played out for now. We might's well break for lunch. We can make one more run, then haul her up and see can we find someplace else as good."

They pulled out sandwiches and potato chips and raw vegetables and pie and coffee. They traded back and forth. Craik had a couple of doughnuts at the bottom of his bag.

"Look like Sandi's doughnuts," Shields said.

"Yeah. Susanna Holder brought them to me," Craik said.

Shields grinned. "Hooo," he said. "Watch your step, son. That girl's got an eye for you, and that's the truth."

"Maybe so."

"That's a beautiful girl there, Craik. Lot of spirit. And she's a nice one too. But her uncle about owns this county, you know. And he's a mean bastard. Like I said, I'd watch my step if I were you."

"I ain't looking, anyway."

Shields eyed him. "You ever been married?" he asked.

"Uh-uh."

"Me, neither. Best way to make a good thing go bad." He chomped down on his sandwich. "You do like the ladies, though?" he said through his food.

"Sure. I'm not against marriage, but I haven't exactly stayed in one spot long enough for anything serious to happen."

"Well, I tell you. When I first saw you, I didn't think I'd say this, but I believe you might have the makings of a waterman. So maybe this'll be it for you. I'll teach you what I can. If we make a team, good. If not, you'll have enough to get you started on your own."

"Thanks," Craik said.

Shields shrugged. "You learn it right, you won't be owing me a thing. Good help's hard to find. But we best be getting our butts in gear. We don't lay in a few more bushels, I'm gonna have trouble making the diesel for this trip."

"Let's do it," Craik said.

They ran the trotline one more time, then pulled it and did some rebaiting. Shields took *Murphy's Law* a little up the coast, to where he knew of another underwater shelf. Pickings there were slimmer.

At three in the afternoon Shields said, "That's good enough. Don't usually get this many runs in this time of year, but you got to do more when there's more of you." He counted the bushel baskets. "Ought to bring us three hundred," he said. "If them Holders don't try to screw us, which'll be the day. Price has dropped since the Fourth of

July. That's your peak weekend. It'll keep coming down till your sooks head south to lay their eggs. Then it'll start up again. 'Course, then, if you want them, you got to dig them out of the mud. Don't care for winter crabbing, myself. But there's those that prefer it over oystering.

"Anyway, you seem to be pretty good luck, boy. We'll split it six to four."

"I'm not sure I deserve that much," Craik said.

"Maybe not. But later you'll be worth more and get the same. It's all gonna balance out, and the boat always comes first. So consider your good fortune. We done this well every day and we could retire in a couple of years. Won't never happen."

"How about if I buy the beer today?"

Shields laughed. "Done," he said. "Let's get moving."

The day was still hot and mostly windless. The boat made good time. In less than an hour it was back in Brawlton. There was no waiting at the off-loading pier. Most of the other boats were already moored in the harbor or had returned home to their private docks.

A man came out of the Holder Seafood Co. shed. He got *Murphy's Law* snugged to the pilings. Shields and Craik gathered the bushel baskets together. A second man joined the first up on the pier. The second man was Rodney Crowe.

"Well, well," Crowe said. "Look who come up a waterman now. Kinda cradle snatching, ain't you, Shields?"

"Mind your business, Crowe," Shields said. "We got some crabs to unload here."

"Yeah, I'll bet you do. You been out robbing pots again?"

Shields looked up, his expression hard. He caught Crowe's eye and held it for a moment. Then he turned his attention back to the baskets. Craik was standing with his arms folded, neutrally watching the interchange.

"Don't pay no mind," Shields said.

"I hadn't," Craik said.

Craik and Shields grabbed opposite ends of one of the baskets and hoisted it up. Crowe and his helper hefted it onto the dock. The process was repeated several more times.

Then Shields said, "Number-one jimmies. Take good care now."

They lifted the basket. Crowe and his helper got hold of it, but Crowe's end slipped out of his hand. The bottom of the basket banged against the edge of the pier and the top flew off. A rain of crabs fell onto the deck of *Murphy's Law*. Crabs scuttled everywhere, waving their claws, darting for holes in the floorboards.

Craik grabbed the tongs and began spearing at the crabs, but Shields shoved him out of the way. The waterman got down on his knees and started grabbing. In a few moments he had a mass of crabs between his palms. He shook them into a basket, banging the ones that wouldn't let go against its side. Then he did it again. His hands moved faster than his quarry could. Soon he had the deck clean.

Craik just stared at him, then up at Crowe. Crowe was leaning against a piling, a half smile on his face.

Shields's hands were bloody. He wiped them on his trousers. "Your hands get as worn as mine, it don't hurt much," he said to Craik.

"Sorry," Crowe called down from the dock. "Just slipped." He was still smiling.

"Don't get into it," Shields said to Craik. "This is his territory. Here he's got the Holders behind him. You get the Judge on your back and you won't last a week in this town, I don't care how tough you are."

"I've learned how to avoid trouble," Craik said.

"Good. Now give me a hand."

Together they heaved the basket up again. This time Crowe pretended to let it slip.

"Oops." He laughed. "Got it. There we go."

Shields climbed the ladder to the dock. He walked over to Crowe. He stood looking down at the shorter man. Crowe regarded him calmly.

"Rodney," Shields said, "you ever pull any shit like that with me again and I'll rip your heart out. I promise you."

"Oh, I'll keep that in mind, boss," Crowe said.

Shields leveled his forefinger at Crowe. "I promise you,"

he said again, then turned and walked to the shed. Crowe's helper had already hauled the bushel baskets inside.

Craik came up the ladder. He sat on the pier, leaning his back against one of the pilings, and looked out over the harbor. Crowe was watching him, but Craik didn't look his way. After a while Craik closed his eyes. Crowe disappeared into the shed.

Shields went into the seafood company's office. Stuart Holder was sitting behind a desk littered with papers.

"Stuart," Shields said.

"Brendan," Holder said. "Good day today, I understand."

"Twelve bushels, less what your goon out there lost for me."

"Yes, I'm sorry, but you understand that the company can't be responsible for transferral accidents."

"Uh-huh. Your boy's gonna get his asshole transferred upside his head one of these days. You be responsible for that?"

"Don't make threats, Brendan," Holder said. "They don't do any of us any good. I'll give you two hundred and eighty for the crabs."

"Shit. They're worth three-twenty. Minimum."

"Market's down, you know that. If you want to try and sell them on the street, go ahead."

"C'mon, Stuart, don't none of us have the time for that. I'll split the difference with you. Give me three."

"Sorry. It's two-eighty. I don't set the prices, I just follow what they tell me."

Shields ground his teeth, then sighed. "All right," he said. "I'll take it in cash."

"Fine." Holder pushed two sheets of paper toward him. "Here's a receipt for the crabs. And you sign the one for the money."

He reached into one of the desk drawers and took out a stack of twenty-dollar bills. He counted out two hundred and eighty dollars. Shields exchanged the slip of paper for the money.

"You know, Stuart," he said, "the best thing Reva ever

done for herself was get away from the Old Man. Him and all the rest of your lot."

Holder glared at him. "Don't you start talking family, Brendan," he said. "You've got nothing to say there."

Shields turned his back. "Yeah," he said, "best thing she ever done," and he left the office.

He walked over to the piling and put his hand on Craik's shoulder. Craik opened his eyes.

"Come on, boy," Shields said.

The two men climbed down onto the boat. Shields handed Craik some money.

"One-twelve for you," Shields said. "We got stiffed."

Craik shrugged. "We'll do better tomorrow," he said.

"Ain't going crabbing," Shields said. "I got a line on some seining. We get lucky and that's some easy money. Mostly just sitting around."

"I need a license?"

"Already got one for me and one assistant. Used to been Beadle. I imagine it'll do for you."

"Okay. Where do you want me to meet you?"

Shields shook his head. "It ain't set up yet. We still need another boat. If it goes, I'll come get you."

"Fine." Craik looked at the money in his hand. He riffled it with his thumb. "Well, it'll pay for the beer," he said.

"Uh-huh. Let's put the *Law* to bed and go have a couple or three," Shields said.

Shields guided the boat away from the marina. Crowe came out of the shed and stood at the end of the pier, watching as they receded in the distance. The late-afternoon sun glittered off the water. Crowe had to squint. He had his knife out and was cleaning under his fingernails. He pried out the grime and wiped the knife on his pant leg. As *Murphy's Law* rounded the breakwater Crowe was still there, cradling the knife in his right hand, hip-high, and watching.

CHAPTER 9

The street was quiet, tree-lined. Only a few blocks away was Wisconsin Avenue and the cacophony of central Georgetown, with its nightclubs, trendy boutiques, swirling, crazed street life. But that was another world. Here was one of the posh sections of Washington, D.C., and it looked like an affluent area in any national capital. The white and yellow and red brick row houses were three stories high. They had wrought-iron balconies and bay windows and tiny gardens in the back. Interiors were thick with crystal chandeliers and ferns. Crazies were not allowed.

A man walked briskly down the street. Heat waves still shimmered from the pavement. The man was in his late twenties. He was slender and moved with the grace of a first-quality flanker back. He wore a pair of tailored gray slacks with a knife-edge crease and a cream-colored silk shirt with the top three buttons open. The shirt hung outside the slacks. There was almost no hair on his chest.

His complexion was dark, almost copper-colored. He had high cheekbones, black eyes, and medium-length black hair razor-cut so that it set off his face like a portrait frame. On his upper lip was a perfectly straight, skinny little pencil mustache. He was smoking a thin brown cigar with a gold band around one end. The cigar was inserted in an ivory holder.

The young man turned in at one of the white-brick row houses, went through a wrought-iron gate, and closed it carefully behind him, making sure that it latched. He took the eight front steps two at a time. The door bell was a small brass breast at chest height. The young man pushed the protruding nipple. Inside, soft chimes sounded.

A middle-aged woman answered the door. She was dressed in black, her dark hair caught up in a tight bun.

"Come in, Aldo," she said.

They entered the beginning of a long hall. There was a closed door to the right and a flight of stairs to the left.

"Your uncle is in his office," the woman said.

Aldo nodded and went up the stairs. He went down the second-floor hall to the door at the end. He knocked. A voice told him to enter. He did. The door closed itself behind him with a whispered sound that suggested solidity.

"Uncle," Aldo said.

"Sit," the older man said.

Aldo took a seat by the window, overlooking the backyard. A bare-chested man in a straw hat was back there, down on all fours, working on the flower bed with a hand weeder. The man's torso glistened with sweat. The muscles of his neck and shoulders slid around under his skin like random mounds of earth.

The older man was seated in an easy chair on the other side of the window. He was dressed in a custom-tailored gray suit, gray tie with a diamond stickpin. His hair, too, was gray. The flesh of his face hung slack, with pronounced folds under the dark eyes. There was a prominent mole over his right cheekbone.

"Aldo," he said, and the younger man's attention turned slowly from the backyard, "we have a problem."

"With the business?"

"Yes."

"And you need me to bail you out, Uncle?"

The older man took a gold cigarette case from the inner pocket of his jacket. He withdrew an unfiltered cigarette from it. He turned the cigarette over in his fingers a few times, as if examining it, then lit it up. He exhaled the smoke in Aldo's direction.

"Aldo," he said, "you are young. You have strength and you have courage. You are also foolish." Aldo began to speak, but the older man held up his hand. "It is not a criticism. I have been young and foolish, and so has your father. It is simply a part of life. You are young and foolish in order to grow older and wiser."

"Forget it, Uncle. I don't want any—"

"Sit down, Aldo. Sit down. You have done much for the business. Things that even your father and I could not have done. We know this. We value this. You are able to take action, to do things that we cannot. There are situations that call for your skills. And there are situations that call for different kinds of skills."

"Don't bother me with a desk job. I'm not interested."

The older man waved the unfiltered cigarette. "This is not a desk job. This is an opportunity to learn. We are in a highly competitive business, Aldo. The only survivors are those who can do many things well. You must learn this or you will lose the business. You have been spoiled, being raised in this country. The true reality for our people is a house made of metal signs wired together, ten persons dividing food for two. If you fail at the business, that is what you will be sent back to. And your neighbors will be much more tough than you. They will destroy you. Without the protection of all this you would not last a week."

Aldo sneered. "I'm not going back," he said. "Never. They can kill me first."

"Admirable. But shortsighted. The authorities here can do with you whatever they wish. That is why we are willing to pay money to them. You are not a true citizen, nor will you ever be one. The business is your sole protection."

"Get on with it, Uncle. If you need something, tell me what it is."

The older man paused. "That is the point, Aldo," he said. "We have a problem that may require your particular talents, yet we hope that it will not. There are times when it does not pay to be intemperate. You must learn to balance action with words. If the words will suffice, they are often preferable to the deed."

Aldo yawned.

His uncle leaned forward. "Listen to me," he said harshly. "And listen well, young man. You will show respect for what your father and I have done. If you wish your proper place in the business, you will learn how it is conducted. You will do it our way. I do not think I have to remind you what would happen if you were forced to seek employment in this city. Do I?"

"No, Uncle," Aldo said tersely.

"Ah, what is the use?" the older man said. "I don't believe that you are ready." He leaned back and smoked, looking out the window.

Aldo let the pause stretch out before saying, "Ready for what? You still haven't told me."

The other man spoke to the window. "Your father was right. I was wrong."

"What did my father say?" Aldo demanded.

"He said that you were not yet ready to become a man."

"And you?" Aldo said through clenched teeth.

His uncle shrugged. "I said that I was not sure."

Aldo slammed his fist down on the arm of the chair. "I have nothing to prove to you!" he said. "No one can question my courage. Not my father. No one!"

"Granted. But a man's balls are not all that must be demonstrated. You must prove to us also that you know how to use your mind." He tapped his temple.

Aldo glared at him. "Are you saying that I am stupid?"

"I know that you are not stupid. But can you persuade someone with your words as well as your balls?"

"Of course."

The older man held the younger's eye for the first time since he had looked away.

"That is what we require," he said. "It is a job your father would ordinarily take. Unfortunately, he is detained in Bogotá for at least another ten days. And I must remain in the city. So we have not the time. I have suggested to your father that you undertake the task. He has left to my judgment whether or not you are up to it."

"I can do anything," Aldo said. He inserted another thin cigar into his holder and lit it. He tilted his chair onto its back legs. "I don't see what you're worried about. Why don't you tell me what the problem is?"

"The problem is the Norfolk facilities. They've just been compromised. It's our best port of entry, and we won't be able to use it any longer."

Aldo shrugged. "We'll find something else," he said.

"Ordinarily, I would say yes. No problem. But these things take time to develop. A lot of time. Doing things that you as yet have not had to deal with. And we do not have the time. There is a shipment coming by sea in less than ten days. A major investment. We must have a place at which to off-load it."

"Well, what about that place in Virginia that Father's been working on?"

The older man got up and went to a heavy steel file cabinet in one corner of the room. He unlocked it, opened one of the drawers, and took out a manila folder. He closed the drawer and relocked the cabinet. He returned to his chair.

"It may be our best bet," he said. "Unfortunately, your father has not gotten very far with it. The man down there does not want our . . . attentions."

"So we force it on him."

"If need be. But we do not wish that. The man has been running his operation for a long time. He has the loyalty of the locals, without whose cooperation there is nothing. In addition, he has a strong organization of his own, nominally within the law. It is not a simple matter of going there and taking over. That is what I meant by learning to choose the proper tactic. Do you understand?"

"Yeah, sure."

"This is imperative, Aldo. He must be convinced that it is in his best interests to side with us. The more peaceably he can be convinced, the better. At the same time, the process must not take too long. It will require a combination of skills. It is a man's job, Aldo."

"I can do it," Aldo said.

"I think so. But you must convince your father."

"The hell with my father."

His uncle smiled. "Nevertheless," he said, "it is he who must be convinced. If you are to be considered his successor in the business, you must be able to do these things."

"Give me the details."

The older man opened the manila folder. He pulled out a five-by-eight black-and-white photograph and passed it to Aldo.

"This is the man," he said. "Forrest Holder, known locally as the Judge, which he used to be. He controls the fishermen. You are familiar with his operation?" Aldo nodded. "It is an ideal setup for us. Traffic on the Chesapeake Bay is heavy. Fishermen are apt to go out at any time of the day or night. It's a big area, difficult for the government to police. Transferring cargo from large craft to small, or vice versa, is simple. The Judge has never been bothered. Of course, he does have the county Sheriff's Department on his side, and some politicians as well. All of that will go to strengthen our position, once we are able to solidify the partnership."

"How far has Father gotten?"

The older man shook his head. "Nowhere. The Judge is a moralist. He feels that what he does is for the good of the country and that what we do is criminal. He cannot see that we both simply deal in supply and demand. Your father tried to convince him of this, unsuccessfully."

"And what am I supposed to do?"

"It is time to try another tack. Show him that not only will he profit by linking with us, but also that he will suffer if he fails to do so. You must be careful not to antagonize him, yet you must be clear. It will take skill. We're confident that once he understands the situation, he'll come around." He passed over several more photographs. "This is the backbone of his organization. Sheriff Bracewell Kemp, Deputies Brent Fyke and Charles Tilghman. They are tough people, and the Judge takes very good care of them. Do not underestimate them."

"I can handle them."

"Aldo, you must not let your confidence become cockiness. If there is trouble, pull back. Should we need to take apart the organization, it is most sensible to do it bit by bit."

"Sure. What else?"

The older man handed over the rest of the folder. "Study this," he said. "It's a description of Holder's operation, background on the people, maps of the area. Commit it all to memory and return the folder to me. Do not make any copies. Come back here tomorrow morning, ready to go."

Aldo got up. "No problem."

"This is important," his uncle said. "If we lose the shipment, it will be very detrimental to the business. Your father will not be pleased. You will not stand tall in his eyes."

"Piece of cake, Uncle," Aldo said. "Piece of cake. You just leave the details to me."

CHAPTER 10

"I don't know," Janine said. "You get yourself mixed up with some strange characters, Susanna Holder. If you want my opinion."

"I ain't mixed up with him, Janine," Susanna said. "I'm just . . . *interested*, that's all."

"I wouldn't be interested in anyone who was on the wrong side of Rodney Crowe, I'll tell you that."

"Shoot, you shoulda seen it, Janine. Rodney's got every man in town afraid of him, outside of the sheriff's office and maybe Uncle Brendan. Craik walked up to him and took the knife away like he was a little kid. I never seen anything like that before."

"Yeah, well, let's close up, what do you say?"

"Sure. That's a good night's work."

The blond girl went over to the door of Sandi's Café and

flipped the hanging sign from the side that said OPEN to the one that said CLOSED, SEE YOU AT and had a little clock under it. She set the hands on the clock to six. Then she set to clearing off the tabletops. Susanna was at work on the bar.

"Susanna . . ." Janine said. "I talked to my dad. About going to college again. I don't think he's ever gonna be able to help me do it."

"Don't let it bother you," Susanna said. "It ain't what it's cracked up to be."

"That's easy for you to say. It's always been there for you. At least you got a choice."

"You think I *chose* Sandi's?"

Janine laughed. "No," she said, "but it all comes so easy for you."

"That's 'cause you never had to live with Stuart and 'licity. Believe me, nothing easy about that."

Janine slumped into a chair. She folded her hands on her lap and stared down at them.

"Susanna," she said, "what am I gonna do?"

Susanna stopped polishing the bar and looked over at her friend.

"Hey," she said, "come on, kid. We'll think of something."

"Like what?"

"I don't know, something."

"I feel like if I had to go on working in this place, if that's all I had to look forward to, I'd rather die."

"Oh, I've felt that way too."

"No, I mean it, Susanna. I would rather die. You know that whatever you decide to do, your folks will back you. Eventually, anyway. Go to college or travel or whatever you want. They'll help you because they *can* help you. My dad'd help me, too, but the difference is, he *can't*."

"You need to find yourself a guy," Susanna said.

"That's not it, damn it!"

"Yeah, I know." Susanna grinned. "But it sure helps. You could have your pick around here."

"Who wants any of these jerks?"

"You're right. Look, Janine, I'll tell you what. Let me talk to Daddy. You're like family to us. Maybe he could help you out. Get you a loan or something."

Janine abruptly looked up. "Do you think he would?" she said.

"Hey, I don't know. No promises. But we won't know unless we try, will we?"

"Oh, God, I don't even want to think about it. Would you do that?"

"Sure. What the hell."

"You're a friend, Susanna." She smiled broadly.

Susanna went back to work. "We gonna get out of here sometime tonight, girl?"

Janine resumed her tasks too. "I hope so," she said. "I don't want to be around when the ghost of Sandi's Café comes out."

"Oh, yeah, bound to be a ghost here."

"No, there really is, actually."

"Come on, Janine."

"I mean it. You never heard that story?"

"Uh-uh."

"It's not really the ghost of Sandi's," Janine said. "This place has been here a long time, you know. It was a lot of different places. Back in the twenties it was called the Night Dredge. After oyster dredging, I suppose. It was a bad place. This was a bad town then."

"I know," Susanna said. "Daddy's told me how some of the watermen used to run in booze that come up on ships from the Caribbean. Back in Prohibition."

"Right. There was some mean folks in Brawlton back then. They used to drink up what they brought in, some of it. Fights all the time. It's a wonder they got any fish packed with all that other stuff going on.

"Anyway, the Dredge was where they'd come on Saturday night. They had a card game going on all night long, they had drinking. The sheriff's office looked the other way. It wasn't on the up-and-up in them days."

"Not like now," Susanna said sarcastically.

"Oh, lordy, no. But the guys that came in the Dredge were about five times tougher than what we got passing for deputies at present. Nobody messed with them. And when they messed with each other, look out.

"Anyway, there was this guy named Tharp. He was a whiskey runner. One of the best. Made a good living at it. But he was away a lot, at night. His wife got lonely. Eventually she took up with his best friend, a guy named Turner. Well, one night Tharp found out, of course. He come down to the Dredge and there was Turner, sitting in that corner right over there, playing cards. Turner waved to him. Next thing, Tharp pulled out his gun and shot his friend through the heart. Died on the spot.

"Well, they carted Tharp away, naturally. I think he died in prison after a while. Mrs. Tharp, she couldn't take it. Killed herself. She'd apparently fallen right in love with this guy Turner. She's the ghost. They say that on certain nights you can still hear her. She comes down here and moans, looking for her man. You never heard that story?"

"Never did," Susanna said.

"Well, if you ask me, I don't think there's too many men that're worth that much."

"Especially not around here."

"You can say that again."

"Of course," Susanna said, "that's not to say there might not be some worthwhile strangers in town."

"God, here we go again," Janine said.

"Think what you want, girl. I'm gonna check this one out. Which reminds me, can you help me out?"

"I ain't gonna do your dirty work."

"It's not dirty work, Janine. Can you maybe cover for me on Sunday?"

"Oh, sure. You know I'd do that for you. What's Sunday?"

"He's working on his house," Susanna said. "I'm gonna go over and offer my . . . assistance."

"Susanna, you be careful now, you hear? This is somebody you don't know nothing about."

"Janine, there's times to take it real careful. And there's times you got to get a hold of something. Before it gets away."

"Yeah, but you still don't even know who he is."

"Mmmm-hmmm," Susanna said. She grinned. "I know. Don't you just love it?"

"I give up," Janine said. "Let's finish up and get out of here, girl. You do whatever you want with your life."

They closed the café and went out into the parking lot. Susanna asked Janine if she wanted a lift home.

"Nah, it's nice," Janine said. "I'll walk."

"Okay. See you tomorrow."

Janine headed down Front Street. As she did, an old convertible pulled into the parking lot. There were four boys in it, about Susanna's age. They were drinking from beer cans and a bottle in a brown paper bag. They stopped next to where Susanna was getting into her car.

"Hey, Susie Q," the driver said. He had long blond hair and wore an earring. "How you been?"

Susanna looked at the boys, then turned back to her car without saying anything.

"I been fine too," the driver said. "Why don't you come with us. Have a drink. Have some fun." The other boys laughed.

Susanna turned around again. She sighed. "Look, David," she said, "once upon a time I made the mistake of dating you. I thought it was important to have played fullback on the football team. But I was wrong. It's over. That's all there is to it. I'm not interested in riding with you, or drinking with you, or hanging around with you or any of your friends. Period."

David's face turned serious. "Yeah," he said. "I hear you go for watermen these days."

"Where did you hear that?" Susanna said angrily.

"Oooh," David said, nudging the boy next to him, "touchy subject, eh?"

"I don't have to discuss this with you."

"Nope, you sure don't. He's a tough guy from what I hear. Real tough guy."

"Fuck you, David," Susanna said. She got into her car and slammed the door.

"Sure you won't reconsider?" David yelled.

Susanna started the car and backed out of the parking lot, spewing gravel. She headed fast down Front Street and was soon out of sight.

"Well," David said to his companions, "what do you think? Should we pay this dude a visit?"

"Sure, sure."

"Right."

"Let's do it."

David slipped the car into gear and drove over to Craik's cottage. He parked on the dirt road. The boys got out and strolled into Craik's yard. One of them had a couple of empty beer cans. He dropped some pebbles into each, then threw them up onto the porch, where they bounced and clattered and rolled around noisily before coming to rest.

"Hey!" another of them yelled. "Come on out and have a beer!" They all laughed.

Craik appeared at the door, wearing only a pair of cutoffs. He came out on the porch, scratching at his head.

"Fellas," he said. "Can I do for you?"

David was standing with his arms folded across his chest. His earring glittered occasionally when it caught some stray light from the house. The other three formed a loose semicircle behind their leader. He was still athletic-looking, with just the beginnings of a heavy drinker's paunch.

"Thought we'd see who was living out here," he said. "Heard you was a tough guy. That right?"

"Sorry," Craik said. "You heard wrong."

"Also heard you been nosing around my girlfriend."

"Wrong on both counts. Now, if you don't mind, I had kind of a hard day and I'd like to get some sleep."

"Trouble is," David said, "the guy I heard these things from, he's my best friend. You calling him a liar?"

"Jesus," Craik said wearily.

"What's that?"

"Nothing. Look, I'd offer you a beer if I had one, which I don't. So why don't you come back another time and we'll sit down and have a drink together. Okay?"

"No, it ain't okay," David said. "I hear there's a tough guy in town, I like to find out how tough, you know what I mean?"

He unclipped a length of chain that had been fastened around his waist and shook it out. He moved toward Craik. The others followed a few paces behind, smiling and drinking their beers.

"How tough?" David asked.

Craik didn't say anything. His arms hung loosely at his sides. He rocked up onto the balls of his feet. David stopped about six feet away. He started whipping the chain back and forth, to his side and over his head, until it was just a whirling blur. He flicked it past Craik's face. Craik pulled his head back a couple of inches.

"Know how to handle one of these?" David asked.

"Yeah," Craik said.

David chuckled. "He does," he said to his friends. He kept the chain moving. "Okay, let's see how."

"Please," Craik said, "you're making a mistake."

"Mistake," David said, chuckling again, the others chuckling with him. He took a step forward.

As the chain went up over David's head Craik moved. He spun his body completely around, pivoting on his right foot, then pushed off. He swept his left foot in a high arc that brought it within an inch of David's nose. David fell back involuntarily, the chain winding itself around his arm. When Craik's left foot touched the ground, he pivoted on it, spinning around again, and swept low with his right, catching the side of David's knee. David screamed and crumpled to the ground.

"My leg! He broke my fucking leg!"

His friends stared stupidly. One of them dropped his beer can. Craik looked hard at them. They all took several steps backward. David continued to moan with pain.

Craik knelt beside him and put his hand on the boy's shoulder. "It's not broken," he said. "I didn't kick you hard enough. Knee's just popped out. Here."

He stretched the damaged leg. He put one hand on the knee, the other on David's shinbone. Then he simultaneously pushed and yanked. There was a soft crack.

"Oh, God," David said.

"Better?" Craik said.

David looked at him. "Who the hell *are* you?" he said.

The others had gathered around them. They were nodding seriously. Craik didn't answer. Instead he got up and reached out a hand. He helped David up. David tested the leg out. He was favoring it, but he could walk.

"Next time we'll have that beer," Craik said, and he went back into his house. The four boys stood in the yard, staring after him.

SATURDAY

CHAPTER 11

The morning was humid and there was still no wind. At six o'clock the heat of the day was already beginning to come on. Shields knocked on the door of the cottage. When there was no answer, he banged violently.

"Come on, boy!" he yelled. Then he opened the door and let himself in.

Craik was just coming out of the bedroom. He was in his underwear.

"Lord God, look at this," Shields said. "You look like something ought to be standing on one leg out in the shallows. Well, get with it. We don't join the group, they ain't gonna wait on us."

"What's up?" Craik asked.

"We're going fishing, what the hell else? It ain't been but a few hours, son. Jimmie and Sook's. What you do, forget?"

Craik rubbed the side of his head. "No, I didn't forget. But I don't believe it was settled at that point."

"Hey, you don't want to go, just say so."

"I want to go. Just . . . gimme a minute, will you?"

"I give you one," Shields said.

Craik dressed. He went into the bathroom and turned on the cold spigot. The pipes groaned. The water ran slightly brown. He splashed some on his face, then ducked his head so the water coursed down through his hair. He toweled off briefly.

The two men walked down to the harbor. *Murphy's Law* was tied up at the dock. Craik pulled the mooring lines and they jumped on board. Shields fired up the engine. The air was thick with the smell of salt and diesel fuel. They headed out into the Bay.

"Good day," Shields said. "We'll do good. There's menhaden all over the place. You ever eat a menhaden?"

"No," Craik said.

"That's judgment. It ain't but a trash fish, though I hear there *are* those who been known to eat it. We just sell them for fish meal and oil around here. Bay's full of them, like I said. Getting ready to head into the ocean for the winter.

"You know, there's more of one kind of fish in all the water of the world, and what do you think that one kind is? Menhaden. That's a fact. Some guy from the university told me that, up here studying Bay ecology or some damn thing. I told him, well, sure there is. Least it's true of the Bay. You take a look around in the summer, you'll believe it.

"And I tell you something else. You get them big schools of menhaden, sure enough you get the blues around them like mutts with a bitch in heat. Now that's something to see. Them blues go stone crazy. You fall in with them when they're feeding, they'd tear you to pieces too. Might as well be sharks."

"I used to troll for blues some when I was a kid," Craik said. "They're mean, I'll give you that."

"Where was that?"

"Massachusetts."

"Ain't that much trolling around here. We all do it, from time to time, when the tourists come. A-course, that ain't really fishing. Bunch of cowboys want to go out and drink beer and get their kicks fighting a six-pound fish. It's no fun. Brings in a little money on the side, though. That where you're from, Massatwoshits?"

"Nah," Craik said, "Philly. Originally. I had an uncle up

there I'd see summers sometimes. He was a funny man. He wore this white suit, vest, tie with a stickpin, the whole thing, and he wore them all the time, except when we'd go fishing. Had a little boat with about a ten-horse outboard. We couldn't go out if it was at all rough." He shook his head. "Uncle Rob. I never did find out what he did for a living, but I don't think it was legal. He loved his country, though. He's the one convinced me I ought to join the army."

"You ended up in the service?" Shields asked.

"Uh-huh. I was eighteen years old. It seemed like the thing to do at the time. And it probably was. Kept me out of trouble when trouble was easy to find."

"How come you didn't?"

Craik looked out at the swells rolling slowly under the bow of the boat. "I wound up in analysis work. I didn't like what I was analyzing."

"And then you went to college?" Shields said.

"Yeah. God bless the GI Bill. It looked like a better bet than working for a living. Now I'm not so sure."

"Teach you a lot of shit you're better off not knowing," Shields said.

"They do," Craik said. "I had a good time, though. I was older than most of the guys coming in. It gave me some advantages."

Shields grinned. "That's what I know. Some of them girls, they like an older man."

"That too."

"What'd you study?"

"Engineering."

"'Scuse me, boss. Maybe you better take the wheel here."

Craik laughed. "Not that kind of engineering. Civil."

"What's that?"

"Building roads and bridges, you know."

"You fight pretty good for a damn road builder."

"My neighborhood," Craik said. "They would've eaten Rodney Crowe for a five-minute snack. I wasn't near to the best."

Shields shook his head. "Don't jive me, son. If that were street fighting, you can kiss my ass 'cause I'm the queen of England and all of her daughters."

"I've got good reflexes. And I maybe trained a little bit too. The army. Some on my own. You learn a few moves and you've always got them."

"That kung fu stuff. You know, you even look like that guy. You ain't him, are you?"

"I ain't him," Craik said.

"Well, whatever the hell it is, it works. Man can't ask more than that. You practice it up after you become a civil engineer? Must've looked funny, out on them roads, doing kung fu."

"I kept in shape."

"Who'd you work for?" Shields asked.

"This and that. The government for a while."

"Doing what?"

"Building roads. The government builds a lot of roads."

"Hnnh. You ever been in jail, Craik?"

"No."

"I didn't think so," Shields said. "You ain't got the look of it to you. But I don't know if all you been telling me is from bullshit or what. Don't suppose I care much. I imagine you're gonna say next you're down here because you got bored building roads or somebody's husband come after you with a .44 Magnum."

"I got bored building roads."

"Well, man's got a right to his privacy. He ain't got nothing else, he's at least got that."

"I'm not hiding anything, Brendan," Craik said. "I didn't like what I was doing, and now I'm doing something different. That's really all there is."

"Okay."

Shields snorted and spat on the deck. He squinted out through glass smeared with salt spray. The light off the water was dazzling, but neither of the men was wearing sunglasses.

Shields plucked the CB mike from its slot and said, "Red-Eye, where in the hell are you, anyway?"

There was a pause, and then a voice crackled back at him, "That you, you mick bastard?"

"I don't believe I'll mention what you're kin to," Shields said. "I've got ladies aboard."

"That what you call 'em?" the voice said. "I got you on the screen, if that's you. Swing west a couple of degrees and hold it steady. You'll see us in about five minutes."

Shields changed his heading.

"You ready to learn how to fish?" he asked Craik.

"Sure."

"Nothing to it, really. Just coordinating the boats and the net. You'll pick it up."

Within five minutes the mother boat had appeared. It was more than twice as big as Shields's and had an arrangement of large booms amidships. A third boat, the same size as *Murphy's Law,* was nearby.

"You reckon you might be ready to go, *Murph*?" came the voice over the CB.

"I'm ready if you'll find some damn fish and quit talking about it," Shields growled back.

The mother boat started northward, with the two smaller boats keeping pace.

"This is the boring part," Shields said to Craik. "First we got to find the bastards." He pointed to a man high atop the mast of the mother boat. "That guy's the spotter. When the menhaden shoal up, they're easy to see, but not from down here. Other hand, they're easy to net, but not from a big mother like *Susie B*. She can't maneuver, you see, and besides, it takes two. That's why we got these little ones out here.

"Then again, we need *Susie*'s hold. You hit a big school of menhaden, you ain't fooling around. You can have a hundred thousand fish in there. Or more. Sometimes with blues chasing them every whichaway. Got to have some place to put all them fish. It works out. I like purse seining. I can make a good day's wage without having to bust my butt. A-course, there's also days we go home empty."

"Thought you wasn't gonna make it, *Murph,*" the CB croaked.

"Sorry, *Eight-High,*" Shields said. "Breaking in a new man."

"Hope he's got a good back on him."

"More than that. He's the one did Rodney the other night."

"Oh, ho. See you keep the leash on, eh?"

"Will do." Then, to Craik, "That's Parnell. He'll be working the net with us. He won the damn boat in a poker game, with an eight-high straight. That's how it got its name. Other fella had three kings. He really took to the drink after that. His daughter works with your girlfriend, down at the café there."

"Blond girl?"

"Uh-huh."

"Yeah, I've seen her. Funny-looking nose."

"Guy broke it a few years back. Tried to get cute with her and she wasn't having any, just a kid at the time. But she fought back, so he busted her nose."

"That's a shame," Craik said.

"It happens. She's still a nice girl. Might try my luck, but she don't want no part of no waterman. She'll get her a rich one, I do believe."

There wasn't much to do. *Murphy's Law* and the *Eight-High* followed the *Susie B*. The sun rose higher. As it did, the temperature rose with it. There was a light breeze that didn't do much. The sea even seemed to smell more like rot.

Shields and Craik took turns at the controls. The other might nap or just stare out over the water. There were long stretches of silence and periods of lackadaisical conversation.

"Seem to be a lot of Irishmen around here," Craik said at one point.

"Sure and we are," Shields said. "You got to learn you some Bay history, son. We been fighting the English just like back in the old country. And near as long too.

"It was real bad a hundred years ago. They had an oyster boom like you never seen. Couldn't meet the demand. So

they went to New York and Philadelphia and dug the paddies
out of the slums. Shanghaied them. The truth. That's how the
Shieldses come to the Chesapeake. Drugged and hog-tied up
in some cattle car. Cops didn't care. They were working for
the English. The Holders and their ilk." Shields paused. "No
offense meant."

"I'm not English," Craik said. "I'm from the Philly slums
too."

"I didn't mean that. I meant I wasn't including your
girlfriend."

"She's not my girlfriend. She's just a young kid who thinks
I'm something I'm not. She'll get over it."

"Yeah, sure," Shields said. "Well, those were some wild
days, anyway. They had a full-scale war going on in the Bay.
People couldn't get enough of them oysters, thought it
improved their sex lives or something. So you had boats
coming clear down from New England, not to mention all the
boys out of Virginia and Maryland. Shooting *all* the time. Us
and Maryland never could decide where the damn boundary
was. They'd fire on our boys if they thought we was in their
water and vice versa. Along with that you had the tongers
fighting with the dredgers, and *every*body turned on them
boats from up North.

"They finally did settle the line, and the oysters ain't what
they once was. But I tell you something, a warning shot here
and there, it ain't unheard-of yet."

"I'll keep my guard up," Craik said.

"You don't have to worry. This is Virginia—"

The CB screeched and a voice said, "Crank her up, boys.
They're shoaling."

Shields grabbed the mike. "Where?" he demanded.

"Port side to us. You got a half a mile, but they're headed
due south, right at *Murph*. You better get to it."

"*Eight-High*, come to me," Shields shouted.

"Ten-four."

The *Eight-High* veered away from the mother boat and
raced over to where *Murphy's Law* waited. Shields slung a

couple of tires from the side of his boat so that the two could lay up close by.

"They got the net," Shields said to Craik. "We got to get our end of it. Keep the edges with the corks on it up, the one with the weights down."

Craik nodded. Parnell maneuvered his boat next to Shields's. The two assistants gaffed their boats together. The end of the net was transferred from one to the other.

"See it don't get tangled," Shields said, and he went back to the cabin. "Red-Eye," he called, "what's it look like?"

"I'd drop now," the voice came back, "and start splitting her. You're still head-on."

"Shove us off," Shields yelled as he returned to the deck.

Craik unhooked the two boats, pulled the tires back aboard. The craft drifted slowly apart.

"You take the wheel," Shields said. "When I give you the word, start her due east. Nice and slow."

The school was visible now—a vast sheet of boiling water—whenever the boat rode up on a swell. Seabirds were beginning to arrive, diving at whatever looked small enough to handle. Craik readied himself at the controls.

"Now!" Shields yelled.

Craik turned the wheel east. Simultaneously, the *Eight-High* turned to the west. The purse seine began to unroll over its side. Shields strained to hold his end steady.

"Slower!" he yelled at Craik.

The weighted end of the net sank quickly beneath the surface, the corks marking the barrier it was forming. The boats steadily drew farther apart. Shields had his feet braced against the stern. The mate on the other boat fed out net at a measured pace.

"That's got her," the CB squawked. "Cinch her up."

"Turn it north!" Shields yelled.

Craik followed instructions, keeping a close eye on the compass. The *Eight-High* turned north at the same time. The school of fish could now be seen halfway between them, thrashing the water, heading heedlessly into the trap. A few minutes later Parnell held up a red cloth. Simultaneously, he turned his boat east.

"That's it!" Shields yelled. "Due west! We got 'em!"

Craik brought the boat around. The two converged on each other. They pulled alongside and gaffed again. The net now lay in a circle half a mile in circumference. Within its boundary was a churning muddle of thousands of fish, accompanied by a cloud of screaming seabirds. The noise level was high.

Craik shifted into neutral and went to help. The *Susie B* was steaming hard toward them. Craik and Shields exchanged lines with their opposite numbers. Shields ran his end to a hand winch he'd set up for the purpose.

"Ring line!" he yelled at Craik. "Feed it to me without the rings!"

He began to turn the winch. Aboard the *Eight-High*, Parnell was doing the same. The ring line slid up through the rings. As it did, the seine slowly closed, like a gigantic purse. The fish kept swimming blindly south. By the time they realized their way was blocked, it was too late. The north end of the net had closed, and the bottom of it was rising to the surface. The trap was complete.

Inexorably, the confused fish were forced into an ever smaller area. The *Susie B* came and stood just off the net. The men aboard swung a massive boom out over the side. Suspended beneath the boom was a large-diameter flexible hose. The men waited.

Turning the winch was hot, backbreaking work. Craik and Shields switched off. The net tightened. The birds went into a frenzy as more and more of the fish were driven within inches of the surface. Finally, Shields and Parnell exchanged a signal.

"Okay," Shields said to Craik. He came over and chocked the winch. "Can't tighten her too much," he said. "This many fish and the net'll just break. Now it's their turn." He jerked his thumb at the mother boat.

Craik sat down on the deck, wiping sweat from his face. The men on the *Susie B* lowered the hose into the mass of fish. A high-pressure pump was turned on. Fish began disappearing up the hose.

"Used to been," Shields said to Craik, "they had to dip them out with buckets. I'd say this is one hell of a lot easier."

The two men rested. From time to time, as the school's numbers were depleted, one of them would winch up some more of the ring line. Harvesting the fish was a time-consuming process. It was over an hour before the last of them was safely stowed in the mother ship's hold.

Then came the job of pulling the net back into the *Eight-High*. This was the most physically taxing task of all. The net was wet and heavy, and there were a few scattered fish still in it. The four men worked together, cursing the midday sun and shortage of breeze, until they were done.

When they were finished, they broke out an ice chest full of beer. Parnell took Shields to one side.

"Who is that new boy, anyway?" Parnell asked.

"Damned if I know. But he's a right worker," Shields said. He grinned. "And don't fuck with him."

CHAPTER 12

"Good day," Shields said. "That old boat was so loaded, you could about take a drink of the Bay without bending over. We'll pick up a piece of change for that. We can probably get it tonight if you need it."

Craik shook his head.

Murphy's Law was making a leisurely run back to Brawlton. There was no reason to hurry. They had nothing more to do. All of the fish they'd caught were in the hold of the *Susie B*. The off-loading would be done by machine, and the menhaden would be fully processed before leaving the Virginia shore.

Craik was sprawled on the bench in the cabin. Shields looked down at him.

"You feel it, huh?" he asked.

"Yeah, I feel it," Craik said.

"Them are muscles you don't often use. But you'll get used to it. I mean, as much as you can. It's always gonna be a strain. Makes for a good break from trotlining, though. You gotta consider we laid around most of the day."

"Thanks. I'll mention that to my chiropractor."

"C'mon, Craik. Look at me. I'm twice as old as you, and I ain't got half the body. I'll buy you a beer when we get in."

"I'll pass. I've got to do some painting tomorrow."

"Well, more power to you. If you can raise your arms above your head tomorrow, that'll be going some."

They were cruising south, about a half mile offshore. From there, much of the land gave the illusion of being uninhabited. There were thickets of loblolly pine, often mixed with water oak, stretching right down to the edge of the Bay. Small creeks ended in swampy marshes stalked by the occasional blue heron. Tidal mud flats leaked their pungent odor into the air.

Shields pointed out a deadrise rotting in one of the marshes.

"Shad Peters's boat," he said "When he went down, so did she. I don't believe she give him five minutes' trouble the most of his life, but when he died, they looked at her and she was about soft enough to eat with a soup spoon. Wasn't use to nobody, so they just let her lie. There's those that'll tell you that's the way it ought to be. Maybe so. Me, I figure if someone can get some miles out of *Murph* when I'm gone, then more power to them."

The marshes gave way to a series of waterfront estates. Twenty-room "summer places" with manicured green lawns. Tall cedar or cypress trees standing on carefully raked ground. Freshly painted gazebos. Shingled boat houses. Forty-foot sloops tethered to private docks, with brown-skinned men polishing teak rails and brass fittings.

On one of the docks was a girl dressed in a white knit

blouse, white slacks, and white shoes. She sat with her back up against one of the pilings, reading a book. As the fishing boat passed her in the distance she waved.

"How'd you like to live like that?" Shields asked.

"Don't believe I would," Craik said.

"Well, maybe just try it for a *little* bit."

They passed a collection of stakes sticking up out of the water.

"Pound net," Shields said. "Now that's the way to go. Just drive on out here each day and pick up the fish, easy as you please. Just like it was one of those automatic money windows. A-course, . . . then you got your poles to pay for. You know what the bastards costs?"

Shields pointed the missing index finger at Craik as if it were still there. Craik shook his head.

"Near to ten bucks apiece," Shields went on. "You run a few pound nets, you'll need a couple hundred poles. And once you set them, that's it. You might get two good seasons out of them. That's provided we don't get heavy ice, which'll tear them up good. Boys that run these things, they can't keep a dime in the bank neither way."

"And you can?" Craik said.

Shields grinned. "Well, that's a different story. Damn Shieldses never been nothing but poor. I got a piece of land back in Connemara they tell me I can claim if I want it. Nothing but rocks. Can't even graze a sheep on it. Hell, the Brits'll give back Ulster before I ever see it. But I tell you, you talk about some fishing! Them Irish boys, they was as tough as it gets. They took a few sticks, covered them with canvas, and laid some tar top of that, and that was their boats. That's the truth. They went out in all kind of storms in them little things. Half the time they didn't do nothing but make some widows. Who can blame them for coming to Philadelphia instead?"

Shields snorted and spat. He ran his hand through his tight sand-and-gray curls. He stared out at the water.

"Shit," he said.

Craik pulled the yellow "Cat" cap a little farther down

over his eyes. He leaned his head back against the cabin wall.
For a while neither man spoke.

Murphy's Law plowed through the monotonous, low
afternoon swells. She rounded a headland and turned southwest. In the lee of the bluff was the wide mouth of a
substantial creek. A small skiff was making its way toward
open water, a quarter of a mile from Shields and Craik.
Shields stepped out onto the deck and waved. The man in the
skiff waved back.

Shields returned to the wheel and nudged Craik. He
pointed at the skiff. Craik looked in that direction.

"Bobby Adams," Shields said. "Now there's a crabbing
fool for you. That boy's got the gift of God, I tell you. You
ever want to get on a mess of crabs, all you do is trail that boy
around. But I warn you, you ever run a trotline and he run
one right behind you, if you don't cloud up the water, he'll
pull up twice as many as you. I'll guarantee it. Young as he
is, and he ain't much past twenty, I follow the boy from time
to time. He don't mind. He knows I'm gonna help him out,
whatever I can. Just ain't no sense in bucking a boy's got the
talent. Funny thing is, kid never did learn how to swim."

"Come on," Craik said, "I don't believe that."

"It's a fact. And Bobby ain't the only one. You'd be
surprised how many go out on the water don't know how.
They trust their lives to their boat, but throw them in the
water alone and they're scared stiff. Think if God meant man
to swim, He'd've given him flippers."

The skiff was moving slowly. In its stern were dozens of
crab pots, in stacks as high as their owner. A recreational
powerboat could be seen in the far distance, heading down
the creek. There were another couple of fishing boats in the
vicinity, one working a trotline near the shore, another slowly
heading north.

"Moving his pots, this time of day," Shields continued.
"One good spot to another, for certain. I don't hold with pots
myself. Too damn much trouble. And I know one boy spends
four thousand dollars on some pots in the spring, he'll be
lucky if half of them are left by fall. That don't make sense to

me. Though I will say you can take a gang of crabs with them. And don't Bobby know about that."

"Maybe I should sign on with *him*," Craik said with a smile. "A younger man."

"Don't bother. Bobby's a loner. Always has been and I believe he always will be. Nice kid, but he don't socialize much. Married young to take care of that end of it. You won't never see him at Sook's, or his wife, either. Religious types. I don't knock it, you understand, but if the Lord didn't put us here partways to have fun, then what'd He make all the good stuff for?"

"Beats me," Craik said.

The skiff was now well out into the mouth of the creek. The other three fishing boats were beginning to diverge, according to their particular plans. The powerboat was bearing down on the skiff. It was a sleek fiberglass twenty-footer with two huge outboards booting it along. There were four people in it, two boys and two girls, teenagers. They were running it flat out.

As the pleasure boaters neared the creek's mouth one of the boys tapped the shoulder of the other, who was at the controls. Both were holding beer cans wrapped in foam jackets. The first boy pointed at the skiff. The second boy nodded and turned the boat so that it was headed dead for the skiff's stern. The other three laughed and waved their beers.

At the last minute the boy piloting the boat spun the wheel and heeled it hard over to starboard, so that it nearly stood on edge. The other teenagers shrieked and clung to the rails. The boat tossed up a wave that flew over the side of Adams's skiff, knocking him to the deck, then turned north and headed up the coast as if there were no time left in the world. There were a few moments of the teenagers pointing behind them and laughing before they lost interest. Their attention shifted to whatever lay ahead.

The wake set up by the powerboat had Adams's skiff rolling from side to side. The young man came up fast off the deck. His stacked crab pots were teetering back and forth, the top ones slipping a little more each time. He rushed to the stern. He shoved madly at the pots higher up, trying to balance the stacks.

A wave pitched him sideways, and then the return wave tumbled one of the pots into the creek. Another headed the same way. He lunged for it. The waves shifted, and he slipped on the slick deck and went down. One of the pots toppled onto him, glancing off his head and striking the point of his shoulder. When he got back up, he braced himself against the roll of the boat and reached out, staggering toward the falling pots.

The roll shifted direction again. It was as if there were a hand at the small of his back, giving him a hard shove. He slipped across the deck, cracked his knees on the gunwale, and went over the side. Two pots splashed into the water after him. The skiff continued slowly out into the Bay.

One of the teenagers had seen the man fall overboard. He caught the others' attention. Together they raised their beer cans to the fisherman and drank solemnly. Then they laughed. They turned away and didn't look back again. The skiff was already dwindling to toy size in their wake.

"Jesus Christ!" Shields yelled. He whipped the wheel to starboard and rammed the throttle to full. The diesel whined and smoked as it tried to respond.

Adams's head appeared above the water. He screamed and thrashed his arms. Then he went under again.

Shields tore the CB mike from its mount. It was set to monitor the emergency channel, nine.

"Man overboard!" he shouted into it. "Mouth of Shot Creek! Emergency! Follow *Murph*!"

He repeated the message and people began to respond. The other fishing boats in sight had turned and were now headed for the empty skiff. Shields was wriggling out of his clothes. He opened a cabinet, pulled out a portable megaphone, and shoved it into Craik's hands.

"Somebody go after the skiff," he ordered. "And have them rig draglines. If we get him up within twenty minutes, we can save him. The coast guard monitors the emergency

channel. Get them to have an ambulance waiting in Brawlton."

Shields was hyperventilating as he piloted the boat close to
where it appeared Adams had gone down. He turned slightly
to port and jammed the throttle into neutral. The boat slewed
to a near stop. Shields ran down the deck, leapt onto the
gunwale, and dived into the water.

He was a strong swimmer. He pulled himself across the
flow of the creek until he was about in the middle, then
jackknifed and went under. He stayed down for two minutes,
surfaced, took a deep breath, and went down again.

The other fishing boats converged on the scene. Craik
shouted what had happened over the megaphone, and the
fishermen set to work. They sent Craik to retrieve the skiff
while they readied drags normally used to retrieve lost crab
pots, half a dozen steel tongs lashed to the end of a line.

Craik turned *Murphy's Law* around and pursued the skiff.
It was heading pilotless out into the Bay. It wasn't going very
fast, and seas weren't high, but halting it was still a tricky
job.

Using the amidships controls, Craik brought his boat
abreast of the skiff. It pitched and slewed, steering itself in a
great arc. Craik pulled slightly ahead, then adjusted his speed
to match the other's. The two boats veered toward one
another, collided, and separated. Craik was thrown, fell to
his knees, but righted himself. He steered into the skiff again.

Just before the inevitable contact, Craik slipped his own
engine into neutral. He put one hand on the gunwale and
vaulted into the skiff. He landed solidly, both feet and hands
on the deck. At that moment the boats collided and Craik was
sent sprawling. He rolled with the force of the blow and
quickly regained his feet. Then he went to the skiff's controls.

Once he had command of the skiff, it was a more simple
matter to maneuver it next to Shields's boat, which was
sitting dead in the water. He roped the two boats together and
towed the skiff back to the mouth of the creek.

Shields was still diving. Craik joined the other two boats,
which were standing off during the attempted rescue. Each

time Shields surfaced now, his breath was more labored. Finally he yelled, "Start dragging!" and swam back over the *Murphy's Law.*

Craik pulled him over the side, and he collapsed on the deck, gasping for air.

"Shit!" he said hoarsely. "Son of a bitch! Can't see a fucking thing down there!"

He pushed himself up and took the megaphone away from Craik. He directed the other boats where to begin the drag. Then he rigged a drag of his own and joined the searchers. They set up a pattern, working bayward and outward from each other.

"Come on," Shields muttered. "Ten minutes. Be there, you bastard. *Be there!*"

"Got something!" one of the men yelled.

The others idled their boats while they waited. The man hauled in the line. On the end was a crab pot. The man quickly yanked it aboard and reset the line. They resumed dragging. The minutes passed.

Then Shields said, "Got him."

The boats idled again. Craik and Shields strained against the line, pulling in nearly a hundred feet of it. Adams's body surfaced within fifteen feet of the boat.

"Got him!" Shields yelled.

Together they lifted Adams's limp body over the stern and laid him out on the deck, ripping open his shirt and draining the water from his mouth.

"Brawlton!" Shields shouted at Craik. "Follow the coast, no closer than we were before. Move it!"

Craik went to the cabin, opened the throttle, and turned the boat south.

Shields tilted Adams's head back and began emergency CPR. First he blew two breaths down Adams's throat. Then he placed his hands two fingers width above the sternum and pressed down and released. He did this rhythmically, ten times. Then he forced in two more breaths. He returned to the chest and repeated the pressure. Over and over he did the same thing. Pump the heart, breathe into the lungs. Pump the heart, breathe into the lungs. His eyes glazed over.

Occasionally, he mumbled, "Come on, Bobby. Come on."

It took another half hour to get back to Brawlton. When they arrived at the dock, the ambulance was waiting. One of the EMTs asked Shields if there'd been any response. Shields shook his head numbly.

They hurried Adams into the ambulance. The EMT was already applying electrodes to his chest. The rear door slammed shut and the ambulance tore out of the parking area. Its siren sounded and died in the distance.

Shields sat slumped over, his hands dangling between his knees. Craik put a hand on his shoulder.

"You did what you could," Craik said.

"Bastards," Shields said to the deck. "They better hope I don't find out who they are."

"I'll take the boat home," Craik said.

Murphy's Law slid away from the pier. Craik piloted it out of the harbor to the Pawchunk, then upstream to Shields's house. By the time they got there, Shields was able to help secure the boat for the night.

Craik asked Shields if he wanted company for a while. Shields nodded, and they went inside the fisherman's small house. Without a word Shields went to one of the kitchen cabinets and took out a nearly full bottle of whiskey and two water glasses. He placed the bottle and the glasses on the mangled circular table. He poured himself a full glass and set the bottle down again without replacing the cap. Then he slouched into an overstuffed chair that once had had considerably more stuffing. He lit one of the unfiltered Camels and inhaled the smoke deep into his chest. The inhalation triggered a brief coughing fit.

"There's beer in the fridge," Shields said when he'd recovered.

Craik got himself a beer, pulled a chair near Shields, and sat down. He drained off half the beer, then leaned forward wearily, resting his forearms on his knees.

"It's no good thinking about it," Craik said. "You did all you could."

"I ain't feeling guilty," Shields muttered.

"Maybe they'll bring him around."

Shields shook his head. "Uh-uh," he said. "We was too long in getting him, I know it. The boy's gone."

They were silent for a while, then Craik said, "They'll find out who was in that other boat."

"I don't even much care now," Shields said. "I'm tired, Craik. Christ, I'm tired."

There was another long pause. Shields finished the one glass of whiskey, refilled it, finished that, and refilled it again. He was well into the third when he spoke next.

"If the boy driving that boat would've been on the dock, I'd've killed him," he said. "But the feeling goes. You can't hold on to it for long. Then who can you blame? It ain't some crazy drunken kids in a boat with more motor than they can possibly use. I wish it was, but it ain't. It's the life, Craik. Nothing else but the life. The life ain't good for a whole hell of a lot to begin with, but what good there is, it's damn well going if it ain't already gone. They taken the best out of it a long time ago. All of them bastards you never see, the ones who double your boat insurance every year, the ones who dump their chemical shit into the Bay, the ones who pay nothing for your catch and sit back getting fat off your work. No goddamn sense in it. Bust your ass every day, put your life on the line, freeze your nuts in the winter and fry your brains in the summer, and for what? Banks end up with the money and the good people die. Shit."

Shields's voice had started off angry but steadily lost its energy until it was little more than muttering. Now he brooded into his drink. Craik didn't say anything. From outside came the far-off sprocketing sound of a boat heading farther up the creek. It was moving slowly. It took a long time to pass. Shields nodded his head at something.

The sound of the boat died away. It was replaced by the raucous cawing of a flock of crows. They flew past the window and alighted in a nearby oak. The conversation continued for a while and then, as if having reached an agreement, they took off simultaneously.

"You know," Shields said, "there's some watermen won't put into the Bay if crows fly across their bow on the way out. Most won't go on the water in a boat painted blue. I've known them to turn back for any kind of reason. It's just a part of the way they was raised up. I ain't one to be superstitious myself, but you never know. You never know about death, do you?"

"I used to not want to die young," Craik said. "Then I saw a lot of guys die young. Now I just don't think it makes much difference."

Shields nodded.

"I don't figure you, Craik," he said, eyeing the younger man. "It seems to me you been some places and you done some strange things. You gonna tell me you seen a lot of guys dying young while they built the road. Uh-huh. Must've been one son of a bitch of a road."

"All right," Craik said. "I did some things I'm not particularly proud of, and I don't particularly like talking about them. And I did some things that I was proud of at the time, but I'm not so sure anymore. It's taking me a while to sort it out. It seems stupid now, but one of the reasons I came to the Bay was to get away from having to watch people die senselessly."

Shields chuckled once, without humor. "You are a damn fool, boy," he said, shaking his head.

The whiskey had begun to thicken his speech. He finished his glass and poured another.

"I know that," Craik said.

"I ain't sure you even know how much of one," Shields said. "My daddy went through the ice twenty winters ago. They never even found him. My mama was a beautiful woman, and she managed to get old. But by that time her hands was so twisted up, they weren't good for nothing. When she finally went down, she was crying all the time with the pain."

"I'm sorry," Craik said.

Shields waved his hand violently. "I ain't looking for your pity." He looked Craik in the eye. "Trouble with you is, you got some damn-fool notion about this kind of life and you think it can help you straighten out your own problems, from being in the war or whatever the hell screwed you up, when you don't know the first damn thing about what you're getting into. You don't want to be a waterman. You *can't* want to be a waterman, 'cause you either are one or you ain't. Choosing don't come into it. If it did, probably wouldn't any of us be here."

Craik got up. "I'll go," he said.

Shields stared hard at him for a long moment, then sighed.

"Ah, shit," he said. "Sit down. Ain't no purpose to taking it out on you."

Craik fetched another beer and sat down again.

"When I was a boy," Shields said, "I spent all my time down at that dock. It wasn't like it is now. There was a *lot* of traffic in those days. Damn Holders still controlled it, a-course. The Judge's father founded that business. You think the Judge is a bastard, shoulda seen the old man. Anyone went into competition with *him*, pretty soon they find their buildings burning down. He killed some folks, old man Holder did. Not that it's so much changed now. There's just different ways of killing these days.

"You wouldn't know to look at it, but that dock was a lively place then. When the boats wasn't in, it was mostly us boys and the old-timers. Men wouldn't let us help any kinda way, said a flock of boys was less than useless, and they was about right.

"The old-timers, they was good to us. They work the water all their lives and they can't leave it alone. Come down in the morning and sit on the dock, just to be around it all. If the men come in with a good catch, them old-timers'd be as happy as if they done it theirselves, though they always did have some piece of advice about how to do it better. We didn't care if the men done good or not. Empty boat looked the same as a full one to us."

Shields paused and drank, then continued. "Sound like your all-American childhood?"

"Yeah, kind of," Craik said.

"Well, maybe it were too. I don't have much to compare it with. It seemed good at the time."

"I played a lot of stickball," Craik said. "I could hit three manholes distant, and I was hell at dodging cars."

Shields laughed. "We had a guy here, on the local team, he didn't have but one arm. Lost the other one to the Bay. But he was a player. Center field. When he caught a fly, he had to chuck the ball back up in the air, drop his glove, catch the ball again, and then throw it. It took him about one second, or maybe less. And I tell you, didn't nobody take the extra base on that boy."

"Stickball and fighting," Craik said. "That's all there was. I didn't have the chance to fish except when we went to visit my uncle. I wish I'd done it more."

Shields had become subdued again. "It's fine if you don't have to make your living at it," he said.

"I've seen worse ways."

"Uh-huh. Well, I hope you liked what you seen around here, 'cause you ain't gonna be seeing it much longer."

"Some say the watermen are dying out."

"Watermen ain't dying out, Craik," Shields said, his voice slurring, "they're dead. We're all dead, walking around and going through the motions, dead. Pretending it still makes sense when it don't.

"All that hanging around the dock when I was a kid, you don't see that no more. The life is gone. There just ain't enough left in the Bay to keep it going. We got too many people fishing, too much pollution, and when we do good, they pay us less and raise the price of everything else. Hell, I might as well take up smuggling. There's plenty that have. That's the only way to make it anymore."

He paused to drink deeply, then continued. "You look around," he said, "and where are the kids? You see any? No. They're gone. The kids don't want any part of it, and I don't blame them. They don't want to get worked to death. They want big TVs and video recorders and satellite dishes, and I don't know what-all kinda shit. They want to flip a switch and have it warm in the winter and air-conditioned in the summer. They want to hold out their hands and have someone drop all the goodies right into them. They want to drink their beer and—" He stopped and frowned. Slowly, the frown was replaced by a half smile. "Ah, to hell with it," he said. "Cheers, Craik."

Shields tipped his glass, then drained it. He leaned his head back and closed his eyes. He sighed deeply. Within a few moments he was snoring.

Craik finished his beer.

"Cheers," he said quietly to his partner. Then he walked out of the house and onto the road back to Brawlton.

CHAPTER 13

The young man settled himself comfortably in the leather chair. He removed a silver cigarette case from his inner jacket pocket and took from it a slender brown cigar. He offered one to Judge Holder. The Judge declined. Instead he took a fat cigar of his own from one of the desk drawers. The young man fitted his cigar into an ivory holder and placed the holder between his teeth. He smiled as he did so. The two men lit their cigars at the same time. Both inhaled and blew smoke out into the room. They regarded each other in silence for a few moments.

Then the Judge said, "Speak your piece, son."

"My father has told me of you—" Aldo began, but Holder cut him off.

"Skip the family stuff," he said. "I'm no more a friend of your father's than I am of yours. I've got no use for you or your kin. The only reason I agreed to see you at all is that we got to get some things straight between us."

"We consider it rude to come too quickly to the point, Judge. How about a drink first?"

"This ain't a social call."

"We are sorry that you feel that way. It would be a lot better if we could speak like the good friends I hope we become."

"Bullshit."

Aldo sat calmly, smoking his cigar. He didn't fidget or hurry his words.

"Judge Holder," he said, "you are a businessman. I, my family, we are businessmen too. Our interests are . . . similar, in many ways. We know a great deal about your . . . business, Judge. Perhaps considerably more than you know about us. We realize that it is necessary for you to maintain a . . . low visibility in the business community. It is important for us also. We do not like to draw . . . attention to ourselves. You, of course, are in the same position."

Holder looked amused. "What?" he said. "Are you threatening me?"

"I don't threaten. Let me put it simply. With businesses like ours it can be very advantageous to cooperate with others. Especially when the two are not competitors. Do you see?"

"Tell your father I'm not interested."

"I am here to persuade you that you should be interested."

The Judge shook his head. "Well, I'm not," he said. "And I won't be. Your business, as you call it, is something I will never be involved in. Nor will anyone who works for me. I can't make it any clearer than that."

"Perhaps," Aldo said, "we should discuss the potential benefits."

"No."

"Judge Holder, all that we need is the use of some of your facilities. You don't have to be involved at all. In return for this we are willing to offer a very generous percentage of the profits. And the profits, if I may say so, are substantial. Even to someone like yourself."

"You couldn't pay me enough to do what you do," Holder said. "It's ugly. Money can't change that."

Aldo shrugged. "We are like you," he said. "No worse. We provide for those who want what we have. There is no difference."

"There are differences, but not ones that a little greaser like you is capable of understanding."

Hard lines appeared around Aldo's eyes and at the corners of his mouth.

"Be careful what you say," he said.

Holder chuckled. "Careful? Of what? What do you think, you're the goddamned Cosa Nostra? Hell, the Italians would eat you for breakfast. You're a bunch of third-rate punks who want to buy something that's not for sale. So look somewhere else. I advise you to stick with your own kind."

Aldo's jaw was tight. "Do not insult us," he said evenly. "I am prepared to offer you more than just money."

"Such as?"

"We can assure you that such misfortunes as you have suffered in the past will not occur in the future."

"What the hell does that mean?"

Aldo said nothing. He smoked and glanced around the room.

"What are you offering me," Holder said, "protection? I don't need your goddamned protection." He leveled his forefinger at the younger man. "And let me tell *you* something. If you think you can come into my county without my say-so, you're dead wrong. Try it and you'll be the one looking for protection."

"My family is not going to like this."

"Tough."

"Listen to me, Judge. I come here and I am very polite with you, and I am repaid with threats and insults. We are making you a very good offer. I suggest that you reconsider."

"Reconsider your ass, son."

Aldo got up. "I don't have to take this shit from you," he said.

"Yeah, you do," Holder said. "This is my county and I do what I want here." He took the fat cigar from his mouth and pointed it at Aldo. "What I want now is for you to get out and stay out. Of my house *and* my county. And that goes for your father and all the rest of you greaseballs. Do I make myself clear?"

Aldo leaned forward and rested his hands on Holder's desktop. His face was twisted with suppressed anger. The Judge brought his own right hand up into view. There was a small revolver in it.

"Don't get any ideas," Holder said. He pressed one of the buttons on his phone console and said into the speaker, "Fyke."

"You are making a mistake," Aldo said.

"Not as bad a one as you'll make if I see you around here again."

Deputy Fyke entered.

"See the young gentleman out, Brent," Holder said. "All the way out the gate, if you would."

Fyke swaggered across the room, his hand resting lightly on the butt of his pistol. Aldo didn't look at him. He continued to stare hard at the Judge. Holder smoked his cigar and calmly returned the young man's gaze. Fyke came and stood next to Aldo.

"Good-bye, son," Judge Holder said.

Fyke took Aldo's arm, but Aldo tore it away and turned on him.

"Don't you touch me," he said harshly.

Fyke shrugged and looked at the Judge.

"Just see him out," Holder said. Fyke nodded.

"I will be talking with you again soon," Aldo said to Holder. Then he turned and went out the door, followed closely by Brent Fyke.

"Don't bother," Holder said after him.

When the two men had gone, the Judge pressed a button on

his phone console. Ten seconds later Sheriff Kemp came into the room.

"Sit down, Brace," Judge Holder said, and Kemp did so. "Well, what do you think? You heard the whole thing?"

Kemp nodded. "I think they're serious," he said.

"Shit," Holder said. "What the hell for? They've got to have other ways of moving their stuff."

"I don't know what for. There's something here that they want. It looks like trouble to me."

"You saying you can't handle it?"

"We can handle it, Judge. It might could be messy, though. Might have to go easy for a while."

"Hnnh," Holder said. "What do you think he was talking about? All those vague hints and shit. You think he was talking about Henry Beadle?"

Kemp nodded. "Could be," he said. "The kid was careful. I think he expected you were recording him. They may know about us, but they ain't gonna let us nail them legally."

"Yeah, you're right. Damn thing could go either way. If they knew Beadle worked for me, then they easily might have disappeared the guy. Then again, they might just as easily use him to make me *think* that they did it."

"I don't see as it really matters, Judge."

"Probably not," Holder said. "What do you think they're apt to do next?"

"Well, we don't know because we don't know just how deep interested they are in Dorset County. Sending someone here personally might make you think they're *real* interested. But then, they sent a kid. Would they do that if they was desperate, say? I don't think so. It'd be somebody more important."

"You don't think that Craik is mixed up in this somehow?"

"Nah, I don't. Which don't mean that I trust him."

"All right," Holder said, "let him be. But I don't want that other boy around. Keep your eye on him. If he's not out of the county by tomorrow, see that he leaves. Politely, of course."

"How much do you want me to tell the deputies?" Kemp asked.

"Just enough. Let them know the greaser's threatening their supplemental income. That ought to do it."

Kemp nodded. "Yeah," he said. "That'll get their attention."

"And, Brace, I don't want any of the rest of his goddamn family in my hair, either."

Kemp nodded again.

The young man picked at the lustrous silk shirt that clung to his body in the heat. He fidgeted, turning this way and that, looking out through the clear plastic walls of the telephone booth. From time to time he swore out loud.

Eventually a voice on the other end said, "Aldo?"

"Uncle," Aldo said. "This place is shit. They're a bunch of fucking idiots down here. Small-town hicks that think they're big-time. I can't do nothing with them."

"The man refuses our offer?"

"Yeah, yeah. The scumbag insulted me, insulted the family—"

"You were gentle with him, Aldo?"

"I should've rearranged his pig face. Told me the Italians could eat us for breakfast. The *Italians*! Yeah, I was *gentle* with him. But you're asking a lot of me, Uncle."

"Keep your temper, young man. We're asking a lot of you because we expect a lot of you. You are the heir to the business, and you must learn to conduct yourself like a businessman. You stressed the many aspects of our offer?"

"Uh-huh."

"Good. Let him have some time to think things over. I believe he will see it our way in the end. Give him a day and then approach him again."

"All right," Aldo grumbled. "But I don't like it. He's an

ignorant old man and he doesn't respect us. As long as he doesn't, he ain't gonna change his tune."

"Keep in control, Aldo. Let him stew until tomorrow evening."

"Okay. One day, Uncle. But I tell you, we could save a lotta time. We're gonna wind up doing things my way in the end."

SUNDAY

CHAPTER 14

The wind had shifted around to the southeast. The air was a little cooler but, if anything, more humid. For the first time in a week, there were large fluffy clouds in the sky.

Craik was up early. He did some stretching, then jogged the back roads of Brawlton. When he returned to the cottage, he did a series of isometric and other muscle-toning exercises. He finished his routine with twenty minutes' worth of the slow, ritual movements of t'ai chi.

After a shower and breakfast he was on his front porch, laying some fresh white paint over the clapboard siding. Susanna walked up behind him and cleared her throat. Craik turned.

"Hello," he said.

"Hello, yourself."

She was wearing jeans and a striped man's shirt that reached to her thighs and was crusted with old paint of many colors. Her brown hair was tied back. She held a thick paintbrush in front of her as if presenting arms.

"Ready for action, sir," she said.

Craik smiled. He had on a T-shirt and denim cutoffs with ragged, frayed cuffs. The skin on his arms was a dark reddish-brown that contrasted with the pale gold of the hair that lay against it. His legs were a lighter brown, and his face was just red. There were dots of paint on his body and clothes, including one on the tip of his nose.

"Good," he said, gesturing at the front wall of the house. "Start anywhere."

He handed her a half gallon of paint, a screwdriver, and a wooden stick. She pried the lid off the paint can and stirred it up.

"Believe we're gonna get some rain," she said.

"We could use it."

"Uh-huh. Except that it's likely to be a thunderstorm, and a lot of it will run off. That won't do the crops any good."

She finished preparing the paint, dipped her brush, wiped off the excess, and went to work on the other side of one of the windows from Craik.

"I understand you met my old boyfriend," Susanna said after she'd been to the bucket a couple of times.

"Word gets around," Craik said.

"Small town."

"Well, he doesn't seem to consider your relationship in the past tense."

"It is."

"Okay."

"Anyway, thanks for going easy on him," she said. "He's not a bad guy. He's just got this stupid macho streak to him. He was always the strongest guy in school, fullback on the football team, that kind of thing. Just not a lot upstairs. He wouldn't've been much of a match for you. Anyway, I appreciate what you done."

"Forget it," Craik said.

They painted for a while, then Craik said, "No fresh doughnuts today?"

"Nah. I'm not working. I've got the whole day off." She

glanced over at him, but he was concentrating on the job. "Janine can handle things, and she'll get some help at mealtimes."

"She's the blond girl."

"Yeah. My best friend, really."

"I worked with her father's old boat yesterday," Craik said. "Brendan told me the guy who owns it won it in a poker game."

Susanna shook her head. "Poor Janine," she said. "She's had a hard life and she's a nice kid. Doesn't deserve it. Her mom died about ten years ago, and since then her dad has been pretty heavy into the whiskey. One way or another, he was bound to lose that boat, which they just couldn't afford to do. She has to work in the café or they wouldn't have enough to make it."

She paused, then went on. "It doesn't seem right. I mean, here I am and have always been able to do whatever I want. And I don't even know what I want to do. Janine, all she wants is to be able to go to college and get a good job, and she can't. I wish it was my money instead of Daddy's, then I'd just give it to her."

She shook her hand to emphasize the point, and paint flew off the brush and spattered on the porch floor. Susanna giggled.

" 'Scuse me," she said.

"I don't believe it'll hurt it," Craik said.

"It makes me mad," she continued. "Daddy's got more money than he needs. I don't want to go back to school. So I said, 'Daddy, look, I need some time off from studying, and Janine really wants to get her education, so why don't you take the money you would've spent on me and float her a loan so she can do it? You'd make me happy and her happy and probably yourself happy too.'

"Well, you'd have thought I was asking for money for a dope deal. What's it to him? She'd pay him back, I know she would. But, no, all I get is a lecture on how I should be grateful for the opportunity to attend the *university* and that I better take advantage of it while I can, because it might not always be there for me." She sighed. "Christ Jesus, what a tightwad."

"I'm sorry it didn't work out," Craik said.

"Not as sorry as Janine. I'd already told her I'd see if I could arrange it for her. She got real excited. Then this morning I had to tell her it was no go. She tried not to show it, but she was crushed. It's like I was her last hope. She gets into these depressions where she sees herself trapped at Sandi's for years and years, and it looks like that's all that's ever gonna happen in her life. I worry about her."

"She'll survive."

"Yeah, we'll all *survive*," Susanna said sarcastically. "But is that enough? Is it enough for *you*?"

"Sometimes I think so," Craik said. "Sometimes it seems like a lot."

Susanna looked at him. "You sure are a strange one," she said, shaking her head. "Were you in the war?"

"What war?"

"*The* war," she said with exasperation. "Vietnam, of course."

"I can think of a few others."

"Sure, me too. But that's the last one back. Well, were you?"

Craik continued to paint, examining his work closely as he went. After a while he said, "I was in the army. But I didn't go to Vietnam."

"You ever kill anybody?"

He turned and they looked at each other for a moment. Then he went back to work.

"That's a peculiar question," he said as he slowly, carefully layered paint onto the siding.

"Well," she said, "I seen that you could fight. I just wondered, that's all."

"Do you wish that I had?"

"Now *that's* a peculiar question, if you ask me. Of course I don't wish that you had! What the hell do you think I am?"

"I have very little idea what you are," Craik said neutrally. "Would it change your opinion of me if you found out I'd killed a man?"

"I—I guess so."

"How?"

She paused. "I . . . I don't know," she said. "Come on, you're making me nervous."

"I never killed anybody," Craik said.

They painted in silence for a while. Clouds gave way to bright sunlight, which gave way to clouds again. It was noticeably cooler with the sun obscured.

"I heard you saw Bobby Adams drown yesterday," Susanna said.

"Yes. Some drunk teenagers were responsible."

"Bobby was a nice guy. It's too bad those creeps done that to him. But what he was working at, it could easily have happened another way. A freak wave, anything. That the kind of life you want, Scotty, where you never know what day you're gonna drown?"

"That's the kind of life I've got." He smiled. "And what is this 'Scotty' shit?"

"Oh, I don't know. Doesn't anybody else call you that?"

"No, nobody calls me that. Not since I was a kid."

"Good. I think that's what I'll call you." She looked at him with amusement. "You don't mind, do you?"

"Suit yourself."

There was a pause, then Susanna asked, "You going to the funeral?"

"When is it?"

"Tomorrow," she said. "Over to the Methodist Church. Ten in the morning. The family decided they want to get it over with as soon as possible. I can see that."

A car rolled slowly past on the dirt road. Susanna looked out and saw the sheriff's department cruiser. Deputy Tilghman was driving. He grinned at her, then pointed at the porch and turned to say something to his partner. Deputy Fyke found whatever he'd said very funny. Susanna raised the middle finger of her right hand and waved it at the two men. Tilghman pretended shock, then grinned some more as they drove off.

Susanna stamped her foot. "Bastards," she said. "They come by here a lot?"

Craik shrugged. "Sometimes," he said. "Their boss probably asked them to keep an eye on me. I believe he thinks I'm up to no good in Dorset County."

"And what are you up to?"

Craik shrugged again. He gestured at the siding. "Painting my house, learning to fish."

Susanna sighed. "Bobby Adams dies young," she said, "and scum like that'll outlive us all." She shook her head. "I knew there was a reason I never went to church anymore."

"But you're going tomorrow?"

She nodded. "You too?"

"Yeah," Craik said, "I'll be there. I suppose Brendan will want to do that rather than work."

"Uncle Brendan wouldn't miss it. He taught Bobby a lot, to where Bobby was better at some things than he was. That's one thing about Brendan. He don't hold back. If you go on to outdo him, it don't bother him at all."

There was a pause, then Craik asked, "Why do you call him 'Uncle'?"

"He *is* my uncle. Well, sort of, anyway. He's my Uncle Forrest's half brother."

"He is?"

"You didn't know that, huh? I'm not surprised. Uncle Brendan wouldn't be inclined to talk about it. He doesn't have a whole lot good to say about the Holders."

"He sure doesn't."

"I can't really blame him," Susanna said. "From his point of view we're the bad guys. His mother, Reva, got mixed up with my grandfather—who they all just used to call the Old Man—when she was real young. He was a hell-raiser, and she was too. Anyway, he knocked her up. He wasn't about to marry her because she was from the wrong side of town, and he probably tried to talk her into getting rid of the baby, though it couldn't have been easy in those days. She went ahead and had it. That was Uncle Forrest.

"After the baby was born, the Old Man took custody and put Reva out in the street. He could do that, since he was rich and she was poor, and besides, she was of 'questionable moral character' for having this bastard kid in the first place. And he never spoke to her again or allowed her to see her child. I suppose she might've killed herself, but Tom Shields took her in, and after a while he married her. He was a waterman. So's Brendan, of course, who turned out to be their only son.

"Eventually, the Old Man got legally married and had Stuart—that's my daddy—by his wife. So Brendan's almost as much my uncle as Forrest, isn't he?"

"Well, not exactly," Craik said. "But that's one way of looking at it. And Brendan still carries a grudge against your family?"

"Sure. He *hates* Uncle Forrest," she said. "What it really is, I think, besides the way the Old Man treated his mother, is that Forrest represents the Holder Seafood Company. The Old Man founded it, and he built it into a monopoly. Not just with fish money, I hear. During Prohibition, word is they run whiskey as well. The Old Man got mighty rich.

"Anyway, as far as the fish goes, anybody tried to compete with the company, they had mysterious warehouse fires, stuff like that. A few watermen who sold their catch elsewhere, their boats sank. It wasn't long before the Old Man controlled the business. After that he could do with the watermen pretty much what he wanted. When the Old Man died, the company passed to Uncle Forrest and things didn't change much. Brendan resents that. He blames all the Holders for the situation—except for me, of course—even though Uncle Forrest is the main one. He cut Daddy out of the real running of the company, and most of the money too.

"On top of that, there's the Irish thing. There's still some of that kind of rivalry goes on around the Bay. It's our history. People of English ancestry owned most of the land. The Irish came later as workers, a lot of the time against their will. They were treated like animals. In fact, the watermen as a whole have always been outcasts, which is why they stick so tight together sometimes. Even I was taught that they're crude and dirty and to pretty much stay away from them.

"Being Irish *and* a waterman, that's a double dose of bad habits. They may not be the next thing to slaves anymore, but someone like Uncle Brendan, he'll always feel like the fight goes on and he's got to be part of it.

"Fortunately my parents couldn't keep me from being friends with him."

"He seems fond of you," Craik said.

"Yeah. You two getting along?"

"I think so. You could fill a purse net with what I don't know about fishing. But he's been patient with me and he's a good teacher. I'm picking it up."

"Whew," Susanna said, wiping her arm across her forehead, "how about a break?"

Craik put his paint bucket down. "Okay," he said.

"Water?"

"I've got some beer now, if you'd rather."

"You're on."

"And I think I might have a couple of homemade doughnuts."

Susanna laughed. Craik went inside for a minute and emerged with two cold beers and two doughnuts. He handed a beer to Susanna and they sat down together on the edge of the porch. He tapped one of the doughnuts against a pillar.

"Little past its prime," he said.

"Let's do them, anyway."

He passed one to her. They crunched down on the doughnuts and sipped at the beer.

"You figured out what to do with your life yet?" Craik asked.

Susanna grinned. "No more than you," she said.

"Okay, no further questions. Except, you mind telling me what you're doing here?"

"I'm a nice person." She shrugged. "I see someone needs a little help, I like to give it."

"Girl Scout."

"That's me."

"C'mon, Susanna," Craik said, "the last time somebody said that to me I slapped my wallet, and damned if it wasn't gone."

"You're a hard man, Scotty, you know that? Okay, I suppose I'm waiting for you to ask me out on a date. If it don't mean I'll get old and gray in the process."

"You don't know anything about me."

"Maybe. But I've got a feeling. I trust my feelings."

"Besides which, I'm a lot older than you are."

"So?"

Craik sighed. "Look," he said, "we were talking about the war in Vietnam. You were about ten years old when it ended."

"Eleven."

"All right, eleven. *My* friends had been getting killed over there. It makes a difference."

"Scotty," she said.

"What?"

"Don't be such a stuffed shirt. That's not the way I want to think of you."

She brushed some lint from his shoulder. He finished his beer and crushed the can with his hand. He got up, turned one way and then the other, finally leaned his forearm against one of the pillars.

"Susanna," he said, "I'm not a good person for you. Can you accept that?"

"Uh-uh," she said.

"You don't even like it that much around here. You've told me that."

"Ah, you won't be here all your life."

"But it's what I'm doing. It's what I want right now. That's not going to change."

"I'll adjust."

"Don't be so damned agreeable," he said. "I'm trying to tell you something for your own good—"

"That's what Daddy says when he doesn't mean it."

Craik sighed. "Got a smart answer for everything, don't you?"

Susanna got up and brushed her jeans. "Nope," she said. "But I'll do until you invent some better questions. How about we paint some house?"

Craik went back to the job and began to paint vigorously. Susanna dipped her brush, then set it on the edge of the can. She went over to him and put a hand on his shoulder. He looked down at her and she smiled at him.

"Loosen up, old man," she said.

CHAPTER 15

The Bay View Motel didn't have one. Those who chose to stay there didn't mind. They were sportfishermen who didn't care, or families on a budget, or travelers just passing through and looking for a quiet place to sleep. Business was never brisk, but it was steady enough to keep the place going.

The sheriff's department cruiser stopped at the Bay View toward the end of the day. Deputy Fyke went into the office. Behind the reception desk was a bored young woman watching a small black-and-white TV. She looked up as Fyke came in.

"The answer is no," she said, and returned her attention to a rerun of *Kung Fu*.

Fyke chuckled. "Too bad," he said. "But this is business."

The woman sighed and got out of her chair with seemingly great effort. She came up to the desk.

"Yeah, what is it?" she asked.

"Small problem," he said. "We'll take care of it. You got a guy from out of town staying here. Skinny guy, dark hair, little bitty mustache?"

"Room 12," she said.

"Uh-huh. Well, we have reason to believe that he may be down here for the purpose of selling illegal substances. We need to, ah, have a talk with him."

"Yeah, I'll bet."

"Just wanted to let you know. In case there's any trouble, you understand. We don't want you to be alarmed."

"Kill the son of a bitch if you want to," the woman said without inflection. "I don't give a damn." And she went and slumped back into her TV chair.

"Thanks, hon," Fyke said. "Always nice talking with you."

The woman waved a limp hand. Fyke turned and left the office. He climbed into the car with Deputy Tilghman.

"You score?" Tilghman asked with a grin.

"Shit. That's a real ragbag," Fyke said. "Let's go get the greaser."

They drove to Room 12. It was just another door in the bland brick facade. The curtains were drawn over the one large window.

A man was leaving the next unit down, Room 10. He saw the two deputies getting out of their cruiser and he turned abruptly, went back inside.

Fyke and Tilghman grinned at each other. They went to the door of Room 12 and knocked.

"Yeah," came the voice from inside.

"Police," Fyke said.

Aldo opened the door halfway. He was wearing a salmon silk shirt and tailored black slacks. The shirt was open to his sternum. Tilghman clucked his tongue.

"Mmmm," he said. "Ain't he pretty."

"What do you want?" Aldo said.

"Talk," Fyke said.

Aldo looked suspiciously from one to the other. "I was just going out to dinner," he said. "How about later?"

"Just a little talk," Fyke said. "Won't take long. Invite us in."

Aldo sighed and opened the door wide. He stepped back into the motel room. The deputies entered and closed the door behind them. Tilghman went over and turned the air conditioner fan on high. It made a harsh rattling sound.

"Against the wall," Fyke said. "Spread 'em. I'm sure you know the routine."

Aldo hesitated. Fyke put his hand on the butt of his revolver and gave a little shake of the head. Aldo went to the wall and assumed the proper position. Tilghman went over and began to pat him down. When he reached Aldo's crotch, he gave it a perfunctory squeeze.

"Nope," he said. "Nothing in there."

Fyke laughed. Aldo took a deep breath and let it out slowly. Tilghman quickly finished up the search.

"He's clean," Tilghman said.

"Good thing for him," Fyke said.

Aldo pushed himself away from the wall, but Tilghman put a hand between his shoulders and shoved him back into the frisk position.

"Stay put, boy," Tilghman said.

Aldo remained where he was. Fyke came over and stood with Tilghman, just behind him.

"Understand this dude's trying to cause trouble in Dorset County," Fyke said.

"That's what I hear," Tilghman said.

"Must think us country folk just up and run away, we hear the bad boys from the city coming out. I don't know, you think that's so?"

"Be a mistake if it is." Tilghman pulled on Aldo's shirt and rubbed the fabric between his fingers. "What do you think this stuff is, anyway? Some kind of new polyester? I never seen nothing like it."

Aldo clenched his jaw. "Take your hands off my shirt," he said.

Tilghman let go. "Oops," he said, "pardon me." He brushed the spot he'd been touching.

Aldo tried to turn around, but Fyke slammed him against the wall again.

"Now listen up, son," Fyke said. "You think we're a bunch of ignorant rednecks out here, you're making a big mistake. I don't care how many greaseball assholes you got behind you, you stay out of Dorset County unless you want to learn about fishing from the fish's point of view. How we doing, we understand each other?"

"You're a sack of shit," Aldo said through gritted teeth. "You fuck with me and you're the one making—"

Fyke kidney-punched him, hard. Aldo fell to the floor and curled into a ball. He began to retch but otherwise made no sound. Fyke kicked him on the point of the left shoulder. The arm flopped off to the side and lay limp on the carpet.

"We communicating yet?" Fyke said.

Aldo said nothing. Tears were leaking from the corners of his eyes. He glared up at the two men. Tilghman prodded him with the toe of his shoe. When he uncoiled a little, Fyke kicked him solidly in the stomach. Aldo gasped for breath. It was a few moments before he caught it, then the gasps alternated with the retching. Eventually he vomited on the rug. Not much came up.

"He's right," Tilghman said. "It was dinnertime."

"You ready to eat?" Fyke asked.

Aldo reached for Fyke's leg with his right hand. Fyke stepped on it and twisted his heel. Aldo finally groaned.

Tilghman went to the closet and took out a dark leather suitcase. "Nice," he said. Then he stripped clothes from hangers, pulled them out of dresser drawers. He hummed "This Ain't Dallas" as he worked. He stuffed everything haphazardly into the bag. When he was finished, he had to sit on it to get it properly latched.

"Good job," he said to himself, and patted the suitcase.

Fyke got Aldo under the arms and lifted him gently to his feet. He brushed the silk shirt.

"It's been a pleasure having you visit our county," he said. "But I'm afraid you won't be invited back. We hope that won't be a problem for you."

Aldo looked him in the eye. "You're a dead man," he croaked.

Fyke clucked his tongue. "Such talk," he said.

He held Aldo up with one hand and punched him again in the stomach with the other. Aldo doubled over. In between gasps he began to cough. Fyke straightened him up with a right to the mouth. Aldo's head spun, and a single tooth flew off to the side. Aldo dropped to his knees. He moved his hands around on the carpet as if searching for something.

"You think he's safe to drive?" Tilghman asked.

"I don't know," Fyke said. He reached down and shook Aldo's body. "Yeah, maybe so. He seems loose enough." Then, to Aldo, "You better be careful, though, boy. State cops around here are hell on drunk drivers. You don't want 'em to think that's what you are."

"Let's go, then," Tilghman said.

"Right," Fyke said.

Together they helped Aldo up and walked him to his car, a rented vanilla Ford. They threw the suitcase into the backseat. Aldo was still coughing as he started the engine.

"You better attend to that cough, boy," Fyke said. "Quit smoking or something." He slammed the car door.

" 'Bye, now," Tilghman said. He waved.

Aldo hung on the wheel with one hand as he backed up, turned, and headed out of the parking area.

"You reckon he'll be back?" Fyke asked.

"No way," Tilghman said.

"Yeah, I agree. Well, let's go get something to eat. I got a right appetite on me tonight. All this exercise."

Tilghman grinned. "I suppose you could use some pussy too."

"Yeah, that too."

When Aldo got to the road, he turned west, away from Brawlton. He drove carefully, keeping under the speed limit. He passed through Dorset, then another twelve miles of rural countryside. Finally, he crossed the county line.

The first town he came to in the adjacent county was small. He cruised slowly through it, looking around. He continued on. The next town was more substantial. It had two large, modern motels. Aldo chose one of them and took a suite of rooms. The desk clerk looked at him a little oddly.

"Are you all right, sir?" the man asked.

Aldo fixed him with a cold stare, and the man said nothing more that wasn't related to checking in.

After settling into his room Aldo took a long, very hot bath. He put on clean clothes. Then he went out and found a telephone booth. He called Washington.

"Uncle," he said, and explained what had happened. There was a pause at the other end.

"I kill the son of a bitch," Aldo said. "For my tooth, his life."

"No," his uncle said. "We may need him later."

"Well, do you think they would have done this if they were going to change their mind?"

"No."

"Then we must persuade them in another way."

There was another pause. Then, "Yes," his uncle said. "But do not get carried away, Aldo. The business will be no good to us if it is destroyed."

"Don't worry, Uncle. I will just send the Judge a brief message. Something easy for us. This deputy can wait for later."

"All right. Be sure the message is understood."

"I will. Now, I'm going to need a few things."

"Within reason."

"Some men," Aldo said. "Three or four, at least. I don't want them catching me alone again."

"That can be arranged."

"And a place. I can't work out of a crummy motel room. I want a house. In Dorset County but out of the way, something you can't see from the road. Big enough for me and the men."

"That may take a day or two. I won't be able to talk to any of the local agents until morning. Even then, it'll be a while before we find the right place, set up the rental. Don't count on it until Tuesday night. Can the men stay with you until then?"

"Yeah," Aldo said. He gave the name of the motel. "Look, do whatever you have to, Uncle. Throw people out of their house, bribe them, give them a free vacation, I don't care. But get me something. If the Judge ignores my message, I'm gonna need to be there for the next step."

"Which is what?"

"I don't know yet. I'm thinking about it."

"All right," his uncle said. "The men will be down tomorrow. Anything else?"

"The usual tools, of course."

"Okay. The men will bring them. I want to talk to you twice a day, Aldo. And if you get pulled in, don't say a word. Katz can be there in two hours."

"For chrissake, don't treat me like a child!" Aldo said. "I know what I'm doing!"

"Yes, we hope so."

CHAPTER 16

The first squall had hit right at sunset. The wind had come whipping off the water, driving rain and spray before it. Little of the rain had penetrated the ground. Most of it pooled, then streamed, feeding the creeks, which eventually fed the Bay once again.

The rainfall cut the heat some. But each time it abated a little, steam rose from the hot land. The air was saturated.

Susanna let the red Toyota coast to a stop, engine off, lights out. Rain beat hard on the roof. It sounded like it was made of tin. She opened the door partway, put her head out, then ducked back inside. She sat there, drumming her fingers on the steering wheel, staring at the water coursing down the windshield as if it were spilling over the edge of a dam.

Fifteen minutes passed before the rain backed off a little. Susanna jumped out, closed the door softly, and sprinted through the yard and up onto the porch. The house was dark and silent.

She paused, deliberately bringing her breathing under control. Then she pulled the screen door out. She turned the knob on the inner door and pushed it open, carefully. It made one tiny squeak. Susanna froze, then quickly entered the house, braking the screen door so that it closed without noise and pushing the inner door until it latched with a small click.

Inside, no clock ticked, no appliance hummed. There was only the sound of the wind and the rain. Susanna took a deep breath, exhaled, repeated the action. She slipped out of her shoes. Then she padded softly across the floor to the bedroom door. It was ajar enough to allow her to slip through.

She paused. Again there was only the sound of the wind

and the rain. The interior of the house was still. She breathed deeply again and stepped into the bedroom. The bed was along the far wall. She crept toward it.

A blow from behind sent her sprawling. Her elbow cracked hard against the thin rug on the floor. She yelped. An instant later hands grabbed her roughly and yanked her to her feet. She was slammed against the wall. One hand snatched a fistful of shirtfront and pulled her forward. Another was raised against her as her face came within inches of Craik's.

He stopped. Slowly his striking hand came down. He let go of her shirtfront.

She smiled. "Hi," she said weakly.

"Jesus H. Christ," Craik said.

"You expecting someone?" she asked.

"Susanna, you are a class-one airhead. What in the hell are you doing?"

She cleared her throat. "I thought I'd, ah, surprise you." She reached up and massaged the side of her neck. "But I guess you don't like surprises. You must be a pretty light sleeper."

"Susanna, since I came to this goddamned place, I've had a run-in with the sheriff's deputies, scuffled with some of your high-school chums, and been threatened by the best knife fighter in the county. Now what do you suppose I'm gonna think when someone comes sneaking into my bedroom at night?"

Susanna shrugged. She stood with water still dripping from her hair, looking at the man standing before her in the dark.

"The past three days," Craik said, "I've had to use some muscles I didn't even know I had." He paced back and forth, gesturing. "Tonight all I wanted to do was go to bed early and get some of the sleep I've missed getting up at five in the morning. But no, this demented girl's got to come tiptoeing into my room, after I've *told* her I'm not the sort of person she wants to know." He stopped in front of her. "I could've *killed* you, for chrissake!"

"You wouldn't have," Susanna said.

"How do you know that? How do you know what I might do?"

She moved toward him. "Why don't you kiss me now?" she said.

"Hnnh—"

She put her arms around his waist and rested her head against his shoulder. He was dressed only in his underwear. She nuzzled him, then raised her head. He looked down at her for a long moment. Slowly he bent and kissed her.

They broke apart, then kissed again, this time longer and more deeply. She ran her hands up and down his back, slipped them inside his briefs, and drew him more tightly to her. As she moved against him the sound of her wet clothes against his skin was lost in the wind and the rain, which lashed in gusts at the windows of the cottage.

Janine hesitated in the doorway of Sandi's Café. She was alone. Behind her, the restaurant was dark.

A car pulled into the parking lot and drifted up close to the door. The window on the driver's side rolled down. Deputy Fyke smiled from within.

"Need a lift?" he called out.

Janine looked at him. "No thanks," she said.

"Come on," he said, "it's pouring down rain. You don't have to worry, my buddy Charles is here with me." He leaned back so that she could see Tilghman sitting next to him. Tilghman smiled and waved.

Janine looked away, up at the sky and off to the east. She didn't say anything. She gathered her jacket around her and huddled farther back into the doorway. Five minutes later the rain was coming down as hard as ever. Fyke rolled down the window again.

"For God's sake, Janine," he said. "In a few minutes you could be home dry. Or you can walk and get soaked. Or you can stand around waiting all night. Ain't nobody else gonna come by for you."

She didn't reply. Another fifteen minutes went by. The rain slackened not at all.

"All right," Fyke said. "I ain't got all night, myself. I'll give you a lift or to hell with you."

Janine looked at him for a long moment. He smiled. She looked around at the night, then pulled the jacket up over her head and dashed to the car. She opened the door and slid into the backseat.

"Just take me straight home," she said.

"Sure," Fyke said. "Anything for you. Anything at all."

The car slipped out of the parking lot, bobbing a couple of times and throwing spray as it hit water-filled potholes. It headed west on Front Street.

Three blocks later Janine said, "You missed the turn."

"What turn?" Fyke said.

"The one to my house, you bastard. You turn this car around right now!"

"Damn, but the seeing's poor," Fyke said to his partner. "You catch the turn?"

"Uh-uh. I don't believe we're there yet."

Fyke reached down and flipped a lever. There was a soft thunk as all four doors locked simultaneously. The rear doors had no inside handles.

"God damn you!" Janine yelled.

She threw herself forward, hands outstretched, clawing for Fyke's face. He fishtailed the car onto the road's shoulder. Janine was thrown across the seat into the door. The car lurched to a stop.

Fyke turned and reached into the backseat. He got a grip on Janine's blouse and pulled her toward him. He slapped her hard across the face. Her head snapped back and then forward. She spit at him. He slapped her again, with the back of his hand. Blood began to trickle from her once-broken nose. He raised his hand again.

"More?" he said.

She stared at him, made no movement, said nothing.

"Good," he said, letting her go. She moved as far from him as she could get.

"Where are you taking me?" she said.

The car shivered in a gust of wind. The sound of the rain on the roof was loud and steady.

Fyke smiled. "That's better," he said. "Relax. Enjoy yourself." He nudged the car into gear. "Keep an eye on her, will you, Charles?"

The car started forward. Tilghman turned and rested a heavy arm on the seat back. He watched Janine. She looked out the opposite window, at the night.

A half mile outside of town the car turned off the main road, onto gravel and, after another half mile, onto dirt. It passed through a dense stand of loblolly pine, rain dripping steadily from the trees' needles. The dirt road was muddy and badly potholed, and the car pitched like a boat on the Bay.

They turned onto a track through the woods that opened, after a hundred yards, into a clearing. In the center of the clearing was a wooden building in an advanced state of disrepair. Fyke stopped the car.

"You're gonna have to kill me," Janine said.

Tilghman still watched her, his chin perched on his forearm. Fyke got out of the car, unlocked the rear door, and opened it. He crooked his finger at Janine. She didn't move.

He bent and reached into the backseat. Janine crammed herself into the corner, kicking at him. She landed one kick on his bicep, then he caught her feet and began pulling her. She scrabbled for something to hold on to, but there was nothing. He dragged her across the seat. Her white nylon uniform skirt hiked up to her waist. Tilghman shifted his position for a better view.

With a final pull Fyke yanked her out of the car. She landed on her back in the mud. The breath rushed out of her.

"Why don't you walk, hon?" Fyke said. "It's a whole lot more comfortable."

As soon as she caught her breath, she scuttled away, trying

to get under the car. Fyke reached down and caught one of her arms, then the other. He dragged her to her feet. She twisted and squirmed, kicking wildly. She bent toward his arm but was unable to get her teeth into him. She screamed.

"No one to hear you," he said. "Not with this rain."

He shoved her toward the building. She dug in her heels but it was no use. He stopped just outside the open door, looked her up and down.

"I love the way that wet uniform sticks to your little body," he said. "That really turns me on."

She spit in his face. He laughed.

"Like your spirit," he said. "Always have." And he hauled her inside.

It was a single, dank room, with thick interior posts supporting a roof that leaked in several places. The floor, where it hadn't rotted, was covered with a mixture of straw and dirt.

"Romantic, ain't it?" Fyke said, and he threw Janine down onto the straw.

She pushed herself away from him. He followed her, across the floor, until she ran up against a wall. Desperately, she snatched up a handful of dirt and crammed it into her mouth. He grabbed her and pulled her up, slapping her face. She coughed, expelling the dirt in a moist cloud. She dropped to her knees, still coughing.

Fyke dropped his trousers, got down beside her, and took her wrists. He pushed her backward until she was supine. He waited until the coughing finally subsided, until she lay still as death. Then he lowered his bulk onto her.

She gasped.

As did Susanna, who dug her fingers into Craik's back. His muscles bunched and shifted as she kneaded at them. She arched her own back, and a hoarse croak came from her throat. Craik groaned, and they moved together, like a single dolphin swimming in open water.

The rain continued to come down. Their damp bodies made a smacking sound as they separated. Craik shifted so that his head lay in the crook of Susanna's arm. She ran fingers idly through his hair as his hand wandered in aimless circles over her slick belly and breasts. From time to time she shuddered.

After a while she said, "See? I told you you should listen to me."

"Susanna," Craik said, "what in the hell am I going to do with you?"

"Well," she said, "I've got one idea. First you do this, and then . . . There, you got the idea."

The wind continued to gust, whipping the branches of the live oaks in the yard, occasionally snapping off small ones and driving them against the cottage wall where they rattled like fleshless finger bones. The rain itself had let up. Water dripped steadily from the eaves.

Beneath the leaky roof of the abandoned building lay Janine curled up in the straw. Fyke was standing by the door, smoothing his hair down and adjusting his clothes.

"Been a pretty quiet night," he said. "Me and Charles cruised around a bit. We was together the whole time. Nothing much doing. You understand what I'm saying to you?"

Janine didn't say anything.

"I sure hope you do," he went on. " 'Cause that's the way we're gonna tell it. Anyone speaks out against us, they're gonna have a hard time being believed, you know what I mean? Two officers of the peace and all. And then there's what might happen to their daddies. I wouldn't want anything to come of that. No, I surely wouldn't. I'm sure you'll be acting sensibly there, girl."

Fyke walked back out to his car and got in.

Tilghman grinned. "Anything left for me?" he asked.

"Nope," Fyke said, starting the engine. He slapped

Tilghman lightly on the cheek. "You wouldn't know what to do with a lady like that, anyway."

They drove off. Janine lay for a long while without moving but eventually got to her feet. She took a few unsteady steps. She shivered and clutched her jacket tightly around her, squeezing her chest.

Then she walked purposefully out of the building, leaving a pair of torn white cotton panties in the straw.

The air was thick with moisture. Every now and then there would be a rumble of thunder and lightning would illuminate part of the distant sky. Janine walked steadily. Only three cars passed her. None of them stopped to offer a ride, nor did she solicit one. It took her an hour to get home.

When she arrived, her father was asleep in his frayed blue velour easy chair. The glass on the end table next to him still had an inch of clear liquid in it. Its companion bottle was nearly full. The TV set was on but the sound was off. The picture showed some Americans from the 1950s doing battle with a squad of giant insects. It wasn't going well for the humans.

Will Devereaux came awake when his daughter entered the room. He wet his lips, muttered something, then started coughing. He got hold of his glass and poured the inch of whiskey down his throat. A small amount trickled from the corner of his mouth. He got the coughing under control, filled the glass from the bottle. He turned to Janine.

"Hello, girl," he said. "How you—"

He squinted up at her. His mouth opened slightly, then closed. He clutched the glass of whiskey.

"Jesus God," he said finally. "What happened?"

In a flat, emotionless voice she told him. The whole thing, down to the last car that passed her on the road without stopping. He finished the one glass and reached for the bottle. Janine kicked the end table. It toppled over.

"Dad!" she said. "*Listen* to me!"

He looked at her, then away from her. The bottle rolled across the floor and came to rest next to the couch.

She finished her story and came and sat on the edge of his chair. She said, "What are we going to do?"

"I don't know, sweetheart," he said. "I don't know."

She put her arm around his neck and rested her head on his shoulder.

"Help me, Dad," she said.

Will stared at the soundless, flickering images on the TV. The tide had turned and the giant insects were now in retreat. He wet his lips.

"Janine, there're a lot of things to consider here," he said finally.

She sat suddenly upright on the chair arm. "What are you *talking* about?" she said.

"We're a poor family. There are things that we can do and things we can't do."

"What are you saying?" she said coldly.

"Janine, if we make trouble for folks who can hurt us, then that's what they'll do. We're not doing much better than getting by as it is."

"Make *trouble*? I don't believe you're saying this. Look at me, Dad! I *told* you what he did to me. We've got to do *some*thing!"

"Now calm down, sweetheart—"

"Calm *down*?"

"Things are gonna look a whole lot different in the morning. If you get this man mad at you, he might do something to really hurt you next time."

Janine stood up, her fists clenched. She looked down at her father and spoke, each word pronounced separately and distinctly.

"You—don't—think—he—*hurt*—me?" she said.

"Please, honey," he said, "I know what you been through, but it—"

"No, you don't. No, you goddamned well *don't*!" She whirled and stalked from the room, saying over her shoulder, "If you won't help me, I'll do it alone!"

Will sighed and levered himself up from the chair. He went

over to the couch and retrieved the bottle. He returned to the chair and sank into it, letting his head fall back. He stared at the ceiling for a moment, then poured half a glass of whiskey. He drank.

Janine closed the door to her room and sagged against it. She closed her eyes and stood, motionless, for several minutes. When she opened them, she was looking across the room at the Arctic scene of snow and ice, the poster that read, "The Sound of Silence." She gritted her teeth.

"No," she said softly.

She got some clean clothes and went into the bathroom. She looked at her face in the mirror over the sink. Suddenly she bent over and vomited. When her stomach was empty, she climbed into the shower. She stood under the hot water until it was completely gone, first scrubbing her body and then just letting the spray bounce off her. She dried herself, brushed her hair and teeth, put on her fresh clothes in a deliberate manner.

She went back into her bedroom, got a clean windbreaker, stuffed the filthy nylon uniform into a paper bag, and took it with her. Then she went into her father's bedroom. There was a key ring lying on his dresser top. She took it.

When she passed the door to the living room, Will turned and called to her, "Where are you going?"

"I'm going to do something about it," she said calmly.

"Wait a minute," he said, coming out of his chair, but his feet got tangled and he fell.

She looked at him for a moment, lying on the threadbare rug, then walked out of the house. She got into the nine-year-old Japanese pickup. Its body was pitted with rust and the salt corrosion of the Bay air. She cranked the engine. She cranked it again. It began to rain, hard.

"Come on," she said. "Come on, please."

The engine caught. She backed out of the muddy yard.

When she reached the main road, she turned west, toward Dorset. The rain was coming down in great, wind-whipped torrents. It hammered on the thin sheet metal of the truck and leaked in where the windows no longer sealed. Janine flipped the wipers to the fast position. They still couldn't keep up with it, but she didn't slow down, kept pushing the pickup along at a steady fifty-five. No one else was on the road.

She kept her eyes, unblinking, glued to the highway. Very softly she began to sing to herself, began to sing the refrain from "Never Surrender."

Three miles outside of Brawlton there was an explosion of thunder directly overhead. The windshield wipers strobed in the blinding staccato light, then the night turned dark again. A diamond-shaped yellow sign loomed suddenly, caught for a moment by the pickup's single functioning headlamp.

The yellow sign had a thick black arrow painted on it. The arrow curved sharply to the right. Below, there was a smaller rectangular sign that read,

SAFE SPEED 25.

MONDAY

MONDAY

CHAPTER 17

"It's quieted up," Susanna said.

"Yeah," Craik said.

The storms had passed, and Monday had dawned with a clear sky. The wind had shifted back into the southwest. Puddles were beginning to evaporate. The still air held the promise of yet more heat, more humidity.

Susanna lay on her side, her head propped on her elbow. "How do you feel?" she asked.

Craik shrugged. "Worried," he said.

Susanna laughed. "Why worried?"

"I'm not used to feeling good about much. When I do, it worries me. I start looking for the catch."

"I guess that's about as much of a compliment as I'm going to get."

"Why, do you need compliments?"

"Oh, I don't know," she said. She kissed the tip of his nose. "Let's try: You are very nice lover, Mr. Craik."

"You too."

"A man of few words. You know, you're damn lucky that I pay more attention to actions."

"Uh-huh."

"Speaking of which . . . what exactly *have* you been doing with your life, Scotty?" She was looking down at him. He met her eyes for a moment, then looked up at the ceiling.

"I'm waiting," she said.

Craik didn't say anything.

"Let me put it this way," Susanna said. "Do you think I pick up a lot of strange men and go to bed with them?"

"No, I don't."

Susanna smiled. "Good going, Scotty," she said. "If you'd hesitated a second longer, you'd now have your balls in your hand and they would be hurting."

"Thanks," Craik said. "And I don't make a habit of picking up strange women. So where does that leave us?"

"I don't know about you, but it leaves me thinking I have a right to know a little something about a man I've shared this much with already."

There was a long pause, then Craik said, "Yeah, I suppose you do."

"So why won't you talk to me?"

"It's not you. It's anybody. It's myself too. There are things I haven't been able to come to terms with."

"Come on. Who are you, Scotty?"

Craik laced his fingers behind his head. He continued to stare at the ceiling. "I'm a civil engineer," he said. " 'Least that's what I majored in in college."

"And then what?"

"Then . . . the government recruited me. They were very pleasant. Said there were countries that really needed my expertise. What did I know, I believed them. It sounded good. Travel. See the world at somebody else's expense. All I had to do was show people how to build roads. Only trouble was, some of these places there was guerrilla activity going on, and I'd better get a little *training* first. So what? I was young. That just made it more exciting."

"You *were* a spy," Susanna said.

"No," Craik said. "Not a spy. I was a dumb kid out there building roads and bridges. Then they started asking me to do them little favors. Here and there. Nothing much. And slowly things changed. Before I really knew what had happened, I found myself doing the favors more than I was building the roads."

"Sounds like you were a *very* dumb kid. It took you that long to figure things out? Didn't you read any spy books when you were growing up?"

Craik laughed. "I didn't read, period, until I went in the army," he said. "And then, that was so boring I didn't do much else except read. I spent four years on my butt, educating myself enough so I could go to college."

"So you could become a civil engineer and then a spy. I don't believe this. How were you as James Bond? Were you good?"

"Susanna, trust me, it's not quite as glamorous as you think. But yes, I was very good at what I did. And . . . I enjoyed it."

She searched his face for a long moment, then said, "You told me once—"

"That I'd never killed anyone, and it's true. I never did."

"And now . . . you're here. You quit. You must've."

He nodded. "I quit."

"Why?"

Craik looked up at her. "It's simple but it isn't," he said. "Some things happened that I couldn't live with. And, I don't know, I . . . changed."

"What things?"

He smiled. "I'll tell you, in my time. I will."

He pulled her down to him and they shared a lengthy kiss. Her long hair enclosed his face. Their bodies pressed close together.

When they separated, she sighed and said, "All right. I trust you." She looked into his eyes for a moment, then added, "I hate to say this, but we've got to get moving." She grinned. "And not *that* way."

"The funeral," he said.

"Ten o'clock. I've got to be there."

He rolled himself up to a sitting position and took a long look at her. His eyes traveled up and down her nude body. She smiled and touched her index finger to her slightly pouting lips. He shook his head slowly.

"You don't like?" she said.

"Hardly, my dear. Hardly. Pun intended."

She examined herself. "Yeah, not bad," she said. "I was on the gymnastics team until I was fourteen and I began to fill out. I still practice now and then. I'm in pretty good shape."

"My thoughts exactly."

She reached over and stroked the hard muscles in his chest. Her finger traced the outline of his nipple.

"You ain't so bad yourself, boy," she said.

He smiled and stretched out his hand. "Come on," he said, getting out of bed.

Instead of taking his hand, she rolled in the opposite direction and dropped to the floor. She crouched, pushed herself up into a handstand. Her tanned body formed a graceful, shallow *C*-curve. She walked a short distance on her hands, then tucked and did a forward roll, coming to her feet in a bathing-beauty pose at the bedroom's doorway, her breasts trembling slightly. Craik still stood next to his side of the bed.

"C'mon," she said. "I thought we were in a hurry."

Craik shook his head slowly again.

They showered together. It was awkward in the tiny space that had been curtained off in the ancient clawfoot bathtub, and they laughed a lot. Then Craik fixed breakfast and they ate, not saying much.

"We're going to have to go there directly from here, aren't we?" Craik asked.

"That'd be simplest," Susanna said.

"Well, do you have something to wear?"

"In the car. I brought a little suitcase. Just . . . in case."

Craik laughed. "Remind me never to underestimate you," he said.

"My, you're just full of compliments, ain't ya?"

"I'm afraid I don't have much in the way of clothes. I've got one pair of dark slacks, and I think there's a blue shirt in there. You think that'll be okay?"

"Sure. This is the Bay here. People will appreciate that you come. They don't care what you look like."

They dressed and drove to the church. It was the church near the turnoff that led to Brendan Shields's place. They arrived just before ten.

The streets of Brawlton had been very quiet for a Monday morning. Businesses had delayed their openings. Watermen had taken the day off. The church parking lot was filled with cars and trucks of every description. A large crowd of people was milling around out front. Marla Vickers was there. Most of the crowd that frequented Jimmie and Sook's. The sheriff and his deputies stood stiffly in freshly cleaned and pressed uniforms.

People were talking in low voices. About Bobby Adams; about the senselessness of his death; about the hazards faced by watermen day in and day out, the hazards of nature and of man; about the judgments of the Lord.

"Ah, well," Susanna said, "I guess you'd better meet the folks," and she took his hand and led him over to the middle-aged couple that had been staring fixedly at them since they arrived.

Susanna cleared her throat. "This is Scott Craik," she said. "A friend of mine. Mama and Daddy. Stuart." Holder's expression was stony as he looked at the young man's clothes. He shook hands formally. "And Felicity." She managed a weak smile. She placed her hand in Craik's and then withdrew it.

"Scotty's new in town," Susanna said. "He's been

working with Brendan. He was there when the accident happened."

"Yes, we know," Stuart said. "And where *is* Mr. Shields today? You'd think he'd be here, wouldn't you?"

"He told me he would be," Craik said.

"Well, he isn't."

"He'll show up, Daddy," Susanna said. "I'm sure he will."

"It must have been awful, Mr. . . . Craik," Felicity said.

"Yes, ma'am," Craik said. "Did they find the kids who were responsible?"

"They did," Stuart said. "Damned idiots. But nothing will happen to them, of course. Their parents are big shots down in D.C. They'll have a fancy lawyer, maybe there'll be a little fine and some probation. Sometimes I wish Forrest was still on the bench."

"It was an accident, Mr. Holder," Craik said. "A stupid one, yes, but an accident. I don't think it would do much good to put those kids in jail."

Holder snorted. "No, maybe not," he said. "And it won't help Bobby none. Maybe what we need to do is keep people like that out of our county in the first place."

"Daddy," Susanna said, but people had begun filing into the church.

Holder offered his arm to his wife. "Let's go, Felicity," he said. They went into the chapel. Craik and Susanna hung behind.

"It is odd that Uncle Brendan's not here," she said to him. "And you know who else isn't? Janine. Her father, neither. She wasn't *real* close to Bobby, but still. We're not supposed to open the café till later, so she's not there. I would've thought she'd be here."

"If she's still depressed," Craik said, "maybe a funeral would be too much for her."

"Maybe." Susanna sighed. "Let's go in."

The church was filled with flowers, their scent sweet in the heavy air. Susanna and Craik sat at the back, in two of the last spots available in the jammed pews. The casket lay near the pulpit. It was of dark, polished wood and it was open. Bobby Adams's face was stark white, as if it had never held the blood of life.

A middle-aged man and woman, two boys in their early twenties, and a girl in her late teens knelt near the coffin. The organ music swelled and trailed off and then ceased. When it did, the people next to the coffin got up and walked to seats in the first row.

"Bobby's parents," Susanna whispered to Craik. "His brothers and his wife."

The family settled itself. There was a general rustling as the rest of the crowd did too. Then there was silence except for the slow turning of two large wooden-bladed ceiling fans. A minister walked over to the pulpit.

The minister was about fifty. A large man in a shapeless black robe. One side of his face was seamed and weathered, the other smooth and waxy-looking. The smooth side did not become animated when he spoke.

"My friends," he said. "We are gathered together today to say our last good-bye to Bobby Adams, a young man beloved of us all. A victim, like so many who have followed his way, of the water." The teenage widow began to sob.

"Death must eventually find us all," the minister went on. "Not in our good time but in God's time. We cannot know when it will come, but we can be ready, as I believe Bobby Adams was ready. And I believe that he looks down upon us now with compassion, for he has realized that peace which none of us will know until that day when we join him."

The minister left the pulpit and came down to stand next to the coffin. He gazed at the boy's chalky face.

"I often think of life as a mystery," he said. "The plot twists and turns, and we can never see ahead to find out where it is going. But as each chapter ends, we know more and more about the overall story. We add together all the sidetracks and the false clues and those things that are real, and we just begin to see the plan that the Author had in mind. In this mystery story death is the final resolution. Only then, when we meet the Lord face-to-face, will it all make sense to us.

"It is especially important for us to remember this now. For there are those, and I am one, who have asked in the night: Why? I have prayed and I have asked that of God. Why this young man? Why this tireless worker, this good husband, this man in the youth of his life?

"But God will not answer. He does not choose to reveal His ways to us. He only assures us, through Jesus Christ, that even in this most seemingly cruel of events, there is plan, there is purpose.

"That purpose we must discover for ourselves. Bobby is gone from us but not in spirit. His legacy is one of hard work, of devotion to his family, of kindness to his neighbors. These values cannot ever die. They are what hold us together through the pressures of modern life that constantly threaten to tear our community apart.

"We know these pressures all too well. Our livelihoods are beset by so many forces beyond our control. By the weather, by chemicals dumped into the Bay, by vagrant cycles of nature, by those who determine what we shall earn by our toil. The temptation is great to say, 'I give up. I cannot earn an honest living and so I will turn away. I will turn to a life of sin.' Many of us here today have faced that temptation. I know that Bobby Adams did.

"And how many have been strong enough to say no? How many have been able to say, 'Get thee away from me, Satan?' I know that Bobby Adams was. He leaves that strength behind for us. Whenever that voice of temptation whispers in our ears, and it will, let us think of Bobby. He had made his peace with our way of life, as must we all. Now he is making his peace with his Lord, as we all will. Until that time we could do no better than to let his life stand as an example for each and every one of us.

"Please pray with me now. . . ."

They prayed together. Then there was a long moment of silence. It was broken by the organ. When it began playing, the family got up and slowly filed out of the church. Behind them, someone closed the coffin and draped it with a white cloth trimmed in gold.

The family gathered on the church steps. One by one the mourners were greeted as they left the church. Craik and Susanna were among the first.

Susanna took the older woman's hands in both of hers. "Annie," she said, "I'm sorry."

"Thank you," the woman said.

"This is Mr. Craik," Susanna said.

Annie looked at him. "Yes," she said, "you're the one who helped Brendan try to save him."

"I'm sorry," Craik said.

"Thank you for your effort."

Craik reached out and the two of them embraced. Then he and Susanna went down the steps, and others took their place.

"Do you want to go to the burial?" Craik asked.

Susanna shook her head. "I'm going home," she said. "I'm going to have myself a cry, and then I'm going to put on my uniform and go down and open Sandi's. I think more than a few people will want to stop in for something. Plus I want to find out why Janine didn't show up. What about you?"

"Ditto Brendan. I've got a strange feeling about his not being here."

They stopped at the edge of the gravel parking area and she looked at him for a long moment. "You are that kind of person, aren't you?" she said.

"What kind?"

"The kind that has strange feelings when something is wrong. And you trust those feelings, don't you?"

Craik nodded.

"Because they're usually right, aren't they?"

Craik nodded again.

"You just naturally psychic?"

Craik shrugged. "The kind of things I used to do," he said, "a lot of the time you had to rely on your instincts. Your gut feelings about people. They're like any skills. They can be developed." He paused. "Any questions?"

Susanna smiled. "Just a couple," she said. "But they can wait."

Craik smiled too. "Thanks," he said. "Can I go look for Brendan now?"

"You may."

They looked into each other eyes. Neither made a move until Craik leaned down and kissed her briefly on the lips.

He sighed. "All right," he said. "Come by tonight. If you want to, of course."

"I want to."

They touched hands, and then she walked toward her car. He turned in the other direction.

"Hey," she called after him, "you want a ride?"

"Nah. Don't bother."

Craik walked through the line of cars parked immediately in front of the church. The pallbearers had brought the casket out a side door and were sliding it into the hearse. Their faces were damp with sweat.

Parked first in the line of cars was the sheriff's cruiser. The three uniformed law officers stood next to it. Craik nodded to them as he passed, and they nodded back. They watched him as he crossed the highway and started down the side road. Other people were gathering near their cars, waiting for the funeral procession to begin. Deputy Fyke looked over at the sheriff and cocked his head.

Kemp nodded. "Later," he said.

CHAPTER 18

Craik walked down the tar road, then the gravel, and finally the curving dirt drive. The Dart station wagon was parked in Shields's yard. The front door of the house was open behind its screen. The air was still. There was only the sound of insects and one outboard motor puttering down the Pawchunk. Craik moved slowly, cautiously, looking around and listening.

When he reached the screen door, he paused, listened, then rapped on it. "Brendan," he said.

There was no answer and he repeated himself, more loudly. No answer. He opened the door and stepped into the house's large central room. It was silent. On the battered table was an empty bottle of whiskey, lying on its side. He called for Shields again, but there was no answer.

The door to the bedroom stood ajar. Craik walked over to it and gently pushed it open. Inside there were only two pieces of furniture, an unpainted oak chest of drawers and an enormous brass bed. Shields lay in the center of the bed, his eyes closed and mouth open. He had on trousers and suspenders but no shirt or shoes. Clumps of matted hair stuck out in a variety of directions. He hadn't shaved recently.

Craik moved quickly to the bed. "Jesus Christ," he said to himself. The air was heavy with the smell of whiskey.

"Brendan," Craik said, shaking the sleeping man.

Shields stirred, blindly tried to push the intruder away. Craik continued to shake him. Slowly, with obvious difficul-

215

ty, the older man's eyes came open. He stared, without at first comprehending.

"It's Craik," Craik said.

"Craik."

"Yeah, come on."

Shields blinked a couple of times. "Craik. Shit," he said. "What the hell time is it?"

"After eleven."

"Monday?"

"Uh-huh. The funeral's over."

Shields levered his body into a sitting position and propped himself against two of the brass bars at the head of the bed.

"I'm an asshole," Shields said. He leaned down and plucked a pack of Camels from the floor. There was a book of matches between the cellophane and the pack. He lit a cigarette, blew out the match, and dropped it on the floor. His hands trembled slightly.

"There's time to go to the burial," Craik said. "If you want."

Shields thought about it, then shook his head. "No," he said. "I'd just be an embarrassment. It won't help Bobby none to watch him go into the ground."

Craik sat on the edge of the bed. "What happened?" he asked.

Shields ran his hand through his hair. Some of the tangles began to come apart.

"Hell," he said, "I don't know, Craik. Used to been I could keep a handle on these things. Now, about the last thing I remember is you and me sitting in the other room. What in Christ were we talking about, anyway?"

"Life," Craik said. "Death. Fishing."

"That pretty much covers it, don't it?"

"Not for you."

"Yeah, I guess you got to add in the whiskey there. But I'm Irish. That get me off the hook?"

"No," Craik said.

"I didn't think so. Well, I'm sorry that I missed the funeral. God damn me if it ain't so. I taught that boy a little bit of everything, and then he turned around and taught me back. But he's gone. It was more than I felt up to taking at the time."

"Bobby's gone, but you aren't. If you lost the past two days, you've got a problem."

"You gonna preach me, Craik?"

"Nope. I'm finished." He got up.

Shields looked at him. "Thanks for not," he said. "You're right. I'm an asshole, and if the son of a bitch life don't kill me, then the whiskey will. And I ain't ever sure which is the harder way to go. Want to go fishing?"

"Wrong time of day for crabs," Craik said. "Or so the master says."

Shields grinned. "I don't mean work fishing," he said. "I mean fun fishing."

"Okay."

"I appreciate your coming to get me."

Craik shrugged.

"Okay," Shields said, "let's let it be. Today we relax. Tomorrow morning we get back after them blue-clawed bastards, eh? You still with me?"

"Yeah, I'm still with you."

Shields got unsteadily to his feet. "Just give me a minute to get some water on my face here," he said. "Then we'll go down to the bait house and see can we fix you up with some tackle."

Craik was outfitted, and Shields took him by boat to a small, isolated stretch of sand beach where they cast for rock bass. They cast for a long while and didn't catch anything.

"This time of year," Shields said, "you got to be more lucky than anything else. You get the blues around, a pack of them'll tear up a rock. Damn rock might be five times their size, but they'll just tear it up. Bluefish is about the meanest thing in the Bay. Before they get here, that's when the rock fishing's best."

"When's that?" Craik asked.

"Spring."

"Maybe I'll get to see it."

"Never know," Shields said.

By mid-afternoon they still hadn't caught anything and they gave up. They packed up the tackle. Shields piloted the boat home.

"Bay's a son of a bitch," he said at one point. "Kills us one at a time. But you know, it could kill us all, just like that, if it wanted to. Man from the university told me that. If it rose up thirty feet, that's all, most of Dorset County would be gone. So would Washington, Baltimore, Annapolis, Richmond, and Norfolk. Just thirty feet. If it fell thirty, three-quarters of it would be dry land, and I reckon wouldn't be nothing but farmers left here then.

"And that's the way it was once, man told me. Flat and dry, covered with grass. There was elephants here. And buffalo. And I don't know what all kinds of animals I never heard of. Must've been a sight. Damned if I know where they all went."

"They got extinct," Craik said. "People killed them, some of them."

"Maybe so," Shields said, and he lit another Camel.

When they'd gotten back home and stowed the gear and had a beer together, Shields said, "How about meeting me down at the dock tomorrow morning. Same time?"

"Okay," Craik said.

"Good. Can I give you a lift home?"

Craik got up and stretched. He shook his head. "Think I'll walk. See you later," he said, and he left.

Shields went over to the cabinet and took down a fresh bottle of whiskey. He cracked the seal with his thumbnail and poured himself half a tumblerful. For five minutes he stared at the glass. Then he poured the whiskey back into the bottle, capped it, and put it back in the cabinet.

Craik had made it nearly to Brawlton when the cruiser pulled alongside him. Tilghman rolled down the side window.

"Like a lift, boy?" he asked.

Craik stopped. "Again?" he said.

"That's right."

"I don't need to see the sheriff. I've got nothing to say to the sheriff. If you've got some charge to pick me up on, tell me what it is. Otherwise I'll walk."

"We don't need a charge," Tilghman said.

"Yeah, you do."

"You know, there's got to be a reason why I don't like you so much."

"You can't figure it, perhaps you don't understand the reasoning process," Craik said, and he started away.

"Get in, Craik," Tilghman said. "It ain't the sheriff. Judge Holder wants to see you. You know who he is?"

Craik nodded.

"Good. I wouldn't advise that you have something else you gotta do."

Craik sighed and got into the cruiser.

"That's a good fella," Tilghman said.

Fyke swung a hard U-turn and headed out the Dorset road. He drove four miles, turned north and then up the Judge's private drive. He stopped at the iron gate and announced who they were to the metal box. The cruiser was admitted. Fyke drove it up the hill and parked in the gravel area in front of the mansion. He switched the engine off. It turned over a couple more times, coughed once, and fell silent. Tilghman got out and opened the back door for Craik.

"I get a ride home this time?" Craik asked.

Tilghman chuckled. "You think we'd leave you here alone?" he said.

"No, I don't suppose you would."

"Smart boy," Tilghman said, and he got back into the cruiser. The two men rolled down their windows and settled back into their seats. "Go on, now," Tilghman said, making a brushing motion with his hand.

Craik went up the brick steps. The front door opened before he reached it. Stayne ushered him in and led him to Judge Holder's library.

Holder came around from behind his desk. He took Craik's right hand, put his left on Craik's shoulder.

"Mr. Craik," he said. "I'm glad to meet you. Please sit down." He indicated the leather chair. "And let me get you something to drink. I have some excellent single-malt Scotch." He raised an eyebrow.

"Sure. Fine," Craik said, sitting.

Holder busied himself at the liquor cabinet. "I tend to take it neat," he said, splashing the twelve-year-old whiskey into crystal tumblers. "Why dilute something this good, I say."

"That's fine," Craik said.

The Judge brought Craik his drink and then went back behind the desk. The two men sipped at the whiskey.

"It's very good," Craik said.

"Isn't it? Not that easy to find in this country, either. But I don't like to let small things like that get in the way.

"And so . . . I heard that you were with my . . . brother when that unfortunate young man drowned."

"Yes."

Holder shook his head. "Terrible thing, terrible. But, unfortunately, far too common. One of the risks we take, living on the water."

"I suppose so," Craik said.

"Well, nothing to be done now. I hope that you don't mind my having the deputies bring you here like this. They do me occasional favors. But I did want to meet you. I understand that you and Brendan worked very hard to save the boy."

Craik shrugged. "We tried. But he'd been under too long. Maybe if the hospital had been right there on the river . . . As you say, though, it's over. I doubt that you had the deputies do you the favor so that we could talk about Bobby Adams."

Holder turned his whiskey glass slowly between his fingers and studied Craik.

"You're right," he said finally. "I'm interested in knowing who you are."

"Why?"

"You're unusual. The men who follow the water, ninety-nine point nine percent of the time, they're born to it. People don't just walk in here with the intention of taking it up. It's hard work, it's dangerous, and it doesn't pay shit. The ones who do it, it's because they have no choice. If they end up loving what they do, that's pure chance."

"I'm unusual," Craik said. "Anything else?"

The Judge grinned. He set his glass down, leaned forward onto his forearms, and laced his fingers.

"Craik," he said. "Look at me. I'm getting old. Most everyone around here my age is helping their kids raise up *their* kids. Me, I don't even have any children, much less grandchildren. My wife is deceased. There's almost no one left for me to care about. Except my niece. I love that little girl, Craik, and she seems to be right smitten with you. I'd just like to know what kind of man it is has caught her eye."

Craik sipped some Scotch. "I guess privacy is something you learn to live without around here," he said.

"Son, the whole town knew about you and Susanna before the sheets dried. It don't bother us. But we are wary of strangers. We've learned from a lot of experience that when they come around, the first thing we better do is check our wallets."

"I'm not here to steal your money," Craik said.

"A figure of speech," Holder said. "You're my niece's boyfriend. Don't you want to meet her family?"

"Judge, I think we're getting a little ahead of ourselves here. I'm not your niece's boyfriend."

"Lover, then."

Craik sighed. He started to say something, then stopped himself.

"Craik," Holder said genially, "we're not antagonists. We both care for the same person. We should be friends."

"If that's what happens."

"Don't you think we should make the effort?"

"No, I don't."

Holder leaned back in his chair. "I'm sorry you feel that way," he said.

Craik shrugged.

"I sense a lot in you that is like myself," Holder went on. "You're stubborn. Not afraid to be your own man. You have courage, you perform well in a crisis. You're not worried what other people think of you. I admire those qualities."

"Actually, all I really want is to be left alone."

"I respect that. But life does have a way of intruding itself into our solitude. Everything we do ends up affecting somebody else. Don't you agree?"

"Yes," Craik said.

"I feel that it's a matter of hanging on to your integrity. You can do that by isolating yourself. But that can wind up being the hard way to go. I try to maintain my integrity in the context of how I deal with people, and I think I've succeeded for the most part. There's a good deal of satisfaction in that."

"Everyone does what works best for them. I've had some dealings with people I'd rather forget."

"Yes," Holder said, pointing at Craik and drawing out the word, "I sense that about you. And you give up your thoughts only in your own time. Well . . . I want you to consider me as someone whose door is open to you. Whenever you feel comfortable about it."

"Thanks," Craik said.

Holder pressed a button on the phone console and got up. Craik stood, following suit. The Judge reached across the desk and shook Craik's hand.

"We'll talk again," Holder said.

"Maybe."

"In the meantime, take good care of my niece. She's a hell of a girl." The door to the library opened, and Stayne appeared.

Craik smiled. He set the tumbler on the Judge's desk. "Good Scotch," he said, and he left.

After he'd gone, the Judge poured a little fresh whiskey into his glass and sat quietly behind the desk for a while. Then he opened a drawer and fiddled with the toggle switches. He punched a two-button combination on the console.

The woman's voice said from the phone speaker, "Congressman Mills's office."

"Allie," the Judge said, "it's Forrest Holder. Is Jess around?"

"Just leaving," the woman said. "Hold on."

A moment later Jesse Mills's voice said, "Yeah, Forrest, what is it?"

"You find out anything about that guy yet?"

"Sorry, nothing yet."

"What's the problem?"

"No problem," Mills said. "I've got one of my people working on it. It's just taking awhile. Sometimes my sources are slow. This is Washington, remember?"

"Okay, just checking. I'd like it soon."

"I'll do my best. Give me a day or two."

"Good."

Mills hung up and summoned his aide. The young man in the blue suit came quickly into his office.

"Richards," Mills said, "what's happening on that background I asked you to prepare for me? Scott Craik."

"I'm working on it, sir. But there doesn't appear to be much information to be had about the man. So far our sources have come up, ah, empty."

"Work harder," Mills said. "I want something by Wednesday morning, latest."

"Yes, sir."

The young man went out. As he closed the office door behind him Tilghman opened the rear door of the tan sheriff's department cruiser.

Tilghman bowed slightly and said, "Door-to-door service."

Craik got out. "Thanks," he said.

"Our pleasure," Tilghman said. "Any friend of the Judge's, well . . . better stay a friend of the Judge's." He looked at Craik as if asking a question.

"Uh-huh," Craik said.

He walked past the deputy into his yard. Tilghman got back into the cruiser and Fyke made a U-turn and drove off.

Craik went on into the house. It was quiet. He was heading for the kitchen area when he stopped. He went over to the table. There was a sheet of paper lying on it. The small porcelain vase held the paper down.

Craik picked up the piece of paper. It was a note, which read: "Janine was in a car wreck. I've gone to the hospital. See you tomorrow. S."

He continued on to the refrigerator, took out a bottle of beer, and carried it to the table. He sat in one of the varnished chairs. The note was still in his hand. He set it on the table and looked down at it. It fluttered a little as a random breeze from outside caught it, turning it halfway around. The breeze died. Craik sucked at his beer and stared at the note.

By the time night arrived, the air was perfectly still. It was hot and humid. Insects of the dark made a cacophonous racket while bats swooped down to pick them off. The waning moon rose, a small, sharp crescent.

Brendan Shields was in his living room, napping in the

ratty armchair. A man opened his screen door and stepped into the house. Two other men followed him.

Shields came awake. He rubbed at his eyes, squinted in the direction of the men. The one in front was young and slender and had a pencil mustache. He was wearing charcoal-gray slacks and an almond-colored silk shirt. There was an ugly bruise on his face.

"Who the hell are you?" Shields demanded. "What are you doing in my house?"

The young man smiled. He walked over to where Shields was sitting. The others followed, fanning out on either side of him. They all stopped next to the chair. The young man reached into his pants pocket and took out a silver cigarette case. He opened it, revealing the slim brown cigars, and held it out to Shields.

"Smoke?" he said.

"Get the fuck out of here," Shields said, pushing himself to his feet.

The young man snapped the cigarette case shut and replaced it in his pocket. He clucked his tongue.

"No way to treat a guest," he said, looking at the man to his left. "No way at all."

TUESDAY

TUESDAY

CHAPTER 19

Craik was at the end of the pier at five, leaning his back against a piling, listening to the sounds of watermen making ready for a day of work. Stars still shone in the night sky. There was no breeze, and the moist air had only the slightest chill in it.

" 'Nother calm day," one man was saying. "But I guess that rain'll have muddied things up a bit. I don't like that calm when the water's clear. Damn crabs get as skittish as a colt. You can't get 'em to the net 'fore they're skittering off every kind of way."

"That's so," another agreed. "You go out any yesterday?"

"Naw. Anybody goes out the day another waterman's been put in the ground, he's just asking for trouble. In my opinion."

Out in the harbor a diesel grumbled to life. Its owner raced it in neutral for a moment to clear out the carbon, then dropped it into gear. The long, low deadrise pulled away from its mooring and chugged slowly for the Bay.

Another had his boat alongside the dock and was hunched

over the engine, banging the end of a long-handled screw-driver with a hammer. A battery-operated lantern illuminated the scene with a garish light.

"Son of a bitch," the man said. "You gotta have arms like sticks to get into this motor. Wonder what kind of person made a thing like this. Sure wasn't no waterman."

Two other men idled near the man working on his engine. From time to time they offered him advice.

Finally, the man looked up at them and said, "You know, you try to work on your goddamn motor and the one thing you never, ever lack for is someone to tell you what you're doing wrong."

The two men shrugged and wandered off.

One by one the work boats were coaxed or cursed into action. In a half hour the only people left at the pier were Craik and the man working on his engine.

The sky lightened, and dawn came from the far rim of the Chesapeake. Craik waited for another hour. Then he went over to the other man.

"Excuse me," he said. "You wouldn't have happened to see Brendan Shields last night, would you? I was supposed to meet him here this morning, and I wonder if something might've come up."

The man looked at Craik. "He wasn't at Sook's," he said. "That's all I know." And he went back to his work, banging and prying and swearing.

Craik walked back to his house. He put his lunch into the refrigerator and made himself a cup of coffee. When he'd finished it, he walked out to the main road. He hitched a ride with a woman hauling a pickup load of seaweed for her garden. She dropped him at the turnoff by the Methodist church. He hiked in to Shields's place.

The wagon was placidly going to rust in the front yard. Craik didn't hesitate. He walked right in through the open door, calling his partner's name. There was no answer. He strode into the bedroom. The bed was empty. He came back into the living room and stood with this hands on his hips, looking around.

The house was silent except for a slight drip from the kitchen faucet. The drops of water plinked down into the drain, making a sound like the topmost note on a piano. Craik went over to the sink and tightened the faucet handle. The drip stopped.

Craik went out the back door. He stood in the yard, looking down toward the creek. Its surface was calm, barely rippled. *Murphy's Law* was tied up at Shields's private dock. The water of the creek eddied around it, causing gentle movements up and down, and from side to side.

Craik walked down to the bait house and pulled open the badly hung door. Its hinges shrieked like a cat in heat. A bird flew out, missing Craik's head by inches. He jerked back involuntarily. He looked inside.

Chaos. Poles and nets and oyster tongs and oars and engine parts and motor oil. Stacked steel drums of salted eel. Carpentry tools and rotting cardboard boxes of nails and cans of paint with stirrers stuck to their tops. Greasy rags and wading boots and old boat cushions with wads of kapok sticking out of them. Clamped to a sawhorse, a small outboard with its housing missing and its innards slick with oil. Craik stared for a long moment, then let go of the door. It slapped shut.

He walked out onto the dock and stood next to *Murphy's Law*. Water flowed around the pilings with a slight sucking sound. The scent of the marsh was heavy in the air. Across the creek, a blue heron stood motionless in the shallows, gazing fixedly at the water. Then it struck. Its head bobbed and its beak stabbed at something beneath the surface. It came up empty.

Craik stooped and picked up something that lay at his feet. He dropped it into the palm of his hand and looked at it. It was the butt of a slender cigar with a gold band around its tip.

He sniffed it, looked at it again, then put it in his pants pocket.

Without any preparation he jumped from the dock onto the deck of the work boat, landing in a crouch. He straightened up and walked to the small cabin, looked around, opened compartments, and peered into them. Then he walked down the starboard side of the boat, the side away from the dock, to the stern. When he reached it, he stood for a moment, looking down at the rudder. His head rose and he was gazing across the creek again.

He turned so that he was looking at the port side of the boat. The stern line was securely tethered to one of the pilings. So was the bow line. Amidships there was a third line. It wasn't attached to anything.

Craik walked over to it and looked down. The line dropped over the side and disappeared into the water. He pulled on it. There was resistance. He pulled harder. The wet line came through his hands and curled itself onto the deck of the boat.

From the shadows under the dock the body of a man emerged, floating face downward. Craik pulled hard. The body bumped against the side of the boat. Craik bent over the gunwale and got his hands under the body's arms. He heaved but couldn't raise it.

Keeping the line taut, he rushed to the hand winch and looped the line around it. He cranked. Slowly, feetfirst, the body rose above the level of the gunwale. Craik chocked the line. He went back over, got hold of leg and belt, and dragged the body into the boat. It thudded lifelessly onto the deck.

It was Shields. There were pocks in his skin where the crabs had begun to pick at his flesh.

Craik squatted beside him. For a moment he placed his hand on the older man's brow, then withdrew it. He wrapped his arms around his knees, began rocking rhythmically, back on his heels, then forward, then back again. His head lolled slightly from side to side; the muscles at the corners of his jaw stood out like knots. He stared into Shields's sightless eyes as five minutes became ten. Another boat passed down the Pawchunk, headed for the Bay. Its pilot gave a little toot on his air horn.

Craik began to hum to himself, a song called, "People Get Ready." He closed his eyes and hummed. The rocking slowed, then stopped. He opened his eyes, reached out, and closed Brendan's. He touched the dead man's lips with his forefinger, just for a moment. Then he got to his feet.

He walked until he found a neighbor with a telephone.

There were just the two of them in the office in Dorset. Kemp asked Craik to run through the story with him.

"Not much to tell," Craik said. "I was supposed to meet Brendan at five this morning, down at the pier in Brawlton. We were going crabbing. When he didn't show, I went out to his house. He'd been dead for some time when I got there. That's it."

"When did you last see him?" Kemp asked.

"Yesterday. You saw me at Bobby Adams's funeral. I thought Brendan would be there, too, and he wasn't. So I went over to his house after the services. Brendan was sleeping off a two-day drunk."

"Any reason for the drunk?"

Craik shrugged. "I doubt Brendan needed a reason. But it probably had to do with Bobby's death. The two of them were close, from what I understand. Being there and not being able to save the boy, that must have hurt."

Kemp looked past Craik, toward the far wall behind him. One of the original oil paintings hung on the wall, exactly in the center. It was of an old skipjack dredging for oysters. The men in the boat were dressed in their foulest weather gear. The sky was cloudy, the sea running high. In the background chunks of ice were floating in the Bay. The men hauled on their dredge nevertheless.

"I imagine so," Kemp said. "So he was depressed after

the drowning. Was he still depressed when you found him yesterday?"

"Maybe some," Craik said. "He was coming out of it."

"Were you with him long?"

"We spent part of the afternoon together. Went surf casting."

"How was his mood?"

"The fishing helped. By the time we got back, he was pretty much like I've known him. He was looking forward to getting back to work today. I'm certain of that."

Kemp frowned. "Well," he said, "I'm inclined to believe it was an accident. There's the bump on the back of his head, the line around his leg, and the fact that he was feeling out of sorts over Bobby Adams's death. Looks to me like he got his feet tangled in one of his mooring lines; maybe he still had a little booze in his system or a couple of shots for breakfast. Then he slipped and fell, hit his head, went overboard, and drowned."

Craik shook his head. "It wasn't an accident," he said.

"Oh. Why do you say that?"

"Brendan was too competent around boats. He wouldn't have made that kind of mistake. And he didn't drink before he went out on the Bay."

"I'm not sure *you're* competent to judge the man's abilities, Craik. Let me tell you that it happens to the best of them. When you've been here as long as I have, you've seen it all before. And for damn sure you didn't know Shields well enough to tell me about his drinking habits."

"I still don't see the sequence," Craik said. "Where was he when he fell?"

"Could've been on the dock. Casting off the mooring lines."

"The mooring lines were tied. Bow and stern both."

"The mid-line, of course."

"Uh-uh," Craik said. "Brendan didn't use a mid-line."

"You remember the storm Monday night? He probably tied an extra line for that."

"Nope. When we got back yesterday afternoon, I tied the boat up myself. Bow and stern."

"Christ, I don't know, Craik!" Kemp said with exasperation. "The weather report last night was uncertain. He probably came out to make sure she'd be ready."

"Even so, what happened when he fell?"

"He hit his head."

"Where?"

"Son, *I* don't know where. On one of the pilings, on the edge of the dock, anywhere."

"He hit his head and then somehow fell into the space between the boat and the dock?"

"It looks that way."

"You'd have trouble doing that if you were trying," Craik said.

"Maybe. But it could've happened that way. Actually, it must've."

"It's very farfetched."

"All right," Kemp said wearily, "you're so bright, what do you think happened?"

"I think he had some help."

"You think he was murdered."

"Uh-huh," Craik said. He fished in his pocket and brought out the little stub of a cigar. He dropped it on the desk in front of Kemp.

"What in hell's this?" Kemp said.

"Cigar butt," Craik said. "I found it on the dock this morning."

"So?"

"Brendan didn't smoke baby cigars. He smoked Camels."

"Like I said, so what?"

"So somebody who does was on that dock recently," Craik said patiently.

"Come on, Craik. Who knows how long this thing might've been out there?"

"I do. I sniffed it."

"And you can tell from that?"

"I can tell fresh from stale. Besides which, we know it wasn't there Monday night. It never would have come through the storm in this good a shape. He was asleep until I got there, or he would never have missed the funeral. And then I was with him until mid-afternoon. I don't smoke the things. Therefore it seems logical to assume that whoever dropped it did so between the time I left and the time Brendan died. My guess is that if you find out who that butt belongs to, you've got a suspect."

"Very good, Sherlock," Kemp said. "And how do I know you don't smoke cigars?"

"I'm telling you."

The two men gazed at each other for a long moment, then Kemp said, "Thank you for your help, Mr. Craik. I'm sorry you've lost your partner. But I think you'll discover in the end that it was just an unfortunate accident."

"What does that mean, that you aren't going to investigate?"

"Don't try to tell me my business, son," Kemp said tersely. "Of course, we'll investigate. But it looks to me like an accident, and I don't see much here to change my mind. A used cigar and a lot of conjecture. I doubt that's gonna be enough."

"I see," Craik said. His face was impassive.

"I'm not sure you do. So let me spell it out for you. How we choose to investigate this matter, or *whether* we choose to, that's our business, police business, and only our business. *We* will decide what happened out there. Do I make myself clear?"

"Very."

"Good. 'Preciate your help, like I said. You can go now."

Kemp switched on the brass lamp that sat on his desk. He

opened a drawer and pulled out a sheaf of papers. He began to examine them.

Craik got up. "Sheriff," he said, "if I see anyone smoking that kind of cigar, you want me to report him to you?"

"Sure," the sheriff said without looking up. "Yes, you do that."

"My pleasure," Craik said. "Help the police."

"Don't hang around, son."

Craik left. Kemp shuffled his papers a while longer, then made a phone call. Less than half an hour later he was sitting in the library with Forrest Holder. Holder had the cigar butt. He was rolling it between his fingers.

"That greaser come to see me," Holder said, "he smoked something like this. I can't swear it was the same, but I'd give you damn good odds. I thought Fyke and Tilghman got rid of him."

"They did. I guess he don't scare easy."

The Judge grunted. "What do you think," he said, "he left it on purpose?"

"Might've," Kemp said. "Or at least he didn't care if he picked it up or not."

"Well, we might not be sure about Henry Beadle, but we gotta be sure about this one. I'd say they was trying to tell us something."

"Might's well assume it."

"Can you keep the lid on? About Shields?"

"I think so. He ain't got no kin. Except you. It looks enough like an accident that that's what we can say it was. We put him in the ground as soon as we can. Nobody's gonna think twice about it."

"What about his partner?" Holder asked.

"Craik? Yeah, he might be a problem. He's convinced it was murder."

"He ain't tied up in this some other kinda way, is he?"

"I don't think so. Something about the boy, people just keep dying around him. But I told him certain, leave cop business to the cops."

"I still don't like it, Brace. The guy's got a feel to him, like he knows a lot more than he's letting on. Besides which, he's a fighter. You heard what he did to them friends of Susanna's?" Kemp nodded. "Well, he's had training. That's training there. Now that the D.C. boys have upped the stakes, having this Craik around, too, it makes me nervous."

"You want me to run him?" Kemp asked.

The Judge thought for a moment. "I don't know," he said. "You do this. He shows any further interest in what happened to Brendan, I want to hear about it. Then we'll decide what to do next."

"Okay. And what about the D.C. boys?"

"We can't let them get their hooks into us, you know that." Kemp nodded. "They do, and the operation won't be ours anymore. It's the end of everything we've built up here. Down the goddamn drain. But it looks like they ain't gonna give up. Can we take them on?"

Kemp cocked his head. "I think so," he said. "But I may need more men than're on the payroll."

"That's all right. Whatever you want. It'll have to look legit, though."

"I know. I can create as many special deputies as I want if I feel there's a clear danger. It's gotta look like they took us by surprise and I had no time to call in state help. Damn thing's gonna be messy, no matter what. We may have to shut down the operation until the smoke clears."

"I don't care, as long as we keep those bastards away from it. You got a plan?"

"I don't think one would do us much good. We don't know where they are, how many of them, or what happens next. I'd say we wait. When they show their face, we hit them with everything we've got."

"Do it," the Judge said.

CHAPTER 20

Craik stood in the middle of the living area of his cottage. He was wearing his cutoff jeans. His torso and feet were bare. He stood with hands on hips, looking around.

The area was clean but otherwise looked much as it had when he'd rented it six days earlier. The sofa and the nonmatching overstuffed chair were in the same place. The tassels on the floor lamp's shade still shivered when the evening breeze caught them. The oval, braided rug was no less worn and faded. Even the magazines that Henry Beadle had left behind were where they had been, lying on the low table in front of the couch. Craik had added nothing to the room, nor taken anything away.

He sighed deeply, then went into the bedroom. He took the duffel bag and metallic suitcase from the closet and began to pack his clothes.

From the front of the house there was the sound of the screen door slamming. Craik went out into the living area. Susanna was standing just inside the door. She was wearing jeans and a sleeveless University of Virginia sweatshirt. On the front of the shirt it said: "Go 'Hoos." Susanna's hair needed washing and her eyes were red and puffy. She stood with her arms by her sides, fists clenched. Her body was straight and rigid.

"Susanna," Craik said.

She opened her hands and her body relaxed a little. Slowly, she walked over and put her arms around him. She rested her head against his chest

"Janine's dead," she said softly, and she began to sob.

Craik stroked her hair. They remained that way for a while, until the sobbing began to abate. Then Craik gently guided her to the couch and they sat down, holding each other.

"I'm sorry," he said.

There was a long silence. Finally, Susanna raised herself up and faced Craik.

"I was at the hospital all day," she said haltingly. "She crashed in the rain on Sunday night and she never . . . woke up. I—" Her voice caught. She swallowed heavily and went on. "I never got to talk to her again."

"I'm sorry, Susanna," Craik said, "but there's just not going to be a good time to tell you this. Brendan's dead too."

She stared at him. "What?" she said, her voice barely audible.

"He drowned. Sometime last night or this morning."

"But . . ."

She continued to stare at him, her face a blank mask. Then she got up. She walked slowly around the room. At the dining table she picked up the salt shaker, put it down again. She went to the rear of the kitchen and leaned against the back door, pressing her face against the glass. Craik came up behind her and put his arms around her waist.

"Something to drink?" he said into her ear. She nodded.

He got two beers from the refrigerator and they went back to the couch. Susanna took several swallows of the beer, sat for a moment staring down at the top of the can. Then she looked Craik in the eye.

"I can't cry," she said, her voice flat. "I just can't cry anymore."

"I understand," Craik said.

"I loved Uncle Brendan, but . . . Janine and . . . It's just too much . . . I . . ." She drank some more beer.

"It's all right," Craik said. "I understand."

"Tell me what happened," she said.

"He didn't show up to go crabbing this morning. I went out to his place. I found him in the water, by the boat. His feet were tangled in some ropes and there was a bump on the back of his head."

"He slipped. He fell and hit his head and . . . drowned?"

"That's what the sheriff thinks."

"It doesn't sound like Uncle Brendan."

"Well . . . I don't know," Craik said.

Susanna shook her head. "Janine," she said, "and Bobby and Uncle Brendan. Scotty, what's going on around—"

She was looking past Craik, in the direction of the bedroom. Very deliberately, she set the beer can on the low table and got to her feet. She walked to the bedroom door and stood there, staring. Then she turned and came slowly back until she was standing in front of Craik. She looked down at him. Her face changed from moment to moment as conflicting emotions passed over it.

"You bastard," she said finally, "you're leaving."

"Susanna," Craik said. "Sit down. Please."

"No, I won't sit down!"

She kicked the low table. The beer cans skittered off it. They lay on their sides, their contents foaming into the braided rug.

"My best friend is dead," she said through gritted teeth. "And you know what? There are some very strange things about the way she died. Which you don't even want to hear about! Any more than you want to hear about how your partner *drowned* himself! You're a cold, selfish bastard, Scott Craik."

"Susanna—"

"You know what it is? You really want to know? Huh? *I'll* tell you! You don't want anything to *happen* in your life. Nothing good, nothing bad. *NOTHING!* You hide out here in this shithole, waiting for *nothing!*"

"Susanna—"

"*No!*" she yelled, and threw herself at him.

She slapped him in the face, hard enough to spin his head. When he raised his arms, she balled her fist and hit him in the stomach. The breath went out of him. She clawed at him with her nails. A cut appeared on his forehead, and blood welled out of it.

He got hold of her arms and pinned them to her sides. She continued to squirm and thrash, trying to kick and bite him. Cries of rage and frustration came from the back of her throat. He got a leg over hers to keep them down and held the rest of her at arm's length. She was immobilized. Her cries changed to dry sobs. Eventually, her anger began to subside, and she sat there, helpless, trembling.

"Susanna," he said, "I'm not leaving."

She stared at him, opened her mouth to say something but didn't.

"Please," he said. "Listen to me."

"Let me go."

He released her. She sat quietly, massaging her wrists. "Bring me a drink," she said.

Craik fetched another pair of beers. Susanna drank some of hers, then asked, "Why are you packing?"

"I *was* leaving," Craik said. He sighed and leaned back against the end of the couch. He turned the beer can slowly in his hand. "There are some strange things about Brendan's death too. I didn't want to face them."

"Why?" Susanna said. "Why, Scotty? What are you running from?"

"Susanna, you still don't know very much—"

"I *want* to know, damn you! I want to know everything about you. Is that so hard to understand?"

Craik shook his head. "No," he said. "It's not hard to understand. It's just that I've seen a different side of life than you have. Things have happened to me. Things that I don't even want to come close to, ever again. If I stay around here, there's trouble . . . to be trouble, and for some reason I seem to be in the middle of it. I don't know why. I didn't seek it and I don't want it. It seemed like the best thing for everybody if I just moved on."

"It wouldn't have been best for *me*," Susanna said. "Or for you either. Don't you know that?"

"I realize that now. It just . . . took me awhile."

"I want you to tell me about yourself."

"I'm not sure this is—"

"Yes, it is," she said through gritted teeth. "My life is coming apart, Craik, and you're about all I have. I want to know who you are."

He gazed at her for a long moment, then sighed. "All right," he said. He looked down, toyed with his beer can, then looked up again.

"I was a civil engineer, like I told you. I went to Africa to help some people build some roads, and eventually I ended up doing undercover work for the government. To me it almost looked like an accident, the way I got involved, although they must've had it planned out all along.

"The thing you have to understand is that I'm not really a very political person. Even when I was younger, I wasn't. I didn't get into long political discussions in college, I didn't join any party, I never went out of my way to vote. I believed in some basic way that we were the good guys, but that's about as far as it went. I did ask questions once in a while, later on, when I saw what some of the people I was working with were like. But usually, no.

"As I said, I enjoyed doing something I was good at, and it could be incredibly goddamn exciting. You get swept along, with no time for any doubts."

He paused, drank some beer, then went on. "There are a lot of people out there like me. They spend their whole lives *doing*, without thinking about *what* they do, or about the consequences of their actions." He shrugged. "It's a way to live. It's not even a bad way to live.

"But then some things happened. I was betrayed. I saw

some innocent people die. In a way, I was responsible. I suppose I should have seen it coming, with all the experience I'd had. So maybe I didn't really want to see. Anyway, even before it all fell apart, I'd realized that for the first time I wasn't sure which side I was on. And then people began to die. Too many innocent people. Too much blood.

"I couldn't take it, so I walked away. Now I move around a lot, and one day I washed up here."

"Can you tell me what happened?" Susanna asked.

"Grenada," Craik said. "1983."

"Grenada the island?"

Craik nodded.

"Is 1983 when we went in to . . . rescue those students?"

Craik smiled without humor. "Yeah, to 'rescue the students.' Susanna, that damned invasion was planned two years earlier. We had a full-scale dress rehearsal off Puerto Rico in 1981 and then we just sat around waiting for a good excuse to do it for real. Nobody gave a shit about the students. Hell, the soldiers we sent in didn't even know where the students *were*.

"That was just one of the lies. You wouldn't believe how many people were lying. The President, the military, the State Department. And almost every newspaper in this country printed the lies as if they were truth. Nobody cared, and now everyone's forgotten, except for me. I can't forget."

"You were . . . there?"

"Yes, I was most *definitely* there."

"Why?"

"Supposedly because of my African experience." Craik chuckled humorlessly again. "Looking back, it seems so ridiculous. They said they were sending me down there because it was a black country and I had a special rapport with black people. And I *believed* them. Well, maybe I didn't completely believe them. They also said it was a juicy assignment and that it would advance my career. And they said that, ultimately, I had no choice in the matter. That's where they were posting me next.

"I didn't particularly want to go, but I did. My assignment was to meet with the prime minister, Maurice Bishop. He was supposedly building a military air base, with Cuban help, for the Russians to use to threaten the oil refineries in Trinidad. I was told to dangle some economic incentives and try to get Bishop to turn back toward the U.S."

"Yeah, I remember now," Susanna said. "It wasn't just about the students. It was that airport. And all the Cuban soldiers on the island."

"Right. Well, when I got there I found out there weren't any Cuban soldiers. There were Cubans working on the airport, yes, but they were just construction workers. Like the British and the Canadians and the French who were working with them. And on top of that, it wasn't a military air base, either. Believe me, I know the difference. The Grenadians wanted jets full of tourists to come to their island and spend lots of money, but they didn't have a runway long enough to accommodate a jet. So they were building one.

"When I realized how much I'd been misbriefed, I wondered why. But when I met with the prime minister, I found that he really *did* want a reconciliation with the U.S. And I liked him. Personally, not politically. His goal in life was to help raise his people's standard of living. I couldn't argue with that.

"So I decided the misbriefing was just the usual Cold War rhetoric, and I ignored it. I went to work, trying to do the job I'd been assigned to do. After a while, as I saw the progress we were making, I began to believe. In what we were doing, and in my ability to bring it off. It was a big change for me. Suddenly I was more than I'd ever been before. I was a diplomat, turning around relations between two countries . . . Little did I know."

Craik stared down at the top of his beer can.

"Know what?" Susanna asked.

"I'd been set up from day one," Craik said bitterly. "All that was ever really happening was that I was being used to lead Bishop straight into a trap. Now he's dead. Along with dozens of the friendliest people you'd ever want to meet. I got to . . . love those people." He shook his head. "Pregnant women, kids. The bastards just slaughtered them. It's still hard to even think about." He looked at Susanna. "Did my job well, didn't I?"

"Scott," Susanna said. "God, I'm sorry. I'm sure it wasn't your fault."

"Yeah." He sighed. "Just another blameless tragedy, and a minor one at that. Dead and buried. But do you understand now why I was packing my bags?"

"Yes."

She slid over and put her arms around his neck. She kissed him.

"And I'm sorry I hit you," she said.

"Don't be. I had it coming."

"Truce, okay?"

"Okay."

She detached herself and said, "Now *you* have to understand why we need you here."

"I'm beginning to see," he said. "Janine?"

She nodded. "And unless I'm way out of it, Uncle Brendan too."

"Yes. Brendan too."

She took a deep breath and let it out slowly. "Okay," she said, "Janine. She was my best friend, Scotty. I knew her better than anyone. The way she . . . died, it just doesn't make sense.

"She was at the café Sunday night. Because I was with you, she had to close up by herself. And that's the last anyone seen of her until she crashed her pickup into a tree in the middle of the night. I talked to Will—that's her father—and he told me he'd had a few drinks and fell asleep in front of the

TV and didn't wake up until the hospital called. I don't know if that's the truth. With Will it's hard to tell sometimes. I need to talk to him again.

"Anyway, here's the strange parts. First off, what was Janine doing heading for Dorset that late, in the middle of a storm? I can't imagine. Usually, after work she just goes home and goes to bed.

"Second, she skidded on a bad curve where the speed limit's posted at twenty-five. For dry weather. Janine knew about that curve, and she was a *very* careful driver. But from what the cops told me she had to've been going over fifty when she cracked up. I don't understand that, unless she was really upset about something.

"Third, I knew Janine a long time and she *never* got in a car or a truck without putting on her seat belt. Never. Not once. But she wasn't wearing it Sunday. Why not?"

She looked at Craik questioningly.

"I don't know," he said.

"There ain't no answer. Not now, anyway. But there's gotta be one somewhere, and I'm gonna find it. I ain't gonna let Janine die like that without finding out what happened."

There was a pause. They finished their beers and Susanna got two fresh ones.

"Tell me about Uncle Brendan," she said.

"I saw him yesterday," Craik said. "He didn't come to the funeral because he was sleeping off a drunk. He was depressed over the drowning. I think he blamed himself for not being able to rescue Bobby."

"He couldn't've."

"I know that. But he really cared for the boy. He was bound to take it hard. Anyway, I think he was glad to see me. It got his mind off Bobby and away from the bottle. We went fishing, just pleasure casting for rock bass. When we got back, he seemed in pretty good spirits. I came home. By way of Forrest Holder's house."

"Uncle Forrest? What'd he want?"

"I'm not sure. He was very friendly, but I got the feeling he was mainly interested in sizing me up. Somebody's told him that you and I were seeing each other. He seems very . . . protective of you."

"Yeah," Susanna said, "he would. I think he thinks of me as one of his valuable possessions. He's got everything else in the world, except for a kid."

"After I saw the Judge I came home. Found your note, but there didn't seem to be anything to do about it. And today I already told you about."

"Except what's fishy about it."

"Uh-huh. Well, like you said, it doesn't seem like Brendan to be so careless. It wasn't raining, the dock wasn't slippery or anything. Also, bumps on the head make me suspicious to begin with. I've seen how people usually get them. Also, how did he fall so as to hit his head and then drop between the boat and the dock? I tried to picture it and I can't. And also, I found a cigar butt on the dock. One of those skinny ones, with a gold ring around the tip."

Craik described a circle in the air with his forefinger. "You know? Now, it couldn't have been there before the storm, and I was with him from pretty early yesterday morning until the middle of the afternoon. I don't smoke the things and neither did he. So somebody else was there between when I left and when he drowned. I'd like to know who."

"You think he was murdered," Susanna said.

"I don't know what he was. But I told all this to the sheriff, and it seemed like he couldn't care less. He seemed happy to call it an accident and let it go at that. That's strange behavior for a sheriff."

"He's a strange sheriff."

"Yeah," Craik said. "I noticed."

"He and Uncle Forrest are very close."

"I noticed that too. His goons picked me up when the Judge wanted to see me."

Susanna grimaced. "Don't remind me," she said. "That bastard Fyke was always bothering—"

Craik cut her off. "Don't think about that now," he said. "It won't do any good."

"Sons of bitches supposed to enforce the law," she said bitterly. "They *make* the goddamn law instead."

There was another pause, then Susanna said, "You don't think what happened to Janine and Uncle Brendan could be connected, do you?"

"I try not to think things when I don't know what the hell I'm dealing with," Craik said. "Why don't you tell me whatever you know."

"About what?"

Craik spread his arms. "Brawlton, Dorset County, anything. It's obvious the sheriff and his thugs keep a tight rein on the county. And the sheriff appears to be in Judge Holder's pocket. That might mean that Holder thinks he's the last of the old-time bosses, or it might mean something else. But it does *mean*. How much do you know about what goes on around here?"

"Right now," Susanna said, "less than I wish I did. I know that Uncle Forrest considers it 'his' county. He controls the fishing business, but not the way his father did. The watermen don't hate him like they did the Old Man. He treats them better, I think. They make a living, most of them.

"But he doesn't take any chances. He keeps the sheriff close so that things get run like he likes it. That means there ain't any drugs in Dorset. Then again, stuff like gambling, cockfights, the boys look the other way. If there's something else going on, I don't know about it. Daddy's never talked about anything but the Holder Seafood Company. That's made a good enough living for him, and I would've thought for Uncle Forrest too."

"That may be all there is," Craik said. "But I'm damned if I believe it. If someone killed Brendan Shields, they did it very carefully and for some very good reason. And if the sheriff is covering up, there's a reason for that too."

"What're you gonna do?"

Craik shrugged. "I don't know," he said. "Start poking around. See what happens when I do."

"I'm gonna find out about Janine," Susanna said firmly. "I at least owe her that."

They looked at each other for a long moment. Then Susanna gave him a half smile and put her arms around him. She stroked his naked back. They kissed.

"Can we go to bed now?" she said.

SECOND
WEDNESDAY

CHAPTER 21

At nine in the morning Craik was in the sheriff's department waiting room in Dorset. He was seated on the bench on the visitor's side of the room divider. There were no magazines to read, just the bench along the wall. On the other side of the divider was an obese deputy with a bristle haircut. He made no attempt at conversation.

Craik waited for an hour before Sheriff Kemp arrived. The sheriff acknowledged his presence, then went through the door that led to his office.

The sheriff called him in half an hour later.

"What do you want, Craik?" Kemp said.

"Checking in about my partner," Craik said. "I was wondering if you'd made any progress."

"Yeah. The medical examiner says he suffered a blow to the base of the skull that was nonlethal. Death was due to drowning. Surprise, surprise."

"An accident?"

"I got no reason to believe otherwise."

"You find the guy who smokes those skinny cigars yet?"

Kemp leaned forward. "Look, Craik," he said, "we have our way of doing things around here. They get done. Now me, I'd say you don't have any legitimate interest in this case."

"He was my partner," Craik said. "I'd like to help."

"I don't see no badge on you, son. I don't believe we need your help."

"I was in the army. I did some intelligence work. I might be able to find out some things that a man with a badge wouldn't get."

The sheriff said slowly and evenly, "Craik, I don't want you fucking around with this."

"Well, maybe I'll just ask around a little. Can't hurt. And you never know. If I find the man with the cigars, I'll be in touch."

Craik got up. Kemp looked at him coldly.

"You've been warned," the sheriff said. "Now go home and leave my business to me."

"Thanks, Sheriff. Be seeing you."

When Craik had gone, Kemp picked up the telephone and punched out a number. A moment later he said, "This is Sheriff Kemp. Put the Judge on." He waited, then said, "Judge, we got a problem. I think we best get together. . . . Yeah, that'll be fine. I'll see you then."

He hung up. For a moment he stared at the phone, then he slapped the top of his desk. "Shit!" he said. He got up and went over to the window. He laced his fingers behind his back and stood there, looking out at the sycamore trees.

A half hour later Judge Holder's phone rang.

"Forrest," Jesse Mills said, "I'm afraid I've got some bad news for you. This fellow you're after, I don't think he exists. What the hell's going on, anyway?"

"What do you mean?" Holder asked.

"I mean, the guy doesn't exist. He's got a social security number but nothing in the account. There's no military record, nothing in the FBI files, and he doesn't pay his taxes.

The only other thing we turned up was a New York driver's license, issued two years ago. That's it.

"I think your boy's created himself a new identity. He might be wanted for something somewhere or he might not. He could be running from the government, the mob, a bad marriage, any damn thing. People do it all the time. If he had some cash to begin with, whoever's after him would probably never find him. Care to tell me what your interest is?"

"He showed up around here. I like to keep track of who comes and goes in my county."

"You think he might be into drugs?"

"I don't know what he might be into. What else can you do for me?"

"I could try the DEA," Mills said. "I haven't tried them yet. But a phony name and a description isn't much to go on. How bad do you want to know who he is?"

"I want to know, Jess. I want to know soon."

"Okay. I'll check with the DEA. And I've got a few other strings I still haven't pulled. I want you to know something, though. If I pull them, it's going to cost me a little. You know how the system works here. There's no free lunches. You sure this is important to you?"

"Pull them, Jess," the Judge said. "The son of a bitch is screwing my niece. I want to know who he is."

Mills cleared his throat. "All right," he said. "I'll do what I can. But no promises. If he's good at covering his trail, it may be impossible to track him down."

"I understand that."

"I'll call you tomorrow."

Mills hung up and called in his aide.

"Richards," he said, "I want a deeper look for Craik."

"Yes, sir," Richards said. "The intelligence agencies?"

Mills nodded.

"They may want to know why," Richards said.

"Play it as tight as you can," Mills said. "Call in that favor we have at Langley. Need-to-know is me and you and whoever you're talking to, and that's it. Clear?"

"Yes, sir."

"I want something, Richards. The guy didn't just drop in from Mars."

"No, sir."

"Give it your undivided attention. I'd like a report on my desk by noon tomorrow."

"I'll do my best, sir," Richards said, and he left.

Mills drummed his fingers on his desk. "Try to run a fucking country," he muttered to himself, "and what do you get?" He shook his head and pulled open one of his desk drawers.

Judge Holder did the same. He put a new tape in the recorder, filed the old one away. He fiddled with the toggle switches. Then he went over to the oiled walnut cabinet and got himself two fingers of Glen Calder.

When he returned to his desk, he picked up a small photograph that lay on it. The photo was encased in an antique silver frame. The Judge held his Scotch in one hand and the photo in the other. He stared at it.

It was a backyard barbecue scene. Stuart Holder could be seen in the background, fussing with the grill. Felicity was carrying a platter of meat to him. In the foreground Judge Holder was stretched out on a redwood chaise longue. He held a thirteen- or fourteen-year-old Susanna in his lap. Susanna was planting a kiss on his cheek. The Judge was feigning astonishment.

Holder looked at the photograph for several minutes, slowly sipping at his drink. Then he put the drink down. He took a handkerchief from his breast pocket. Meticulously, he cleaned the glass in the silver frame. He breathed on it and wiped it once more, then replaced it on his desk. He picked up the Scotch.

About noon, Sheriff Kemp arrived.

"Heard anything?" the sheriff asked.

Judge Holder shook his head. "I think they believe they're sweating me," he said. "You got a line on where they might be?"

"Not yet. But they can't hide out forever, not in Dorset County. Somebody'll see them. We'll find them." He sipped the whiskey the Judge had provided him.

"Meantime, we got another problem," Kemp said.

"Craik?"

The sheriff nodded. "He come to see me this morning," he said. "He was right there when I got in. Started bugging me about Brendan's death. What was I doing, had I found out anything, that kind of thing."

"You told him it was an accident?"

"Yeah, but he's a stubborn bastard. He knows it wasn't no accident as well as we do. I believe he means to ride us for I don't know how long."

"You told him to mind his own business?"

"Yeah, sure," Kemp said. "Then he offered to 'help' us in the investigation."

"Doing what?"

"Damned if I know. He said he was in the army and done some intelligence work. Said that not being a cop, he might be able to dig up stuff that we couldn't. I told him to keep his fucking nose where it belonged or he'd regret it. He told me he thought he'd ask a few people some questions, anyway, and he left."

"He wasn't in the army," Holder said. "At least not under the name of Craik."

"How'd you find that out?"

"I talked to Jesse this morning. He's been trying to trace the boy for me. There's nothing on him. No army record, no cop record, no government records, nothing. We got ourselves somebody living under a false name."

"Shit," Kemp said, "that could mean anything."

"Yeah, except that he's probably not a federal agent down here to check us out."

"We can't be sure of that."

"I know. But it ain't likely they'd withhold that information from a U.S. congressman who specifically asked. I think he's something else."

"What?"

The Judge leaned back and put his hands behind his head. "I don't know," he said. "Maybe just a retired drug dealer. Maybe a guy with a wife and three kids back home that he doesn't want to see anymore."

"That don't explain it. Not after the way he handled Rodney and them friends of Susanna's. Plus, I've had the boys keep half an eye on him today. He's doing right what he said he would. Talking to people, friends of Brendan's. He's put his nose in this thing. Don't ask me why, but I don't think he's gonna take it out again until he finds what he's looking for."

Holder sighed. "You're right," he said. "We can't afford to have him here right now. I don't especially want him hanging around my niece, either."

Kemp nodded. "I can understand that," he said.

"Can you get rid of him? Quietly?"

"Sure. I'll talk to him myself. He'll be gone by tomorrow."

"And if he doesn't leave?"

"I think it's worth making sure he leaves. If he doesn't listen to me, he'll listen to Charles and Brent."

"How about Crowe?" the Judge asked.

"What do you mean?"

"I mean that he has a history of involvement with the man. Crowe's likely to be holding a grudge and he's on the payroll. If I tell him the deputies might be needing him, he'll go along. Gladly, I'm sure. They could use his talents, couldn't they?" Kemp nodded. "Give them one more person. This Craik is not to be underestimated, which I'm sure you know by now. And then, if anything should happen to go wrong . . ."

Kemp smiled. "Fyke and Tilghman'd have someone to arrest," he said.

"Crowe's useful," Holder said, "but not indispensable."

"Done. Though it'd be a damn sight better if Craik leaves without a fuss."

"Uh-huh," the Judge said.

Not long after Kemp had left, the telephone rang once again.

"You get my message, Judge?" the voice asked.

"I don't speak with people who don't identify themselves," Holder said.

"You know who this is."

"We have nothing further to discuss."

"Yeah, we do. We're getting a little impatient with you, Judge. I think it's time we got together and worked some things out."

"Don't bother," Holder said. "I'm not interested."

"You should be. Accidents have a way of happening closest to home."

"What are you talking about?"

"But who could be closer than a brother?"

"What—"

"Think about it. I'll call you tomorrow, Judge. Better change your mind by then."

"Where are you?"

"You don't need to know that. Tomorrow, Judge."

"Listen, you little greaser—" Holder said, but the line had gone dead.

CHAPTER 22

Marla Vickers was on the porch of the neat white house with the shiplap siding. She was in her bentwood rocker, dressed in bib overalls and a short-sleeved plaid shirt. The brown-and-white dog was asleep next to her. The short, stubby pipe protruded from her mouth. She sucked and blew smoke, sucked and blew smoke.

Craik came walking down the road and turned into her yard. The dog raised its head, eyed the visitor for a moment, then went back to sleep. Craik stepped onto the porch.

"Mind if I join you?" he asked.

"Long as your looks don't do you no harm," Vickers said, "you're welcome here."

Craik grinned. "Thanks," he said, and sat on the stoop. He wiped his face with his T-shirt. It was getting on toward dusk, but it was still hot.

They were silent for a while, then Vickers said, "Gonna miss Brendan."

"Yeah."

"Heard you found him."

"Uh-huh. What else did you hear?"

Vickers tapped the pipe on her false leg. A lump of ash fell out. There was a small live coal mixed in with it. Vickers ground the ash with her foot until the coal was out. She reloaded the pipe and got it going again.

"Not much," she said. "Heard he fell and hit his head and drowned."

Craik looked up at her. "Marla," he said, "it's a load of crap. It wasn't an accident and it never will be."

"Figured as much. Brendan might've drank too much, but one thing he never was, drunk or sober, was clumsy. He could keep his feet in the middle of a winter northwester. So what happened?"

"I don't know. I talked to the sheriff. He thinks it was an accident. He wants it to be an accident. I told him it didn't look that way to me, and he warned me to mind my own business. He's obviously got some reason for getting Brendan into the ground as soon as possible and forgetting the whole thing."

Vickers nodded noncommittally. "Could be."

"Today I went back to see the sheriff again," Craik went

on. "I asked him about the cigar butt. I found one of those skinny cigar butts"— he described its size with his fingers— "on the dock when I found Brendan. It was fresh. I haven't seen anybody around here who smokes them. The sheriff told me he didn't think it was important. Chrissake, of course it's important. Unless you've already made your mind up.

"So I've been seeing what I could turn up on my own. I've been all over this county today, which took me a while since I don't have a car. I've talked to some of Brendan's friends, and some of his enemies too. Or maybe I shouldn't say talked 'to,' maybe I should say talked 'at,' because nobody would talk back to me. Nobody's seen anything or heard anything or has any ideas about it at all.

"Of course, I don't really know any of these people, so I wouldn't be surprised if they don't trust me. But I do know you. And I trust you. So here I am."

"Lord," Vickers said, "that's the most words I *ever* heard you say at one sitting."

Craik smiled. "Well?" he said.

"Well, what?"

"Can you help me?"

Vickers puffed at the pipe. "Don't know," she said. "If I can, I will."

"Marla, there's something going on around here. Something that involves the sheriff, and those deputies of his, and Judge Holder, and probably some of the watermen. Whatever it is, it has to do with why Brendan died. If I knew what it was, I might be able to find out what happened to him. I figured if anyone could tell me, you could. Can you?"

Vickers laid her pipe hand on her knee and looked out at the road that ran past her house. A sheriff's department cruiser went slowly past.

"Craik," Vickers said, "you can't come into someplace and a week later expect to understand things that've been—"

The cruiser had halted and was backing up. It stopped in front of Vickers's house. The driver's-side door opened and

Sheriff Kemp got out. He left the engine running. He came around the car and stopped at the picket fence. The dog raised its head and growled.

"Quiet, Lucky," Vickers said.

"Craik," the sheriff called. "Miz Vickers."

"Sheriff," Vickers said.

"Like to talk to you, Craik," Kemp said. "Won't take long."

Craik sighed. He got up. "I'll see you later," he said to Vickers, and he joined the sheriff.

"This is getting to be a habit," he said.

Kemp gestured at the cruiser. It was empty. Craik got in the front. Kemp climbed in behind the wheel and they started off.

"Where to?" Craik said.

"Your place okay?"

"I suppose."

They drove to Craik's cottage and parked.

"Invite me in," Kemp said.

"You don't need that."

"This is an unofficial visit, Craik. Friendly like. So invite me in."

"My pleasure," Craik said, and the two men got out of the cruiser and went into the house.

"Sorry about the air-conditioning," Craik said. "Can't find a decent repairman these days. Beer?"

Kemp nodded. He sat down at the table in the dining area. Craik poured two beers and brought them over. They drank a few swallows and wiped their mouths on their bare arms.

"What can I do for you, Sheriff?" Craik asked.

Kemp took off his silver-rimmed spectacles. He breathed on the lenses and carefully cleaned them on his khaki shirt. Then he hooked the curving cable ends back over his ears. He adjusted the glasses until they sat just so on his face. The pale blue smudges of his eyes called so little attention to themselves that it was as if they weren't even there.

"Craik," he said finally, "you probably think I'm just some hick country sheriff."

"Not really," Craik said. "I've been in your office, remember?" Kemp half-smiled and nodded. "It's not your typical sheriff's office. I assume that you decorated it yourself?" Kemp nodded again. "So you have taste in art. You know something about antiques. I wouldn't mistake you for a hick."

"You're an observant man, Craik. Doubt you've missed much around here. I also assume that you're intelligent. And I know you don't scare easy."

"You come here to dish out compliments?"

"And then you got this edge to you. Big chip on your shoulder. That's too bad. Except for that, we might find we got things in common. Might be able to talk. But there it is. You put people off, son."

"Not if people leave me alone."

Kemp shook his head. "World don't work that way," he said. "We all keep bumping into each other. You bump me, sure enough somebody else is gonna get bumped, too, just like stones in the bottom of the creek."

They drank some beer in silence.

"You know what I had growing up," Kemp said. "Nothing. My daddy was wiped out in the Crash, and I mean wiped *out*. He rode iron during the thirties. Only the war saved his ass. He couldn't fight 'cause one of the freights had got his foot, so he had his pick of the work, and the women too.

"One of 'em was my mama, but I don't know which to this day. Daddy lit into her a little much one time and she was gone. Left me there. He was a hard man, but say this about him: I ain't got a school education, but he taught me good. He'd been around, traveling the country all those years, and he knew a lot. Books and art and Cajun music and the 1928 Yankees and what the weather'd be like in Bakersfield. You name it, he could talk your ear off about it.

"After the war, Daddy was old and there were all these young guys around. He lost his job. Drank too much. Died.

Basically, I been on my own since I was ten. Wasn't but pretty early I realized that I was gonna end up on one side of the law or the other. So I decided that well, that being the case, I might's well end up on the side that keeps me outta jail."

Kemp paused. "I didn't have anything, either," Craik said. "The streets of Philly and cold water most of the time. Law there was whatever we decided it was gonna be. The cops didn't like to screw around in the streets much."

"You made it to college, though, I believe."

"Luck. It was the same choice as yours, really. It was gonna be that or jail. I lucked out because I discovered the GI Bill in time."

"So we ain't that different," Kemp said, "you and me."

"In some ways."

"Except that you give it all up for some reason." Craik started to say something, but Kemp held up his hand. "Which is your business," he went on, "and I don't care about it. Man's got a right to live as he pleases. There ain't nothing else. But . . . well, here we be. I got a good life here, Craik. There ain't no way in hell I'm gonna end up like my daddy. I'll do whatever I have to do to protect my life."

"I didn't think I was threatening your life."

"Oh, you ain't. Not yet. If you was, I woulda figured a way to have you in jail long time ago. But you come in here and all of a sudden you're in the middle of everything. You might want to be left alone, but you attract flies to you like a lump of shit, son."

"I don't know what you mean," Craik said.

"Yeah, you do. You getting in fights and people dying all around you. Now, I ain't saying it's your fault, mind, but there it is."

"Shields was my partner, Sheriff. Somebody threw him off that dock."

Kemp looked at Craik for a long moment. Neither man betrayed any emotion. A sudden breeze rattled the screen door against the frame.

Kemp said, "The law ain't always a simple thing."

Craik shrugged. "Somebody still helped him into the water."

"Damn it, I'm trying to tell you something!"

"I've heard it before, Sheriff," Craik said sharply. "It's called expedience. Oh, yeah, I know about that, all right. I'm a fucking expert at that. And you know what it means? The same thing every time. It means that some poor sucker at the bottom of the pile takes the heat."

"You don't know what you're talking about."

"Yeah, unfortunately I do. Dorset County is the same as Philly, is the same as Washington fucking D.C. or any other place on the planet you care to name. Somebody at the top makes a decision, and some innocent bastard down below pays for it." Craik sighed. "I'm sick of it, Sheriff," he said softly. "And I'm sick of running away from it."

"Life ain't gonna be the way you want it to," Kemp said.

"Except for the part I touch with my own hands. That I can make into what I want."

Kemp shook his head. "You're buying a hard ride, son."

"Maybe. But somebody killed my partner. I'm gonna find out who it was."

"In my county *I* find out things like that."

"But you're not going to."

"I never said that. One of your problems, Craik, you think everything's got to go according to *your* schedule. That ain't the way it works."

"At least by my schedule it'll get done," Craik said.

"God damn it—" Kemp stopped himself, then continued more calmly. "Craik . . . Shit, I don't know what to do with you. I'm trying to tell you something for your own good, in a nice friendly way, and you won't listen to me."

"Not at all, Sheriff. I'm listening. You want me to get the hell out of Brawlton and leave you to keep doing whatever it is you're doing."

"I wouldn't put it quite like that."

"Don't insult me."

"All right," Kemp said, "let me tell you how I would put it. I think it would be best for you, and I mean *for you,* if you left town for a while. I'm not trying to run you off, Craik. But I got a lot on my mind right now; it'd be easier I wasn't worrying about you too. It don't have to be for long. A month, six weeks. Then see how you feel about coming back here. That sound okay to you?"

Craik paused. He turned his empty beer can in the wet ring it had made on the table.

"I don't know," he said. "I'd have to think about it. You promising you'll nail whoever killed Brendan?"

"Sure," Kemp said. "If there's someone to get, we'll get him."

"You *do* know it wasn't an accident."

Kemp got up. "Get yourself a good night's sleep," he said. "Tomorrow's supposed to be nice. Good travel day."

Craik nodded. "I'll think about it."

"Thanks for the beer," Kemp said. "And, Craik, try to remember something, will you? Sometimes folks give you advice, you might not like it, but it really is what you need to hear."

The sheriff left. Craik got another beer and sprawled out on the couch. He drank slowly, staring at the ceiling, and was just finishing when Susanna walked in the door.

Susanna's face was drawn and white. Her fists and jaw were clenched and her lower lip trembled slightly. She walked slowly to the couch and stood over Craik.

"What is it?" Craik said.

"I saw Will," she said.

"Janine's father?"

Susanna nodded. "He just got back an hour ago. From the hospital and the . . . funeral arrangements. They killed her." She beat steadily on her thighs with her fists. "God damn the bastards, they *killed her.*"

Craik got up and took her by the shoulders. Gently, he

guided her down onto the couch. He tried to put his arms around her, but she pushed him away.

"You want a drink?" he asked.

"No."

"You want to tell me about it?"

"Give me a minute, will you?"

She sat with her hands folded in her lap, staring past Craik. She took several deep breaths. Then she focused on him.

"Fyke and Tilghman," she said evenly. "They killed Janine."

"I don't understand," Craik said.

She told him about the rape.

"Where was she going in the truck?" he asked when she'd finished.

"I don't know. Will doesn't know. He was drunk," she said disgustedly. "It could have been anywhere. To see a doctor or the sheriff, or to kill Brent Fyke, or to drive herself on purpose into the tree. What does it matter?"

"You're right, it doesn't."

"I'll kill the son of a bitch myself."

"No."

"Don't you tell me what to do!"

"Susanna," Craik said, "I know you feel like that right now and I don't blame you. Your place, I'd feel the same. But there's only a couple of things that can happen. You can fail, in which case he might very well kill *you*. And you can succeed, or almost, in which case you'll go to jail."

"What do you care?"

"Don't say that."

"Well, what *do* you?"

"I care," he said quietly.

"Craik," Susanna said slowly, "a lot of the time you're a miserable shithead, but I seem to have fallen in love with you, anyway. Do you love me?"

She held his eyes with hers.

"I don't know," he said without hesitation. "Maybe. It's . . . difficult for me. I've been alone for a long time."

"If you did, you'd help me," she said.

"I will help you, but not to kill Brent Fyke. There's been too much killing already. Besides which, there's a connection somewhere. The sheriff and your uncle and the deputies and Brendan Shields are all connected up somehow. Whatever connects them is so important that Kemp asked me to leave town."

"Today?"

"Uh-huh. He came here. He was as charming as I think he knows how to be. But the message was clear. He wants me gone by tomorrow."

"What'd you tell him?"

"I said I'd think about it."

"Are you afraid?" she asked.

Craik shrugged. "A little," he said. "Fyke and Tilghman are dangerous people. Together they're four times as big as I am. More important, they're allowed to carry large-caliber guns. And I doubt they're hesitant to use them. For all we know, they may be the ones who killed Brendan, though I don't think so. Doing something subtle like planting a cigar butt doesn't seem within their grasp."

"Well, frankly, at this point I care more about Janine."

"That's what I'm trying to tell you. Janine will tie in too. Fyke obviously felt he could do what he did and not have to worry about the consequences. That's important. The reason has to connect back to whatever got Brendan murdered. It all fits together, I can feel it. We need to find out how."

"And then what?"

"I don't know," he said. "I admit it. The sheriff's department certainly isn't going to help us. We might be able to go to the state cops, but we might not. Some of them might be on the take, and we wouldn't know which ones. The feds are probably our best bet. I've got some . . . contacts that I might still be able to use."

"And what happens to you if you do?"

"What do you mean?"

"Craik, don't treat me like a child!" she said sharply. "I know you were doing some shady job for the government, and I know you quit and maybe it wasn't the kind of job you can just kiss good-bye one day. Then you come to Brawlton and act like you haven't got a past. So what am I supposed to think? Are there people looking for you?"

There was a long pause. "I don't know," Craik said finally. "They might be."

"Shit."

"I won't walk away from this, Susanna."

"Oh, for chrissake!" She beat on the back of the couch with her fist. "What'll they do to *you*, Craik? What'll they do if they *find* you?"

"Probably nothing," he said. "They probably just want to talk to me."

"Or?"

"Or . . . . I don't know."

"Or they might want to kill you?"

"No," Craik said. "They don't want to kill me. They have no reason to want that."

She stared at him. "I don't know if I believe you," she said.

"You have to," he said.

She got up and crossed her arms under her breasts. She walked over to the front door and stared out the screen. It was dark. There was nothing to see. Craik left her alone.

She stared for five minutes. Then she returned to the couch.

"What do you want to do?" she asked him.

"I want to get whoever killed Brendan. You want to nail Fyke for Janine. I think that's the same purpose. And I think we can do it, if we keep our heads. First we've got to pry the lid off whatever's going on around here."

"How do we do that?"

"We ask someone who knows. I think Marla Vickers might, but I'm not sure. I was just getting around to asking her this evening when the sheriff interrupted us. But now there's something better. Will Devereaux. I don't care if he was drunk; his daughter had just been raped and he didn't lift a finger to help her. That means he's afraid of something, and that something is what we want to know."

"You think he'll tell us?"

"Susanna, right now he's home alone and feeling guilty as hell. I have no doubt that he's drunk again. He'll tell us."

"Let's go see him," she said.

They drove in Susanna's red Toyota to the small gray-shingled house with the crumbling chimney. They walked up the creaky steps to the front door and knocked. There were lights on inside, but there was no answer. Susanna looked at Craik. He put a finger to his lips.

Cautiously, he opened the screen door, then the inner door. He stepped inside. Susanna followed. There was light coming from the kitchen at the end of the hall, and through the doorless frame on the left. Craik eased his head around the door frame and peered into the room.

The black-and-white television on the metal cart was off. There was a labelless bottle of clear liquid on the end table, three-quarters empty. An empty glass tumbler was nearby, on the floor.

Will Devereaux was sprawled in the blue velour easy chair. His legs were together and stuck straight out. His arms were splayed to either side and his head lolled back, as if the chair were a cross and he the sacrifice.

His breath came in short, mucus-filled gasps.

Craik and Susanna went into the room. Except for the sound of Devereaux's intermittent breathing, the house was silent. Susanna sat on the velour couch. Craik went over to Devereaux and shook him.

Devereaux slapped at Craik's hands. Craik shook him harder. The older man opened first one eye, then the other. He blinked and squinted. The whites of his eyes were splotched with red smudges and cross-stitched by spidery red lines. With the pale blue of the irises, the effect was of a schizophrenic American flag. In the center of the eyes the pupils were shrunken and hollow.

"Wh—" Devereaux said. "Who?"

He looked around, focused for a moment on Susanna. Then he reached out for the bottle next to him. He uncapped it and took a long swallow. When he tilted it again, Craik reached out but stopped himself in mid-action. Devereaux drank.

He held the unstoppered bottle in his lap. "What you want?" he asked.

Craik went and sat on the couch, facing Devereaux. Susanna said, "Hello, Will."

"Wh—what you doing here?" He took another swallow from the bottle.

"We want to talk to you," Susanna said.

"I told you—told you everything." He looked at Craik suspiciously. "Who—who's this man?"

"This is Scott Craik," Susanna said. "He's a friend of mine."

"What's he want?"

"He wants the same thing I want, Will. I want to put Brent Fyke away for a long time."

"No," Devereaux said sharply.

"Why not, Mr. Devereaux?" Craik said.

Devereaux set the bottle on the end table. He folded his hands in his lap and stared down at them.

"Nothing to do," he mumbled. "Too late."

"Will—" Susanna began.

Devereaux laughed suddenly. Craik and Susanna started.

"Will!" he shouted, pointing a finger at them. "Ha, ha! That's a good one, isn't it? Only place there's any left, in my name!" He laughed some more and the laughter turned into a coughing fit. He snatched up the bottle. The whiskey made him cough some more. His eyes teared and he hacked up a gob of mucus. He spat it on the bare wood floor.

Susanna looked at Craik. He gave her a slight shake of the head.

"Will," Susanna said, "we can do it." Devereaux was looking morosely at his hands again. "We can put the bastard in jail. We can get some justice for Janine."

"Justice," Devereaux mumbled.

"Craik has friends in the government," Susanna said. "We can do it."

"Government," Devereaux said, chuckling.

"Mr. Devereaux—" Craik began.

"Sure!" Devereaux shouted. "Call in the judge!" He made a beckoning motion with his arm. "Come on in, judge! Bring in the justice!"

Devereaux reached for the bottle. Susanna looked at Craik, and this time Craik nodded slightly. He moved to the end table and grabbed the bottle before Devereaux could get his hand around it.

"Who the—bastard," Devereaux said.

He struggled to raise himself up. Halfway to his feet, he abandoned the fight, collapsed back into the chair. He twisted his head rapidly one way, then the other, as if looking for something. He ran his tongue over cracked lips. Craik sat on the couch, holding the bottle by its neck.

"Will," Susanna said, "we need your help."

"Me," Devereaux said. "Can't help you. Nothing to do."

"Devereaux," Craik said. "I'm very sorry about your daughter. I didn't know her, but she was Susanna's best friend and that's enough for me. I'm also sorry about my partner. Brendan Shields."

"Drowned," Devereaux mumbled.

"Devereaux!" Craik said. Will's head jerked. He looked at Craik. "He didn't drown by himself. Somebody killed him. The same people who killed your daughter."

"Fyke." Devereaux spat out the word.

"Yeah, Fyke and Tilghman and Kemp and Judge Holder and all the rest of them. They're all in something together.

Something that causes innocent people to die. I want to know what it is." He leaned toward Devereaux. "I want you to tell me."

Will looked from Craik to Susanna and back again. He stretched out his arm toward the bottle. Craik held it just beyond his reach. Devereaux's hand was trembling. Craik cocked his head slightly and Will gave a small answering nod. Craik passed the bottle over. Devereaux drank, hesitated, then returned the bottle to Craik. There was only an inch of liquid left at the bottom.

"Tell me," Craik said.

"Tell *us*," Susanna said. "It's important, Will."

Devereaux gazed at the empty television, his eyes unfocused.

"Guns," he said finally.

Craik sat forward. "What?" he said.

"Guns," Will repeated. "Judge Holder buys and sells them. Guns and . . ." He waved his hand in the air as if at a bothersome insect. "I don't know what else. Military stuff, I guess. The guns is all I ever saw."

"Where does he get them?" Craik asked.

"Don't know. Judge has friends in Richmond, friends in Washington, friends everywhere. Gets what he wants. Y'always get what you want, you can pay for it. Can't pay anymore, so I got nothing."

"Where does he sell the guns?"

"Don't know. They come in long black boxes. Nailed shut. Come at night in Holder Seafood trucks." Devereaux chuckled. "Black fish, we called 'em. Greasy black fish. Load 'em on our boats. Don't have mine anymore. Had three kings. Son of a bitch filled a inside straight. Still have it if Molly hadn't've died."

"Whose boats are involved?" Susanna asked.

"Watermen," Will said. "Some of 'em. Can't blame 'em. Bay's dying. Run black fish and at least you get paid for it. Money's good, work's easy."

"Where do you take the guns?" Craik asked.

"Into the Bay. Freighter meets you, coming down from Bal'more. Freighters up and down, all day and night. One of 'em stops and you transfer the boxes. Don't take long. Then you get the money. Need the money or you could lose . . . everything."

"And the sheriff and his deputies protect the operation," Craik said.

Devereaux shrugged. "Do what they say," he said.

"Who? Anyone else?"

Devereaux shrugged again. "Crowe, I heard. Some of his friends. Don't matter. Watermen are happy to get the work, them that take it. They don't talk."

"You didn't know what was in the boxes?" Craik asked. "None of you? The boxes didn't say anything on them?"

Will shook his head. "Money to us. Money."

"How'd you find out it was guns?"

Devereaux reached for the bottle. Craik gave it to him and he drained what was left in it.

"Molly," he said to its emptiness.

"The *boxes*," Craik said. "How'd you know what was in them if they were nailed shut?"

" '72," Will said. "Gar Dent."

"Gar Dent," Susanna said. "Lester's brother. I remember him. He disappeared. I was just a kid. People thought he probably drowned, but they never found his body."

"I killed him," Will said.

"What?"

"Didn't tie the boxes right. Winch got 'em halfway up and they come loose. Fell top of Gar. Killed him." Devereaux paused, looked down at his hands, then over at Craik. "One of them broke open," he went on, "and I seen the guns. They hauled Gar's body up on the freighter and he was gone. Later the Judge told me he knowed what had happened. I killed a man. If anybody ever found out, I'd go to jail. I never told nobody. Not Molly. Not . . . Janine."

Devereaux looked down at his hands. His shoulders trembled and he began to sob.

Craik looked at Susanna and motioned with his head. The two of them left the room. They walked down the hall into the kitchen. They embraced, kissed briefly, and separated.

"I'd rather be with you," Susanna said, "but I don't think I should leave him alone tonight."

"I'd rather too," Craik said. "But I agree with you." He began opening cabinets as he talked. "Get him to bed. In the morning take him to the café with you. Put some food and coffee in him." He finished his search of the kitchen. "There doesn't seem to be any booze left," he said. "See if you can keep him sober. We need him."

"I don't know if I can go to the café," Susanna said. "Fyke and Tilghman come there for their morning coffee. Every day around seven. I'm liable to kill them."

"You're going to have to get used to seeing them until we get them put away. Don't kill them, please."

"It's going to be tempting."

"I realize that. But remember, you can't even let on that we know as much as we do. Fyke thinks that no one knows, or that only Will does, so he's not worried. If he finds out that you know, too . . . well, don't let it happen. Think you can control yourself?"

She nodded unenthusiastically.

"It's important," he said. "And look . . . how do you feel about your uncle being in the middle of all this?"

"It's hard," she said. "He was always good to me. He used to take me and . . . Janine on the boat . . ."

"I'm sorry, Susanna. But he's part of it. In a way he's just as responsible."

She nodded. "I'll be all right. But I don't know if I can stay at Sandi's all day, wondering what you're doing."

"I'll check in with you. If there's anything you can do, I'll ask, don't worry."

"You got a plan?"

"Not much of one. Give me the car keys."

She handed them over. "You got a license?"

He smiled. "New York," he said. "It hasn't lapsed."

"Where are you going?"

"Home. I need some sleep. Then I'm going to try to find a guy who smokes skinny cigars. And I'll see what I can do about getting us some help. I'll meet you at my place no later than five." He paused, then said, "Okay. If something comes up, I'll leave you a note. The pad and pen will be on the table. I'll slip the note inside that yellow tide-table book. If I'm not there and you have to go out, you do the same."

"Uh-huh." She stood on her toes and kissed him. "Be careful," she said.

Craik nodded. "Don't let Will do himself any harm," he said.

"I won't."

SECOND
THURSDAY

CHAPTER 23

Susanna awoke without an alarm at five-thirty. She looked around her at the walls of Janine's room, at the calendar from Sandi's Café, at the posters of the Arctic and Huey Lewis. Tears welled in her eyes, and for a moment she sniffled. Then she threw back the covers. Hurriedly, she stuffed herself into the clothes she'd been wearing the previous night.

She went to the bathroom and washed her face, ran some toothpaste over her teeth with a finger. Then she entered Will's room. Gently, she shook him awake.

He came to with a start, raising himself up on his elbows. His hands clutched at the sheet. He squinted and focused on the young woman.

"Susanna," he said, "what are you doing here?"

She put a hand on his arm. "I stayed with you last night," she said. "You were tired and depressed after the funeral arrangements."

"I—" His voice caught in his throat. He coughed up some phlegm and swallowed it. "I don't remember."

"That's okay. I'm going to work now."

"What time is it?"

"Quarter to six. Look, Will," she said, "I want you to promise me something. I want you to come down to Sandi's when you get up. I'll make you some breakfast. On the house. We can . . . talk then. Will you promise to do that?"

He was looking past her. His face suddenly softened, as if he'd seen someone in the door. Susanna half turned, but there was nothing.

"Uh, sure," he said, his voice steady. "Just give me a half hour or so."

She patted his arm and smiled. "No hurry. Whenever you get up, like I said."

His head fell back on the pillow. He laced his fingers over his stomach. He was staring hard at the ceiling.

"Don't worry," he said. "I'll be there."

"Good."

For a moment she looked at him lying there, staring at the ceiling, then she shrugged and left the house.

When she'd gone, Will Devereaux stripped off the covers and got out of bed. He removed the T-shirt and briefs he'd slept in. Slowly, methodically, he tore them to shreds.

Then he stood naked before the mirror over his dresser. He looked at himself from the front. His eyes were sunk deep in his head, the pupils like pencil points. His hair was unkempt, his beard gray and stubbly. The hair on his chest was gray too. The flesh of his upper body hung slackly above his protuberant stomach.

He turned sideways. From that angle his stomach bulged outward even more. He sucked at it with little effect. Quickly, he turned to face front again. He stretched out his hand toward the mirror. When his arm was fully extended, his fingers jumped and twitched. He closed them into a fist and banged it on the dresser top. Then he raised his arm again. His hand still trembled. He banged it again. He repeated the procedure until the shaking diminished noticeably.

He walked naked to the bathroom and took a long, hot

shower. Then he got out his razor. He lathered up and scraped at his face until the stubble was gone. He opened the medicine cabinet and took out some after-shave lotion. The cap to the bottle was stuck. He grunted and swore and finally got the bottle open. He poured some lotion into his hand and slapped his face, hard.

Then he brushed his teeth. His teeth were yellow, and the brushing made no visible difference. Afterward, he gargled with mouthwash. He applied deodorant to his underarms. He combed his hair.

He returned to the bedroom and put on clean clothes. A sleeveless undershirt, briefs, khaki slacks, a white shirt, brown socks, and brown loafers.

At the foot of the bed was a battered old trunk with decaying leather hinges. Will walked over to it and raised the curved lid. Inside was a jumble of old clothes, knickknacks, cigar boxes with rubber bands around them. Will plunged his arms in and began to feel around the bottom. A moment later he pulled up a linen package, tied with twine. He untied it and slowly folded back the cloth.

A .22-caliber revolver lay in his hand. He lifted it by the butt. He pressed a lever and shook it. The cylinder fell open to the side. It was a six-shot, and there were six cartridges in it. He closed the cylinder.

He stood up, straightened his arm, and held the pistol out in front of him. His hand was not steady. The pistol vibrated as if it had an internal motor. He nodded, pushed the gun behind his belt. The white shirt, hanging free, concealed it.

He went over to the mirror and looked closely at his face. He felt his shaven cheeks. He smoothed his hair. Then he went into the kitchen. He looked in all the cabinets. What he was after obviously wasn't there. He swore and looked purposefully around the room, stopping at the refrigerator. He knelt before it and detached the grille at its bottom. Inside the cavity there was a pint bottle full of clear liquid. He took it out.

Sitting in the middle of the kitchen floor, he drank deeply.

At seven o'clock the deputies came into Sandi's Café. They were laughing about something. They clomped over to one of the wall booths and sat down, across from each other.

Susanna brought them coffee. She set the heavy china mugs in front of them and turned away.

"Hey," Fyke said, "no kind word for the day?"

"Not for you, Brent Fyke," Susanna said.

"Aw, what'd I do now?"

Susanna started to say something, then clamped her mouth tightly shut and continued to walk away. She went back behind the counter and busied herself with morning chores.

Fyke turned to his partner. He flapped his hand, palm upward, in front of his chest.

"Rag on," he said.

"That's okay," Tilghman said with a smirk. "I don't mind that."

"How would you know?"

Fyke looked seriously at him for a moment, then began chuckling. Charles joined in, without much feeling. When the humorless laughter faded, they sipped at their coffee. Their talk turned to a couple of departmental matters. They were still at it five minutes later when the door opened and Will Devereaux entered Sandi's.

Susanna looked up from the counter. "Will," she said brightly.

Devereaux nodded to her and went over to the table where the two deputies were sitting. He stood over them. They ignored him for a while, continued their conversation. He waited. Finally, Fyke, who was sitting closest to him, looked up.

"What is it, Devereaux?" he said.

Will reached under his shirt and pulled out the pistol.

"I just don't care anymore," he said.

He pointed the pistol at Fyke. Tilghman reached for his own gun, but Devereaux swung his arm and Tilghman put his hand back on the table. Devereaux's hand was shaking badly as he moved the pistol.

"Will!" Susanna yelled. "For God's sake, put it down!" She hurried toward the end of the counter.

"Put it away, Devereaux," Fyke said coldly.

Will swung the gun back in Fyke's direction, cocking the hammer as he did so. The gun went off. The .22-caliber bullet went across the table and out the front window. It broke one pane of glass.

Susanna froze at the end of the counter.

Fyke turned in his seat and lashed out with his foot, catching Devereaux in the stomach. In the same motion he drew his gun. It was a Colt Python, a .357 Magnum. The .22 went off again. The bullet grazed Devereaux's shoe and buried itself in the floor.

When Devereaux straightened up, Fyke shot him once in the chest. The massive Magnum bullet tore open his chest and exited from a fist-sized wound in his back. Blood sprayed as far as the counter. Some of it spattered onto Susanna's shirt. The bullet continued on. It penetrated the counter, shattered some glasses racked behind it, and punched through the wall into the kitchen. There was the sound of rending metal and a final rattling before it stopped.

The point-blank range of the slug threw Devereaux back into one of the circular tables in the middle of the café. He slid across the top of it, leaving a red smear behind, and toppled over the far side. His body crumpled on the floor. Blood pulsed from his chest like a miniature geyser.

Susanna screamed. She rushed over and knelt beside Devereaux. She pressed her hand over the wound. Blood spurted between her fingers. She gathered his shirt and tried to plug the hole.

Fyke was standing over her. "Don't bother," he said. "At that range there ain't nothing you can do. Charles, call

Brace," he said to his partner. "Fill him in. Tell him there's no need of an ambulance."

Tilghman went to the phone behind the counter and called the sheriff.

Fyke reached down and took Susanna by the shoulders. He tried to raise her up.

"Susanna," he said, "I'm sorry. But you seen what happened. I don't know what he—"

She whirled and kicked him hard in the shin. When he let go of her arms, she punched him in the stomach. The punch bounced off. He grabbed her wrists.

"Son of a bitch!" she screamed. "Let me go!"

She wriggled in his grasp, continuing to kick at him. He was able to hold her away from him. She shrieked and bent her head, sank her teeth into his arm. He shook her, snapping her head back. He let go of her wrists and slapped her across the face. The blow staggered her. She sat down, hard. She shook her head.

Fyke leaned down. "Holder," he said coldly, "we're gonna wait for the sheriff now. I want you to get up, find yourself a chair, and sit in it till he gets here. You give me any more trouble and I'll really hit you. And I'll arrest you for interfering with me in the performance of my duties. You got it?"

She stared at him, didn't say anything.

"Good," he said.

A couple of people had wandered in from the street. Tilghman was shooing them from the café.

"Show's over, folks," he said. "Come on, move it on out of here."

He stretched his arms wide and herded them back out the door. When they were gone, he locked the door and turned the CLOSED sign facing outward. Faces appeared at the window; noses were pressed to the glass. Tilghman closed the curtains. They were of a light, diaphanous material. Through them the faces could still be seen, trying to peer inside.

Two hours later Susanna was sitting with Sheriff Kemp in his office in Dorset.

"That's it," she was saying. "I ain't gonna tell it no different." She folded her arms across her chest.

"Susanna," Kemp said wearily, "my men say that Will Devereaux came in with a gun and started firing. They have a legal right to defend themselves. With deadly force, if necessary."

"He shot him in cold blood," Susanna said. "Will would never've hurt no one."

"Nevertheless, he shot first. Twice. We *know* that. He certainly couldn't have fired after Deputy Fyke *shot* him."

"He killed that old man. In cold blood."

"Susanna, why would he do that?"

"Oh, for chrissake, because—" She stopped and paused. "Why don't you ask him? Why don't you ask him why Will came in there with a gun in the first place?"

"I intend to," Kemp said tersely.

Susanna uncrossed her arms and leaned forward. She leveled a forefinger at Kemp.

"Yeah, you fucking well better," she said. "You better do something about that murdering bastard and you better do it soon—"

"Listen, young lady—"

"No, you listen to *me*, Bracewell Kemp. I know goddamn well you and my uncle are close as sin, but he doesn't own the whole world. You don't do something and do it now, and I'm going to the state cops, and if they won't listen, I'm gonna go down to Richmond and sit in the Attorney General's office until I find somebody who will. You got that?"

The sheriff's face was impassive. "Don't you threaten me, Susanna," he said.

Susanna got up and stood over Kemp's desk. She banged her fist on the desktop.

"I'm not threatening you!" she said angrily. "I'm telling you to do your goddamn *job*!"

They stared at each other for a long moment.

Then Kemp said icily, "Thank you for your cooperation, Miss Holder. I'll have someone to take you home."

"Don't you dare send me home with those murdering scum."

Kemp pressed a button on his phone console. A voice said, "Yes Sheriff," through the speaker.

"Hawes," Kemp said, "come in here, please."

"Yes, sir."

The obese deputy with the bristle haircut came into the office.

"Take Miss Holder home," Kemp said to him. "And send Brent and Charles in here."

"Yes, sir."

Susanna glared at the sheriff, then turned and went out with Hawes. A few moments later Fyke and Tilghman entered. Kemp was standing with his back to them, looking out at the sycamore trees. They fidgeted.

Finally, Kemp turned around. He fixed his attention on Fyke.

"What the fuck do you think you're doing?" he said coldly.

"C'mon, Brace—"

"Don't give me that *shit*!"

Kemp strode rapidly across the room to where the two men were standing. He looked up at Fyke, his face twisted with anger. Then he slapped Fyke, hard, cupping his palm. The big man staggered a step backward. He put his own hand to the side of his face. Kemp pointed a trembling forefinger at him.

"Don't we have *enough* trouble around here?"

Fyke didn't say anything.

"*Answer me*!"

"Yes, sir," Fyke mumbled.

"You're goddamn *right* we do! Now tell me what that old drunk was doing in there shooting a gun off."

Fyke shrugged. Kemp turned abruptly to Tilghman.

"Charles," he said, "what the fuck is going on?"

"I don't know," Tilghman said quickly. "Devereaux was upset. His daughter dying and all. He prob'ly wanted to take it out on somebody. Maybe he knew Brent used to make passes at the kid, so he picked him."

Kemp turned to the other man and said, "That what you think, Fyke?"

"Shit, I don't know, Sheriff," Fyke said. "He was a crazy, drunk old man. Who knows what goes on in their heads?"

Kemp began to pace back and forth in front of the two men.

"A crazy, drunk old man," he muttered. "And you two couldn't figure out some way to disarm him without blowing him away. Jesus Christ! I know you ain't geniuses, but how hard could it have been?"

Neither of the deputies said anything.

"You know, we got some problems around here," Kemp went on, "in case you've forgotten. There are some very bad people trying to move into this county, and it's gonna be up to us to clean them out. I can't afford to have one of my men on suspension for a couple of weeks. I *need* every man I can get. Now I got to worry about the Commonwealth Attorney's office on my back because my deputies are out there shooting civilians." He stopped in front of Fyke. "You understand what I'm saying?"

"Yes, sir," Fyke said. "I thought the Judge—"

"Yeah, *maybe* the C.A. owes the Judge," Kemp said, "and *maybe* he can keep it quiet. But that's a hell of a lot of *maybes* at this particular time." Kemp paused, then said, "Shit!"

He turned and walked away from the two men. He walked to the window and then back. The deputies didn't say anything.

"All right," he said to them. "I'm keeping you both on active, but only because I don't have any other choice. I've got a lead on our friends. If it pans out, we may know where they are by morning. In the meantime . . ." He paused, then emphasized his words. "In the meantime, I want you to stay close to the office for the rest of the day. If you have to go out, I want to know exactly where you both are at all times. And I don't want either of you drawing your guns until I personally tell you to do so, is that clear?" The deputies nodded. "And, Fyke, if I find out there's any more to this Devereaux thing than you've told me, I will *have* your ass, you got me?"

"Yes, sir," Fyke said.

"Now get out of here," the sheriff said. "Both of you."

The deputies left, and Kemp went over to his desk. He sat down with a heavy sigh and punched out a phone number.

"Judge," he said, "you heard the news?"

"A little," Holder said. "Fill in the details."

Kemp told him what had happened at Sandi's Café earlier in the day.

"Shit," Holder said when he'd finished.

"My sentiments exactly," Kemp said. "Can you keep the C.A. off our backs?"

"I don't know."

"How about for a few days? I've got a line on our friends from D.C. I think we may be able to get rid of them by the weekend. But I need Fyke and Tilghman."

"Okay. I can at least stall him."

"The other thing," Kemp said, "is your niece. She raised holy hell and I ain't surprised. She was pretty good friends with those two, Janine Devereaux and her old man. She's threatening to go to the state cops if I don't lock Brent up by yesterday."

There was a lengthy pause.

"All right, I'll take care of Susanna," Holder said finally.

"And what about Craik?" Kemp asked.

"I want him gone," the Judge said firmly. "But for chrissake, no more killing."

"Don't worry. I put the boys on the tight leash."

"Use Crowe."

"Okay."

"And, Brace, the next few days, I want to know everything that happens, when it happens."

"Right."

"Make it some good news, will you?" the Judge said.

CHAPTER 24

Congressman Jesse Mills picked up his phone. He listened, then said, "Okay, send him in."

A moment later the door to his office opened and a man entered. The man was dressed in a gray suit with vest and an unobtrusive striped tie. The outfit was not dissimilar to Mills's own, except that Mills's suit was navy blue.

That, however, was the extent of the physical similarity between the two men. The congressman was dark and ruggedly good-looking, with stylish razor-cut hair that called attention to itself by its seeming casualness. His visitor was moon-faced and completely nondescript. He peered at the world from behind glasses with neutral plastic frames.

The visitor didn't seat himself. Instead, he stood before Mills's desk, looking down at the congressman.

"Sit down, Mr. Smith," Mills said.

Smith ignored him. "You've been briefed on who I am," he said.

"Yes."

"Good. Then let's take a walk. It's a lovely morning, actually."

"Mr. Smith, I'm quite a busy—"

"I am too, Congressman. Let's go, shall we?"

"Look, I know you people think you can do anything you want to. But I don't happen to subscribe to that view. What's this about, anyway?"

Smith shrugged. "Dorset County," he said.

"It's in my district. What about it?"

Smith smiled and looked the congressman in the eye. There was a lengthy pause.

"Shall we go?" Smith said finally.

Mills sighed and got up.

"It's quite warm," Smith said. "You won't need your jacket."

Mills looked at Smith's outfit. Smith gave him a little half smile and said, "I never take mine off."

"Yeah, I'll bet," Mills said.

The two men walked out of the Longworth Office Building, onto Independence Avenue. With Smith leading the way, they turned east. It wasn't a warm day, it was a hot one, the air dense with Washington's summer humidity. Mills had left his suit coat behind. Smith was still wearing his.

"Don't you ever get hot?" Mills asked his companion.

Smith looked over at him. "No, I don't," he said.

Mills shook his head. "Jesus," he said, then asked, "And where are we going, Smith? If that's your name."

"It's my name, and we're not going anywhere in particular." He looked around at the heavy stone buildings that surrounded them. "Isn't this a beautiful city?" When Mills didn't respond, he went on. "The operative assumption, Congressman, is that you don't come to work wired. I would not, however, want to make that assumption about your office."

"Oh, for chrissake," Mills said.

"No, for my own sake. And for yours. Would you have wanted to discuss what's going on in Dorset County in your office?"

Mills stopped and stared at him. Smith took his arm and guided the congressman across Independence Avenue. They started up First Street, the Library of Congress immediately to their right.

"Don't act so shocked," Smith said. "Did you think you could carry on such activities without us noticing?"

"What the hell are you doing in domestic surveillance?" Mills said angrily.

Smith, unruffled, said, "It's hardly entirely domestic. Nor are you, might I add? But let's not quibble about jurisdiction. We've known what's going on down there for some time. In fact, we don't even keep close track of it anymore."

"Why don't I know that you know?"

Smith waved his hand. "No need," he said. "Come on, relax, Congressman. We approve. It wouldn't still be going on if we didn't. I'm sure you realize that. So what point would there be in our bothering you?

"You see, we tend to have a more realistic view of the world than you sometimes do." He gestured at the Capitol Building on their left. "Them, too," gesturing at the Supreme Court on their right. "We're in a war, Mr. Mills, and the other side has one objective: our destruction. And please spare me any of the fashionable platitudes. I know that you basically agree with me, or you wouldn't be mixed up with someone like Forrest Holder.

"Now this war, it has a lot of fronts, dozens of them, all over the world. Sad to say, the Congress doesn't always see fit to properly supply the people who are manning these fronts for us. The ones who are on *our side*. Need I mention Nicaragua? Or Grenada? Would you have approved of what the President did there if you'd known ahead of time?"

He looked at his companion, but the congressman didn't say anything.

"So . . . Fortunately, in this country we still have the private sector. That's where your friend Holder, and others like him, comes in. We watched him carefully at first, but it

didn't take long for us to be convinced. The man is a patriot.
He sells only to our allies. By extension, so do you. This
does not cause us any conflict. We can't openly encourage it,
of course, but we can operate under a policy of benign
neglect.

"Does all of this make you feel more comfortable?"

"I . . . don't know," Mills said.

They started down the long slope that led to Union Station.

"Well, it should," Smith said. "Like I said, relax."

"I don't understand," Mills said. "You don't want to talk
about what's going on in Dorset County?"

Smith shook his head. "That was just to get your attention.
To show you we're on the same side."

"Don't put frosting on it," Mills snapped. "You got my
attention by very gently threatening me."

"Look at it however you need to," Smith said casually.
"What we're really interested in is the request for information that you made to us."

"I wasn't aware—"

"Scott Craik."

Mills stopped. "Craik?" he said.

"You did request a check on the gentleman."

"Why? Do you know who he is?"

"As a matter of fact, we do," Smith said, getting them
moving again. They had turned west on D Street and were
skirting the open, grassy area that lies in front of Union
Station. "But that's not the 'why' that concerns me,
Congressman," Smith went on. "The one that concerns me
is: Why are you requesting data on this man?"

Mills thought for a moment, then said, "I don't believe
I'm required to answer that."

"You are when it's a matter of national security."

Mills laughed. "That's good, Smith," he said. "Tell me
what isn't national security these days."

"Congressman," Smith said. He wasn't amused. "I
thought we might be able to have a civilized conversation

as two people with similar objectives. I was hoping not to encounter this kind of stupid prejudice against my agency."

Mills stopped chuckling. "All right, then," he said. "Let's deal. You tell me what you've got on this character and I'll tell you what I know about him."

Smith thought about it as they came around on Constitution Avenue and walked along the north side of the Capitol grounds.

"Mr. Mills," he said finally, "I'm not kidding about national security."

"Okay, it stops here."

"Very well. When we received your request, we checked the person by name, which is always our first step. Nothing turned up. We tried a few other things, with no success, then we ran the data with a special computer program that we use routinely when the request comes from as high a source as your office.

"This program checks names and descriptions against a file that we keep of persons whose whereabouts we'd like to know. The program looks for physical similarities and also phonetic similarities in the name itself. In this instance we got a double match. There's little doubt that this is a man we've been looking for for some time."

"What's his real name?"

"Immaterial," Smith said. "It wouldn't mean anything to you, anyway."

"Okay. Why are you looking for him?"

"He's a renegade operative of ours."

"Meaning?"

"Meaning that he didn't resign from the service, he just disappeared. We have reason to believe that he may be carrying a grudge against us."

"I can't understand that," Mills said sarcastically.

Smith ignored him. "We'd like to know where he is," he said. "Do you mind?"

"He's in Dorset County."

It was Smith's turn to stop. He stared at his companion.
"You're sure?" he said.

"Of course I'm sure," Mills said. "Someone there wanted
to know who he was."

"Who?"

Mills hesitated, then said, "Holder."

"Craik is mixed up with Forrest *Holder*?"

"I don't know 'mixed up with.' The guy wandered into
town, and Forrest thought he was a suspicious character.
He wanted to know if I could find out anything about him."

"And?"

Mills shrugged. "Not much," he said. "No police or
military records. He's got a Social Security account with
nothing in it. And a New York driver's license that's almost
two years old."

"New York?"

"Uh-huh. Is that important?"

Smith began walking again. "I don't know," he said. "I'll
have to check."

"What do you think," Mills asked, "that this guy's down
there because of Holder's activities?"

"It's possible. Where in Dorset County is he?"

"Brawlton, I think. Holder knows."

They passed the Supreme Court again, from the opposite
direction. Smith put his hands in his pockets and moved
along, neither fast nor slow, looking slightly downward.
Neither man said anything further. They crossed Independence
Avenue and walked west, until they stood in front of
the Longworth Building.

Smith shook Mills's hand. "Thank you, Congressman,"
he said. "You've done us a great service in locating this man.
We won't forget your cooperation. And, of course, we never
had this conversation."

"I already agreed to that," Mills said testily. "What am I
supposed to tell Holder?"

"Leave that to us," Smith said. "We'll take it from here."

He walked off down the hot sidewalk without looking back. The Capitol Hill weekday-morning foot traffic was heavy. Tourists and secretaries, congressional aides and lawyers and influence peddlers, gofers running from here to there with attaché cases. Smith immediately blended with his surroundings. In a few moments he could not be distinguished from the crowd.

Mills returned to his office. He picked up the phone and punched a number.

The voice said, "This is Holder."

Mills stared down at his desk.

"Who is it?" the voice said impatiently.

Mills continued to stare at the desktop. Then he put the receiver back in its slot.

"Fuck it," he said.

CHAPTER 25

Felicity Holder was in her kitchen.

The kitchen was a bright, airy space. It had three windows that looked out over the green expanse of well-kept backyard, with its brick patio, redwood lawn furniture, and hooded, natural-gas grill.

Felicity scrubbed the countertop. It was white Formica with tiny flecks of gold. The appliances—stove, refrigerator, dishwasher, microwave—were all in harvest gold. There was a stainless-steel double sink. The cabinets were handmade and of a polished blond hardwood. The floor was of springy composition tile, beige, set in a repetitive pattern of starkly outlined diamonds. There were vents set into the baseboards along two of the walls. They were expelling chilled air.

The countertop stretched nearly the full length of the fifteen-foot kitchen. There was a toaster oven on it, as well as a butcher-block knife-and-cheeseboard set. There were two wood carousels that held spatulas, whisks, ladles, potato mashers, and similar implements.

Felicity was cleaning the area around the blender when the front door slammed. Susanna came into the kitchen. She stared at her mother, her face crimped with anger, until Felicity finally said, "What is it, dear?"

"Fyke killed Will Devereaux," Susanna said.

Felicity's hand went up and rested in the hollow of her throat. "What . . . what are you saying?" she said.

"Exactly that. I was there," Susanna said, and she told her mother what had happened that morning. When she'd finished, Felicity went over and hugged her daughter. Susanna's arms hung limply at her side.

Felicity released her but kept a hand on each shoulder. "Oh, how terrible," she said. "But why? Why would Will do a thing like that?"

"Fyke raped Janine. That's why she was out in the truck that night. She was going for help."

"Oh, no."

"Oh, yes. We've got to do something, Mama. The sheriff isn't going to."

"But what can we do?"

"Mama," Susanna said, her voice low and intense, "those fucking animals—"

"Susanna!"

"—have got the blood of two people on their hands. Good people. We need to see that they're put away somewhere they'll never get out of."

Felicity turned away from her daughter. She rested her hands on the countertop and gazed out one of the windows.

Her shoulders rose and fell visibly with her breathing. She stretched her slender body until she was raised up on her toes, then lowered herself again. She examined the backyard for a while before turning back to her daughter.

"Susanna," she said, her lips barely parting as she spoke, "I know that Janine was your friend. I know how you must be feeling. But I don't think you should involve yourself in—"

"Goddamn it, Mama! How can I not be *involved*?"

"Dear, I'm sure that if there's anything to be done, Sheriff Kemp will—"

"He will *not*! That's what I'm trying to tell you! They all protect each other because—"

She was interrupted by the sound of the phone ringing. There was a gold handset hanging on the wall next to the refrigerator. Susanna went over and answered it.

"Susanna," Judge Holder said, "I'm glad I caught you at home."

"Yeah, I'll bet. You know what's going on around this place, Uncle Forrest?"

"Yes, I heard. That's why I called. I know you must be very upset. Why don't you come out here and we'll talk about it. Between us, maybe we can figure out what to do."

"Don't you trust your sheriff?" Susanna said sarcastically.

"It's not that. I just thought you'd like some reassurance that we're going to get to the bottom of this."

"I wish I believed that."

"It's true, Susanna. Trust me, I want it as much as you do. Please come out to my house and we can talk about it."

"All right."

"Good. See you in a little while."

Susanna hung up and turned to her mother. "Give me the keys to the BMW," she said.

"Why? Where are you going?"

"To Uncle Forrest's."

Felicity looked to one side, then the other. "I don't know," she said. "I'm not sure—"

"Give me the goddamn keys, Mama!"

"Now, Susanna, don't you raise your voice to me."

Susanna whirled and stalked out of the kitchen. She went into the dining room where she picked up a pocketbook that was lying on the table. She dumped out its contents.

Her mother had followed her. "Susanna, what are you doing?" Felicity said.

Susanna snatched up a set of keys. "What does it look like I'm doing?" she said. "I'm taking the car."

"But where is your own car?"

"I don't have it right now. Thanks, Mama. I'll be back in a while."

Susanna drove to Holder's estate. At the wrought-iron gate halfway up the winding drive there was an armed guard. He was a tall, muscular man in a khaki uniform with damp half moons under the armpits. He was unsmiling as he came over to Susanna's car. She rolled down the window.

"I'm Susanna Holder," she said. "My uncle's expecting me."

The man grunted and bent to the speaker box. He described the car and its occupant to someone at the other end. Then he nodded to Susanna. The gate opened and she drove in.

She parked in the gravel area in front of the mansion. She went up the broad brick steps. In the shaded area between the columns a man had set up a folding chair and was sitting on it, rocked back on its two rear legs. The man wore a khaki uniform and he was armed.

Stayne opened the front door before Susanna had a chance to, and led her to the library.

Judge Holder came around from behind the desk and took Susanna's hands. "Susanna," he said, "I'm so sorry. But thank you for coming. Please, sit down." He indicated the chair, but Susanna remained standing.

"What's with all the rent-a-cops, Uncle Forrest?" she said.

"Just a precaution," Holder said. "I hope it's nothing. A man I once sent to prison has been paroled. He's been telling people he's going to kill me. I'm sure it's nothing but . . . I decided to hire a couple of men for a week or two." He dismissed them with a wave of the hand. "These things happen. Now let me get you something to drink."

"I don't want anything to drink."

"Some Perrier then, at least. And please sit down."

Susanna sat, and Holder went to the walnut cabinet that held his bar. He kept his back to her.

"How are you doing, Susanna?" he said over his shoulder. "How are you holding up? Such terrible things, all at once."

Susanna's gaze wandered around the room. "Oh, I'm great," she said. "Just great."

Holder tumbled some ice cubes into a crystal goblet. Next to the goblet was a small capsule. He broke open the capsule and emptied its contents over the ice cubes. Then he filled the goblet with Perrier. He took a wedge of lemon from a silver bowl, squeezed it over the mineral water, and dropped it in. Into another goblet he put two fingers of Glen Calder, neat.

He carried the Perrier to Susanna. "A lemon spritzer," he said. "Nonalcoholic."

With Scotch in hand, he went and sat behind his desk. Susanna sipped at the sparkling water, then drank down about half of it.

"Thirstier than I thought," she said. "Thanks."

"No problem," Holder said cheerfully. Then, more seriously, "Susanna, do you want to tell me what happened today?"

Susanna leaned back, drank some more. She belched, then sighed. She looked at her uncle for a long moment without speaking. Finally, she told her story again.

"God, that must have been horrible," Holder said when she'd finished.

"It was," Susanna said.

"It just seems so out of character. Will Devereaux wasn't that kind of man. Since his wife died and he lost the boat, well . . . why would he do something like that?"

"He had a little bit of courage left in him," Susanna said. "He wanted his daughter's murderer."

"What are you talking about? Janine died in an accident."

Susanna shook her head. "Brent Fyke raped her," she said.

"*What?*"

"Earlier Sunday night. Janine was upset. She was on her way to report it when she crashed. He might as well have put a gun to her head and pulled the trigger."

"How do you know all this?"

"Will told me yesterday."

"And you're convinced it's true?"

"Of course it's true!" Susanna said angrily. "Nothing else would've made Will do what he did. Besides, Janine must've been incredibly upset. Normally she was a very careful driver. It wasn't like her to go out in a storm like that if she didn't have to. And she *always* used her seat belt."

Holder leaned back and sipped his Scotch. "I—I don't know what to say," he said. "It's all so . . . ugly. Have you told the sheriff what Will said?"

"What good would it do?"

"Bracewell is an excellent sheriff."

"It doesn't matter. Fyke is his boy. He'll protect him."

"Susanna, you don't know what you're saying. This is a serious charge."

"You know damn well what he'd say," Susanna said. "He'd say, 'It's hearsay, Susanna. I can't arrest a man on hearsay.' Will Devereaux can never testify. So what's he . . . gonna . . . do? You . . . tell me." Susanna shook her head quickly a couple of times.

"I have some influence with the sheriff," Holder said. "I assure you that I will use it. We can't let things like this go on in Dorset County."

"Brendan . . ." Susanna said. Her head fell forward. She jerked it upright again. "Janine . . . Will . . . too . . . much death. There's something . . . can't seem . . . to keep my eyes . . . Uncle Forrest . . . what . . ."

Her head dropped again and her eyes closed. She slumped in the chair. The goblet she'd been holding in her lap slipped out of her hand. It rolled down her thigh and fell to the floor, bouncing out the lemon wedge and the remains of two ice cubes. Droplets of water glistened against the dark nap of the carpet.

Holder set down his drink and came over to her. He peeled back her eyelid a little. Only the whites showed. He slapped her face gently. She didn't stir. He returned to the desk and punched a button on his phone console. A moment later Stayne entered.

"Stayne," he said, "Miss Holder appears to have fainted. She's had quite a number of shocks lately. Would you please take her to the Remington room? Just lay her on the bed and maybe put a cold cloth on her forehead. I'll call Dr. Lintle and see what he thinks we should do."

"Certainly, sir," Stayne said. He took Susanna in his arms and carried her from the room.

When they were gone, Holder made a phone call.

"Lintle," he said, "Judge Holder. I'm at home. My niece was with me and she fainted while we were talking. . . . Yes, she's out now. I think she may be having a nervous breakdown. She's been under quite a strain. There was my brother dying, then her best friend was in a car wreck, and the girl's father was killed this morning. I wonder if you could come over here. . . . Cancel them, Lintle. . . . Yes, and reserve a spot for her at the clinic, would you? I'm *sure* you're going to want to take her over there for observation. . . . All right, see you then."

The Judge hung up and made another call.

"Brace," he said angrily, "Susanna just told me what

happened. . . . Yeah, I know that, but you know *why* he
was taking a shot at him? Because the idiot raped his
daughter. . . . Of course I believe it. It's just the sort of
thing he'd do. No wonder Susanna's got such a bee in her
pants. I don't blame her. I just can't believe he picked now
to do it. Jesus Christ, the man doesn't have a brain in his
head! . . . Look, don't give me the hearsay shit. I don't
give a fuck whether we can legally hang him or not. The
stupid son of a bitch is a liability, Brace. He'll bring us all
down if we give him enough time. So you listen up. Once the
D.C. boys are gone, I want *his* ass out of here too.
Permanently, you understand? . . . I don't care. You find a
way, Brace. You damn well *find* a way!"

He slammed the phone down.

CHAPTER 26

Kemp barked into his speakerphone: "Yeah, what is it,
Hawes?"

"Scott Craik to see you," Hawes said.

"Jesus Christ," Kemp muttered. "All right, Hawes, send
him in."

A few moments later Craik entered the office. He walked
over to Kemp's desk and sat down, facing the sheriff.

"It looks like we ain't gonna be friends," Kemp said.
Craik shook his head. "In which case, I'm not too happy to
be seeing you still around."

"I've been busy," Craik said.

"I hope I'm not gonna hear what I think I'm gonna hear."

"Sheriff, I don't really care what you hope. I've been driving up and down this county all morning long. I've been banging on doors and talking to people. One of them told me that Will Devereaux is dead. Now, that fucking upsets me."

"He tried to kill one of my deputies and got himself shot," Kemp said through his teeth.

"Uh-huh. And what was he doing going after your deputy?"

"Look, Craik, what business is this of yours?"

"It's my business because it happened while I was out doing your job," Craik said.

Kemp's eyes narrowed. "Get out of here," he said. "And while you're at it, get out of my county."

Craik looked back just as hard. "Will Devereaux was a harmless old drunk," he said, "and you know it. Fyke never had to shoot him in self-defense. The bodies are starting to pile up here, Kemp. You've got to do something, and I'm offering you my help. You throw me out and I'll get help someplace else."

Kemp slammed his fist down on the desktop. "Who do you think you are?" he shouted. "Are you *threatening* me?"

"Uh-uh. I'm filing a report. Somebody else talked to me today."

Kemp started. "Who?" he said uneasily.

"A woman at the Bay View Motel. She remembered a guest who smoked little cigars with a gold band."

"Oh, for chrissake—"

"Skip the act, Sheriff. Said person left after a visit from your deputies. It's not at all certain that he departed, ah, voluntarily."

Kemp started to say something, then closed his mouth.

"Come on, Kemp," Craik said. "I'm doing you a favor. Give me another day or two and I'll have a murderer for you. I'm good at this. All you have to do in return is a small favor for me."

"What?"

"Put Fyke in jail where he belongs."

"God damn you," Kemp said in a low, choking voice. "Don't you tell me who I should arrest. I've been in charge of enforcing the law around here since you were in grade school."

"Good. Do your job, then. That's all I want and I'll get out of your hair."

Kemp aimed a forefinger at him. "Craik," he said, "I thought we come to an understanding yesterday, but I guess not. So let me make it real plain to you. Today is the end of your visit to Dorset County. I don't want to see your face again. Is that something you can understand?"

Craik got up. "The Bay View Motel, Sheriff," he said. "I guess that's where we'll have to start. I'm sorry you can't see your way clear to cooperate. Be a lot easier working with you than against you."

He left. Kemp stabbed furiously at his phone console.

"Yes, sir," Hawes said.

"Send Fyke and Tilghman in here. Now!"

The deputies hurried in a moment later.

"Follow Craik," Kemp said. "If he don't leave town, help him. I don't want no more dead bodies, but I want the son of a bitch out of Dorset. You'all think you can do that without fucking up?"

He was looking at Fyke, but Fyke didn't say anything.

"Yes, sir," Tilghman said.

"Well, get moving, then."

Craik got into Susanna's car and pulled out of the parking lot. When he got to the main road, he turned right, headed west. A sheriff's department cruiser fell in behind him. He drove at a leisurely pace. The cruiser kept a measured distance between them.

Craik continued to drive west. In twenty minutes he crossed the county line. At that point the cruiser pulled off onto the shoulder. It stayed there for five minutes, then made a U-turn and headed back the way it had come. The return trip to Dorset took considerably less time.

The deputies reported to Sheriff Kemp.

"All right," Kemp said, "but I don't believe for a minute that he's gone for good. He's your assignment. I want you two to cruise around today, and I don't want you quitting before midnight. Check the likely roads, go by his house from time to time. Don't assume that he'll still be in the girl's car.

"If you see Craik in this county, grab him and make sure he leaves. Make *sure,* you follow me?" The two men nodded. "If he needs persuading, let Crowe do it. Crowe knows he might be hearing from you. I don't want any more *killing.* I don't want any more *shooting.* I don't want either of you to *touch* him, you understand me?" The deputies nodded again. "Just see he knows better than to stay around. And witness that he shouldn't've screwed with Rodney Crowe. Clear?"

"We'll do it right, Sheriff," Tilghman said.

"You'd better," Kemp said. "I got a shitload on my mind here, and I can't be worrying about an asshole like Craik every time I sniff the air."

"Yes, sir," Tilghman said. "Don't worry."

"All right, get going. And keep in contact."

The deputies returned to the cruiser and went out on the road.

Craik had driven only a few miles, until he came to the first small town. It had one modest motel, called the Chesapeake Rest. The Chesapeake Rest was ten units done in fake brick, with a tar shingle roof. A number of shingles had blown off and had not been replaced. Craik drove up to the office.

The boy behind the desk gave him a room for one night. Craik paid in cash. He asked the boy where the nearest outside pay phone was and was referred to a service station two doors down.

He parked Susanna's car in front of his room and walked to the service station. The attendant gave him change for a dollar. He went into the phone booth and dialed a long-distance number. A woman came on the line and repeated the number back to him.

"I want to talk to Smith," Craik said.

"I'm sorry, there's no one here by that name," the woman said.

"Right. Find him and tell him I'll call back in two hours. It's important."

"I'm sorry—"

"Tell him it's Kirk," he said. He hung up and walked back to the motel room.

GRENADA

October 1983

CHAPTER 27

There was a very soft knocking at the outer door. Kirk had been lying on his bed, not sleeping. The occasional hollow crack of a gunshot reverberated among the hills in the pitch-dark night. Very few people would be able to sleep.

Kirk's apartment was dark too. The generator had overloaded again, and there was no power in St. George's. The only illumination came from the headlights and searchlights of the roving military vehicles.

When the knock came, Kirk grabbed a heavy flashlight from his bedside table. He rolled silently off the bed. He padded on bare feet across the living room. At the door he straightened up and stood off to the side.

"Who is it?" he whispered.

"Quahtahmain," came the return whisper.

He quickly opened the door, and the slender young black man slipped inside. Kirk shone the light on him. He was wearing black shorts and a cutoff dark gray sweatshirt. On the sweatshirt was a faded drawing of a bird in navy blue. The bird had a funny haircut and was saying "Peace."

Underneath were block letters reading "The Message of Woodstock."

The man's skin was ebony black. It glistened with sweat in the hot, damp air, like the surface of a highly polished shillelagh. The man had hair cropped close to his scalp and the faintest wisp of a mustache on his upper lip. His body seemed to be constructed entirely of small, flat slabs of muscle.

"Jesus Christ, Quartermain," Kirk said. "There's a shoot-to-kill curfew on. What the fuck are you *do*ing?"

"No time, Mistah Kirk," Quartermain said. "Come now."

Kirk lit some candles. The room partially emerged from the dark. He switched off his flashlight.

"Come *where*?"

"You must leave now."

"Quartermain, what are you talking about? We can't go out there. The bastards will shoot us."

Quartermain had taken a small tin from his pocket. He popped the lid on it and handed it to Kirk. The tin contained some kind of black makeup grease.

"Put on, mahn," Quartermain said.

Kirk stared stupidly at the thing in his hand.

"On face," Quartermain said, smiling gently. "Hahnds. You don't hahve the nahtural protecshahn. Dahk clothes too. Soonest."

"Tell me what it is, Quartermain," Kirk said. He was already moving across the small apartment to his bedroom. He went to the bureau and fished around in the gloom, taking out jeans, black socks, and a dark cotton sweater. From the closet came some blue-on-blue jogging shoes. Stripped to his briefs, he went back into the living room and began dressing.

"They come for you soon, mahn," Quartermain said.

"Who? The RMC?"

Quartermain nodded. "They know who you ah."

"You guessing?"

Quartermain shook his head vigorously. "Is not specu-lashahn," he said. "You a enemy of the new revahlushahn."

"You got orders to pull me out or you acting on your own?"

"Orders, mahn. But I do it, anyway, when I know. I doan let you die heah."

Kirk smiled slightly. "Thanks," he said. The smile passed. "All right. But how the hell are we supposed to use the safe route when the army's all over the fucking streets?"

"No safe route, mahn. We go in my boht."

"Somebody be there to pick us up?"

Quartermain nodded. Kirk had finished dressing and begun to smear the greasepaint on the exposed whiteness of his body.

"You know you won't be able to come back to Grenada," Kirk said. "Not as long as those murdering bastards are in power."

"I know, mahn."

"We got any choice?"

"No choice. You don' go, you be dead by mahnin'. You be one dead spy. Mistah Coahd, him show you body in Mahket Squayah."

Kirk grimaced. "Thanks a lot," he said.

"Hurry, mahn," Quartermain said.

Kirk finished blacking himself. Quartermain held out one of the dark, knitted, circular caps favored by the islanders.

"You hair, mahn," he said. "Don' sweat, if you please. You get black-and-white face daht way."

Kirk grinned and fitted the cap over his pale blond hair. "I pass for Grenadian?" he said.

Quartermain shook his head. "Don' mattah," he said. "Them shoot you if you Grenadiahn, them shoot you if you Americahn. Come now."

Kirk went around and blew out the candles. When they

were all extinguished, Quartermain was only a moving shadow.

"Don' bring light, mahn," Quartermain said. "You might use it, ya know. Stay by me."

"Okay," Kirk said. "Where we going?"

"Yacht Servahces. My boht theyah."

"Then what?"

"Americahns meet us offshoah. Take you hohm."

"What about you?"

"I goin' to Barbados. I wait it out theyah."

"Wait what out?"

Quartermain chuckled. "The new revahlushahn, mahn," he said. "Waht you thinkin'?"

Kirk took a deep breath. "Let's go," he said.

Quartermain carefully opened the door, and the two men left the apartment. There was no difference in light level, inside or out. There was no sound or light coming from any other part of the small building. There was only the incessant screeching of the tree frogs and the occasional distant rumble of a truck negotiating one of the steep hills of St. George's.

The two men were on a patio adjacent to the entrance to Kirk's basement apartment. Stone steps led up to the main road into town. Kirk and Quartermain went in the opposite direction. They crossed the patio. At its far end was a wrought-iron railing. Quartermain went over it and stood on the other side.

"Six foot, mahn," he whispered, and he dropped into the darkness.

Kirk did the same, with Quartermain breaking his fall. Both men slipped on ground still wet from an earlier evening shower. They held on to each other and kept their footing.

The ground sloped downward. It was generally soft and mushy, with occasional outcroppings of volcanic rock. They stayed close together, following the course of a stream that carried runoff from the street above. The slope was thick with trees that were shedding large droplets of water, but there was very little underbrush. The people who owned the building also owned a goat. They passed near to where it was tethered. It bleated at them and they quickened their pace.

They reached the far end of the property. The browsing goat had not yet defoliated the area. There were some low-lying brambles that caught at the men's clothing. They picked their way slowly, carefully. Kirk worked at keeping his clothes from being torn and his white flesh from being exposed.

In a few minutes Quartermain reached back and stopped Kirk with his hand. He crouched. Kirk followed suit.

The two men were squatting behind a screen of immature banana trees. Beyond the trees lay Lagoon Road, and on the other side of it was the lagoon where the yacht basin was located. There was no movement on the road, and none on the water save the ghostly bobbing of boats riding at anchor.

Quartermain tugged on Kirk's sweater, and they edged out onto the perimeter of the road. They headed southwest, skirting the lagoon.

For a while there was only the sound of the night animals and the sea. Then Quartermain froze. Kirk, right behind him, stopped too. There was a sound in the distance, from the direction in which they were headed. No light, no movement, just sound. It was the hiss of tires and occasional clanking of a vehicle coasting with its engine off.

There was a stand of screw pine to the two men's left. Without a word they melted into it. They lay prone.

As the vehicle reached the bottom of the hill at the western end of Lagoon Road, the night came suddenly alive. Its engine groaned and then rumbled. There was the gnashing of ancient gears. Spot and headlights came on simultaneously.

The jeep moved slowly down the road, lighting up the houses and thickets that lined it. The light flickered here and there as the jeep jounced through the frequent potholes. Kirk and Quartermain buried their faces in their arms and wriggled as if to dig themselves into the soil. The jeep rolled past. In front were a driver and a man operating a portable spotlight. In the back were two soldiers. Each was carrying an American M-14 on his hip. Their heads swiveled with the movement of the spot. The whites of their eyes gleamed in the reflected light.

The sound of the jeep receded. Kirk and Quartermain kept their faces hidden until the driver could be heard downshifting. The engine whined as it pulled the jeep up the hill toward the road into St. George's.

Quartermain peered out through the maze of stilt roots that supported the trunk of one of the screw pines. He placed a hand on Kirk's shoulder to keep him down. A tiny red glow could be seen on the road, and then the outline of two armed soldiers, one of them smoking a cigarette. They moved down the road, looking around, talking so softly that their words were inaudible a few feet away. One of them stepped in a pothole filled with rainwater. He swore in a low voice while his companion giggled quietly.

Kirk and Quartermain waited, huddled among the thickly leafed shrubs. Five minutes passed. There was no further sound or movement on Lagoon Road.

Cautiously, Quartermain eased himself up and edged out onto the road. Kirk followed a moment later. They moved west again, always keeping to the road's landward side.

"No moah pahtrols, mahn," Quartermain said. "Not on this rohd."

They went at a trot. After a few hundred yards Quartermain stopped and crouched. Kirk imitated him. Quartermain squatted stock still and turned his head from one side to the other. Then he pointed toward the lagoon. Just offshore, a small, dark shape rode up and down on the gentle swell of the water.

The two men removed their shoes, but Kirk left his dark socks on. They crept across the road and entered the water. It was warm as blood. Kirk kept his hands raised.

They waded out to the boat, which was moored in chest-deep water. It was a sleek sixteen-foot runabout with a seventy-five horsepower outboard clamped to the stern. Quartermain went first. He put his hands on the gunwale, levered himself up, and rolled into the boat. Kirk did the same. Neither man made much noise.

"Down, mahn," Quartermain whispered.

Kirk lay on the forward floorboards. Quartermain untied the boat from its mooring, then went to the controls amidships. The boat drifted slowly until its bow was pointed north, toward the mouth of the harbor. At that point Quartermain punched the electric starter.

The engine turned over once, then caught. Quartermain pulled one lever backward. The transmission engaged with a low chunk. He then shoved another lever all the way forward. He put both hands on the wheel. The engine whined, and the bow of the boat rose straight up out of the water. For a moment it seemed to hang there, then it came back down and the boat shot forward. In a few seconds it was up to speed.

The channel out of the yacht basin wound among buoys and moored boats of all kinds. Quartermain weaved the craft in and out, running without lights, keeping the throttle wide open. The runabout was fast. It had nearly reached the mouth of the lagoon before spotlights came on behind them. They were well out of range of small arms.

At harbor's mouth, the port of St. George's lay just north and slightly west. Quartermain turned to the southwest and headed out into the open Caribbean. The gentle sea became choppy.

The boat rounded the bluff on which stood Butler House, formerly government offices, now under control of the Revolutionary Military Council. There were men up on the bluff. They opened fire.

Quartermain aimed the boat due west. Its hull banged violently against the waves. The gunfire slackened. Eventually, it ceased. When it did, Quartermain turned back to the southwest. He ran the engine flat out for another ten minutes, then cut it back. At the diminished speed the engine turned over very quietly.

Kirk raised himself up and sat in the forward seat. He looked around. To the east the ghostly crescent of Grand Anse Beach was visible in the starlight.

Quartermain handed Kirk a small pump. "One bullet hohl," he said.

Kirk slid the end of the hose under the floorboards and pumped. A stream of water splashed over the side. At the rate the boat was leaking, he could pump for a few minutes, then rest for an equal amount of time.

"Where we going?" Kirk asked.

"Islahnd," Quartermain said. He coughed.

"Chopper or boat pickup?"

"Choppah."

They rode in silence for a while, then Kirk said, "Shit, Quartermain, we really blew it, didn't we?"

"Who, mahn?"

"I don't know, all of us. I felt like some good things were beginning to happen there, and now it's all turned around."

"Is Grenadiahn politics. You cahn't tell."

"You can tell that those bastards murdered every decent person in the government."

"Coahd not a bahd mahn," Quartermain said. "General Austin not bahd—"

"Not *bad*? They killed Maurice in cold blood. *And* Unison. *And* Jacki. Jacki Creft was pregnant, for chrissake!"

"Daht I know."

"They fired into the *crowd*. How could they *do* that? Their own brothers and sisters and cousins . . . Jesus. How could it all have gone so bad so fast?"

"Is Grenadiahn politics, Mistah Kirk," Quartermain said. "Americahns don' understahnd. This will pahss. When you hahve you own revahlushahn, many people die. We too. We ahsk for you help, but we make our mistakes."

"Killing all those innocent people is a pretty bad mistake."

"Yes. Maurice and Unisahn and Jahki gone now. My cousahn too. Ahnd now we staht again. If Mistah Coahd truly a bahd mahn, then we be rid of him and I cahn go home. In such time."

Quartermain had another coughing fit.

"You okay?" Kirk asked.

"Yes," Quartermain said. "Is the night air ohnly."

"God, I wonder what's going to happen next."

"Americahns come in, I believe."

"You think so?" Kirk paused. "Christ, I don't even know how I feel about that."

"Is not you prahblem."

"It just means more people will be killed, doesn't it? But then, *some*body should throw those murdering bastards in jail." Kirk paused again, then continued. "You know, Quartermain, I love this place. All the places I've been posted, I never loved any of them. But I love Grenada. I love the people here."

"Grenadiahns love you, too, mahn."

"It isn't fair," Kirk said. "The people haven't done anything to deserve all this."

"It will pahss," Quartermain said. "Grenadah people, they don' change. You come bahck next year, they will welcahm you."

"Yeah. And what happens in the meantime?"

"Don' worry. Americahns always hurry, always worry.

You a bettah mahn since you runnin' on Caribbeahn time, but you still Americahn."

Quartermain's teeth were visible when he grinned. Kirk shook his head slowly and pumped water from the bottom of the boat. They rounded Grenada's southwestern tip, still well offshore. Quartermain changed course, headed them east. A small island loomed dead ahead in the dark.

The boat churned its way around the small island. The south side of it was in the lee of the tradewinds. It was also the far side, looking from Grenada proper. Quartermain steered for a tiny cove, with a slice of sand beach and a dark hill rising behind it.

Twenty yards from shore, the boat hit a submerged rock. It was going slowly enough that only a small hole was torn in the hull. Water began seeping in. Quartermain cut the engine.

"Go ashoah heah," he said.

Kirk dropped over the side. The water came up to his shoulders.

"Sink boht," Quartermain said.

"Okay," Kirk said. "Come on."

Quartermain coughed. "Cahn't, mahn," he said.

"What are you talking about?" Kirk said. He pulled himself along the gunwale of the boat until he was next to Quartermain. He reached up and touched the other man's arm. The cotton sweatshirt was soaked and sticky.

"Jesus Christ," Kirk said. "You're shot."

"I be okay, mahn," Quartermain said. "Let boht sink."

"*Quartermain!*"

"Quiet, mahn. Let me be now."

The boat settled slowly toward the bottom. Eventually, there was enough water that Kirk could ease Quartermain over the side. He supported the Grenadian's head and towed him to the beach. He laid his friend out on the still-warm sand.

"Thank you, mahn," Quartermain said.

"When's the chopper get here?" Kirk asked.

"Dahn."

"God damn it," Kirk said. "Goddamn fucking shit . . ."

The boat burbled and sank completely. Kirk tried to get Quartermain's sweatshirt off, but the other man stopped him.

"Is okay," Quartermain said. "Is stopped now."

"Any water here?" Kirk asked.

"No watah."

Carefully, Kirk dragged his friend up among some rocks, screened from the open sea. He smoothed the sand. Then he climbed the hill behind the beach. He found a traveler's palm. At the base of its leaf stalks rainwater had collected in little hollows. He tore off several of the stalks and went back to the beach.

"Quartermain," he said.

The other man groaned. Kirk knelt and raised his head. He tipped some water into his mouth. Quartermain drank, then coughed.

"Shit," Kirk said.

He tried again, but Quartermain's lips remained closed. Kirk sat on the sand, cross-legged, cradling the Grenadian's head in his lap. A half hour later Quartermain coughed violently, expelling blood, and then his breath ceased.

Kirk stayed in the same position all night. No boat passed. The cove was protected from the great ocean swells that rolled out of the east. The waves that broke on its sands were small and steady. They broke and retreated, broke and retreated. There was little other sound. The two men waited, the living one moving only slightly more than the dead one.

First light arrived with tropic suddenness. With it came the chopper, a U.S. Navy Seasprite. It hovered over the tiny beach and dropped a harness. Kirk wrapped it around Quartermain's body, and the Grenadian was winched up. The body revolved slowly at the end of the line.

The harness returned and Kirk, too, was hoisted aboard. The Navy men solemnly shook his hand.

One of them said to him, "We'll get the bastards," through gritted teeth.

Kirk looked into the man's eyes for a long moment, then said, "Fuck it," and turned away. He sat down and spoke to no one.

The chopper tilted over and set a course just south of due east. It followed the rugged southern coast of Grenada, at no great distance from the island. There was no danger of it being intercepted. The RMC had, along with the militia and a collection of World War I rifles, inherited the Grenadian Air Force, which did not exist.

After the Seasprite had cleared Grenada, it turned northeast and flew over open water the hundred and twenty-five miles to Barbados. Kirk was given fresh clothes and the chance to sleep for a couple of hours.

At eleven o'clock the following morning he was in the office in Washington with the white walls and the black furniture. Smith faced him from the other side of the barren executive's desk, as he had that morning in June. Smith was rotating his leather swivel chair slightly as the two men looked each other over. Then he smiled.

"Hell of a job, Kirk," he said.

"Yeah, great," Kirk muttered.

"No, I mean it."

"Don't powder my ass, Smitty. The operation was a failure. It may not have been my fault, but it was a failure. I got close to Bishop and now he's dead, along with every other decent person they had down there. It was a wasted three months."

Smith looked at Kirk with disbelief. "Come on, Steven," he said. "You're going to get a commendation. From the top. I've got all the paperwork right here in my desk. I don't understand why you're so down. This isn't like you."

"I'm down because I did my best and nothing came of it."

"Of course something came of it. We got the PRG out of power."

"Oh, yeah, we did that, all right."

"But that's what we wanted."

Kirk stared at the man across the desk. A minute passed. Slowly, Kirk's expression changed. The weariness and resignation were gone. His features set into an icy mask.

"Come on, Steven," Smith said finally, nervously. "Lighten up."

When Kirk spoke, his words were measured, each spoken clearly and distinctly. He said, "What do you mean, Smitty? What do you mean, *we* got the Provisional Revolutionary Government out of power."

"What do you mean, what do I mean?" Smith said with exasperation. "*We*. The United States. Collectively. With a lot of the credit going to you. Personally."

"I think you'd better explain a few things to me."

"Oh, for chrissake, Kirk! What the hell did you think you were doing down there?"

"I know what my assignment was, and so do you."

"Of course I know. But what did you think you were *doing*?"

"I thought I was doing my assignment," Kirk said evenly.

"Jesus. I can't believe I have to explain this to you. You're an experienced field man."

"Well, you do. Pretend I'm one of your green recruits who got a job because he has a degree in Islamic studies. Make it that simple." Kirk folded his arms. "I'm waiting," he said.

Instead of answering, Smith got up and went to the window. He stood, looking down at the busy avenue eight stories below. He took several deep breaths. When he returned to his desk, he was composed.

"Look, Steven," he said, "the PRG was a government hostile to the U.S. It was building another Cuba in the southern Caribbean. You knew that. You knew we were working hard to destabilize. What did you think, that we were going to turn around and make *friends* with them?"

"Yes, that's what I thought. That it was at least an option."

"Don't be naive."

"Don't you dare call it naïveté," Kirk said coldly. "I'm as good a tactician as anyone in the agency. What I was doing was sound tactics."

"Look, what you were doing was helping bring down the PRG. That was always the objective. Is that simple enough for you?"

"You used me, you son of a bitch."

"Cut the crap, Kirk. Of course we use our operatives. That's their job. To be used in the attainment of this country's objectives."

"You've never used me like this. Why wasn't I told of the real objective?"

Smith shrugged. "Would you have done as well?" he asked.

Kirk stared at him for a long moment. "I don't believe it," he said finally. "I can't believe how fucking cynical you are. You have a mole in the PRG council too?"

"You don't have a need-to-know on that."

"Yeah, I'll bet you did. And who provoked the soldiers to fire on the crowd at Fort Rupert? You have your lily-white fingers in that one?"

"That was unfortunate," Smith said. "But sometimes—"

"Yeah, I know. Sometimes innocent people get hurt. Spare me, will you? I was *there*, Smitty. The bastards turned their guns on an unarmed crowd. Women, kids, old people, they didn't give a shit. They slaughtered them. When it was over, even you would have thrown up."

"I don't see—"

"Now, that's sure an understatement. You don't see fucking anything. That's your problem."

"Look, Kirk," Smith said angrily, "I don't have to take this shit! You seem to be forgetting that I am your superior."

"Oh, don't worry, I haven't forgotten that. I couldn't

possibly have gotten myself into this without your superior help. Actually, I gotta hand it to you, Smitty. It was a great plan and it worked perfectly.

"You knew there was tension between the Bishop and Coard factions. You knew Coard wanted to be top dog himself. So you send in some dumbass who thinks he's there to improve relations, who's been instructed to communicate with the prime minister in strictest secrecy. Me. Then you betray the dumbass to the other side. They watch him closely, find out about his secret meetings with Bishop, and immediately assume the prime minister is negotiating to sell the country out to the hated Yankees."

Kirk nodded his head. "Very effective," he continued. "The Bishop wing of the government gets disgraced and the hard-liners take over. Coard and Austin and the rest of those murdering scum. Just as you'd hoped.

"The next step's pretty easy to see. We invade, right? Uncle Sam to the rescue. To 'restore democracy'? Sure. The country's in turmoil, twenty-four-hour curfew with shoot-to-kill, serious Marxists in charge. And the students! Of course. American students on the island. We can't have another Iran! That's a couple more excuses to invade than we really need, isn't it? Which was the idea all along. Jesus, how could I not have seen it?"

Kirk leaned back in his chair. Smith said quietly, "Are you finished now?"

"No, I am not fucking *finished*! Two nights ago a man died in my arms, Smith. A good man who gave up his life saving mine. Before that I watched dozens of innocent people get butchered. And why? Because we caused a decent government to be replaced by a gang of thugs, just so we'd then have an excuse to go in and play liberator. I don't suppose you'll be able to understand this, you prick, but I hate the fact that I was a part of it."

"Steven, Steven," Smith said solicitously. "I know how you're feeling. But it'll pass. There's a war going on in the world. I know that you know that. And I know that you believe we're on the right side. In any war there're going to be casualities, people who don't deserve to die but do just the same. Right now you don't have any perspective about what's happend in Grenada. You got a little charmed by a tinhorn dictator. You'll see that eventually. You'll see that we did the right thing there. Please, take a couple of weeks off. Think things over. Will you do that?"

Kirk stared at his boss for a long moment, then said, "You patronizing son of a bitch. You really are a cold fish, aren't you? You think any amount of time is gonna change the way I feel? Well, fuck ya." He got up and leaned his hands on the edge of Smith's executive desk. "Fuck you, Smith. Fuck the agency and the government and all the simple shits who do this every day of their lives. I quit. Take that fancy commendation and stick it up your ass." He turned slowly on his heel and walked away.

"Steven . . ." Smith said. When Kirk didn't respond, Smith said more sharply. "Steven! Don't you walk out that door. You can't do that. You owe the agency. There are procedures to follow. You don't just stroll away from a job like this. It's your country you're turning your back on. Don't do it, Steven."

Kirk paused when he reached the door. He put his hand on the knob, then withdrew it. He turned to face Smith.

"Don't threaten me," he said.

"It's for your own good," Smith said. "If you want to leave the agency, you need to be debriefed, all that. You know the routine. Don't make me read you the regs, for chrissake."

"Eat your regs, Smitty. I'm walking and there isn't a damn thing you can do about it. And maybe while I'm at it I'll tell someone what really happened in Grenada."

"Oh, that's great, Kirk. That's really terrific. You know what? You just go right ahead. Tell *The New York* fucking *Times* if you want. They won't believe you. And even if they do, you're going to learn something. They don't care,

Steven. No one in this country cares what happens in some Third World backwater unless it directly affects them. Sure, we'll use the students. Americans are gonna care about those poor sniveling little rich kids. But the natives? Don't kid yourself. You can waste them from now until they're wiped out, and *no body gives* a shit."

He paused, but Kirk didn't say anything.

"Go on, Kirk." He sneered. "Walk, you sanctimonious shit. Go tell someone what you *know*. See where it gets you."

There was a lengthy silence. Anger showed at the corners of Kirk's eyes, but otherwise it was as if he were deep in thought. From the street below came the muted wail of a siren. Its pitch rose steadily, then suddenly and rapidly diminished.

"You know," Kirk said finally, "someday, some way, I'm gonna pay you back for this. You keep that right there in your head, Smith. Keep it there all the time."

Kirk pulled open the heavy oak door and walked out of the office.

DORSET COUNTY, VIRGINIA

August 1985

SECOND
THURSDAY

CHAPTER 28

Craik called back two hours later. The same female voice insisted that there was no Mr. Smith at that number. Craik said that he understood but that it was important and they should make every effort to locate Smith. He said that he'd call back in another two hours.

He went back to his room and watched afternoon soap operas on the black-and-white TV. When the two hours had passed, he placed the call once again. The woman continued to insist that he had the wrong number. Craik told her to have Smith leave a message for him and that he'd check in later in the evening.

When the sky began to darken, Craik drove back to Brawlton. He went directly to his cottage and parked the red Toyota in the dirt yard. Inside, he flipped through the yellow tide-table book. There was nothing there. Then he went into his bedroom and put a few things into the metallic suitcase.

He carried the suitcase to Marla Vickers's house. He rapped on her door. She was at home and hollered him inside.

As he opened the door a gray Ford passed the house. Craik turned, but it was just an anonymous set of receding taillights. He went in.

"Marla," he said, "I came here yesterday to find out what was going on in Brawlton, and now I know."

"Right much," Vickers said.

"Yeah, and just between you and me, it's about to blow. For some reason I seem to be in the middle of everything. It's not what I wanted but it's happened, and there's no point to bitching about it now. Thing is, there are people who want me to leave town in a bad way."

"Which you ain't gonna oblige them."

"No."

"I didn't think so," Vickers said with a sigh. "I expected first time I met you that you was trouble. But like you say, no use bitching about that now. You want me to help you, I suppose I will."

"Thanks. I guess, outside of Susanna, you're the only person in town I trust."

"Just tell me what you need, Craik. You don't have to put the icing on it." She sucked at her pipe, expelled a small cloud of bluish smoke.

"I don't think it's much," Craik said. "I want you to keep this suitcase for me. You have someplace you can hide it?"

"Yeah. Anything illegal in there?"

"No. You can look if you want. It's just some things I want to be sure I can lay my hands on if I need them."

Vickers waved the pipe in a gesture of dismissal. "I believe you," she said. "Who might be coming after your stuff?"

"I'm not sure. The sheriff and his deputies. Maybe some people I don't know. No one has a reason to think I'd leave anything with you, so you shouldn't be bothered. If anyone comes looking for me, you don't know where I've gone. The suitcase won't even come up."

Vickers looked into Craik's eyes for a moment, then said, "Susanna's a nice girl, Craik. You gonna do right by her?"

"As best I can."

"See you do. Okay, I'll hold this thing for you."

"Don't do anything with it unless I tell you personally."

"All right."

"Thanks, Marla."

Vickers smiled. "Ain't but your looks, Craik," she said. "You don't keep 'em, you're gonna be in a pile of trouble. But for now they'll do ya."

Craik left and walked back to his cottage. The gray Ford was parked out front. Craik slipped quietly into the yard. He skirted one of the live oaks and came around the side of the house. He edged up to the wall, peered into the window that gave onto the dining area.

The dining area was empty, but from his vantage point Craik could see across the cottage. There was a man sitting on the threadbare sofa. The man was wearing a lightweight pale blue summer suit. He had a featureless, round face and plastic-frame glasses. He was scanning one of the copies of *Popular Mechanics* that had been lying on the low table. He steadily turned the pages, apparently looking only at the pictures.

Craik walked around the house and in the front door. The man set the magazine down and smiled.

"Steven," he said, rising from the couch. He extended his hand. Craik ignored it.

"Hello, Smith," Craik said. "You got my call?"

Smith hesitated, just for an instant, then said, "Yes, of course. How are you, Steven?"

"What'd they tell you?"

"Well, not much, actually."

Craik nodded. "The name's Craik," he said. "Scott Craik. Might save us some embarrassment along the line."

"Of course. It's as meaningful as Kirk, I suppose."

"Uh-huh. You want something to drink?"

"Sure. Whatever you're having," Smith said. He sat back down again.

Craik went to the refrigerator, got out two beers, and
punched open the tops. He carried one to Smith, then folded
himself into the overstuffed chair that didn't match the couch.
The two men looked at each other and drank a little beer.

"How'd you know where I was?" Craik asked.

"Well, we've been looking for you, of course," Smith
said.

"I'll bet."

"You're good, Kir—ah, Craik. But then, I always knew
that about you. You were one of the best. Still, two years is a
damned long time, isn't it?"

"You have found me if I hadn't called?"

"Uh-huh. We've developed some pretty sophisticated new
software since you left."

"Sure," Craik said. "But I don't care what kind of
computer searches you can run; you still don't have a data
base for the whole country to run them against. Who tipped
you?"

"You know I'm not going—"

"Forrest Holder?"

Smith casually sipped at his beer. "What's your interest in
Holder?" he asked.

"I sell him fish."

Smith chuckled. "You're a fisherman?"

Craik tapped with his fingernail on the edge of the beer
can. "That's right," he said.

"Come on, Craik. I know what you are, and I know that
you know. It isn't a fisherman."

"What are you doing here, Smitty?"

Smith shrugged. "Why'd you call?"

The night breeze had picked up. Some cooler air had
moved in from the northwest, and it wasn't nearly as hot as it
had been during the day, but the front door and windows were
still open. The screen door rattled gently against its frame. It
was the only noise in the room except for the slurping sound
of beer being consumed.

"All right," Smith said finally, "I want you to come to Washington with me."

"What for?"

"We want to talk to you. Hell, we'd even have you back, after all this time. But at the least, you were never properly debriefed, as you well know."

"I told you two years ago that I didn't want any part of the agency."

"I respect that. We just want to talk. Then you'll be free to go. Become a . . . fisherman, or whatever you care to."

"Talk for how long?" Craik asked.

"A day or two. You know how these things go. There's a lot you haven't told us about your last . . . assignment."

"I wouldn't think you'd care. Everything went just the way you planned, didn't it?"

"We attained our objectives, yes," Smith said. "And you can't deny that the people there are a hell of a lot better off than they were. If you don't think we did the right thing, just ask *them*."

"Yeah, the end justifies the means and all that. I really don't want to discuss this with you."

"Look, come back to D.C. with me and we'll talk about it there, okay? That's all *we* want. How about telling me what *you* want?"

Craik rubbed the side of the beer can across his forehead. It left a sheen of moisture on his skin.

"When I mentioned Holder, you recognized the name," Craik said. "Why?"

"When we found out where you were, I did a little prelim on the area, of course. Holder's an important man hereabouts. And he has considerable clout in Washington. We have a file on him. What of it?"

"You know about the scam he's running?"

"What scam?"

Craik paused to study the other man's face. There was nothing to see. The eyes behind the glasses didn't blink. It was an innocent face. Craik blew out a long breath.

"All right, look, Smitty," he said. "It's been a long time. I'm not as angry as I once was, and maybe I'll even go to D.C. with you. But I can't right now. First of all, there's a lot of bad shit going on in this county, and by my own well-earned fate I've landed right in the middle of it. I've got no choice but to deal with it.

"Now, I'll believe you don't know anything about it. Thing is, it may be too big for me to handle by myself. If I need help, I want to be able to get it from you."

"That's all you're going to tell me?" Smith said.

"For now. Stay in the area and let me know where. I'll keep in touch."

"How much help are we talking about?"

"Government. There's federal crime going on here."

"I can't involve the agency in domestic."

"Yeah, but you can get the goddamn bureau down here in an hour if you start yelling."

"I don't know," Smith said. "It *has* been a long time, Steven. I've changed too. I'd like to say we'll help, but . . ."

"I'm doing you a favor, Smitty. Look at it that way. I'm giving you a chance to earn some favors from the bureau."

"Well, maybe. I won't do anything until I know a hell of a lot more than I do now."

"You'll have the whole story," Craik said. "But you might have to make up your mind fast."

"I can handle it. That, I assume, is your 'first of all.' Is there a 'second of all'?"

"Yes. I have to make sure that someone is safe. I won't budge until I do."

"The second," Smith said, "is more important than the first, I take it."

"It is."

"And what's the time frame?"

"I can't be sure. A day. No more than two."

"Then you'll come to Washington with me."

Craik hesitated. "Yeah, then I'll come to Washington with you."

Smith got up. "I'll be at the Dorset House," he said. He extended his hand and Craik shook it.

The Dorset House was a huge nineteenth-century brick mansion set on two acres of sweeping lawns and formal gardens just north of Brawlton. It fronted on the Chesapeake and had a hundred yards of private sand beach. The grounds contained a famous maze constructed of carefully clipped ornamental shrubs. At the center of the maze was a flower bed laid out in the shape of a heart.

Smith registered at the Dorset House and went immediately to one of the private, wood-paneled phone booths in the lobby. He punched an eleven-digit number. A woman answered at the other end.

"It's Smith," he said.

"I'm sorry, Mr. Smith," the woman said, "he's got someone in the study with him. He didn't want to be disturbed. I think it's someone from the State Department."

"Can you buzz him?"

"I shouldn't."

"It's very important. Just buzz him and say that I've found Kirk and I need to know what to do. He'd want you to."

"All right," the woman said. "Hold on, Mr. Smith."

The line went dead for half a minute, then the woman came back on. "He says to call back in fifteen minutes," she said. "He wants to know if you've got a good connection."

"Tell him it's fine. Thanks."

Smith hung up. He went to his room, lay down for fifteen minutes, then returned to the lobby. This time a man answered the phone.

"It's Smith," he said.

"You've got a clear line?" the man said.

"Hell, I don't know if there's a clear line in the country anymore, but as far as I know, yes."

"You found him?"

"Yes."

"How does he seem?"

"It's hard to tell. He wants me to think he's become a fisherman. I'm not inclined to buy it, but I'm damned if I can figure out what he's up to. He said he'd called the agency. That true?"

"He did. After you left today. He wanted to speak to you and nobody else, and we put him off until you could get to him. We don't know what he was after."

"He told me he needs help," Smith said. "He wants to bust some illegal activity going on here."

"Holder?"

"Could be. But it doesn't make any sense that he came to *us* for help with that. He must know that we already know about Holder. Otherwise he wouldn't be targeting Holder as part of a payback to us. Of course, there's the possibility of a deep double cross, but he's making himself pretty vulnerable to set it up."

"I think he's bent."

"If he is, he's got a good front. He doesn't seem different than he ever was. Anyway, what should I do? He says if I give him a day or two, he'll come in voluntarily. After he cleans up whatever he's involved in, and after he makes sure 'somebody's safe'—I assume a woman."

"Negative on the delay," the man said. "Your report said he was in New York before Virginia. Last year we lost that operative in New York, you remember? It took a long time to work him to where he was, and then he comes to New York and he's gone."

"You think Kirk . . ."

"Safest to assume he's bent. We can't have him out there screwing around with our operations. Bring him in."

"Yes, sir," Smith said. "How persuasive do you want me to be?"

"Sufficiently."

"Extremely?"

"I said, bring him in, Smith. Do you require assistance?"

"No. No, I don't think so," Smith said. "I've got good hardware along, and he seems to want to trust me. I think I can get close to him. If I do need help, I ought to be able to get it locally. Holder will be inclined to cooperate with me. He can give me some law, if nothing else. Where should I take Kirk?"

"Take him to the farm, then we'll decide what to do next."

"Fine. Sometime tomorrow."

"Yes, tomorrow."

The line went dead.

CHAPTER 29

Deputies Fyke and Tilghman had been cruising the roads of Dorset County for hours. For about the seventh time they swung down the dirt road past Craik's cottage. The red Toyota was parked in the front yard.

"That's the girl's car, ain't it?" Tilghman asked. He drove past without stopping.

"Yeah," Fyke said.

"You suppose he's in there?"

"I don't know, but I'm gonna find out. Drop me off."

Tilghman pulled to a stop a hundred yards farther down the road. Fyke got out.

"Go get Crowe," he told Tilghman.

"Okay."

It was dark. Fyke walked slowly back down the road, his hand on the butt of his pistol. When he neared Craik's cottage, he circled around so that he came at the house from the rear. He crept up and peered in the kitchen door. There was no one to be seen. He edged to the window near the dining area. From there he could see Craik moving around in the bedroom.

Fyke drew the Colt Python. He went quickly around to the front and in the door. Craik looked out at him from the bedroom.

"What the fuck do *you* want?" Craik said.

Fyke smiled. "Pack some clothes," he said. "Nice and slow." He came and stood in the doorway to the bedroom, gripping the Python with both hands.

"You got a warrant?"

"Don't need one. You don't live here anymore."

Craik sighed. "Jesus Christ," he muttered.

"Do it now," Fyke said. "I don't usually shoot people for resisting arrest, but you never know."

"All right, take it easy," Craik said. He got his duffel bag from the closet, pulled clothes out of the dresser, and stuffed them in. When he was finished, he looked at Fyke questioningly.

Fyke backed away slowly, the .357 Magnum still aimed at Craik's chest. "Now come out here," Fyke said. "Both hands on the bag, nothing fast."

The two men emerged from the bedroom. "Sit there," Fyke said. He pointed with his gun at the couch. Craik obeyed, dropping the duffel bag at his feet. Fyke sat in the chair across from him, the pistol now held loosely in his lap.

"And then?" Craik said.

"Sheriff asked you to take a little vacation, Craik. Seems like you don't hear so good."

Craik stared at him impassively.

Fyke shrugged. "Soon as my partner gets here, we're gonna help you leave," he said. "Thought we'd got rid of you this afternoon. Well, this time I suggest you stay gone for a while."

Craik didn't respond. The two men sat in silence until a car stopped out front.

"Let's go," Fyke said, getting up. "You do anything weird and I will shoot you. I mean it."

"Don't worry," Craik said disgustedly, "I believe you."

Craik picked up his duffel bag and went out the door, Fyke close behind him with the Python trained on his back. The cruiser was idling out in the road. It was dark inside the car. Craik had nearly reached it before he could see that there were two men in the front seat. He reacted quickly, dropping the bag and spinning on his foot, but Fyke was too close. The big deputy brought his gun down hard on the back of Craik's skull.

Craik crumpled. Fyke holstered his gun and opened the back door of the cruiser. He threw Craik's unconscious body inside, and the duffel bag after him. Then he climbed in himself.

"That place by the river?" Tilghman asked.

"Yeah," Fyke said. "Good as any."

Rodney Crowe turned and looked down at Craik. He smiled.

They drove out the main road to Dorset. They took the same turnoff that led to Shields's place but, before reaching it, turned onto a dirt road that led back east, toward the Bay. The road twisted through the woods, until it terminated at the Pawchunk, with no bridge or ford across. There was a small dirt area next to the creek. No cars were parked in it. Beyond it, the water rushed noisily by, a vague, flowing shape in the dark.

Tilghman stopped the cruiser and turned off the engine. Fyke dragged Craik and his bag out onto the dirt. He and Crowe stood over the unconscious man.

"Do no good if he ain't awake," Crowe said.

"Charles," Fyke said, "what you got to hold water besides your pisser?"

"Thermos," Tilghman said.

"Fill it and bring 'er over here."

Tilghman got his thermos from the cruiser. He went to the

creek and filled it with water. Crowe held out his hand and
Tilghman handed the thermos to him.

Crowe poured water onto Craik's face. There was no
reaction. He tilted Craik's head and poured again, making
sure some went down Craik's nose. Craik spluttered. He
wriggled on the ground, waving at his face with his hands.
He opened his eyes. Crowe poured some more water onto his
face.

Craik rolled over, coughing. He got to his hands and
knees. He felt the back of his head, where there was blood
and sticky, matted hair. His hand went back to the ground as
he began to topple. He steadied himself. For a moment he
swayed back and forth, then he threw up. His body spasmed
with the effort.

Crowe laughed. "He don't look so tough now, boys," he
said. The others laughed too. Crowe kicked Craik hard in the
ribs. The blow doubled him over. He continued to retch.
Crowe kicked him again. Craik curled into a ball, protecting
himself, but the coughing and retching kept opening him up.
Crowe continued to kick him here and there. The deputies
were leaning against the cruiser, their arms folded.

"Hey, Craik," Fyke called out. "You suppose the sheriff's
got a good idea there? About you taking a vacation and all?"

Crowe reached down and pulled Craik up by the shirtfront.
When he had him on his knees, he kicked him hard in the
stomach. Craik fell forward, gasping for breath. His body
shook uncontrollably and he clutched at the dirt. Crowe took
a small switchblade from his pocket. He pressed the button
and a three-inch blade clicked into place.

"Easy, Crowe," Fyke said.

Crowe waved his hand. He pulled Craik to his knees again.
With one deft motion his wrist flicked out and a gash
appeared on Craik's cheek. Blood streamed down the side of
his face. Crowe stepped back to admire his work. One of
Craik's hands went to the wound. The blood flowed between
his fingers.

With the other hand Craik threw the dirt he'd scratched up. It hit Crowe in eyes that were wide with admiration for what he'd done. He screamed and dropped the knife. He clawed at his eyes.

Craik rolled backward and came up on his feet. He ran in the direction of the water. The deputies were twenty feet behind him before they reacted. Tilghman drew his pistol. He brought it up into firing position, but Fyke put his hand on his partner's arm.

"No shooting," Fyke said. "Remember? The sheriff'll have our ass."

Tilghman lowered his arm. Craik stumbled into the creek, gasped a deep breath, and dived beneath the surface. Crowe was still screaming about what he was going to do and scrabbling around trying to find the knife.

"I think he got the message, don't you?" Fyke said to Tilghman. His partner smiled and nodded, reholstered his gun. They watched Crowe's antics with amusement.

Craik's head broke water downstream. He took a breath and went under again. The swift current carried him into an area of woods and marsh. The next time he surfaced, he was out of sight. He gulped air and went under again.

Fyke picked up the duffel bag and dumped its contents out on the ground.

"Come on, Crowe," he said. "You done your part."

"I'll kill the sumbitch," Crowe was saying. "I'll kill him."

"You ever see his sorry ass around here again," Tilghman said, "you go right ahead."

The three men got into the cruiser, the deputies laughing, Crowe still muttering to himself. They drove off.

The third time Craik surfaced, he looked around. There were woods on both banks. He turned onto his back, tilted his head, and let the creek carry him, moving his hands only enough to stay afloat.

When he'd drifted about a quarter of a mile, he rolled onto

his stomach and laboriously pulled himself to shore. It was a marshy spot. He dragged himself through mud and sharp-edged swamp grass. Eventually he hit solid ground. He flopped onto his back. He lay there, his breath coming hard.

The old man heard the splashing and picked his way along the bank of the creek. He had a flashlight in one hand and a long, pointed stick in the other. He was wearing high rubber boots, khaki pants, and a plaid flannel shirt. There was a knotted twine bag over his shoulder. The bag was half full of frogs.

He moved in and out among the pines, water oak, and sycamores that grew right down to where the land merged with the water. He played his flashlight over the ground. The splashing ceased. He switched his flashlight off and moved more cautiously. He stopped, listened. There was the sound of tortured breathing. He headed toward it. When he was right on top of it, he flicked on the light again and gasped.

The young man's hand came up to block out the light. He was wet and muddy. Blood ran from the open wound in his cheek.

"Nnnh," Craik said.

The other man moved the light away from his eyes.

"Jesus," he said. "You need a doctor, son."

"N-no doctor," Craik mumbled.

"I know you. You're the boy was working with Brendan Shields."

Craik gave a slight nod.

"He talked about you, down to Sook's," the old man went on. "Thought right much of you. Now, there was those didn't have no use for Brendan Shields, but he always did right by me. Who done this to you?"

Craik didn't say anything.

The old man knelt next to him. "You can tell me," he said. "I ain't gonna do you no harm. I at least owe Brendan that much."

"Deputies," Craik said.

"Yeah, I shoulda knowed. Sons a bitches. Well, I gotta hand it to you, they done this to you and you still got away. How bad is it?"

"N-not bad. Need to rest."

"You don't want to go to the doctor because they're still after you, right?"

Craik didn't say anything.

"All right, whatever the reason. Well, you sure hell can't stay here. You need to get cleaned up, get some sleep. Anything broken?"

Craik shook his head slightly. "Cracked rib, maybe."

"All right, I'll take you to my place. That suit you? It's off by itself. Won't no one think to look for you there."

"Okay."

"We get you cleaned up, you don't get a infection, you should pull through. Come on, I'll help you." The old man got Craik to his feet. "My name's Frank Whately, by the way," he said.

"Craik," Craik mumbled. "My pleasure."

The going was slow, but eventually they made it to the end of a dirt road, where a decrepit Dodge pickup was parked.

"Don't let her looks fool you," Frank said as he helped Craik into the cab. "Don't take her much but to the Bay for fishing and out here to gig frogs. The salt done ate up her body, but the engine's sound as a horse."

He patted Craik on the knee and dropped the twine bag of frogs on the floorboards.

Ten minutes later they were in Whately's cottage, a three-room wooden structure that rested crookedly on uneven piles of rock. It was upstream from Shields's place and about a quarter of a mile from the Pawchunk. It sat in a half-acre clearing, surrounded by woods, at the end of a long, twisting driveway of dirt and crushed oyster shells.

Whately guided Craik to an easy chair. "You'll be safe here," he said. He glanced around at the rough board paneling. "She's like the truck. Short on looks, but she'll be here long after they plant us. Okay, first get you cleaned up."

He scurried off to the small bathroom and started water into the tub. Then he went into the kitchen area. He opened a cupboard and took down a quart mason jar of golden liquid. He poured two water glasses full.

"Here," he said to Craik.

"What?"

"Brandy. Just drink it. Make it myself. It's pure, I guarandamntee it."

Craik took a swallow and caught his breath.

"Good," he croaked.

The tub filled, and Whately helped Craik into it. He washed the younger man. When they were finished, Craik was clean but showed the effects of the beating. His upper body was a welter of colorful contusions. There were bruises on his thighs, and his knees were scraped.

Whately sat him naked in a straight-back chair and looked into his eyes.

"How you feeling?" he asked.

"Better."

"You sound better. How many fingers I'm holding up here?"

"Two."

"Okay. You might've been concussed, but I can't tell for sure. You don't look it. Nothing I could do about it, anyway. You want to take the chance, that's your business."

"It doesn't feel like it," Craik said. "I've been before."

Whately grunted. He felt Craik's rib cage. Craik winced a couple of times.

"I think we got some cracks," Whately said.

"Yeah."

"I'll tape 'em. Now let's see your head. Lean it forward a little."

Whately examined the wound. It was scabbing but still sticky. The hair around it was matted, dirty, and bloody.

"It ain't too bad on the outside," he said, "but I gotta clean it."

"Okay."

Whately washed the wound and shaved around it. Then he made a dressing from gauze and an aloe plant and taped it to Craik's skull. Lastly, he examined the knife wound. It was raw and still oozing.

"This one's deep," he said. "I ain't got no antibiotics, and I can't stitch anything more'n my trousers. We're gonna have to sterilize it, Craik."

"What you got?"

"All's I got's iodine."

Craik flinched.

"What I'd do," Whately said, "I'd put on some iodine and leave it open tonight. Tomorrow I'd clean it again and put a dressin' on it."

"Do it," Craik said.

Whately washed Craik's cheek and patted it dry. He inspected it closely.

"Okay," he said, "now we move into the bedroom."

"Why?"

"That's where you're gonna sleep, and I don't want to haveta carry you. Come on."

Craik shuffled to the bedroom under his own power. Whately sat him on the edge of the bed, then went and got some cotton and a bottle of iodine.

"You ready?" Whately asked.

Craik gripped the sheets and nodded. Whately soaked the cotton with iodine. Gently, he leaned Craik's head to the side. He placed the cotton against Craik's face and squeezed. The iodine ran down into the wound.

"Nnnnh," Craik moaned, and he passed out.

"Better'n sleeping pills," Whately said to himself.

He stretched Craik out on the bed. He dabbed at the knife wound with the cotton until he was satisfied. The gash looked like a smiling orange mouth.

CHAPTER 30

When Susanna woke up, there were two men standing over her. She blinked her eyes.

"Susanna," one of the men was saying. "Susanna, it's your Uncle Forrest. Can you hear me?"

Susanna nodded.

Holder gestured at the other man. "This is Dr. Lintle," he said. "Do you understand what I'm saying?"

Susanna nodded again. She moved her mouth but no words came out. She licked her lips, tried again. "Wh-what happened?" she said.

"You fainted," Holder said. "You've been out for several hours. Dr. Lintle has examined you. He thinks you've had a slight nervous breakdown. Nothing to be concerned about now, you understand. But it's been a terrible couple of days for you, and your system just couldn't take it anymore. You need some rest. Dr. Lintle's going to take you to the clinic for a complete physical. Just to be on the safe side."

"What—what day is it?" Susanna asked.

"It's still Thursday, dear."

"Don't want to go to the clinic."

"Susanna, please, it's important that you get proper medical attention."

"Yes," Lintle said. "I need to do some things that I can't do here. You won't have to be there more than a day or two."

"Can't," Susanna said. "Too much to do."

"Whatever it is can wait," Holder said. "Your health comes first, young lady."

Susanna closed her eyes. When she opened them again, she said, "Groggy. Never happened to me before."

"That's what severe shock will do," Lintle said.

"I have my car waiting," Holder said. "Stayne can drive you. And Dr. Lintle will ride along. How's that?"

Susanna sighed deeply. "All right," she said.

"Good, good. Would you like to wash up or something first?"

Susanna sat up. "No," she said. "Be okay."

The two men helped her to her feet. She walked unsteadily. At one point her knees buckled, and they caught her under her arms. With their help she made it outside. The sky was dark. A shiny black Mercedes waited in front of the house, engine running.

Stayne was in the driver's seat. He was alone in the luxury automobile. Susanna got in and slid over directly behind him. Lintle joined her in the back. The interior of the car had already been chilled by the air conditioner. Holder closed the door and leaned against the car's roof. He made a cranking motion with his hand. Lintle flipped the lever that opened the window. It slid down with a soft electric whir.

"I'm sorry I can't go with you," Holder said to Susanna.

" 'S all right," she mumbled. Her head lolled forward.

"Too damned much to do tonight. But I'll come visit you, you can count on that. Tomorrow for sure. And don't worry about your folks. I'll call them and tell them what's happened. They'll probably be waiting for you when you get to the clinic." He smiled. "And you take good care of her, Lintle. She's still my baby."

"I will, Judge Holder."

"You drive carefully, Stayne."

"Yes, sir."

Lintle flicked the lever, and the window crept up again. The Mercedes rolled slowly down the driveway. The gate was standing open for it. As it passed through, the guard waved and Stayne waved back. The gate swung closed immediately.

At the bottom of the driveway the car turned right. It headed along the county road toward the main highway. Stayne drove at a moderate speed. Half a mile passed. A beige sedan came into view behind the Mercedes.

There were no houses along the road, just woods on both sides. Susanna raised her lolling head. She looked quickly at Dr. Lintle, out of the corner of her eye. He was staring blankly out the side window. Susanna's attention returned to the road ahead. The black car was approaching a sharp curve. As it did, Stayne slowed a little. Susanna leaned forward.

"Stayne," she said.

He turned slightly and said, "Yes, m'am?"

"Stayne, I was wondering if—" Her eyes opened wide and she yelled, *"Look out for the dog! Look out!"*

Stayne braked automatically. When he did, Susanna opened the door and jumped. Her feet hit, and she immediately tucked and went into a skillful shoulder roll. The Mercedes screeched to a stop down the road. Susanna's momentum carried her up onto her feet and forward some more, so she tucked and did another shoulder roll. This time she had slowed enough that she could come up running. She ran into the woods.

The Mercedes backed up along the shoulder, spraying gravel. The beige sedan went around it and continued down the road without pausing. Stayne stopped the Mercedes and killed the engine. He and Lintle got out. They looked around in the dark. The woods were silent.

"Shit," Lintle said. "Holder's not gonna like this."

"I'm sorry, sir," Stayne said.

"It's not your fault. She's a smart cookie. I don't suppose there's any point in beating the bushes for her."

"I don't think so."

Lintle sighed. "All right," he said. "Come on, we'd better go tell him."

The two men got into the black car and returned to the estate.

Susanna picked her way carefully through the woods. She began talking softly to herself.

"Drug," she said. "Got to've been a drug. Come on, Susanna."

She pinched herself on the arm. "Ouch. Okay, I'm awake. Uncle wants me out of his hair. Hnnh. No way, José. Get back to Brawlton, find Scotty, start all over again." She paused, leaned against the trunk of an oak. She looked left and right. "Damn," she said. She slapped the tree. Slowly, she turned herself completely around. "Got to be," she muttered, and she headed at a ninety-degree angle to the direction she'd been going. "Got to be this way," she said. "Know this county in the goddamn dark. Can't be far."

The beige sedan drove out to the state road and turned east, toward Brawlton. It went two miles down the road, made a U-turn, and retraced its steps. It went two miles past the turnoff to Judge Holder's, made another U-turn, and returned. It went down the county road. A mile past Holder's, it swung around and went back over the same territory. Then it repeated the previous pattern.

The fifth time through, the sedan was heading west on the state road when a white station wagon passed it, going the other way. The driver checked his rearview mirror. A girl ran up out of the ditch next to the road. She flagged down the wagon and got in. When the wagon was out of sight, the beige sedan made a leisurely U-turn. It sped up until the wagon's taillights were visible ahead, then it slowed until its speed matched the wagon's.

The white station wagon took Susanna to the cottage in Brawlton. She thanked the lady for the ride and assured her that she didn't need any further help. The wagon drove off.

Susanna looked around. There was a light on in the cottage, and her red Toyota was parked in the yard. She walked into the house.

"Scotty," she called.

There was no answer. She went into the bedroom, looked

into the closet, pulled open the dresser drawers. Her face was creased with lines of anger.

She stalked into the living area. The pad and pen were on the table. She wrote a quick note and stuffed it between the pages of the yellow tide-table book. Then she went back outside.

She walked over to her car and peered in the window. The keys were in the ignition.

"Thank Jesus for small favors," she muttered to herself.

As she went to open the car door the man's arms went around her. One of them pinned her own arms securely to her sides. His other hand clamped over her mouth. He was very strong. Her scream was a meager gurgle in her throat.

"If you make a sound," he said softly into her ear, "if you fight at all, I'll break your neck. You understand?"

She nodded weakly.

He dragged her and she didn't resist. Another man was standing in the darkness next to the beige sedan. The other man opened the rear door of the car. The man who held Susanna shoved her inside and followed right behind her.

She opened her mouth and sucked in air, and then there was a gun next to her face.

"Don't," the man said.

CHAPTER 31

Smith pulled up in front of the cottage. With the engine off, the night was still. He sat quietly for a moment. The red Toyota was parked where it had been before. The light was on inside. Smith slipped a snub-nosed .38-caliber revolver into his jacket pocket. He got out of his car and walked quietly to the door. He listened, peered in through the screen.

"Kirk?" he called.

There was no answer. Smith took out the revolver. Cautiously, he let himself into the house. There was no one in the large room, no one in the bedroom. There were few clothes left in the closet and dresser. Smith put the gun back in his pocket.

"Shit," he said. He sat on the edge of the bed and ran a hand through his hair.

He thought for a moment. Then, wearily, he set about searching. He was thorough. He looked inside everything, banged on walls, inspected floorboards. He searched the shed in the backyard. He got a flashlight from the gray Ford and looked under the house.

When he was finished, he took nothing away from the cottage. He got into his car and drove back to the Dorset House. In the lobby he placed another phone call.

"He's gone," Smith said.

"How is that possible?" the man said.

"I don't know. I can't believe that I misread him. He's got something important here, I'm sure of it. I don't think he's left the area. He's probably started doing whatever it is he has to do. Since he didn't call me, we have to assume he's going to try to do it on his own and then get away."

"What do you suggest?"

"I can only cover so much ground," Smith said. "And I'm a stranger here. I suggest we get some local help. Have him picked up. We don't have to get too specific with them."

"All right. How do you want to handle it?"

"Get in touch with Congressman Mills. Have him phone Holder and tell him I'm on my way over. I'll talk to the Judge. Once he realizes that we know about him, he'll bust his ass to get Kirk into our hands. I won't tell him more than he needs to know."

"I'll call Mills personally," the man said. "I agree that

Holder should be very cooperative. Now, Smith, there is . . . one other thing. We do want Kirk brought in. We don't want to spend another two years worrying what he's up to. You do understand that the first priority is to protect our interests?"

"I understand."

"Good. Please try not to let him get away again."

After the connection had been broken, Smith said softly, "Screw you."

He got a suitcase out of his car and went up to his room. He took a shower, put on some fresh clothes. Then he drove to Forrest Holder's estate. The man at the gate told him that he was expected and to go right up. Stayne met him at the door and showed him into the library.

The Judge shook his hand and the two men seated themselves.

"Jesse wasn't too specific," Holder said. "May I ask who you are?"

"Judge Holder," Smith said, gesturing around him, "is this place wired?"

"I beg your pardon."

"Are you recording this conversation?"

"Whatever makes you think—"

"Cut the crap, Judge," Smith said. He leaned forward and said very precisely, "If you record this conversation, I guarantee you you're going to be in very serious trouble. Now turn it off." He stared at Holder, his face a bland mask that somehow suggested menace.

Holder held his eyes for a moment, then looked away. He opened the desk drawer, flipped a switch, closed the drawer again. He looked back at Smith.

"Thank you," Smith said. "I trust that you are not bullshitting me. If I ever find out that you've got another wire in here, you can consider your operation shut down. Permanently."

"I don't know what you're talking about," Holder said. "What operation?"

"For God's sake, your export business, of course."

"My . . . Who the hell are you, anyway, Smith?"

Smith smiled. "I'm your tax dollars put to use," he said.

"I see. Just what do you think you know?"

"Enough to put you out of business. Look, Holder, I didn't come here to talk about how you make your money. If we'd wanted to stop you, we would have done so a long time ago. As it is, we don't even bother monitoring you anymore. You deal with the right people, you sell American products, so frankly, we don't give a shit how rich you're getting. Okay?"

"I don't know," Holder said guardedly. "What *do* you want?"

"Not what. Who."

"Who?"

"The man you know as Scott Craik," Smith said.

The Judge pursed his lips. "Ah," he said. "I think the time has come to have a drink. I've got some excellent single-malt Scotch."

"No thanks."

"Let me help myself, then."

Scott nodded, and Holder fetched a glass of Glen Calder, settled himself back into his chair.

"I knew there was something about that boy," Holder said. "What's he done?"

"He's a former government employee," Smith said.

The Judge smiled. "I get you," he said.

"A *low-level* government employee. Unfortunately, he got hold of some sensitive material, including some on your operation. Now, apparently, he sees himself as a tilter at windmills. We feel that he may be here to interfere with what you're doing."

"He may be 'low-level,' but he's awfully good at taking care of himself."

"He's had some training in that area, yes. Also, he has some natural ability."

"He took a knife away from the best knife man in the county, with his bare hands. That's ability, all right."

"Judge, look," Smith said, "we're getting off the subject. I know that Craik can handle himself, and so apparently do you. The point is that it's not in the national interest to have him running around loose. He's an unstable man. He could do us harm. What I want to know is where he is."

"Beats me."

"All right, let's find him, then. He was in Brawlton an hour ago. I know that, because I was with him. I had to leave for a bit, and when I got back, he was gone, most of his clothes with him. But from the way he talked, I don't think he intended to leave Dorset County, at least not tonight. That means he's out there somewhere. Now, you have resources, I believe."

"Sure," Holder said. "I can call on the sheriff's office."

"Good. Let's find him. When you pick him up, you can hold him at the county jail or wherever you want. I'll come and take him off your hands. If you need any kind of authorization, I'll get it for you." Smith got up.

"No, that won't be necessary. We'll find him, Mr. Smith." Holder got up and shook his hand. "Just leave everything to me."

"Fine. You can get word to me at the Dorset House. I'm going to be looking myself, but I'll check in with them periodically."

"We'll have him by morning, I'm sure of it."

After Smith had gone, Holder sat for five minutes, slowly sipping his Scotch. Then abruptly, he put the glass down and made a phone call.

"Brace," he said. "Can you get over here? . . . Yeah, right away. . . . Huh? What do you mean, Craik's taken care of? . . . *Shit!* . . . No, I'm not all right! Look, I'll explain later. Just get the hell over here." He banged the phone down.

A half hour later Kemp was sitting across from him.

"Bracewell," Holder said, "what in hell happened?"

"Look, I'm sorry, Judge," Kemp said. "But we decided to get rid of Craik, and that's what the boys done."

"Tell me the story."

"They taken him down by the Pawchunk, and Rodney worked him over a little bit. Cut him. You know. And then Craik escaped—"

"Escaped!" Holder cut in harshly. "Escaped! Two deputies twice his size and the best knife man in the county and the son of a bitch escaped! I sent my niece off to the clinic with Lintle and Stayne, half full of drugs, and *she* escaped! Everybody around here is fucking *escaping*!"

"Take it easy, Judge."

"And those clowns from D.C. Where in the hell are they?"

"I don't know yet," Kemp said. "But I'm working a good lead. If it pans out, we should have them located by tomorrow."

"Shit! You know who was just here?"

Kemp shook his head.

"*Smith*, he called himself. Some asshole from the *CIA*. Or the NSA, or one of those goddamn agencies ends in *A*. That's what our boy Craik is, my friend. Some kind of government spy!"

Kemp shifted uneasily. "What did he want?" he asked. "He know about us?"

"Damn straight he knows about us! Him and Craik and the greasers and the whole fucking world for all I know!"

Holder slammed his hand down on the desktop. He glared at Kemp for a moment, then shoved himself abruptly from his chair. He went over to the cabinet and fixed himself a Scotch. He drained half of it in one swallow. When he went back to his chair, he was more subdued.

"What does the CIA have to do with anything?" Kemp asked hesitantly.

"Jesus, I don't know, Brace," Holder said. "They want

Craik. He's running around loose with some secrets or something." He began chuckling. "The screwy thing is," he continued, "they've known what we were doing here, right from the beginning. And they don't even care. As long as we sell to the right people. Hell, we're almost on the goddamn government payroll."

"I'll be damned," Kemp said. "So what do we do now?"

"First we find Craik."

"I'll put Fyke and Tilghman on that. Tell them they can forget sleep until they pull him in."

"Take the county apart, Brace. I want that son of a bitch before Smith gets hold of him."

"You think——"

"Yeah, I think," the Judge said. "That boy has nine lives, and I'm damned if he don't. If we play our cards right here, Craik just might be the answer to all our problems."

"Use him against the greasers," Kemp said, nodding his head in agreement. "Okay. But I don't see how."

"You just find him. I'll come up with the reason he wants to work for us."

"First, find Craik. All right. Second?"

"Second, find my niece. Last they saw her, she was running around in the woods off my road here. There's too much shit going on for that. I don't want her to come to harm, Brace."

"What do you want done with her when we find her?"

"Call me, then have someone take her to the clinic. Put her in one of those cruisers with no inside door handles. Soon as I hear from you, I'll arrange for Lintle to meet her there."

"Okay," Kemp said. "Anything else?"

"Yeah. We better keep looking for the D.C. boys too." Kemp nodded, got up.

"Brace," Holder said, "you gotta help me keep this together. You understand that, don't you?"

"Sure, Judge," Kemp said, and left.

To the south and east, on the other side of Brawlton, Smith

parked his gray Ford in the cul-de-sac. He strode purposefully up the front walk and knocked on the door of the brick
rancher. The dark, stocky, middle-aged man answered.

"Mr. Holder?" Smith said. "Stuart Holder?"

"Who the hell are you?" Holder demanded.

"I'm from the government," Smith said.

He produced his wallet, flipped it open, and held it out.
Holder pushed open his screen door and examined the ID
under the yellow porch light. The credentials assured him
that Smith was from the Immigration and Naturalization
Service.

"What the hell does this mean?" Holder asked him.

"It means I'm a U.S. government employee," Smith said,
"like I said. May I come in? I'd like to speak with you."

"What about?" Holder asked suspiciously.

"Your daughter."

Holder stared at him. "Susanna's in trouble with the
government?" he said finally.

"Not at all, Mr. Holder. If we might go inside . . ."

"Who is it?" a woman's voice called from within.

"Well, all right," Holder said. "But look, Mr. . . . ?"

"Smith."

"Yeah, Smith. Look, my wife is pretty upset. Susanna's
missing and we don't know where she is. I don't want you
making things any worse."

Smith held up his hand. "I understand," he said genially.
"I'm here to help, Mr. Holder."

Holder stood aside and Smith went in. Holder followed
him into the living room. The focus of the room was a suite
consisting of a couch and two matching chairs, done in a
brown-and-gold wool fabric. The furniture was grouped
around a glass-topped coffee table with beveled edges.

The slender woman with chestnut hair was seated on the
couch. Holder joined her there. Smith sat in one of the
chairs.

"Who is this man?" the woman asked.

"He's from the government, Felicity," Holder said. "From—"

"Smith, ma'am," Smith said. "From Immigration and Naturalization."

"It's about Susanna," Stuart said.

Felicity's hand went to her throat.

"Please," Smith said, "both of you. It's not Susanna we're after. We don't bother good citizens of this country. But I understand that your daughter has befriended a man you know as Scott Craik."

"That awful man," Felicity said. "I knew it."

"I don't want to alarm you," Smith said. "Actually, he isn't an awful man. But he is in the United States illegally."

"We don't know where in the hell he is," Stuart said.

"I understand that," Smith said. "Perhaps your daughter does."

"Mr. Smith," Felicity said, "Susanna has . . . disappeared."

"I'm sorry."

"Well, I'm sure she'll turn up, of course. But she's had several shocks lately. My husband's step-brother, whom she cared for, he drowned. And her best friend was killed in an auto accident. And then, just this morning, her friend's father started firing a gun in the restaurant where Susanna works, and one of the sheriff's deputies had to . . . to shoot him. Susanna was there and saw the whole thing." Felicity gazed into the distance. After a moment she added, "My Lord, it sounds so . . . awful." She shifted her gaze to Smith and looked at him as if for help.

"I am sorry," Smith said.

"She's only twenty-one," Felicity said.

"She had a breakdown at her uncle's earlier today," Stuart said. "The doctor was taking her to the clinic for examination when she jumped out of the car. That's the last anyone's seen of her."

"How involved was she with Craik?" Smith asked.

"Well, you know how they are at that age," Stuart said. "I guess she fancied him. I don't know if it meant anything. Hell, she's only known him for a week."

"Do you think it's possible that she ran away with him?"

"Oh, I hope not," Felicity said.

Stuart shrugged. "Kids," he said. "You never know. Where's the guy from, anyway? Seemed like he spoke English okay."

"Africa," Smith said. "He's a South African. English is his language."

"South African," Felicity said. "How terrible."

"No, I think he was on the side of the good guys," Smith said. "That's why he didn't want to go back."

"South African," Stuart said. "Jesus, Susanna'd probably go for that. Anything weird."

"Has this Craik done anything wrong over here?" Felicity asked.

"Not that we know of," Smith said. "His visa's expired, that's all. We heard he was looking for work up here, which he can't legally do without a green card, and he doesn't have one. I'm sure that when we find him, we can work it all out.

"In the meantime, if you should hear from your daughter, or if you hear anything about Craik, let me know, will you? I'm staying at the Dorset House. Please leave a message if I'm out."

The two Holders nodded and Smith got up.

"You . . . you don't think he's dangerous, this man?" Felicity said.

"No, ma'am," Smith said. "Not at all."

"If he marries an American," Stuart said, "that's the end of his troubles, right?"

"Well, not exactly," Smith said. "Though I suppose that *could* be his intention. If it is, I'm sure you'll be hearing from the two of them soon. Call me, like I said. No matter what."

"We will," Felicity said.

"Yeah, sure," Stuart said. "And if you hear anything about Susanna, you let *us* know."

"Of course," Smith said. "Anything to help."

SECOND
FRIDAY

CHAPTER 32

Craik opened his eyes. Slowly, he turned his head on the pillow. Whately was sitting next to the bed, reading a book on herbal medicine, keeping an eye on him. He raised himself onto his elbows and winced.

"Reckon it hurts a bit," Whately said.

Tentatively, Craik touched his left cheek. He withdrew his finger rapidly. "Feels like it's on fire," he said.

Whately nodded. "Somebody cut you nice," he said. "Not as bad as it could be, though. Considering, I'd say you don't look like you probably feel."

"Thanks," Craik said. "Is it Friday?"

"Uh-huh. Afternoon. How's the ribs?"

Craik took a deep breath, let it out. "Hurt, but not more than cracked."

"Keep the compress on. You should be able to get around all right. I soaked it in a herb tea. That's what the smell is. The bump on your head is clean, so I don't think there'll be any problem there. But like I said last night, you could be concussed, and I wouldn't know it."

"Head's clear," Craik said. "My face?"

"Iodine."

Craik sucked in air. "I scream a lot?"

"Nope. Just passed out. You moaned a bit in your sleep, but you didn't wake up till just now."

Craik paused, then said, "What's your name again?"

"Frank Whately."

"Why you doing this, Frank?"

Whately took off the reading glasses he'd been wearing and set them on the table next to the bed.

"Deputies got you, son. So you said. Well, I've lived here all my life, and it used to been a good life until the fishing went to hell and hoodlums like them started to take things over. Me, I'm too old to do anything about it now. You're still young. You can do anything about it, do it."

"Okay," Craik said. "I just might. But first I have to check on somebody. You got a phone?"

"Sure." Whately got up. "Come on, I'll help you."

Whately assisted, and Craik made it to his feet. Together they shuffled into the living room. Craik asked for a local phone book, looked up a number, and dialed it.

"Marla," he said, "it's Craik."

"How you doing?" she said.

"Not great. Remember I told you I might be getting in some trouble? Well, I did."

"Where are you?"

"I'm okay. Listen, I need for you to do me a favor. I need to get word to Susanna that I'm all right, and I need to know that she's all right too. Can you do that?"

"Sure," she said, "I suppose so."

"Just tell her that I had a run-in with our friends but that I'm okay. But tell her that it'd be better if we didn't see each other for a little bit. Tell her to stay home and I'll be back in touch as soon as I can."

"Anything else?"

"Call me back here after you talk to her." He gave her Whately's number.

"No problem," Vickers said. "And look, Craik, I heard that there was some guy asking after where you lived last night. Stranger."

"He found me," Craik said. "Then he lost me again. His name's Smith, and he'll tell you he's from the government. If you see him, don't let on that you've talked to me."

"Thought as much. Be back to you shortly."

Vickers was on the phone again in a half hour.

"Can't find her," she told Craik. "Nobody seems to know where she is. Her folks told me to let them know if I heard from her. Or you. What's going on?"

"I don't know, Marla," Craik said. "You'd better bring me that suitcase I left with you. I'm at Frank Whately's place. You know where that is?"

"Uh-huh. You need it now?"

"Yeah, I guess as soon as possible. And along the way could you please stop at the cottage? There's a yellow tide-table book on the front table. Look and see if there's a note inside it."

"That it?"

Craik paused, then said, "No. You've gotta be sure you're not being followed. If you even *think* you might be, don't come here. Go home and call me."

"That bad, huh?"

"I'm not sure. It may be."

"Susanna in trouble?"

"That's what I need to find out."

"Okay, I'm on my way."

Vickers retrieved the suitcase from its hiding place. She moved quickly, loading the suitcase into her car—an old Chevy Bel Air—and drove to the cottage. As she leafed through the yellow tide-table book Stuart Holder was answering his phone.

"It's Smith," Smith said.

"Mr. Smith," Stuart said, "something odd just happened. We got a call from Marla Vickers. You know who she is?"

"Yes."

"She wanted to get in touch with my daughter. They're friends, but . . . Well, it's unusual."

"You think she was calling for Craik?"

"I thought maybe."

"Was she calling from home?"

"I don't know. I assumed so."

"All right," Smith said. "That's very good, Mr. Holder. Thank you. I'll go see her right away."

"You'll let us know . . . ?"

"Of course. As soon as I find out anything at all."

Fifteen minutes later Craik had the note in his hand. It read: "Your stuff is gone, but I can't believe you've run out on me. A lot has happened. I'm on my way to Marla's. She'll know everything. Find me. Love, S."

"You never saw her?" Craik said.

Vickers shook her head. "Nope. No telling when the note was written, but I was home, last night and this morning both. Where in hell did she go, Craik?"

"She's somewhere," Craik said. "I'll find her."

Vickers looked him over. "You don't look in shape to find your own shoelaces," she said.

Craik dismissed the thought with a wave of his hand. "It's not the outside that counts," he said. "But I'm gonna need some help. Can you drive to D.C. today?"

"D.C.?"

"Near there. I just need you to pick up some stuff for me. It'd be better if I rested this afternoon rather than going myself."

" 'Spose I could," Vickers said. "But the old Chevy is slow. Take me a couple of hours each way."

"That's all right." He opened his suitcase, lifted a patch of fabric, and pulled out a key that was taped underneath. He handed it to her. Then he took a sheet of paper and wrote for a minute. When he was done, he gave her that, too, along with some money.

"The key is to a self-storage locker," he said. "Those are the directions to the locker. Inside you'll find another suitcase. Settle up whatever I owe the guy and bring me back the suitcase."

Vickers gave him a searching look. "What's in it?" she said.

There was a lengthy pause. "Guns," Craik said finally.

Vickers nodded slowly to herself.

"Will you do it?" Craik asked. "I need to be able to defend myself. Look at me." He gestured at his face with one hand.

Vickers met his gaze. Deliberately, she took her pipe from her shirt pocket, tamped down the tobacco, and ignited it. Her eyes stayed with his as she inserted a small cloud of bluish smoke between them.

"Tell me who you are, Craik," she said.

He paused, then said, "I used to work for the government."

"And now you work against it?"

"No. No, I . . . I just wanted to be left alone."

"But they're after you."

"Sort of. They didn't like the way I quit the service."

"What's all that got to do with Kemp and his deputies?"

"I don't know. Nothing."

"But *they're* after you too. They're the ones got you beat up, aren't they?"

"I'm sorry," Craik said. "Why I'm in the middle of this doesn't make a whole lot of sense to me, either. But somebody murdered Brendan Shields, Marla. And somebody did something to Janine Devereaux that made her drive into a tree and got her father killed as well. And somebody wants me out of this county. And now something's happened to Susanna."

"You think it's all connected," Vickers said.

"Yes. But not to my former job."

"And you're gonna put it all together?"

"Yes."

"Then what?"

Craik shrugged. "I don't know," he said. "First we find Susanna. Then we try to do something to blow the whole thing wide open. I've still got some friends in the government. Maybe I can make it happen. After that, Susanna and I just get the hell out of here."

Vickers smiled. "Well," she said, "don't suppose it'd hurt to clean this place up a bit. Okay, I'll get your guns. But, Craik, you see that girl's safe. That's more important than anything you can do to the turd-hoppers around here. You understand what I'm saying?"

Craik nodded.

"Good," Vickers said. "Let's see what the old Chevy can do." She turned and walked out of the house, limping only slightly.

CHAPTER 33

The heat from the mid-afternoon sun rose from the soft tar of the road in visible, shimmering waves. There had been a morning Bay breeze, but it had died. The air was lifeless, with even the normally frantic insect population taking a break.

The cruiser passed small farms and solitary homes. Dogs lay in a stupor in the shade of trees. The gaunt metal frames of sprinkler systems stood in fields of soybeans, idled until evening. A single hawk perched high in a spidery, dead oak, turning its head, waiting for something to move.

Inside the cruiser, the air conditioner was going full blast, yet the front of Tilghman's uniform was soaked with sweat. There was a fine line of perspiration on his upper lip. He was drumming his fingers on his knee, out of synch to the sound of Alabama coming from the radio.

Fyke, driving, appeared cooler. His hair looked freshly blow-dried and there was no moisture in his neatly trimmed mustache. He hummed along with the anthem of the eighteen-wheeler as if it were all that was on his mind.

"I don't know," Tilghman said. "I don't like it, Brent."

"Relax, will you?" Fyke said.

"They said they wanted to see the Judge. Why doesn't he go himself?"

"We're his negotiators, Charles."

"What the hell does that mean? I ain't a goddamn negotiator."

Fyke sighed. "It means," he said, "that we go in there and see what kind of a deal they got in mind. We take their proposal back to the Judge. That's all there is to it."

"I still don't like it."

"Come on, Judge Holder ain't gonna do anything that'll be a risk for us. He *needs* us. We're the best he's got. That's why he's sending us in the first place. It means he's confident we can do the job. That oughtta be worth something down the road."

"You think?"

"Yeah, I think," Fyke said. "Trouble with you is, you don't see the big picture."

"What the fuck does that mean?"

"It means you think small, Charles. People throw you

nickels and dimes and you get hoarse as a bullfrog thanking them. Didn't you ever wonder how the Judge got that fancy house he lives in?"

"I know how he got it. His daddy give it to him."

Fyke sighed. "That's what I mean," he said. "For chrissake, it don't matter who first got it, the point is that they got it and you don't. And the reason is because you don't see the big picture. The way you get a house like that is to have something that somebody else wants so much, they'll give you whatever *you* want."

"And how do you get that?"

"Use your head, Charles. What makes this whole business run?"

"Uh, Judge Holder does. Him and Brace."

"Nope," Fyke said. "It's Holder's business, all right. But he don't make it *run*. *We* do. We take care of all the shit he can't do for himself. Without us the business breaks down, partner."

"I don't know," Tilghman said. "Guys like us, he could find others."

"Maybe so. That's why we got to become more valuable. When we get so he *can't* replace us, then we can cut ourselves off a bigger piece. So we want to do good here."

"With the D.C. boys."

"Uh-huh. This is our chance. Brace and the Judge are in some deep shit. They need someone to bail them out. When we do it, I been thinking it's about time we got a little raise, got a little closer to the action. That's what I mean about seeing the big picture."

"Yeah," Tilghman said, "I see what you mean." He drummed his fingers against the dashboard, accompanying a hard-driving number by Hank Williams, Jr. "We *deserve* it, God damn it!"

The cruiser slowed as it came to a deserted intersection in the woods. There was a car waiting, with two men in it. Fyke parked the cruiser, and the deputies went over to the other car.

A window slid electrically down. "Where's the old man?" the driver of the other car asked.

"We're his negotiators," Tilghman said.

The two other men looked at one another.

"Just take us to your boss," Fyke said. "The Judge'll be along when the time's right."

The driver shrugged. His window slid up and he dropped the car into gear. The deputies got into their cruiser and followed him.

The two cars went by back roads. They drove to the opposite end of the county, fifteen miles southwest of Judge Holder's estate. The lead car turned off onto a tar road that was posted with signs reading, PRIVATE ROAD, NO TRESPASSING, and END STATE MAINTENANCE. The deputies were close behind.

A hundred yards in, the road bent around and there was a high brick wall with an iron gate. On the wall to the right of the gate was a large brass plaque bearing the word *Spindrift* in ornate script. To the left was a white gate house.

The man in the gate house glanced at the two cars, and the heavy gate swung slowly open. The two cars passed through. They drove another couple of hundred yards and stopped in front of a Victorian mansion. The house was painted brown. There were no people and no other cars in sight.

The two men got out of the lead car. The one who'd been driving was short and wiry. The other was short and stocky. Both were clean-shaven, with black hair and dark complexions. They were joined by the deputies. Tilghman looked the house over.

"Nice," he said.

The two men didn't say anything. The wiry one motioned with his head for the deputies to follow. The four of them went in the front door of the mansion.

Inside, there was a large, cool foyer. There were also two other men waiting. Each of the men was armed with a boxy automatic machine pistol. The pistols were trained on Deputies Fyke and Tilghman. Central air-conditioning hummed unobtrusively in the background.

Tilghman nervously looked over at Fyke. Fyke appeared unconcerned.

"What do you want us to do?" Fyke asked. "Put up our hands?"

The two men who'd been in the car came over and relieved the deputies of their guns, then patted them down quickly to make sure they were carrying no other weapons. The deputies offered no resistance.

"Keep calm, Charles," Fyke said. "We're just here to talk."

The wiry man looked at Fyke. For a moment his face was expressionless, then it broke into a broad grin. Gold and white vied for the predominant color in his mouth. He tried to take Fyke's arm, just above the elbow, but Fyke shrugged his hand off.

"Tough guy," the wiry man said.

He led the deputies down a corridor to the left. They were followed by the men with the machine pistols. The stocky man stayed behind in the foyer.

The five men entered a large formal dining room. The long, narrow table had a dozen heavy antique chairs drawn up to it. At the head of the table sat a slender young man with a pencil mustache. He was dressed in a lime silk shirt with the top three buttons open and was smoking a skinny brown cigar with a gold band around it. The bruises on his face were still evident.

The young man smiled. One of his front teeth was missing. Tilghman looked nervously at his partner, but Fyke's attention was fully on his host.

"Ah, gentlemen," Aldo said. "Perhaps you do not expect

to see me again so soon." He gestured down the table. "Please come in. Sit down."

The two deputies did as Aldo said. He motioned for the wiry man to come over, and whispered something in his ear. The wiry man nodded and left the room. Aldo leaned forward. He rested his arms on the tabletop.

"Now," he said, "where is the old one?"

"Where's *your* boss?" Fyke countered.

Aldo shrugged. "I *am* the boss," he said. "If the old one wishes to deal, he deals with me." His expression got hard. "And if you do not show me respect," he added, "I will cut your nose off."

Tilghman wet his lips and looked from Aldo to Fyke and back again. There was a man with a machine pistol standing close behind each of the deputies' chairs. Fyke took a pack of cigarettes from his breast pocket. He extracted a cigarette, tapped it down, and set it afire. He shook out the match and dropped it on the table.

"You do not care for antiques," Aldo said.

"No, not particularly."

"Do you care for your life?"

"Look," Fyke said, "we didn't come here to bullshit, we came here to listen. You want to make some kind of deal. The Judge wants to know what it is. We're listening."

"No," Aldo said, shaking his head, "you are wrong. It is you who must offer to deal. Your Judge will understand this. He will have sent you with instructions."

"Uh-uh," Fyke said. "You make an offer, we take it back to him. That's how it works."

The wiry man came back into the room and stood by the door. Aldo got up and walked the length of the table until he was opposite the deputies. He put his hands on one of the heavy chairs and leaned toward them. His face was a mask of tightly controlled anger.

"You are pigheaded men," he said to them. "In the

country of my ancestors you would have been thrown out with the rest of the garbage. You will cooperate with us or we will destroy you all. Beginning with the girl."

"How do we know she's not already dead?" Fyke said.

Aldo smiled faintly for a moment. "You don't," he said. "And it doesn't make the slightest difference. Not to you."

He raised his hand slightly to the wiry man by the door. The wiry man came over and stood next to Fyke. He took some lengths of leather thong from his pocket. Then he grabbed Fyke's forearm and attempted to pin it to the arm of the chair.

Fyke flung him aside as if he were a child. Aldo just smiled and nodded. One of the other men shoved his machine pistol hard into the base of Fyke's skull.

"Brent—" Tilghman said. The word came out with two *B*'s and three syllables.

Aldo's smile was gone. "Trust me," he said to Fyke. "If you do that again, I will make your friend clean your brains off this beautiful table. Perhaps I will make him eat them."

Tilghman blanched.

The wiry man returned. This time Fyke allowed himself to be securely tied to the chair. First his arms, then his legs. The final thong went around his chest. When the wiry man was finished, only Fyke's head could move freely. The wiry man went to stand by the door again, and the man with the gun stepped back a few paces. The other man kept his gun trained on Tilghman, a fact that Tilghman checked more than once.

Aldo turned his back on the table. He walked casually to the side of the room, where a rolling bar had been set up.

"Anyone like a drink?" he said over his shoulder.

"Ah. Well . . ." Tilghman said. He stopped himself when he saw Fyke give a slight shake of the head. "Ah, no thanks."

There was a shiny ice bucket on the bar. Next to it lay a

long, sterling silver ice pick. Aldo took the pick and broke up some of the ice in the bucket. He dropped some pieces of ice into a shallow glass and poured something clear over it. Then he walked back to the table, carrying the glass in one hand and the ice pick in the other. He sipped from the glass a couple of times before setting it on the table, where it immediately began forming a ring.

"Good," he said, as if trying to get the deputies to change their minds.

When there was no response, he shrugged. He walked around the end of the table and stood next to Fyke. He turned the ice pick over in his hand.

"Silver," he said. "If it was worth the same, I would rather have it than gold. Don't you agree?" Fyke didn't say anything.

"And this is a tool of many uses," Aldo went on. "You can pick your teeth with it, for example."

He tugged on Fyke's lower jaw and tried to insinuate the pick into his mouth. Fyke kept his jaw clenched tight. Aldo nodded his head once, and the man with the machine pistol stepped forward and butted it into Fyke's skull again. Fyke's face was tight with rage, but he opened his mouth.

"Nice," Aldo said as he picked delicately between Fyke's teeth. "You have a good dentist. Take care of your teeth."

He inserted the pick in the space between Fyke's two upper front teeth. Then, abruptly, he whacked the end of the pick with his other hand, driving it deep. In the same motion he twisted the hand holding the pick. One of the teeth broke off and dropped into Fyke's mouth.

"Nnnh," Fyke said. His jaw snapped shut automatically. Aldo calmly withdrew the pick from the hole he'd created and looked at it as if in wonder. Fyke spat out the broken tooth and some blood. His eyes were small slits in his face. One corner of his mouth twitched repeatedly.

Tilghman was gaping at the scene. Aldo walked around

behind him and pressed the point of the pick against his neck. Tilghman jumped when he felt the prick.

"What do you think, my friend?" Aldo said. He leaned down so that Tilghman could see his face. His lips curled back, showing the gap in his own smile. "What do you think?" he repeated, pointing at the gap with the ice pick. "Are we not brothers, your friend and me?"

"Uh, yeah," Tilghman said. "Sure."

Aldo moved so that he was facing both deputies again. He set the pick on the table.

"It is fair, no?" he said. There was no response. "But now," he continued, holding out his hands, "we must talk of the future. Look around you. Go ahead."

There was nothing to see but three impassive men, two of them with machine pistols.

"We *are* your future," Aldo announced. He rubbed his hands together. "So let us have no more talk of deals, all right? From now on you will be working for us. Your Judge, he is an old man with no knowledge of the modern world. We will introduce you to the modern world.

"Tell me, how much money do you make?" No response. "Not much, as I suspected. An operation such as this one, you should be making ten times as much, a hundred times as much. And with us you will."

Aldo paused, then said, "Of course, those who join us early will be in a . . . favored position." He looked at Tilghman. "How about you, are you ready to begin working for us?"

Tilghman cleared his throat. "Ah, well, if you—"

Fyke shot him a furious look. "Shut up, Charles," he said, and Tilghman did. Then he turned to Aldo.

"All right," he said, "you've had your fun. Now I suggest you let us go. If we're not back soon, you're gonna have more law down on you than you've ever seen in one place before. The sheriff can deputize as many as he needs. Ain't no lack of people would be happy to get you out of town or into the ground."

Aldo had a long, hearty laugh. When he'd finished, he said, "You threatening *me*?" He turned his attention to Tilghman. "How about you, fat boy? You agree with what this man is saying?"

"I don't know," Tilghman said quickly. He didn't look at his partner.

"Good," Aldo said. "That's good. But you're gonna have to make up your mind—"

"Look, greaseball," Fyke growled. "Cut the shit. You got your tooth. Now put us in the car and we'll tell the Judge you want the whole thing."

Aldo chuckled. He went to the table and picked up the ice pick again. Then he stood next to Fyke but angled himself so that he was looking directly at Tilghman.

"How about it?" Aldo asked Tilghman. "You made up your mind yet?"

Tilghman's mouth opened slightly but he didn't say anything. Aldo placed the pick so that its point was directly under Fyke's jaw and seized a handful of the nicely styled hair. He pushed the pick a little. Fyke's head tilted back reflexively.

"What do you think of this pig?" Aldo asked Tilghman. "You like him?"

Tilghman paused, wet his lip, then said, "No. No, I don't. He's . . ." He closed his mouth.

"I didn't think so," Aldo said. "You know, you'll be much happier working with us. Especially without him taking your share, and his too."

He pushed harder on the pick. Fyke's head bent farther backward, until his throat was exposed all the way from breastbone to chin. Aldo pushed until the pick point broke the skin.

"You gutless bastard," Fyke said through gritted teeth. "I

catch you when I'm not tied down and I'll kill you with my bare hands."

Aldo clucked his tongue. "How about it?" he said to Tilghman. "You want to see him die like the dog he is?"

Tilghman looked from Aldo to Fyke and back again. "I don't know," he said.

"Sure you do," Aldo said. "If he dies, you will be our number-one man around here. You'd like that, wouldn't you?"

Tilghman looked wildly from Aldo to Fyke and back again.

"*Wouldn't* you?" Aldo demanded.

"Uh, I don't—" Tilghman said. "I guess—"

Aldo gave the ice pick a hard shove. The point slid cleanly upward, through Fyke's mouth and palate and into his brain. Aldo wiggled the handle a little. Fyke's body jerked a couple of times before he died. There was surprisingly little blood.

Tilghman stared, his mouth wide open. Then he gagged, swallowed hard.

Aldo let go of the pick. Fyke's head flopped forward. The pick handle rested on his chest. Aldo got the glass of liquor and offered it to Tilghman. Tilghman drank. He came up coughing, took another drink.

"Now," Aldo said, "you're one of us. His job is your job. Go on, get out of here. Bring me the old one."

They gave Tilghman back his gun. He looked at it as if he didn't know what it was for. Then they led him out to the cruiser. He drove slowly back to Judge Holder's estate, glancing into the rearview mirror frequently. No one followed him.

Tilghman was shown immediately into the Judge's library. Holder was waiting there for him, along with Kemp, Crowe, and two other hirelings. Tilghman told them what had happened.

When he finished, there was a stunned silence. Tilghman turned and started to walk away.

"Wait a minute," Holder said. "Where the hell do you think you're going?"

Tilghman stopped. "I'm leaving," he said.

"No, you're not. I need you."

"Yes, I am. I ain't letting what happened to Brent happen to me. I'm going as far away from this shithole as I can get."

He started moving again. Judge Holder looked around him at the other men.

"Well, come *on*," Holder said. "He can't just walk away like this."

No one stirred. The Judge himself rushed after Tilghman and caught him by the arm. But the big deputy just brushed at him. Holder, despite his bulk, was thrown violently backward. He landed on his butt.

Tilghman exited the room, leaving the door standing open behind him. Holder got to his feet, somewhat dazed. He glared at the remaining men.

"Well, what about the rest of you bastards?" he said coldly, moving his eyes from one man to the next. "You going to desert me too?"

The others looked down at the floor.

CHAPTER 34

Clouds had moved in from the southwest. They hung over the Bay, trapping the heat, but no breeze blew. The night was close and soggy, the cloud cover hiding the stars but reflecting the lights of the land below. Mist rose slowly from the marshes and estuaries. Rain seemed promised, but no rain fell.

The creaky Bel Air rolled to a stop. The woman got out and went inside the small house. She moved slowly and with more of a limp than usual.

"I'm sorry it took so long," she said wearily. "I got lost. And the Chevy overheated once."

"It's all right," Craik said. He took the brown leather suitcase from her. "Thanks, Marla."

"Susanna turn up?" she asked.

Frank Whately shook his head. "Nope," he said. "I put one of my boys to work on it, but no one's seen her that he could find."

"Marla," Craik said, "will you call Judge Holder for me? I don't want him to know for sure that I'm still around."

"Okay," she said. "You just want me to ask him if he knows where Susanna is?"

Craik nodded. Vickers went to the phone and put the call through.

"Judge," she said, "Marla Vickers. I was wondering if you knowed where Susanna was at. I talked to her folks and they ain't seen her since yesterday."

"Ah, no," Holder said. "No, I don't. She was here yesterday, too, but I don't know where she might have got to."

"Just thought I'd try."

"Look, Marla, while I've got you, there's maybe something you could do for me."

"What might that be?"

"Your tenant, Craik, is he around anywhere?"

"Not that I know of," she said.

"Well, if you *do* happen to see him, tell him I'm looking for him, would you?"

"Sure, Judge. You do the same for Susanna."

"I will."

Vickers hung up and said to Craik, "He says he doesn't know about Susanna, but he's looking for *you*. Personally, I think he knows about Susanna."

"Yeah," Craik said, "I guess if anyone would know, he would."

"Well," Vickers said with a sigh, "I'm tired. Anything else you need?"

"No. Thanks, Marla. You've been more help than I had a right to expect."

"I'll be going home, then."

Craik put his arm around the older woman. "I'll find her," he said.

Vickers seemed a little embarrassed. "You do that," she said, and she left.

"Frank," Craik said to Whately, "could you leave me alone for a while?"

Whately nodded. Craik toted the leather suitcase into the bedroom and closed the door.

He unlatched the suitcase and opened it out on the bed. There was a flap fastened over one side. The other side was open. The open side was a customized jumble of pockets and loops, pouches and bags, small jars and glassine envelopes. It was filled with hardware. Everything recognizable was a weapon of one kind or another.

Craik unfastened the flap on the other side of the suitcase and raised it. Beneath, there were rubber-banded stacks of money, packed solid to the rim. American dollars predominated, but there was a scattering of British pounds, Swiss francs, and German marks. Craik reclosed the flap.

Slowly, carefully, he loosened straps and opened pockets. He lifted things from the suitcase and arranged them on Whately's bed. Eventually, he nodded to himself, shut the suitcase, and put it on the floor. With meticulous attention to detail he prepared his tools. He cleaned and assembled and inspected. Then he concealed the chosen weapons on his person.

To the east, in Brawlton, Marla Vickers pulled herself out of the Bel Air. There was a gray Ford parked a little farther down the road, on the same side. She didn't look at it. She walked carefully across her yard.

When she reached the front steps, she stopped, her eyes screwed up in the darkness. There was a man sitting in one of the chairs on the porch. Lucky, the brown-and-white mongrel, was curled up at his feet. The man was scratching Lucky behind the ears. The dog occasionally whimpered with pleasure.

"Mrs. Vickers," the man said, getting to his feet.

"Could be. Who're you?" Vickers said.

"Please join me. I'd like to talk with you."

Vickers grunted. She kept her eye on the stranger as she hoisted herself onto the porch and settled into her rocker. She squinted at the man. Then she took out her pipe and tobacco and got a load going.

"I know you now," she said when she'd begun puffing smoke. "You're the one was looking for Craik."

"Yes, ma'am. My name is Smith," Smith said. "I'm still looking for him."

"What for?"

Smith chuckled. "Well, it's kind of a long story," he said.

"You got my attention," Vickers said. "I'll listen until bedtime. Which ain't that far off, so you might want to shorten it up some."

"All right. Do you know who Craik is?"

"He's my tenant."

"And before that?"

"Don't much care. Long as he pays the rent on time, which he ain't even been here long enough to do."

Smith took off his glasses and polished the lenses on his shirt. When he put them back on, he looked at Vickers as if he could see her better.

"Mr. Craik used to work for the federal government," he said. "He was sort of a . . . troubleshooter."

"Thought it might be something like that." She puffed a little smoke directly at Smith's face. He reacted not at all.

"Craik was a valuable man," he went on. "He did a lot of work for us—overseas, primarily."

"He's a spy," Vickers said.

"No, not exactly. In fact, that's sort of the crux of the problem. There are those who think that Craik knows considerably more than he does."

"Uh-huh. So what's he doing in Brawlton?"

Smith shrugged. "Man has a right to live anywhere he wants. He left the government and chose to live here. We have no difficulty with that. It's his life. Unfortunately, there are certain parties who want to interfere with that. They want the information that they think he has and they're . . . they're very anxious to have it. He needs help, Mrs. Vickers."

"Uh-huh," she said again. "And how do I know it ain't you he needs help from?"

Smith pulled out his wallet and extracted an ID card. She inspected it by the flame of her lighter. It was laminated in plastic and identified Smith as an Under Secretary for Caribbean Affairs, United States Department of State. It had his picture on it. In the photo he was well dressed and smiling pleasantly. She looked at it, then held the lighter near his face. She handed the ID back to him.

"How bad is it?" she asked.

Smith pocketed his wallet. "We truly don't know," he said. "But you know the Sov— You know how it is with sensitive information. We have reason to believe that the, ah, opposition would be willing to kill for it."

"And Craik doesn't have it."

"No, he doesn't."

"So you're saying they might kill him for something he hasn't got."

Smith nodded.

Vickers puffed at her pipe for a while.

"He never told anything like this," she said finally.

"He wouldn't. He's a private man, and he defends his privacy with all he's got. It's one of his strengths, but it's one of his weaknesses too. He's not the kind of man who seeks help, even when he knows he's in trouble. And like I say, I'm not sure he *knows* he's in trouble this time."

"How come there ain't more of you here?"

"First of all," Smith said, "I can't *force* him to do anything. He's a free American. Basically, I'm here to warn him. We're still a couple of steps ahead of the other guys. If he hears what I have to say and turns his back on me, then that's it. He goes his way and we go ours. He doesn't know anything that will compromise our national security. On the other hand, if he wants protection, then I'm empowered to offer it to him. He's served his country well. He's earned that much."

"I don't know what to say to you, Mr. Smith."

"If you know where Scott Craik is, please tell me, Mrs. Vickers. The two steps we're ahead of the opposition today, tomorrow that could be gone. I'm asking for your help. If Craik is anything more to you than a tenant, help me. You may well be doing him a greater favor than he can ever repay."

"I don't know," Vickers said. "You got me all mixed up now. He said he didn't want no one to know where he was. I got to honor that."

"Of course you do. I can understand your reluctance to break a promise. But let me show you something."

Smith got up and walked to the gray Ford that was parked down the road. When he returned, he had a handful of papers and a flashlight.

"Here," he said, "look at this."

Vickers inspected the document. It was from the Office of the President of the United States and it commended Steven Kirk for meritorious service to his country.

"Who's Steven Kirk?" she asked.

"That's his real name," Smith said. "Here."

The next document was a directive from the U.S. Secretary of State to Smith. It requested that he immediately locate Steven Kirk, a.k.a. Scott Craik, for the benefit of Kirk's well-being.

"This is very confusing," Vickers said.

"I know that."

He handed her another sheet of paper. This was a memo from Kirk to Smith regarding his assessment of the political stability of a certain African country. The memo was written in the informal style of a man who knew the recipient well.

"There was a time when I depended on him," Smith said, "for things like this. Now he's dependent on me, even if he doesn't know it. Would you like to see more?"

Vickers shook her head. "No," she said, ":I don't think so. I . . . still don't know what to say."

"Please, Mrs. Vickers. Help me. Help Craik."

There was a long pause while Vickers smoked and thought about it. Finally, she sighed.

"He's in more trouble than just from these fellows you're talking about, I think," she said.

"All the more reason that I get to him soon."

"Well, I can't guarantee anything. But I'll see what I can do."

"Thank you. Thank you very much."

Smith followed her as she got up out of the rocker and went inside. She made a brief phone call.

"Don't know where he is now," she said after she'd hung up. "Place he was at, he ain't anymore. Man wouldn't tell me more than that."

"What do you think?" Smith asked.

Vickers gave him a long look before saying, "Well, my guess is he would be at Judge Holder's."

"All right, I'll try there. And thank you again, Mrs. Vickers." Smith hurried out.

Vickers returned to the porch, where she sat in the rocker and smoked her pipe.

"Well, Lucky," she said to the mongrel, "I hope to Jesus you're right about that man. I ain't questioning your judgment, now. But you got to admit you always were a sucker for them smooth talkers."

She scratched the dog behind the ears and blew smoke into the hot, moist darkness.

CHAPTER 35

Frank Whately looked at Craik over his reading glasses. He'd been reading the Bible. Craik was dressed in jeans and a navy blue short-sleeved shirt, blue running shoes, and a light-weight black watch cap.

"Take the truck," he said.

"Jesus, Frank," Craik said, then caught himself. "No offense."

"Jesus don't mind what you say. He only minds what you do."

"Look, Frank. You've done plenty. If I take your truck and something happens to me, they'll know it's you that's been hiding me. I don't know what might happen to you."

"It's all right," Whately said. "Take it. You need it."

"You've got no reason . . ."

Whately set the Bible and the reading glasses on the small table next to his chair.

"I got more reason than you know," he said. "You ever hear of Garfield Dent?"

Craik shook his head. "No, I don't think so. Is he . . .
Wait a minute, yeah, Will Devereaux mentioned the name the
night before he died. Gar Dent."

"My sister's boy," Whately said. "He disappeared, close
to fifteen years ago. The . . . body never did turn up." He
cleared his throat. "My nephew. He was a good kid. I tried to
find out what happened to him. No one knew, supposedly, but
this is a small town. I heard the rumors. Gar was working for
Judge Holder on the side. He got killed during some
smuggling operation. That's what they say.

"I don't doubt it, either. It ain't easy to make an honest
living in this business. Never has been. But it's even harder
when they wave that dirty money in front of your face. Poor
kid like Gar never had a chance."

"I'm sorry," Craik said.

"Don't be. It's long over now. I tried to do something
about it and I couldn't. The bastards are slippery. Now, you're
my chance to even the score a little. Take the truck."

Craik started to say something, then stopped. He simply
nodded and walked out of the cottage. The leather suitcase
was in one hand, the metallic one in the other. He hoisted
them into the back of the pickup.

He drove south. A hundred yards from the intersection
with the main Brawlton–Dorset road, he pulled off onto the
shoulder. There were no other vehicles in sight. He lugged
the two suitcases into the woods and left them propped
behind a tree.

Then he continued on. When he reached the entrance to
Forrest Holder's estate, he found the gate open. There was no
one on guard. He lifted the tail of the sport shirt and slipped
the small .38-caliber revolver out of his waistband. He rested
the gun hand in his lap. Cautiously, he drove up to the
mansion.

There were no cars parked out front, no sign of anyone
around. Craik dropped down from the cab of the pickup. He

scanned the area, then went up the broad steps. The door was open. He went inside.

He called the Judge's name, but there was no response. Moving slowly, gun in hand, he made his way to the library. The door was ajar. From within came the sound of someone humming to himself. Craik stood off to the side and shoved the door with his foot. As it swung open, he went into the room in a crouch.

Holder was seated behind his desk. Craik spun on the ball of his foot. He held the gun chest-high and kept his arms extended, both hands stabilizing the weapon. There was no one else in the room. The Judge stopped humming and began to laugh. It was a deep, sputtering laugh.

"Craik," he said, holding his crystal tumbler up in salute, "welcome to the party." He drank. There was a half empty bottle of Glen Calder next to him, from which he refilled the tumbler.

Craik was still holding the gun. "Though, of course," the Judge said, "you are a bit *overdressed* for the occasion." This caused Holder to laugh again. Craik slipped the pistol back behind his belt. He went and sat across from the Judge.

"Have a drink," Holder said. "World's finest Scotch." Craik shook his head.

The Judge waggled his forefinger at Craik. "I know who you are now," he said.

"Where's Susanna?" Craik said.

"Ah," Holder said, grinning, "my niece. My beautiful niece. And tell me, sir, is your interest in her personal or professional?"

"I'm not a professional anything. I'm looking for Susanna. I think you know where she is."

Holder set his glass down, hard. Whiskey sloshed over the rim and onto the desktop. Holder ignored the spill. His manner was more serious.

"Do you, now?" he said. "How come you can't find her yourself, Mr. CIA hotshot?"

"I'm not CIA."

Holder paused. He gazed at Craik for a long moment. His head trembled slightly, and his eyes seemed not to focus.

"How much do you know about me, Craik?" he said finally.

"Look, Holder," Craik said, "I don't care who or what you are. It's Susanna I'm interested in. After I find her you can go on living your life any way you want."

"You answer my questions and I'll answer yours."

"Holder," Craik said through gritted teeth, "if I have to beat it out of you, I will."

"You won't succeed. You want Susanna. I want you just as badly."

Craik paused, looking the other man over, then said, "Yeah, I believe you. In your condition I'm not sure the pain would mean anything."

Holder smiled and took another large swallow of whiskey. "Very good," he said. "Please continue."

Briefly, Craik told him what he'd learned of the Judge's smuggling operation.

"That's fine, as far as it goes," Holder said when he'd finished. "But there's one other thing. Your former colleagues know what's going on. One of them came to see me. A Mr., ah, Smith."

Craik nodded noncommittally.

"He told me the reason they've let me continue is that they know I don't do anything that isn't in the country's interest. It's true, I don't. All I'm doing is what the Congress lacks the will to do."

Holder waved his hand at something only he could see. When he did, he upset the tumbler of Scotch. The whiskey puddled on the desktop. Holder paid it no attention. He set the glass upright and refilled it without looking.

"No matter," he went on. "Your Mr. Smith didn't come to see me about that. He came about you. Apparently your colleagues are looking for you. Whatever the reason, I don't care. Do you want to go with them?"

Craik stared impassively at the other man.

"No," Holder said, "I don't believe you do. Good. Now let me tell you what's wrong with the rest of your little story. Look around you." He slurred the words slightly and waved both arms, this time missing the whiskey glass by a couple of inches.

"You see anything?" he asked. "Well, that's what's left of my so-called lucrative business. Nothing." He slapped his chest twice. "Me, that's all that's left. Fyke's dead."

"What?" Craik said.

"The late, very unlamented Brent Fyke. A useful man but not a good one. The bastards killed him with an ice pick."

"Who did?"

"Your friend with the gold-tipped cigar. His name's Aldo. You were right about him, of course. He murdered your partner, and now he's killed my deputy. I'm finished, Craik." The Judge stared down at the desktop for a moment, then took a drink. "The rats have been leaving the sinking ship faster than even I thought they would.

"Tilghman went first. They executed Fyke in front of him, and that was all it took. He stopped here long enough to tell us what happened and then he was gone. Kemp was right behind him. Said he'd heard of an opening for a county sheriff out in Wyoming. The rest of them, my loyal watermen, they just drifted away. They're scared, and I don't much blame them."

"Who's Aldo?"

"Drug smuggler from D.C. South American. His whole family's into it. They want to use my setup to bring in their filthy drugs. I *hate* drugs, Craik. They're ruining this country. And these people are animals. They kill anyone who gets in their way, like you'd shoot a groundhog in your garden. I know I haven't always operated strictly within the law. But I never did anything to undermine my country. And I never *killed* anybody."

"Yeah, sure," Craik said. "Where's Susanna?"

"Aldo's got her." The Judge's tone was morose. He reached down and opened one of the desk drawers. He punched a button on the tape recorder.

It was a tape of a telephone conversation. Aldo was careful not to come right out and say anything. But the gist was that Susanna's safety was being offered straight up in exchange for control of the Judge's business.

Craik flinched when he heard her being bartered.

"You believe him?" Craik asked after the tape had played.

Holder shook his head wearily. "I don't know," he said. "It's probably on the level. He has nothing to gain by harming Susanna. But I don't have anything left to trade."

The Judge raised his head and looked at Craik. His eyes were moist.

"Look at me," he said. "I'm whipped. I'm drunk and I've got nothing to offer. All I have left is my niece, and they've got her too. It's almost funny, isn't it? I've got more money than anyone in this county, and yet I've got nothing."

Craik leaned forward and swept his hand across the desktop, sending the glass and bottle flying. Holder watched soddenly.

"What did you plan to do, you bastard?" Craik said. "Drink her out of there?"

"Craik, for God's sake, I want her safe. That's why I need you. Help me."

"Where is she?" Craik said through his teeth.

"Spindrift. It's an estate on the other side of the county."

"Can we go in in force?"

Holder shook his head. "My forces are gone," he said.

"State cops?"

"Uh-uh. Those animals would kill her the minute they knew what we were doing. They want me to come alone." The Judge looked at his watch.

"When?"

"Half an hour. Out near the main road. Or else . . ."

"And you want me to go instead."

Holder nodded. "There's nothing left," he said. "They'd realize that in five minutes. When they did, they'd kill us both and get the hell out of Dorset County. But you, you've had training. You're good. If you can get in there, I believe you can get her out. You're all there is."

"Shit," Craik said. He got up and paced back and forth for a minute. He returned to his chair but remained standing, resting his hands on the chair back.

"How many of them?" he asked.

"I don't know. Maybe half a dozen."

"I need backup. Once we're free, I don't want them coming after us. What can you do?"

"There's some deputies left," Holder said. "They don't know what's going on, so I can probably get them. Some of the watermen, too, the ones that don't know."

"How long?"

"An hour or so."

"Surround the place. I want state cops too."

Holder hesitated. Craik walked over to him and slammed his fist on the desktop. He pointed his forefinger and spoke directly into the Judge's face.

"Do it," he said. "They aren't gonna find anything that some fancy lawyer can't get you out of. But if you fuck up, *I'm* coming after you, and when I find you, you'll wish I was Aldo instead. We clear?"

The Judge nodded.

"All right. Where's the meet?"

"This side of the main road," Holder said. "They'll be waiting."

"How do I get to where they're holding her?"

Holder told him.

"You know the layout of the place?"

"Vaguely," Holder said, and told Craik what he knew.

"I'll need to be able to contact you," Craik said.

"Call this number." Holder gave it to him. "It's the phone here. When I leave, I'll have it forwarded to my car."

"That's fine if I can neutralize whoever's in the house. If I can't, we need someone watching. I'll head for a point on the wall about a hundred yards south of the gate house. Put someone in a tree near there. Someone who can shoot. Give him the best rifle you've got. If they're right behind us, I don't want to have to look back."

"I know the right man," Holder said.

Craik was still standing next to the Judge. When he spoke, it was with a grim intensity.

"All right," he said, "that's about all the preparation we can make. But I want you to understand something, Holder. You're a prick. You don't kill anyone personally, but you sell guns that do, and you hide behind the flag. I've known people like you all my life and I'm real tired of them. I don't believe you care one way or the other what happens to Susanna. You want me to go in there to save your own ass. Which I will do. But afterward I'm gone. You clean up the mess. That's the deal."

Holder nodded.

"And last but not least," Craik continued, "Susanna better come out of this in one piece. If she doesn't, you take all that money of yours and go hide someplace far away, because you don't *ever* want to see my face again. Understand?"

Holder nodded again.

"Now sober up," Craik said, "and get on the phone. You got a lot of work to do." He turned and walked out of the room and out of the house.

Craik was moving quickly, but Smith was quicker. Smith came from the shadows as Craik reached the bottom of the front steps. Craik picked him up in peripheral vision and had begun to react when Smith hammered him hard with a rabbit punch to the back of the neck. Craik dropped in his tracks.

Smith frisked him with a practiced efficiency. He took the pistol from Craik's waistband. Then he stood and placed his foot on Craik's shoulder. There was a small automatic in his own right hand. He jostled the unconscious man.

Reflexively, Craik grabbed for the foot, but Smith jerked it away. Craik pawed the air for a moment, then rolled onto his stomach. He pushed himself to his knees, shaking his head. He looked up.

"Jesus," he said. "You're about all I need right now."

"Come on, Steven," Smith said. "It's time to go home."

Craik got to his feet.

"I'm serious," Smith said. "Don't try anything."

Craik blinked and shook his head once again. He brushed himself off. Then he looked Smith in the eye.

He sighed and said, "I'm not going, Smitty. You can shoot me if you want, but if you do, an innocent girl is going to die too."

"Holder's niece?"

Craik nodded.

"Where is she?"

Briefly, Craik explained the situation.

"Now, I've got about ten minutes to make the meet," he said. "I intend to do it unless you kill me."

"I can't let you go again, Steven."

"Then help me. The Judge is supposed to back me up, but I don't trust him any farther than the end of my arm. You back me. After we get Susanna out I'll . . . I'll go with you."

Smith stared at him for a long moment.

"Come on, Smitty. We don't have much time."

Finally, Smith took Craik's pistol and tossed it back to him.

"Don't screw me over," he said. "If you do, I swear to God I will kill you."

Craik stuck the gun back behind his belt. "Where's your car?" he asked.

"By the gate."

"Let's go."

They rode down to the gate in the pickup and got out. "Did you bring a full kit?" Craik asked.

"Of course," Smith said. He opened the gray Ford's trunk. Inside were a number of leather bags and cases.

"Give me a directional for the truck," Craik said. "I don't know exactly where I'm going and I couldn't tell you so it'd make any sense, but you know the general direction. I'll just follow them in the truck and you can follow us out of sight. If it seems like they're taking me someplace else, there's something wrong. Use your judgment."

Smith fished out the transmitter. It attached magnetically to the back of the pickup's bumper.

"I'll take out the gate guard," Craik said. "You wait for us near the house. If we're in trouble, do what you can."

"You need any hardware?"

"I'm armed." Craik thought a moment. "You got a formaldehyde pen?" he asked.

Smith went into one of the leather satchels and took out a small cylinder that looked like a ballpoint pen. He gave it to Craik, and Craik clipped it to the inside of his shirt pocket.

"Okay," Craik said. "And thanks, Smitty."

Smith nodded silently. The two men got into their respective vehicles.

Craik drove down the driveway and out the county road. The beige sedan was waiting for him, parked on the shoulder near the intersection with the Dorset–Brawlton road. Craik pulled off. A car turned down from the main road. Craik waited until it had passed, then got out and walked over to the sedan.

There were two men inside. The driver was short and wiry. His window slid down and he said, "We were expecting the old man."

"Take me to Aldo," Craik said. "The Judge is ready to

deal, but you can hardly expect him to go with you after what
you did to the deputy. When the girl's safe, then he'll meet
with you. Someplace neutral."

The driver looked at his partner, a short, stocky man. The
partner shrugged. The driver looked back at Craik.

"Get in," he said.

Craik shook his head. "I'll follow you in the truck," he
said.

"Suit yourself," the driver said. His window slid back up
and he started the engine.

The sedan drove to the main road and turned west. Craik
followed. A mile later the sedan pulled into a small service
station. The station was closed. Craik stopped behind them.
The two men got out and strolled over to the truck.

"I gotta make a call," the wiry man said. "Stick around."

He left his partner with Craik and went to the old-
fashioned glass outdoor phone booth. He made a short call,
then returned to the pickup. He nodded to the stocky man,
who produced a revolver from beneath his polyester jacket.
The revolver had a silencer screwed to the barrel. It was
pointed at the center of Craik's forehead.

"Out," the wiry man said.

Craik complied. While the stocky man held the gun the
wiry one patted Craik down. He took away Craik's pistol,
along with the two full speedloaders Craik had in his back
pockets. He tossed all the hardware into the cab of the
pickup.

"Let's go," the wiry man said.

Craig shrugged. The two men led him to the sedan. The
one with the silenced revolver motioned him into the
backseat, then slid in beside him. He had Craik sit with his
back to the door. The two men faced each other across the
seat. The gun was centered on Craik's heart, and the hand
that held it was steady. The wiry man continued to drive.

Craik began to cough.

"Shut up," the stocky man said.

"Can't help it," Craik said between coughs. "Summer cold." He coughed some more, his body shaking. Slowly, the fit subsided.

"Sorry," Craik said.

"Don't give it to me," the stocky man said. His face was expressionless and the gun hadn't moved.

The car turned south, onto a smaller county road. The countryside was dead flat. Small farms with patches of woods in between. A mile or so along the road, the car pulled over. There were dense woods on both sides. The wiry man switched off the lights.

"Don't trust this guy," he said. "Let's just see who comes along." He watched the rearview mirror.

The stocky man grunted. He didn't shift his attention from Craik. They waited for five minutes. No one came. One car passed, going in the opposite direction.

The driver restarted the car, shifted into gear, and pulled back onto the road. As he did, Craik began to cough again. The violence of the coughing doubled him up. He bent forward and turned his body slightly.

When his arm moved, it was a blur. He slapped the gun against the seat. It went off. The bullet exploded the seat's fabric and stuffing. Tiny shreds of fiber puffed into the air.

In the same motion Craik pivoted, pushed off with his left leg, and drove his left fist into the side of the stocky man's throat. The man gurgled and slumped forward. The pistol dropped from his hand.

Craik snatched it up just as the driver began to react. He spun the wheel and slammed on the brakes. Craik was tossed around, but when the car came to a stop, the gun was pointed at the driver's head.

"Keep both hands on the wheel," Craik said. He cocked the hammer. The wiry man didn't move.

Craik slid over until he was directly behind the driver. He

nudged the base of the man's skull with the silencer. The man stiffened.

"Nod if you have a gun," Craik said.

The man nodded.

"Take one hand off the wheel. Take out the gun by the barrel. Reach over the back of the seat and drop the gun. Then put your hand back on the wheel. Move slowly and do it right. I *will* kill you."

The driver followed directions. A heavy automatic thumped on the seat next to Craik.

"Now," Craik said, "I want the interior layout at Spindrift. I want to know where the girl is, and I want to know where Aldo will probably be. I want to know how many men are in the house and where they're stationed. If there's anything that I don't like the sound of, I'll start hurting you and I won't stop until I'm satisfied. Tell me now."

The wiry man started talking immediately. He went on in great detail. As he did, Craik reached down with his free hand and detached one of the small syringes that was taped to his calf.

"And that's it," the wiry man said. "That's everything, I swear it."

"I believe you," Craik said, and he plunged the syringe into the base of the man's neck. The man slapped once at Craik's hand, then collapsed on the seat.

Craik slid the silenced revolver behind his belt. He took another of the syringes and injected the stocky man. Then he dragged the stocky man out of the car and into the woods.

As he returned for the other man a shiny new pickup came down the road, from the opposite direction. It had extra-high tires and a silver roll bar. The sedan was sitting on the shoulder with its two offside doors open and the interior light on. The pickup stopped on the other side of the road.

The pickup's driver rolled down his window. "Hey!" he called. "You'all in trouble?" He was young and had shaggy hair and a neatly trimmed beard. He was smoking a hand-rolled cigarette.

Craik crossed the road and stood by the pickup. The scent of marijuana drifted out into the night air.

"Nah," Craik said. "Just had to take a piss is all. No problem."

The young man nodded and held out the cigarette. "Want a hit?" he asked. His eyes were focused on something in the middle distance.

Craik sniffed the smoke. "Mmmm," he said, "I'd like to. But the old lady catches me with it on my breath tonight, she'll have my ass. Thanks, anyway. And thanks for stopping."

"Okay." The young man lowered his voice. "And watch yourself along here. There's some weird people out tonight." He touched the corner of his eye and nodded knowingly. "If they try to take you, don't let them."

"I won't," Craik said.

The young man held out his hand. When Craik extended his, the young man slapped his palm.

"Take care," he said. "And remember what I told you."

The pickup drove off. Craik hurried back to the sedan, got the wiry man, and pulled him into the woods. The wiry man had begun to snore. Craik propped him against a tree, next to his partner. He looked down at the two men.

"Have a nice evening, gentlemen," he said.

CHAPTER 36

Craik drove past the asphalt driveway. A quarter mile down the road, he pulled off and buried the sedan in a field screened from the road by a stand of loblolly pine.

On foot, he made his way back, at a forty-five-degree angle to the road. The pine thicket was dense and the going was slow. Swirls of mist rose from the ground. The branches that brushed him were wet with condensation. The bed of needles crunched delicately beneath his feet.

A light appeared in the mist. Craik moved toward it, more slowly than before. He took each step with care, making almost no sound.

Inside the gate house was a burly man with dark curly hair and a vivid scar near his left eye. He was fidgeting, picking his teeth. Every few minutes he'd step outside and look around.

The phone in the gate house buzzed. The man with the scar answered, listened for a moment, then said, "No, not yet. Don't worry, I'll call you."

He hung up the phone. There was a sound outside. Something rattling against the iron gate. The man drew a long-barreled .357 Magnum pistol. He held it close to his body. Cautiously, he edged out of the gate house, his eyes scanning the area around the gate.

Craik came from below and behind him. Before he had a chance to react, Craik had crashed the silenced revolver against the base of his skull. He crumpled. Craik used the third of his syringes.

He didn't bother to move the burly man. He went inside the gate house. There was a phone and a panel with several toggle switches. Beneath each switch was a strip of black plastic with raised white letters. Craik flipped the one marked GATE. Nothing happened.

"Bastards," he said softly.

He hurried out of the gate house, jamming the pistol into his waistband. He pulled himself up the ten-foot-high iron gate. When he neared the top, he felt carefully between the spikes. There was nothing there. He hoisted himself over and dropped down onto the grounds of the estate.

By the time his feet touched earth, he was already running, the pistol back in his hand. There was a broad expanse of lawn sloping gently upward to the brown Victorian mansion. Most of it was open. The driveway was bordered with Japanese cherry trees, and there were some giant cedars here and there. A low mist hung over everything.

Craik moved along a straight line for the house. He was twenty-five yards away when his path was intersected by the dog. It was an attack Doberman, trained to move in complete silence. It sped through the mist and launched itself at Craik's throat without a sound.

Craik was able to turn just a few inches, but it was enough. The dog's jaws clacked as they slid past his throat. Its chest slammed into his shoulder. The two of them fell to the ground, and the pistol skittered away. Craik rolled, pulling the ballpoint from his pocket.

The dog rolled, too, and in an instant had returned to the attack. Its lips were curled back, and its white teeth stood out against the rest of its dark body. The white teeth loomed phosphorescent in the reflected light from the house.

Craik aimed the ballpoint at the teeth and pushed the plunger. A thin stream of liquid squirted out. It hit the dog on the point of its snout, splashing into its nose and eyes. The acrid smell of formaldehyde filled the air.

The dog stopped as if it had hit a wall. It burrowed its head into the grass, raking its paws across its face, writhing furiously, as if trying to bury itself. Still it made no sound.

Craik retrieved the silenced revolver. He put the barrel next to the agonized dog's skull and fired one shot. There was a muffled whump, and the dog died.

Immediately, Craik was moving again, sprinting for the shrubbery massed next to the house. A man came around the corner from his right.

"Hold it!" the man shouted.

He had a Spanish accent and a machine pistol slung from his shoulder. The gun had an attached suppressor nearly as long as its body. A cluster of silenced bullets tore the earth near Craik's feet.

Craik dived into the bushes. He slithered on his belly until he was against the base of the house. He moved along the wall. To the left there was a small basement window, just above ground level. He crept over to it. It was barred.

"Throw the gun out!" a man shouted. He was off to Craik's right.

"You cannot escape from there!"

This was a different voice, and it came from his left. The command was punctuated by a round of automatic gunfire. The bullets stitched themselves into the wood a foot above Craik's head. He pressed himself against the earth.

"The next round is lower," one of the men said. "Then we fire into the bushes. Come out now."

Craik started to crawl, but more bullets slammed into the house, a few inches above where he lay.

"All right!" he yelled.

"Throw the gun out."

Craik lofted the pistol through the shrubbery. One of the men picked it up and stuck it behind his belt.

"Now you," the man ordered. "On hands and knees. Backwards."

Craik complied.

"Stop," he was told. He did.

The two men moved close to him. They had him stand. One of them stood off to the side, machine pistol at the ready, while the other patted him down. Then he, too, moved away from Craik.

They motioned him inside. One stayed in front of Craik and slightly to the side, facing him obliquely. The other was always two paces behind him. They led him down a long hall and into the formal dining room.

The slender young man was seated in one of the heavy antique chairs. He still had on the lime silk shirt. It was still open down the front. He was in the process of lighting up a thin cigar with a gold band around the tip. He looked up as the three men entered.

Craik walked slowly over to him, stopping at an unthreatening distance. The two gunmen covered his back.

"Where's Susanna?" Craik said.

Aldo got up and looked Craik over. "Ah, yes," he said. "You're the boyfriend. My name is Aldo."

"Where is she?"

"In good time. And the fisherman's partner as well, if I am not mistaken. I know of you. I am truly sorry about . . . your partner." He smiled.

Craik's face was expressionless. "The Judge sent me," he said.

"You work for the Judge too?"

"I represent him."

"Ah." Aldo walked completely around Craik, examining him as if deeply interested in his clothing. Craik didn't move.

"And where are the men I sent to meet the Judge?" Aldo asked.

"They're delayed," Craik said.

"And my man at the gate? My dog?"

Craik didn't say anything. Aldo was standing in front of him, looking him in the eye.

"You're good, mister," Aldo said. "Damn good. I don't think that I trust you."

Aldo backed off a couple of yards and snapped his fingers. He pointed at one of the gunmen. The man came over while the other continued to cover Craik. Aldo took the man's machine pistol and leveled it at Craik's chest.

"Strip him," he ordered.

The man hesitated.

"Come on," Aldo prodded. "He won't try anything. If he does, it will give me great pleasure to see how many rounds it takes to kill him."

Reluctantly, the man went over to Craik. He lifted off his cap and tossed it to the side. Then he removed the sport shirt. Next came the running shoes and socks. When he got to the jeans, he hesitated again. Then he stripped them off, along with Craik's briefs. Craik never moved except to cooperate with the undressing.

"The tape, too," Aldo ordered. The man pulled off the tape that bound Craik's ribs. He gave the ribs a little poke, like a boy doing something particularly daring, but Craik didn't flinch.

He stood naked, his clothes piled out of reach. His arms hung limp at his sides. The musculature of his upper body was finely etched, his waist and hips narrow. He had the sinewy legs of a long-distance runner.

The man who'd stripped him retrieved his gun and moved away. Aldo chuckled as he looked at Craik.

"Very interesting," Aldo said to himself, then to the others, "If he looks like he's going to move, shoot him."

Aldo walked over to Craik and carefully removed the weapons from his body. The throwing knife that was laced to the small of his back. The length of piano wire that was looped around his waist. The thin, needle spikes that were strapped to one ankle. And, finally, the strip of tape around the other ankle that now held only one syringe.

Aldo hefted the syringe and looked at Craik questioningly. Craik didn't say anything. Aldo shrugged and carried the weapons over to the table. He set them down. Then he pulled one of the chairs over to Craik.

"Sit down," he directed.

The naked man did as he was told. Aldo got himself a chair and sat near Craik, but not too near.

"Now," Aldo said, "what does the Judge say?"

"He's ready to deal," Craik said.

"Deal what?"

"His operation for the girl. He'll give you the whole thing. Where is she?"

Aldo ran his forefinger along his mustache. "She's all right. I *think*. She's . . . entertaining one of my men right now. I hope that he hasn't . . ." He shrugged.

Craik's body stiffened and jerked forward slightly. The muscles at the base of his jaw bulged.

"What is it, boyfriend?" Aldo asked casually.

Craik didn't respond.

"Good," Aldo said. "I don't know whether I will have to kill you, but I surely don't want to do it now. I need to meet with the Judge. Why isn't he here?"

"He's afraid of you," Craik said flatly. "He thinks you killed one of his deputies."

"Yes, the fool didn't know when it was time to change sides."

"Fyke's no loss to the world, Aldo. You've made your point. Let me take the girl and you can have whatever you want around here."

"How do I know that I can trust you?"

"You don't, except for this. I could have killed you at any moment since I walked into this room. Your men over there would've gotten me, but you'd be dead, too, before they could pull their triggers. I didn't do it. All I'm interested in is getting Susanna out of here. I don't give a shit what you and the Judge do when we're gone."

Aldo studied Craik for a long moment.

"Yes," he said finally, "I believe you could have. And that is the problem I have with you, gringo. You have killed my dog and maybe three of my men, and you could, as you say, have killed me too. And what I wonder is: Why is this? Who is this man who can do these things? Some fisherman? I think not, mister. I think that before I can trust you, I must know who you are."

"I'm just a guy looking for his girl."

Aldo laughed. "Very good. The knight in shining armor, eh? But I'm afraid you fight like something more than a boyfriend."

Craik shrugged. "I was a street kid," he said. "Probably like you were."

"A street kid," Aldo said sarcastically.

"I studied karate for a while. I was in Vietnam. I picked up a few things."

Aldo chuckled again. "A soldier," he said. He motioned to the two gunmen. They came over and stood close to the chair. One aimed his weapon at Craik's head, the other at his chest.

Aldo got up. He pointed at Craik's cheek. "How'd you get this?" he asked.

"Shaving," Craik said.

Aldo slapped him on the wound, hard. It split open and began to ooze. Tears welled in Craik's eyes. Aldo slapped him on the other side of the face and then on the wound again. Blood ran down the side of his face.

"And these, mister?" Aldo pointed to some of the bruises on Craik's body.

Craik gritted his teeth. He didn't say anything. Aldo punched him in the stomach. Craik doubled over and Aldo slapped his face again, knocking him off the chair. He kicked Craik's ribs, his shoulders, his ribs again. Craik curled into the fetal position, moaning. Aldo continued to kick him.

Finally he stopped. He took one of the guns while his man got Craik back onto the chair. Then he began the interrogation again. He grabbed Craik's chin and shoved his head back, demanding to know who he was. Craik said nothing. He sat clutching himself, teetering on the antique chair.

Aldo let Craik's head drop. He strode down the table. He looked back at Craik and gestured at the collection of weapons. "What's this shit?" he said.

Craik shook his head.

Aldo snatched up the syringe and stalked back to where Craik was sitting. He stood behind the chair, leaned over, and spoke into Craik's ear.

"Tell me who you are."

"I've told you," Craik mumbled. His voice cracked.

Aldo pricked the back of Craik's neck with the syringe. "And what's in this little thing?" he asked.

"Just a sedative." Craik licked his lips.

"Just a sedative," Aldo echoed. He shoved the needle into Craik's flesh. Craik winched. "You sure?"

Craik trembled.

"Okay, let's find out," Aldo said. He put his thumb on the plunger. "You think it's so fucking easy to kill me. Let's see if you can kill me before I shoot this stuff into you."

"Wait!" Craik said.

Aldo smiled. "Why?" he said.

"Because—" Craik's voice broke. "Jesus, take the goddamn needle out, will you?"

"Who are you, mister?"

"All right," Craik said, "all right. My name's Scott Craik. I work for the federal government."

"Ah," Aldo said. He withdrew the needle and moved around to the chair facing Craik. "Tell me more."

"Drink," Craik said. It was little more than a croak.

Aldo motioned to one of the men, who brought a small glass of whiskey from the sideboard. Craik swallowed some. He coughed, holding his ribs.

"Talk," Aldo said.

The coughing fit passed. "Treasury Department," Craik said wearily. His voice was steadier, but he was shivering. "We've been investigating Judge Holder's illegal arms shipments. I was sent in under cover to get hard evidence. I took a job as a fisherman because that looked like the best way to get close to the operation."

"You're gonna come down on him?"

"Yeah. As soon as we can."

"You're not really here to deal."

"No."

Aldo stroked his mustache. "That changes things," he said.

"From your point of view," Craik said, "I suppose it changes things a lot."

"Shit," Aldo said. He paused, then said, "I still don't understand what you're doing here in place of the old man. You couldn't be that close to him, he'd want you to deal for him."

"I'm not. I'm here for Susanna. That's real." He shrugged. "You do your job the best you can. You can't help who you fall in love with."

Aldo smiled. "Ain't it the truth? You know, I believe you, mister."

"Thanks," Craik said. "Let me give you some advice, Aldo. Pull the hell out of Dorset County. It isn't gonna work for you. This place'll be crawling with federal heat before you get a dime out of it. You let the girl go, I don't give a fuck what you do after that. I'm not DEA. I don't even *like* the DEA. As far as I'm concerned, I never met you. It's Holder I'm after."

Aldo considered it for a minute. "I gotta talk to some people," he said, then to his gunmen, "Lock this guy up in that other room."

The two men came for Craik.

"I don't think I can walk," he said.

The men looked at Aldo, who had gone to a phone at the far end of the room.

"Help him for chrissake," he said to one of them, and to the other, "but don't take your eyes off him for a second. Shoot him if he even looks at you funny."

The two men took Craik down the hall. They opened a door, and the one who'd been supporting him threw him into the room. Craik crumpled on the floor. He lay there, groaning. The two men laughed. They closed the door and threw the new, heavy iron bolt.

Craik was still for a few moments. Then he curled himself into a ball. He reached back and slowly, carefully, inserted two fingers into his rectum. When he withdrew them, they were clutching a slim metal tube.

He sat up and looked around. The room was a small study. There was a leather couch, antique rolltop desk and chair. Bookshelves lined the walls. The carpet was a thick Oriental with a huge red dragon woven into it.

Craik unscrewed the top of the tube. He shook another tiny syringe into his hand. Then he crawled to the wastebasket next to the desk and dropped the empty tube into it. He crawled back to where he'd been lying. He fitted the syringe into his palm and closed his fist, so that the needle protruded slightly between the tips of his middle and forefingers and the plunger rested on the base of the same fingers. Then he arranged himself on the carpet.

The two men returned ten minutes later. They slid back the bolt, turned the knob, and pushed open the door. They remained in the hallway, both machine pistols pointed into the room. Craik lay where they had thrown him earlier. He was curled up, and his body was quivering.

The gunmen walked into the room. One of them stood back while the other prodded Craik with his toe.

"Come on," he said, "get up."

Craik turned his face upward. "Help," he said, his voice cracking.

The man sighed and slung the automatic weapon on his hip. While his partner covered him, he bent down and helped Craik to his feet.

Craik got his arm around the man's shoulder. He took a couple of hobbling steps, which brought them closer to the other man, before he jabbed the syringe and pushed the plunger. The man reached up with his free hand, stopped, started to say something, and pitched forward.

Craik released the falling man and used his momentum to carry him into a shoulder roll toward the other gunman. As he came out of the roll he swept his left leg in a broad arc and knocked the man's feet cleanly out from under him. The man fell prone, his gun flattened under his body.

Before he had a chance to move, Craik had leapt onto his back and seized him under the chin. Craik pulled the man's head backward, pinning his jaw shut.

"One sound and I'll break your neck," Craik said into his ear.

With his other hand Craik clamped two fingers over the man's carotid artery. He pressed hard. The man squirmed a little at first, then his movements slowed, and finally he was still. Craik eased the pressure.

Craik stripped the man closest to him in size. He put on the man's trousers and shirt. The trousers were too baggy and the shirt too tight. He slung one of the machine pistols over his own shoulder, removed the clip from the other. He slipped the spare clip into his pocket and left the second gun in the hall. Then he locked the two men in the room.

He made his way back to the formal dining room. Aldo was sitting at the far end of the table, next to the telephone, smoking a cigar. He made no move against Craik. Craik held the gun steady as he walked the length of the room. Aldo just shook his head wearily.

"Let's go," Craik said.

Aldo got up. "Jesus," he said. "You're ever out of work, you come see me."

"Turn around," Craik said. "Lean on the table. You know the drill."

Aldo did as he was told. Craik frisked him with one hand, balanced the gun with the other. Aldo offered no resistance, and Craik discovered no weapons on him.

"Okay," Craik said. "Anyone left?"

Aldo stood up again. He shook his head.

"Who was with Susanna?" There was a hard edge to Craik's voice.

"Nobody."

"Good boy," Craik said. "That was the right answer. Now turn your back again. See what you can see out the window."

Aldo complied. Keeping the gun steady, Craik made a phone call.

"Craik here," he said. "The place is neutralized. How soon can you get here? . . . Good. Bring the cops. There's four men here. At least one of them was with Brendan when he died. You can sort it out."

He hung up and motioned to Aldo to lead the way. They went upstairs and halfway down a hall. The door had another new bolt on the outside. Aldo threw it and let them in. It was a bedroom. There was a four-poster bed and a mahogany dresser with a large oval mirror. Susanna was sitting on the edge of the bed.

"You look like hell," Craik said to her.

"You look swell yourself," Susanna said. "Who's your tailor?"

Craik chuckled. "Come on, lady," he said. "We can talk about this later."

Susanna got up. "Just give me one minute," she said.

She walked over to Aldo. Craik stood a few paces behind, the gun centered on the man's back.

"Bastard," Susanna said, and she spit in Aldo's face. When he reached up to wipe it, she kicked him in the groin. Hard. He screamed once as he dropped to the floor, then he began to retch.

"Okay," Susanna said to Craik. "I don't want to see the rest of this."

They went out, and Craik bolted the door. They shared a quick kiss.

"You alone?" she asked.

"At the moment."

She nodded. "Pretty good." She touched his cheek next to the knife wound. "Though not without its cost."

"Your uncle is supposed to be coming later. With help. But he was drunk and alone. Fyke's dead. Kemp and Tilghman have run off. So I don't know what to expect. Best thing for us is just to get the hell out of here."

Susanna shrugged. "Let's go," she said.

Craik put a hand on her shoulder. "I don't quite know how to say this, and I sure don't know what it means, but are you ready to leave?"

"Leave Brawlton?"

Craik nodded.

"Jesus, Scotty, I been ready to leave half my life."

"I mean tonight. For good. With . . . me."

"I know what you mean. Let's quit talking about it, okay? I've got a real bad feeling the shitstorm isn't over yet. The sooner we leave this place behind, the better."

They went downstairs. In the front hall there was a table with a phone on it.

"One second," Craik said. "Just to be on the safe side. I'm not ready to trust your uncle."

Craik dialed the operator. When he came on, Craik told him to call the state police and inform them that there had been a homicide at an estate called Spindrift, in southwestern Dorset County. Then he hung up.

Susanna and Craik went outside. The hot, humid night air was filled with a fine mist that was almost like rain. They walked past the high white columns. When they reached the top of the steps, they stopped.

Below them, looking up, were Forrest Holder and Bracewell Kemp. The Judge's Mercedes was parked nearby. Holder was smiling. Kemp's hand rested on his holstered pistol.

"I'm glad to see that you're all right, Susanna," he said.

Craik stared long and hard at Holder, his face knotted with suppressed rage. "Good going, Judge," he said finally. "The drunk act was perfect. You fooled me. The rest of it a lie too?"

"Here and there," Holder said. "Fyke *is* dead. Tilghman's gone. But Brace hasn't deserted me, as you can see."

"You forwarded the phone to your car, of course. Then all you had to do was wait out there and see what happened. I don't suppose there's any help coming."

"No, you were on your own. Though I'd say you didn't need much assistance considering you come strolling out the front door like you owned the place. What's that make, six men you went through?"

"You're a calculating son of a bitch, Holder," Craik said. "You think the two of you can clean up here?"

"I think so," the Judge said.

"So what do we do now?"

Holder shook his head slowly. "I don't know," he said. "You're something of a problem to me."

"A problem with an automatic weapon," Craik said, displaying it prominently. "The way you risked Susanna's life here, I don't feel much concern for yours."

"What do you want, Craik?"

Craik looked at Susanna. "Just let us leave, Uncle Forrest," she said.

"Give me the gun," Holder said to Craik, "and you can go. But my niece stays here."

"Uh-uh," Craik said.

"If you leave now, I won't stop you. If you don't, I will turn you over to your Mr. Smith."

"No deal."

"Well, I tried," Holder said with a sigh. "But it just don't look like we're gonna reach agreement."

He made a small gesture with his hand. Rodney Crowe stepped quickly from behind one of the columns. He grabbed Susanna around the neck and pulled her head back. With the other hand he held a revolver to her head.

"You shoulda taken my advice a long time ago, Craik," Kemp said. "Left town for a while."

"How about it, Craik?" Holder asked. "You still want to shoot me?" He spread his arms, offering the front of his body as a target.

"Uncle Forrest!" Susanna shouted. "I don't believe this! What are you *doing*?"

"Just have your friend hand over his gun, dear, and Rodney will let you go. That's all. I don't want to see you hurt."

"It's a trap, Craik," Susanna said. "Don't do it. They're bluffing."

Craik turned his head so that he could see her and still watch Kemp and the Judge with his peripheral vision.

There was a moment of silence. Then Crowe grinned, and the silence was broken by the sound of his cocking the hammer on the revolver. The sound seemed to echo in the night.

Craik dropped his weapon.

"Now, you with the pistol." The voice came out of the misty darkness. "You do the same. Everyone stand right where they are."

Crowe turned in the direction of the voice. Simultaneously, he relaxed his grip on Susanna's neck. She brought her arm forward and rammed her elbow back into his gut. Then she dropped to her knees.

Crowe reacted quickly. He leveled his gun hand and fired three quick shots toward the voice. There was one answering shot. A small hole appeared in the center of Crowe's forehead, and the rear of his skull was blown away. He was thrown backward. He lay supine, his eyes open and sightless, the blood pooling around him.

No one else moved.

Smith walked slowly into the lighted area near the house. He was carrying a high-powered rifle. It wasn't pointed directly at anyone, but it was ready.

"Smitty," Craik said. "Long time."

"You two," Smith directed, "down on your bellies. Arms out in front of you."

Kemp and Holder followed instructions.

"Craik, get down here."

He and Susanna walked down the steps. They stood next to the two prone men on the ground. Smith joined the little group.

"You didn't really think I'd trust you, did you, Craik?" Smith said.

Craik shrugged.

"Who's this?" Susanna asked.

"He's from the government and he's here to help us," Craik said.

"I slipped another directional behind your belt buckle," Smith said. "While you were unconscious. My ass is hamburger if I lose you again."

"I didn't try and ditch you," Craik said. "The boys didn't cooperate."

"What's the scene here?" Smith said.

"One man on the gate," Craik said. "Two in the house. They're all napping. The boss is here too. He's having some trouble with his testes, courtesy of Susanna. The other two are back along the road about five miles. They won't wake up till tomorrow morning."

"Nobody greased?"

"No. Except the late Mr. Crowe. The guy you just shot. His mother may miss him, but that's about it."

"I think we can handle it. What about these two?" He pointed at Holder and Kemp with his foot.

Craik walked over to the Judge. He squatted down and fished in Holder's pocket. He pulled out a silver key ring with about a dozen keys dangling from it. He got to his feet again.

"I don't know," Craik said. "What do you want to do with them?"

"What're the choices?" Smith said.

"I called the state cops. At their speed they should be here in, oh, half an hour or so. You can throw our friends to them. They're into smuggling, extortion, obstruction of justice, conspiracy to do something or other, I don't know what all.

"Of course, if you do that, then you're probably gonna blow the fact that the agency knew about the criminal activity that was going down around here. I'm not sure the boss would like that. So you may end up having to make a deal with Holder here. I'm sure he's ready to make you a nice offer. Right, Judge?"

Holder didn't say anything.

"On the other hand, I wouldn't turn my back on these guys. It'd be a whole lot easier for them if you were dead. They could claim they thought you were one of these thugs from Washington, shot you in self-defense. Who'd dispute them?

"But as I say, it's up to you. Do what you think's best." To Susanna he said, "Let's go." He took her hand.

"Go?" Smith said. "Where? What're you trying to pull, Steven?"

"Steven?" Susanna said.

"Tell you later," Craik said.

"Hold on!" Smith shouted. "You can't leave here!"

Craik stopped. "Why not?" he said.

"You—I—God damn it, you can't leave me holding the bag! Steven!"

"Sure I can," Craik said. "I don't work for the government, you do. I didn't kill a man, you did. You've got to stay for the explanations or you're in the worst trouble of your life. Me, I'm used to moving around. Remember?"

"You shithead! That was years ago!"

"Seems like yesterday to me, Smitty. Way I look at it, this only begins to even the score."

"Don't you *dare* take another step."

"What're you gonna do?" Craik said. "Shoot me? Shoot an innocent woman? I don't think even you can do that."

Craik and Susanna resumed walking. Smith stamped his foot and hurled obscenities after them. Kemp raised his head slightly.

"Stick your fucking nose in the dirt!" Smith screamed at him, and Kemp quickly did just that.

Craik and Susanna had reached the Mercedes. Just before he got in, Craik said, "Come on, Smitty. Think of how much fun you'll have trying to find me again."

Smith ranted some more as the car started to pull away. Then he became suddenly calm. He dropped to one knee and aimed the rifle at the retreating automobile. It had almost disappeared into the mist when he fired.

One of the rear tires exploded. The Mercedes veered but straightened out. It continued down the driveway, riding on the rim.

CHAPTER 37

Craik drove the crippled Mercedes as far as the field, where he exchanged it for the beige sedan.

"Where are we going?" Susanna asked as they started moving again.

"I don't know," Craik said. "Where do you want to go?"

Susanna thought for a moment, then said, "Europe. South America."

Craik looked over at her. "Okay," he said. "We'll have to get you a passport. But I think that can be arranged. Europe it is. If not South America."

They spoke little, each pursuing his or her own thoughts. Craik stopped and picked up the two suitcases. Then he continued down the main road. He turned north at the church. A few minutes later they were parked in Brendan Shields's yard.

They unloaded the suitcases. Then Craik drove the sedan a short distance into the woods.

"That ought to be enough," Craik said. "We don't need much of a head start."

"Got any clothes for me?" Susanna asked.

"We can get them in the morning."

"You've got money?"

"Enough."

They carried his suitcases down to the boat.

"Now," Craik said, "if I can remember how to operate this thing."

"I do if you don't," Susanna said, and Craik smiled.

The engine started right up. Susanna cast them off, and Craik eased the boat out into the creek. They puttered east, along with the tide, toward the still distant day. Mist rose from the water in streamers.

Susanna stood in the cabin as Craik strained to guide the boat into the Pawchunk in the foggy darkness.

"Can we get away with this?" she asked.

"Uh-huh," he said. "I'm good at it, remember? In a couple of hours we'll be in Norfolk. From there we can go anywhere we want. It'll be days before they figure out what we did. And even then, someone or other will find a way to put a lid on the whole thing. In the end, Smitty's probably the only one who cares."

"Jesus," Susanna said, "do I really want to live like this?"

Craik shrugged. "If you don't, you can go home. You haven't broken any law."

"I barely know you, Craik."

"That'll change. And the name's Carson. Steve Carson."

Susanna laughed. "And who am I?"

"Whoever you want to be."

"You know something, this is insane. Totally insane."

"Yes," Carson said. "Yes, it is."

A little later *Murphy's Law* nosed out of the Pawchunk. Hugging the coast, it headed down the Chesapeake. Over the sound of the engine a distant foghorn could be heard.

Susanna walked to the stern of the boat. She rested her hands on the rail, leaned out, and gazed down at the swirling black water below. Tears formed at the corners of her eyes and trickled down her cheeks. She flicked them off. They fell, mixing with the brine of the bay.

"Thanks, Uncle Brendan," she said softly, and she turned her back on the water.

EPILOGUE

WASHINGTON, D.C.
April 1986

The two men faced each other across the massive executive's desk. The man behind the desk was older. He had a moon face and was dressed in a smoke-gray suit. He wore glasses with neutral plastic frames. His expression gave away nothing.

"The hair will have to go, of course," the moon-faced man was saying. "The Front doesn't have haircuts like that."

The younger man unconsciously ran his hand through his thick, expensively styled black hair. Then he gestured toward the man behind the desk. He shook his hand backward and forward.

"This is *crazy*," he said, gesturing vigorously. "You want me to set up a ten-million-dollar cocaine deal and then you want me to get *caught*?"

"That is correct, yes."

"And I'm supposed to be some revolutionary from Bananaland?"

"I should think you can adequately portray a Central American."

The younger man stopped gesturing and shook his head slowly. There was a lengthy silence.

"Right," the younger man said finally. "I get arrested and

I sing like a bird about raising money for the goddamn People's revolution."

"Yes."

"And then?"

"Then we get your case thrown out on a technicality. You'll be free."

"And this is the payback for keeping me out of jail last summer."

"You may consider the debt canceled, yes."

"You people are fucking nuts. I ain't gonna do this."

The moon-faced man appeared unperturbed. He spread his hands.

"Suit yourself," he said. "The cell in Bogotá is still there. I understand that it is not comfortable."

The younger man stared cold and hard across the space between them. Without taking his eyes from the other man's he fumbled a silver cigarette case from his pocket.

"You cocksucker," he said bitterly. "Why should I trust you?"

The moon-faced man's expression softened a trifle. "You can trust me," he said.

His hand nearly steady, the younger man took a cigar from the silver case. It was a skinny little cigar with a gold band around the tip.

MORE MYSTERIOUS PLEASURES

HAROLD ADAMS
MURDER
Carl Wilcox debuts in a story of triple murder which exposes the underbelly of corruption in the town of Corden, shattering the respectability of its most dignified citizens.   #501 $3.50

THE NAKED LIAR
When a sexy young widow is framed for the murder of her husband, Carl Wilcox comes through to help her fight off cops and big-city goons.
                                                            #420 $3.95

THE FOURTH WIDOW
Ex-con/private eye Carl Wilcox is back, investigating the death of a "popular" widow in the Depression-era town of Corden, S.D.
                                                            #502 $3.50

EARL DERR BIGGERS
THE HOUSE WITHOUT A KEY
Charlie Chan debuts in the Honolulu investigation of an expatriate Bostonian's murder.   #421 $3.95

THE CHINESE PARROT
Charlie Chan works to find the key to murders seemingly without victims—but which have left a multitude of clues.   #503 $3.95

BEHIND THAT CURTAIN
Two murders sixteen years apart, one in London, one in San Francisco, each share a major clue in a pair of velvet Chinese slippers. Chan seeks the connection.   #504 $3.95

THE BLACK CAMEL
When movie goddess Sheila Fane is murdered in her Hawaiian pavilion, Chan discovers an interrelated crime in a murky Hollywood mystery from the past.   #505 $3.95

CHARLIE CHAN CARRIES ON
An elusive transcontinental killer dogs the heels of the Lofton Round the World Cruise. When the touring party reaches Honolulu, the murderer finally meets his match.

JAMES M. CAIN
THE ENCHANTED ISLE
A beautiful runaway is involved in a deadly bank robbery in this posthumously published novel. #415 $3.95

CLOUD NINE
Two brothers—one good, one evil—battle over a million-dollar land deal and a luscious 16-year-old in this posthumously published novel. #507 $3.95

ROBERT CAMPBELL
IN LA-LA LAND WE TRUST
Child porn, snuff films, and drunken TV stars in fast cars—that's what makes the L.A. world go 'round. Whistler, a luckless P.I., finds that it's not good to know too much about the porn trade in the City of Angels. #508 $3.95

GEORGE C. CHESBRO
VEIL
Clairvoyant artist Veil Kendry volunteers to be tested at the Institute for Human Studies and finds that his life is in deadly peril; is he threatened by the Institute, the Army, or the CIA? #509 $3.95

WILLIAM L. DeANDREA
THE LUNATIC FRINGE
Police Commissioner Teddy Roosevelt and Officer Dennis Muldoon comb 1896 New York for a missing exotic dancer who holds the key to the murder of a prominent political cartoonist. #306 $3.95

SNARK
Espionage agent Bellman must locate the missing director of British Intelligence—and elude a master terrorist who has sworn to kill him. #510 $3.50

KILLED IN THE ACT
Brash, witty Matt Cobb, TV network troubleshooter, must contend with bizarre crimes connected with a TV spectacular—one of which is a murder committed before 40 million witnesses. #511 $3.50

KILLED WITH A PASSION
In seeking to clear an old college friend of murder, Matt Cobb must deal with the Mad Karate Killer and the Organic Hit Man, among other eccentric criminals. #512 $3.50

KILLED ON THE ICE
When a famous psychiatrist is stabbed in a Manhattan skating rink, Matt Cobb finds it necessary to protect a beautiful Olympic skater who appears to be the next victim. #513 $3.50

JAMES ELLROY
SUICIDE HILL
Brilliant L.A. Police sergeant Lloyd Hopkins teams up with the FBI to solve a series of inside bank robberies—but is he working with or against them? #514 $3.95

PAUL ENGLEMAN
CATCH A FALLEN ANGEL
Private eye Mark Renzler becomes involved in publishing mayhem and murder when two slick mens' magazines battle for control of the lucrative market. #515 $3.50

LOREN D. ESTLEMAN
ROSES ARE DEAD
Someone's put a contract out on freelance hit man Peter Macklin. Is he as good as the killers on his trail? #516 $3.95

ANY MAN'S DEATH
Hit man Peter Macklin is engaged to keep a famous television evangelist *alive*—quite a switch from his normal line. #517 $3.95

DICK FRANCIS
THE SPORT OF QUEENS
The autobiography of the celebrated race jockey/crime novelist. #410 $3.95

JOHN GARDNER
THE GARDEN OF WEAPONS
Big Herbie Kruger returns to East Berlin to uncover a double agent. He confronts his own past and life's only certainty—death. #103 $4.50

BRIAN GARFIELD
DEATH WISH
Paul Benjamin is a modern-day New York vigilante, stalking the rapist-killers who victimized his wife and daughter. The basis for the Charles Bronson movie. #301 $3.95

DEATH SENTENCE
A riveting sequel to *Death Wish*. The action moves to Chicago as Paul Benjamin continues his heroic (or is it psychotic?) mission to make city streets safe. #302 $3.95

TRIPWIRE
A crime novel set in the American West of the late 1800s. Boag, a black outlaw, seeks revenge on the white cohorts who left him for dead. "One of the most compelling characters in recent fiction."—Robert Ludlum. #303 $3.95

FEAR IN A HANDFUL OF DUST
Four psychiatrists, three men and a woman, struggle across the blazing Arizona desert—pursued by a fanatic killer they themselves have judged insane. "Unique and disturbing."—Alfred Coppel. #304 $3.95

JOE GORES
A TIME OF PREDATORS
When Paula Halstead kills herself after witnessing a horrid crime, her husband vows to avenge her death. Winner of the Edgar Allan Poe Award.   #215 $3.95

COME MORNING
Two million in diamonds are at stake, and the ex-con who knows their whereabouts may have trouble staying alive if he turns them up at the wrong moment.   #518 $3.95

NAT HENTOFF
BLUES FOR CHARLIE DARWIN
Gritty, colorful Greenwich Village sets the scene for Noah Green and Sam McKibbon, two street-wise New York cops who are as at home in jazz clubs as they are at a homicide scene.
#208 $3.95

THE MAN FROM INTERNAL AFFAIRS
Detective Noah Green wants to know who's stuffing corpses into East Village garbage cans . . . and who's lying about him to the Internal Affairs Division.   #409 $3.95

PATRICIA HIGHSMITH
THE BLUNDERER
An unhappy husband attempts to kill his wife by applying the murderous methods of another man. When things go wrong, he pays a visit to the more successful killer—a dreadful error.   #305 $3.95

DOUG HORNIG
THE DARK SIDE
Insurance detective Loren Swift is called to a rural commune to investigate a carbon-monoxide murder. Are the commune inhabitants as gentle as they seem?   #519 $3.95

P.D. JAMES/T.A. CRITCHLEY
THE MAUL AND THE PEAR TREE
The noted mystery novelist teams up with a police historian to create a fascinating factual account of the 1811 Ratcliffe Highway murders.
#520 $3.95

STUART KAMINSKY'S "TOBY PETERS" SERIES
NEVER CROSS A VAMPIRE
When Bela Lugosi receives a dead bat in the mail, Toby tries to catch the prankster. But Toby's time is at a premium because he's also trying to clear William Faulkner of a murder charge!   #107 $3.95

HIGH MIDNIGHT
When Gary Cooper and Ernest Hemingway come to Toby for protection, he tries to save them from vicious blackmailers.　　#106　$3.95

HE DONE HER WRONG
Someone has stolen Mae West's autobiography, and when she asks Toby to come up and see her sometime, he doesn't know how deadly a visit it could be.　　#105　$3.95

BULLET FOR A STAR
Warner Brothers hires Toby Peters to clear the name of Errol Flynn, a blackmail victim with a penchant for young girls. The first novel in the acclaimed Hollywood-based private eye series.　　#308　$3.95

THE FALA FACTOR
Toby comes to the rescue of lady-in-distress Eleanor Roosevelt, and must match wits with a right-wing fanatic who is scheming to overthrow the U.S. Government.　　#309　$3.95

JOSEPH KOENIG
FLOATER
Florida Everglades sheriff Buck White matches wits with a Miami murder-and-larceny team who just may have hidden his ex-wife's corpse in a remote bayou.　　#521　$3.50

ELMORE LEONARD
THE HUNTED
Long out of print, this 1974 novel by the author of *Glitz* details the attempts of a man to escape killers from his past.　　#401　$3.95

MR. MAJESTYK
Sometimes bad guys can push a good man too far, and when that good guy is a Special Forces veteran, everyone had better duck.　　#402　$3.95

THE BIG BOUNCE
Suspense and black-comedy are cleverly combined in this tale of a dangerous drifter's affair with a beautiful woman out for kicks.　　#403　$3.95

ELSA LEWIN
I, ANNA
A recently divorced woman commits murder to avenge her degradation at the hands of a sleazy lothario.　　#522　$3.50

THOMAS MAXWELL
KISS ME ONCE
An epic *roman noir* which explores the romantic but seamy underworld of New York during the WWII years. When the good guys are off fighting in Europe, the bad guys run amok in America.　　#523　$3.95

ED McBAIN
ANOTHER PART OF THE CITY
The master of the police procedural moves from the fictional 87th precinct to the gritty reality of Manhattan. "McBain's best in several years."—*San Francisco Chronicle*.   #524 $3.95

SNOW WHITE AND ROSE RED
A beautiful heiress confined to a sanitarium engages Matthew Hope to free her—and her $650,000.   #414 $3.95

CINDERELLA
A dead detective and a hot young hooker lead Matthew Hope into a multi-layered plot among Miami cocaine dealers. "A gem of sting and countersting."—*Time*.   #525 $3.95

PETER O'DONNELL
MODESTY BLAISE
Modesty and Willie Garvin must protect a shipment of diamonds from a gentleman about to murder his lover and an *un*civilized sheik.   #216 $3.95

SABRE TOOTH
Modesty faces Willie's apparent betrayal and a modern-day Genghis Khan who wants her for his mercenary army.   #217 $3.95

A TASTE FOR DEATH
Modesty and Willie are pitted against a giant enemy in the Sahara, where their only hope of escape is a blind girl whose time is running out.   #218 $3.95

I, LUCIFER
Some people carry a nickname too far . . . like the maniac calling himself Lucifer. He's targeted 120 souls, and Modesty and Willie find they have a personal stake in stopping him.   #219 $3.95

THE IMPOSSIBLE VIRGIN
Modesty fights for her soul when she and Willie attempt to rescue an albino girl from the evil Brunel, who lusts after the secret power of an idol called the Impossible Virgin.   #220 $3.95

DEAD MAN'S HANDLE
Modesty Blaise must deal with a brainwashed—and deadly—Willie Garvin as well as with a host of outré religion-crazed villains.
                    #526 $3.95

ELIZABETH PETERS
CROCODILE ON THE SANDBANK
Amelia Peabody's trip to Egypt brings her face to face with an ancient mystery. With the help of Radcliffe Emerson, she uncovers a tomb and the solution to a deadly threat.   #209 $3.95

THE CURSE OF THE PHAROAHS
Amelia and Radcliffe Emerson head for Egypt to excavate a cursed tomb but must confront the burial ground's evil history before it claims them both. #210 $3.95

THE SEVENTH SINNER
Murder in an ancient subterranean Roman temple sparks Jacqueline Kirby's first recorded case. #411 $3.95

THE MURDERS OF RICHARD III
Death by archaic means haunts the costumed weekend get-together of a group of eccentric Ricardians. #412 $3.95

ANTHONY PRICE
THE LABYRINTH MAKERS
Dr. David Audley does his job too well in his first documented case, embarrassing British Intelligence, the CIA, and the KGB in one swoop. #404 $3.95

THE ALAMUT AMBUSH
Alamut, in Northern Persia, is considered by many to be the original home of terrorism. Audley moves to the Mideast to put the cap on an explosive threat. #405 $3.95

COLONEL BUTLER'S WOLF
The Soviets are recruiting spies from among Oxford's best and brightest; it's up to Dr. Audley to identify the Russian wolf in don's clothing. #527 $3.95

OCTOBER MEN
Dr. Audley's "holiday" in Rome stirs up old Intelligence feuds and echoes of partisan warfare during World War II—and leads him into new danger. #529 $3.95

OTHER PATHS TO GLORY
What can a World War I battlefield in France have in common with a deadly secret of the present? A modern assault on Bouillet Wood leads to the answers. #530 $3.95

SION CROSSING
What does the chairman of a new NATO-like committee have to do with the American Civil War? Audley travels to Georgia in this espionage thriller. #406 $3.95

HERE BE MONSTERS
The assassination of an American veteran forces Dr. David Audley into a confrontation with undercover KGB agents. #528 $3.95

BILL PRONZINI AND JOHN LUTZ
THE EYE
A lunatic watches over the residents of West 98th Street with a powerful telescope. When his "children" displease him, he is swift to mete out deadly punishment. #408 $3.95

PATRICK RUELL
RED CHRISTMAS
Murderers and political terrorists come down the chimney during an old-fashioned Dickensian Christmas at a British country inn.

#531 $3.50

DEATH TAKES THE LOW ROAD
William Hazlitt, a universtiy administrator who moonlights as a Soviet mole, is on the run from both Russian and British agents who want him to assassinate an African general.   #532 $3.50

DELL SHANNON
CASE PENDING
In the first novel in the best-selling series, Lt. Luis Mendoza must solve a series of horrifying Los Angeles mutilation murders.   #211 $3.95

THE ACE OF SPADES
When the police find an overdosed junkie, they're ready to write off the case—until the autopsy reveals that this junkie *wasn't* a junkie.   #212 $3.95

EXTRA KILL
In "The Temple of Mystic Truth," Mendoza discovers idol worship, pornography, murder, and the clue to the death of a Los Angeles patrolman.   #213 $3.95

KNAVE OF HEARTS
Mendoza must clear the name of the L.A.P.D. when it's discovered that an innocent man has been executed and the real killer is still on the loose.   #214 $3.95

DEATH OF A BUSYBODY
When the West Coast's most industrious gossip and meddler turns up dead in a freight yard, Mendoza must work without clues to find the killer of a woman who had offended nearly everyone in Los Angeles.   #315 $3.95

DOUBLE BLUFF
Mendoza goes against the evidence to dissect what looks like an air-tight case against suspected wife-killer Francis Ingram—a man the lieutenant insists is too nice to be a murderer.   #316 $3.95

MARK OF MURDER
Mendoza investigates the near-fatal attack on an old friend as well as trying to track down an insane serial killer.   #417 $3.95

ROOT OF ALL EVIL
The murder of a "nice" girl leads Mendoza to team up with the FBI in the search for her not-so-nice boyfriend—a Soviet agent.   #418 $3.95

JULIE SMITH
TRUE-LIFE ADVENTURE
Paul McDonald earned a meager living ghosting reports for a San Francisco private eye until the gumshoe turned up dead . . . now the killers are after him.   #407 $3.95

TOURIST TRAP
A lunatic is out to destroy San Francisco's tourism industry; can feisty lawyer/sleuth Rebecca Schwartz stop him while clearing an innocent man of a murder charge?   #533 $3.95

ROSS H. SPENCER
THE MISSING BISHOP
Chicago P.I. Buzz Deckard has a missing person to find. Unfortunately his client has disappeared as well, and no one else seems to be who or what they claim.   #416 $3.50

MONASTERY NIGHTMARE
Chicago P.I. Luke Lassiter tries his hand at writing novels, and encounters murder in an abandoned monastery.   #534 $3.50

REX STOUT
UNDER THE ANDES
A long-lost 1914 fantasy novel from the creator of the immortal Nero Wolfe series. "The most exciting yarn we have read since *Tarzan of the Apes.*" —*All-Story Magazine.*   #419 $3.50

ROSS THOMAS
CAST A YELLOW SHADOW
McCorkle's wife is kidnapped by agents of the South African government. The ransom—his cohort Padillo must assassinate their prime minister.   #535 $3.95

THE SINGAPORE WINK
Ex-Hollywood stunt man Ed Cauthorne is offered $25,000 to search for colleague Angelo Sacchetti—a man he thought he'd killed in Singapore two years earlier.   #536 $3.95

THE FOOLS IN TOWN ARE ON OUR SIDE
Lucifer Dye, just resigned from a top secret U.S. Intelligence post, accepts a princely fee to undertake the corruption of an entire American city.   #537 $3.95

JIM THOMPSON
THE KILL-OFF
Luanne Devore was loathed by everyone in her small New England town. Her plots and designs threatened to destroy them—unless they destroyed her first.   #538 $3.95

DONALD E. WESTLAKE
THE HOT ROCK
The unlucky master thief John Dortmunder debuts in this spectacular caper novel. How many times do you have to steal an emerald to make sure it *stays* stolen? #539 $3.95

BANK SHOT
Dortmunder and company return. A bank is temporarily housed in a trailer, so why not just hook it up and make off with the whole shebang? Too bad nothing is ever that simple. #540 $3.95

THE BUSY BODY
Aloysius Engel is a gangster, the Big Man's right hand. So when he's ordered to dig a suit loaded with drugs out of a fresh grave, how come the corpse it's wrapped around won't lie still? #541 $3.95

THE SPY IN THE OINTMENT
Pacifist agitator J. Eugene Raxford is mistakenly listed as a terrorist by the FBI, which leads to his enforced recruitment to a group bent on world domination. Will very good Good triumph over absolutely villainous Evil? #542 $3.95

GOD SAVE THE MARK
Fred Fitch is the sucker's sucker—con men line up to bilk him. But when he inherits $300,000 from a murdered uncle, he finds it necessary to dodge killers as well as hustlers. #543 $3.95

TERI WHITE
TIGHTROPE
This second novel featuring L.A. cops Blue Maguire and Spaceman Kowalski takes them into the nooks and crannies of the city's Little Saigon. #544 $3.95

COLLIN WILCOX
VICTIMS
Lt. Frank Hastings investigates the murder of a police colleague in the home of a powerful—and nasty—San Francisco attorney.
#413 $3.95

NIGHT GAMES
Lt. Frank Hastings of the San Francisco Police returns to investigate the at-home death of an unfaithful husband—whose affairs have led to his murder. #545 $3.95

DAVID WILLIAMS' "MARK TREASURE" SERIES

UNHOLY WRIT

London financier Mark Treasure helps a friend reaquire some property. He stays to unravel the mystery when a Shakespeare manuscript is discovered and foul murder done.   #112 $3.95

TREASURE BY DEGREES

Mark Treasure discovers there's nothing funny about a board game called "Funny Farms." When he becomes involved in the takeover struggle for a small university, he also finds there's nothing funny about murder.   #113 $3.95

■ ■